Copyright © 2018 by Craig Rainey Creative, LLC

All rights reserved. No part of this publication may be reproduced, distributed or transmitted in any form or by any means, including photocopying, recording, or other electronic or mechanical methods, without the prior written permission of the publisher, except in the case of brief quotations embodied in critical reviews and certain other noncommercial uses permitted by copyright law. For permission requests, write to the publisher, addressed "Attention: Permissions Coordinator," at the address below.

Craig Rainey/Craig Rainey Creative, LLC
Austin, Texas, USA
www.craigrainey.com
www.massacreataguacaliente.com

Publisher's Note: This is a work of fiction. Names, characters, places, and incidents are a product of the author's imagination. Locales and public names are sometimes used for atmospheric purposes. Any resemblance to actual people, living or dead, or to businesses, companies, events, institutions, or locales is completely coincidental.

Cover Design by ParamitaCreative.com

Massacre at Agua Caliente, A Western Tragedy/ Craig Rainey. -- 1st ed.
ISBN 978-1-7339867-4-8

Novels by Craig Rainey

Massacre at Agua Caliente

Stolen Valor, A Carson Brand Novel

Dark Motive, A Carson Brand Novel

Reasonable Sin, A Carson Brand Novel

The Art of Sales, Handbook for the Career Seller

Reviews

"MASSACRE AT AGUA CALIENTE BY CRAIG RAINEY IS WELL-EDITED. THE WRITING IS DONE ADEPTLY AND THE CHARACTERS ARE REALISTIC AND FLAWED. EVERY TURN IN THE BOOK IS SURPRISING AND UNEXPECTED. FOR EVERY READER WHO IS FASCINATED BY THE ADVENTURES OF AN OUTLAW, MASSACRE AT AGUA CALIENTE IS THE BOOK TO READ. I RATE IT 4 OUT OF 4 STARS,"
- ONLINEBOOKCLUB.ORG

"RAINEY KEENLY DEPICTS AN UNFORGIVING LANDSCAPE THROUGHOUT THIS NOVEL – A NEARLY LAWLESS WORLD WHERE BRUTAL VIOLENCE CAN ERUPT AT A MOMENT'S NOTICE,"
-KIRKUS REVIEWS

"I AM AMAZED THAT THIS IS THE FIRST BOOK WRITTEN BY THIS AUTHOR. THERE ARE... MOMENTS THAT ...SPEAK TO AN AUTHOR'S STORY TELLING IN ANY GOOD BOOK, AND THIS STORY HAD QUITE A FEW. BRAVO, I LOOK FORWARD TO MORE OF MR. RAINEY'S WORKS! RECOMMENDING TO MY FRIENDS AND FAMILY,"
-AMAZON READER REVIEW

"I LOVED THE AUTHENTIC LANGUAGE AND THE COMPLEXITY OF CHARACTERS AND THEIR HARDSHIPS AND DRAMAS. THE CONCLUSION IS RIVETING AND EMOTIONALLY CAPTIVATING,"
-READER REVIEW

"I love reading western stories... but this book is a must read as it is an outlaw story," -
READER REVIEW

CRAIG RAINEY'S MASSACRE AT AGUA CALIENTE IS A WELL WRITTEN MASTERPIECE. DETAILED DESCRIPTIONS AND CAPTIVATING STORYTELLING. HOW HE MANAGES TO GET THE READER TO STOMACH BOYD HUTTON AND HIS DESPICABLE NATURE IS A WONDER, GREAT JOB!"
-READER REVIEW

For Alexandra

As with most worthwhile goals, this novel is the result of a lifetime of wanting and a few months of doing.

–CRAIG RAINEY

Contents

Foreword 1

The Mormons 7

Trail Boss 15

The Bank 41

Boyd Hutton 71

Helen's Battle 93

Cab Jackson 105

Quinceanera 131

Pursuit 147

Rigo 157

Bounty Hunter 179

Cantina 195

Fear 213

Murder 227

Dark Stranger 241

Alone 257

Love 281

Pis Aller 303

Gonzaba 315

Foreword

an Angelo, Texas was not much different in the 60's, when I grew up there, than it was in the late 1800's and the early years of the twentieth century when my ancestors settled in the region. The car had replaced horse and buggy and we had a TV in every house with at least 3 stations available. But all one had to do was step outside, and the waning remnants of a passing era were easily recognizable in the fast-moving clouds and the warm acrid dust in the ever-present winds.

"Angelo," as it was called by the natives, moved at its own pace. That pace was slow but not plodding. The hot days were oppressive, but you got used to it. Country wisdom was known simply as wisdom. Anyone without a west Texas drawl was a yankee, even if he was from only as far north as Dallas.

You respected your elders - and that was a tall order in a town populated by a large number of older west Texans. We didn't give the respect reluctantly. We youngsters depended on the unerring guidance of our predecessors.

West Texas culture is not carried on as one might a religious dogma. The culture is something with which one is born: not necessarily a birthright, but rather an instinct as vital as the will to survive.

In the sixties, my grandparents, great grandparents and their immediate families were celebrities in my view: they were the remaining witnesses and players in a rugged adventure only read about now. The significance of their first-person accounts was never lost upon me.

It seemed that the Old West lingered in west Texas as a passing stranger reluctantly leaves the comfort of a welcome fire. In those final days of the wild west, my great-uncle was the sheriff in Eldorado. After a vicious outlaw threatened to murder him in his sleep, he sat in his old rocker on his front porch where he waited through the night. A 12-gauge shotgun rested across his knees as he rocked and smoked cigarettes, ready for the vengeful outlaw to arrive in the dark to carry out his threat. My great-uncle was killed in the line of duty some years later, but he survived that night.

My great grandmother, Nanny, told stories of her youth where her family crossed Indian country in a covered wagon. Even in my boyhood, I remember the wagon livery which stood behind her old house, a large mound protecting the wagon and the occupants of the house from Indian attack. Many of my ancestors lived in nearby *Paintrock* where they battled angry redskins as a matter of course.

Growing up in the company of those who represented the last participants of a rich western heritage, and having been touched throughout my life by the magic of that oasis town at the edge of the vast sage and sand deserts to the west, it was no wonder that I craved the stories of the old west.

In those days, western novels were popular and inexpensive. Max Brand entered my world from the disorganized contents of an *ML Leddy and Son* boot box on a table at a garage sale. My mother purchased several books there for she and my father to read – they were, and still are, voracious readers.

The western novels were quick reads for them. I was younger and slower at the skill. The stories were wonderous in their similarities to those stories of my forefathers and mothers. Privately, I read slowly, savoring every word. Publicly, I blamed much of my slow reading pace on my father as he directed me to keep a dictionary handy rather than trouble him incessantly for the definitions of unfamiliar words.

Max Brand was the master of western dialogue. His prose were exquisite turns of phrase, seasoned with a genuine delivery as only denizens of the old west could achieve.

Zane Gray soon entered my worn paperback collection. My first Zane Gray novel was "Man of the Wilderness," His descriptions were palpable and compelling. If he described cold and wet misery, I reached for a blanket. Hot desert scenes had me on my feet desperate for a glass of water.

My first efforts as a writer were less than admirable. I wrote my first story in my early teens. The characters were too perfect, and their motivations were painfully contrived. Although poorly conceived, those early imaginings were the tender seedlings of a strong desire which would beckon me all my life.

I entered the film business in my late 30's. I have heard that 90% of all film actors make less than $2,500.00 per year at the craft. My claim to fame was that I was among the top 10% - just barely. Recently I was described as a failed actor. That is a painful observation based upon how low the success bar is set.

After more than 60 films, commercials, industrials, and other video productions, I was considered a minor celebrity within the Austin/San Antonio film market. I rarely auditioned, yet I appeared in 3 to 4 projects per year.

One of the directors with whom I worked on more than 15 films cast me exclusively as the heavy in many of his movies. Once, I asked him why he never cast me as a lead in any of his films.

As he considered his response, he pursed his lips and shook his head sadly. Finally, he told me that in the limited talent pool of the local industry there was no actor who could successfully convince an audience that a Craig Rainey character would have anything to fear from them. He blamed the predicament on my strong screen presence. He told me when he found a script where the bad guy was the lead character, he would surely cast me in that role.

Years later I worked with another film company, *Mutt Productions*, which made larger budget films with better known actors. I managed to land the lead antagonist role of *The Mayor* in the grindhouse film

The Return of Johnny V. After acquiring the film, the distribution company requested a follow-up film falling in one of any of three genres including: science fiction, movies featuring animals, or westerns.

One of the producers with Mutt Productions asked if I knew of any available scripts for any of the genres. I said I didn't, but of those listed I liked westerns.

As we talked further, I recalled my conversation with the director with whom I had asked for a leading role. A glimmer of an idea struck me. I snapped out of my reverie and interrupted the producer's continued conversation, announcing to him that I had an idea for a western film. After a few questions about my idea, which I could not answer, I promised to produce a summary or possibly a treatment for a screenplay.

Less than a month later, I had the treatment completed for *Massacre at Agua Caliente*. The producer loved the premise and offered to forward it to Hollywood where vetted screen writers would create a full script. I asked if I might have a try at writing the screenplay. Reluctantly, the producer agreed. 30 days later, I had the first draft of the script completed.

The script was passed around to several production houses including two major film studios in Hollywood. Offers were made for the rights to the script. I turned them down, doggedly holding to the desire to play the main character – the villain.

With the return of the script came notes on how the film companies thought the story might be improved. Everyone agreed that the story was too long and complex. The most common criticism I heard repeatedly complained that it was two movies in one and would be too expensive to make.

Ultimately, the script was shortened, and the main character was softened to increase his likeability with audiences.

I submitted the screenplay to several festivals where it won many awards and official selections. Although the story was well received, over time the offers dwindled until the script was no longer the hot property it once was.

After 3 years, I felt driven by a desire to write the complete story I had originally created before the edits and redactions. The novel would contain every scene and present the main character as I had intended in the original script.

As I began the novel, I saw in my imagination the story told in the style of the books I had read as a child. I wanted the novel to be an ode to those turn of the century authors I loved, and who had influenced me so greatly.

To succeed, the dialogue had to be important and the imagery needed to jump off the page and grab the reader, pulling him or her into the midst of the characters.

Because a novel is filled with description that a script never contains, I found it necessary and critically important to research many of the places, people and events peripheral to my story. With few exceptions, the locations and references to outlaws and Indian tribes mentioned in the book are accurate. Hurrah City is a real place. The name was changed in the early twentieth century, but it is authentic to the period.

I completed the novel five years after the final version of the script. Four additional edits refined the style until I was satisfied with the work. I knew I risked a great deal by departing from the quick prose and spare descriptive styles of modern novels, but I wrote the novel with the idea that it would ultimately be a monument to the genre.

I am a reader, and I know the styles of popular authors. I enjoyed the *Sackets* of Louis L'Amour. The grit of Larry McMurtry enthralls me still. Both are masters of their craft: their styles wisely modern and swift. Still, I dared to risk the dangers of my throwback novel.

My intention was to bring my readers a taste of those turn-of-the-century authors with the modern sharp edge of my present-day favorites. I hope I have succeeded. Only you, the reader, can know for sure.

No matter the reception of *Massacre at Agua Caliente*, my goal was achieved.

I was in San Angelo recently – my first visit in more than 15 years. A new expressway runs through the middle of town. The Twin Buttes seem smaller and less significant, and one must drive as far as Mertzon to feel the few remaining ghosts of the old west. Dear reader, I believe you will find that same rare spirit I knew as a boy in the pages of this singular novel.

Thank you for your time invested in the reading of the book. May your visit be entertaining and memorable.

Craig Rainey

CHAPTER ONE

The Mormons

Hurrah City was a bustling gateway to the frontier. To her east, the Ozarks began an intricate stair step to gain their ultimate heights. To the west and to the southwest, the terrain gave up its arduous complexities for smoother lowlands and less densely wooded greenery. The most heavily travelled routes carried hardy adventurers to sparsely settled lands and the territories west amongst the lower elevations and to semi-arid regions. Less popular routes led into harsh regions containing Indian territories and savage lawless lands beyond the grip of civilization and its constraints.

Like a healing wound, soon to achieve the permanence of a ragged scar, a bright slice of railway was under construction and had reached within 10 miles of the outlying district, east of Hurrah City. The growing city's expansion had been rapid – in fact, nearly panicked in its efforts to keep pace with the demand for goods, trades and personnel serving the approaching railway and its associated wealth. Commerce established with departing settlers' trains had made the town as robust as was thought possible. The promise of lucrative railroad activity was likely to cause the little town to fairly explode with additional opportunity.

The main thoroughfare serving the village resembled a tree's trunk from which intersecting lanes were random as branches. These paths of necessity were formed by wild growth rather than any real plan. Many of the buildings were rude wooden structures, hastily erected. However, the overwhelming number of business establishments and spare shelters for wayward families comprised dingy white sided tents.

Of the wooden structures, the largest and most impressive, by frontier standards, contained the general mercantile and saloon. The narrow saloon was no more than a broad hallway occupying the space to the side of the store. It spanned the depth of the building, separated from the mercantile by a thin plank wall. The chief feature of the smoky, dank establishment was the elbow worn top and boot scarred foot rail humbling the long high bar guarding the entirety of the outer wall. Entry to the raucous room was made either through the general store or by double doors at the front of the saloon.

As was common during the mild evenings of early spring, windows and front doors were cast open, pounding the night air with the din of the mad frivolity within the crowded saloon. The bar was lined with all manner of patrons. Some appeared to be lean-hipped, broad shouldered cow punchers. Others wore the soft clothing of settlers enjoying a last night of civilization before heading out for the territories. A small constituent was made of neatly dressed card sharps, weasel-faced grifters and a small contingent of female consorts.

Unnoticed at a corner table was Crease Cole, accompanied only by a dull bottle of Rye whiskey. His sandy hair and rakish moustaches served to sharpen the pointed gaze of his blue eyes. He tossed down a shot then leaned back to take in his surroundings more fully. He was in the habit of being aware of all who were in proximity. He absently fingered the death black butts of his pistols, poised impatiently in a well-oiled two-gun rig. His gaze met many, but few weathered the look.

Seemingly satisfied at his safety and comfort, he poured another slug and rapidly downed it, pinching his lips and moustache with thick blunt fingers to remove excess moisture. He clinched his strong teeth and exhaled warm vapor between them as heat made its way to his belly.

Crease's gaze was drawn to the front doors where four men entered together. The first was a raw-boned whipcord of a man with his hat pushed well back on his head. Two of his companions were obviously easterners, probably settlers, due to their heavy clothing and round hats. The last man to enter was an unhappy, barrel-chested, gray whiskered man in suspenders and shirt sleeves.

All four were occupied in a sincere but mobile conversation. Led by the set jaw and singular intent of the raw-boned man, the four made their way to the bar. The stubborn leader placed a spurred boot on the foot rail then turned to the three men. He uttered an emphatic protest. Buried within the general din of the saloon, his words found no reach beyond his followers. His jutting jaw and defiant pose said much about his resistance to the other side of the conversation. With a gesture, he ordered a drink and listened to the older man of the shirtsleeves with an arched brow and an ugly grin. The drink arrived, and he downed it in an instant. He stopped the bartender abruptly and ordered another.

His companions looked about in protest and despair as if to implore some cool head around them to persuade this recalcitrant rebel to sense. The three men continued to state their case with lowered heads and firm gestures. Their entreaties went unheeded as that worthy downed three more drinks in quick succession.

By this time, nearby patrons focused more than casually upon the drama playing out at the bar. Many of those spectators regarded the scene with genuine interest and guarded smiles.

Some feet away, a buxom, thick limbed saloon girl eyed the newcomers with a wry smile as she stood from her table. She smoothed her dress carefully, giving her attention to her companion at the table: a man in a garish hat. He seemed to encourage her in her endeavor. She nodded to her companion a half attentive reply. She shook her luxuriant mane and made her way towards the group. She hid her intentions poorly as she feigned interest in other patrons: wandering, as it were, haphazardly, toward the group.

The rebellious drinking man noticed her as she approached. The spirits-fueled gleam in his eye hardened as he considered her with obvious desire. She moved in behind him and gestured to the bartender for a drink. She 'accidentally' bumped her quarry and uttered a demure "excuse me, cowboy" or so it seemed from Crease's vantage.

With a daring look towards his wide-eyed companions, the leader turned with exaggerated surprise, doffed his hat, and said something to the woman - probably meant to be clever.

She smiled, then said something in return. The embarrassment and growing displeasure of the other three was obvious as they became more aware of their undesired roles on center stage.

The bare-headed leader moved in closer to the woman and bared his long-stained teeth as he shared another thought with her. The woman's face changed by degrees as this last sunk past her mischievous front. Her intent had been to enter the limelight, but it was apparent she was not prepared for her role as it was playing out with the drunken stranger.

Enjoying her discomfiture, he followed up his last remark with another, still inaudible in the loud room. Her mouth dropped open and those who knew her also knew what would come next. Her mouth slowly closed, and her lips stretched into a smile which only a woman can wield. She batted her eyelashes then dashed her full drink into the man's face. Amber liquid dripped down onto his collar. Her face transformed into a mask of fury, and she began dressing down the insulting cowboy. She punctuated her narrative with a sound slap across the man's face.

Quick as a wink, the cowboy's fist shot. His fist was large enough that his blow completely covered her face. She went down with a sickening suddenness, completely unconscious. The bar fell immediately into silence. By degrees angry murmurs lifted like a rising plague. The assailant's three companions recoiled from the scene with a very real horror and distaste.

The man of the garish hat, who had apparently launched her upon this mission, stood slowly, never taking his eyes from the bare headed attacker. He was a diminutive man with close-set eyes and a pencil thin moustache. His hat was a tiny hat with a red band, a green feather tucked beneath. He approached the assailant with stiff strides. As the small man approached the drunken cowboy, Crease could not resist an overpowering impression of the tiny man's stature as that of an attacking leprechaun.

Apparently, the same thought occurred to the small man's quarry because a cruel leer grew upon the taller man's face as the slight man approached. The leprechaun paused above the prostrate woman. He bent and helped her to her feet. He removed a red kerchief and dabbed at the blood around her nose and mouth. She stood unsteadily. Her eyes rolled as she struggled to clear the mist from her mind. Two saloon girls approached and gently helped her away. They cast dark looks rearward at the assailant.

The villain crossed his arms and stared down at the smaller man. His sneer was now fully matured. He curled his lip in disdain. It was apparent that he was not intimidated by this angry dwarf.

The room was sufficiently quiet now for the words between the men to be heard by all.

"So, you like to hit women?" said the leprechaun. His Irish brogue completed the picture for the other.

The villain laughed heartily. He held his sides as he said, "You'd better get back to your toad stool or cobbling or whatever it is you keep busy doing when you're not drinking with full grown men."

This sally was not greeted with the raucous laughter the villain had expected. Conversely, if it were possible, the room became even more silent. The crowd was a study in reactions. On some faces there were expressions of veiled horror – even fear, on others, one could almost make out traces of pity.

"You are funny," said the smaller man. "It is a sad thing these are your last words."

The smaller man moved with surprising quickness towards his target. As he did, he drew a gleaming blade as large as his arm. The grinning villain hardly had time to straighten and reach for his pistol when the blade sunk to the haft into his chest. The smaller man rode him to the floor gripping his neck as he would a saddle horn. The bigger man's body hit the dusty floorboards with a dull, heavy chunk. The dwarf kneeled on the dying man's chest, looking at his surprised face with a grim countenance of squinting eyes and bared teeth.

As the villain died, the dwarf stood, withdrawing the blade slowly until the wound was empty save for a spreading blood stain upon the man's shirt. He looked about the crowd. Those close by felt his gaze single them out.

"I am Liam 'Kabash' O'Flaherty. I fled my loving Isle for the killing of better men than this sack of shit that lies before me."

His eyes scanned the room. Finally, he turned to the remaining three newcomers.

"Take your friend and go...now."

The last was low but menacing.

The older gentleman said, "This poor soul was no friend of ours. We met him just yesterday. He was to lead our party through the Indian lands to our new homes in the territory."

O'Flaherty didn't move a muscle. He stood with his knife dripping crimson onto the worn floorboards. He waited for the three to obey.

Speaking to the throng in general, the old man continued.

"Is there anyone who knows the country well enough to guide us through?"

Not one of the patrons replied, nor did they show the slightest interest. Liam O'Flaherty was a known man who had recently made Hurrah City his home. He had been tested on other occasions with similar results. When his passion was high, it was unwise to make oneself noticed.

The larger of the settlers placed hands upon the other two and drew them through the front doors. The Irishman watched them until they disappeared. He glanced at the dead man as if he had forgotten him. He turned to two men at the bar.

"You two muster up and haul this mess out into the street. We've drinking to do."

Crease sat holding his empty glass aloft. With a start, he looked down and realized he had been frozen in this way for some time. He lowered the glass unsteadily and capped the bottle. He watched as the two men went to the body and obediently carried it out the front doors. Silence fell away once again, replaced with the slow gain of saloon sounds. Soon the saloon was once again bathed in its former clamorous noise.

Crease stood resolutely then made his way toward the front doors.

CHAPTER TWO

Trail Boss

The settlers' wagons were encamped in a small valley just outside of town. The rising sun warmed the new day as Crease sat his horse atop a rim overlooking the valley. The settlers were slowly going about their morning chores. Smoke from breakfast cook fires rose lazily over women bent to their tasks. Men occupied themselves with any number of preparatory duties required of those looking to break camp for good.

Crease clucked to the bay mare as she picked her way easily down the slope towards the encampment.

Travis St. Peter, the older man from the saloon, puffed at his pipe as he watched the stranger at a distance making his way towards their camp. St. Peter was the leader of their group. He again wore suspenders and shirtsleeves as he had the previous evening at the saloon. He listened to the elders nearby debating alternative travel plans necessitated by the death of their guide.

Kyle Spears, the large farmer who had drawn the others from the bar, rubbed his chin in thought. He was a giant of a man with a large shaggy head.

He looked away from the discussion and towards St. Peter as the conversation continued without him.

16 | CRAIG RAINEY

His voice was low, booming gently as he finally said, "We can't make the trip without a guide, Father."

Shin Bruce, the third of the men in the saloon, was smaller but dressed similarly to Kyle.

He favored Kyle with a sneer. "I reckon that's true. With a keen brain like yours, we should put you in charge."

Kyle looked down at the smaller man. His gaze was mild, considering the words of the other. After considering him for a moment, Kyle said wearily, "Do you ever get tired of hearing yourself talk?"

"A stranger," St. Peter said through a cloud of sweet smoke.

The others turned to watch the stranger's approach. Crease had gained the edge of the encampment. He rode with a casual relaxed posture. He looked around at the Mormons with mild interest.

Much of the work stopped as other settlers turned to watch Crease.

"Welcome, stranger," said Travis St. Peter when Crease was close. "State your business, sir."

Crease stopped his horse and dismounted. He approached the three, looking around him as if he were memorizing each settler's position.

"Crease Cole," he said putting out his hand. "I hear you're in need of a guide of late."

The elders sized up the stranger as Travis St. Peter accepted his hand.

The leader shook his head. His eyes darkened at the memory of the grisly killing.

"I was there," Crease said, seeming to read St. Peter's thoughts. "That feller didn't act with much sense."

Travis nodded in sad agreement.

"We had just met him. We had commissioned him in writing. He met us at Hurrah City only a day before he was..."

"Bodine was crazier than an outhouse rat," said Shin in disgust.

"Hush, Shin," said Travis. "What are your qualifications, Mr. Cole?"

"I reckon I know this country better than most and I don't drink much on the trail and carouse even less. Judgin' from the man I'm replacin', that is a big step up."

Crease grinned at his own awkward humor. His expression sobered when his words were not met with lightened moods.

St. Peter cleared his throat to indicate a return to business.

"Have you made the trip before?"

Crease removed his hat and wiped his brow, looking around him.

"I ain't been as far as the territory, but I've passed through your Indian country many times. Indians are the tricky part. Once we get through Tontantin Mesa, we're in the clear. After that, it's all keepin' the Sun in front or behind from there."

Kyle looked at Travis and Shin fixed a critical stare on Crease.

"Give us a moment, Mr. Cole," Travis said as he turned and led the other two a distance away.

Once out of earshot, Shin said, "I don't trust him, Father."

Kyle rubbed his chin. Travis looked at Shin, weighing his own feelings. Shin took the gaze as invitation to give his opinion.

"He could be anybody: a robber, murderer, thief."

Shin glanced over his shoulder at Crease, standing in the distance with his back to the three.

"He wears two guns. He is probably a gun fighter and criminal. We got our women to think of."

St. Peter nodded as his mind busied itself with private thoughts. His assessment of their situation offered a limited number of prospects upon which he could count.

Shin took the nod as agreement and continued.

"Maybe we could wait until a little later in the season."

St. Peter's eyes lifted from their thoughts, regarding Shin with a blank look. Shin realized that the older man had not been listening to him. He pursed his lips as he endeavored to keep his frustration to himself. Kyle looked at the smaller man, amusement pulling at the corners of his mouth.

Shin looked up at Kyle and his eyes narrowed in anger.

"Shin," St. Peter said finally, "You and Kyle pass the word: Go back to your families and make ready to move out at first light."

Helen was nervous. It wasn't the hardships of the long journey that made her uneasy. The oxen's slow laboring gait was comforting. Her surroundings were vastly alien to what she was accustomed in her young life, but the rough desert country was a continual source of wonder and discovery. Her discomfort sprung from many quarters. She labored eagerly at her chores with the others, but she didn't feel a part of the Mormon group. She was a gentile, by their definition. She felt homesick despite the many weeks since she had left her home to join them.

The chief source of her uneasiness came from her new husband, Shin Bruce. The marriage had been arranged by her mother and executed despite her protests.

To call the woman 'mother' seemed unfitting of late. Helen's father perished in the war, after which her mother had retreated into a world unwelcome to all but herself. Helen tried, on many occasions, to council her troubled mother to no avail. Indeed, her advances had been parried with a cold indignation, that tool wielded by those elders who hold little respect for youthful opinion.

It became apparent, soon enough, that Mother desired to be alone in her efforts to replace her dead husband. It wasn't that her mother was slovenly. Rather, she sought a companion to occupy the lonely void within her which she would, in Helen's opinion, never fill. Her father's passing had broken her mother's fragile heart. Helen believed broken hearts incapable of containing love. One could as easily ask a broken pitcher not to leak - so it seemed with her mother.

Helen came from modest means. Her prospects were numerous, though not substantial. She feared fate would relegate her to the role of sodbuster's wife or perhaps the wife of a wild cowboy. As in so many things in life, her heart yearned for more. She felt from childhood that she was meant for more. Adventure dwelled in her soul and she felt she would die if that resource was not tapped.

The Mormon group, led by Father St. Peter, arrived in her small town as the leaves began to turn. Their intent was to winter near her village and wait out the snow for fairer weather by which to trek west.

She remembered the day she saw Shin for the first time. She noticed his attention towards her at the market where he accompanied the Mormon women tasked with purchasing supplies for the encamped assemblage.

She was accustomed to male attention from both young and old. Her Auburn hair and green eyes never failed to draw male notice initially. Her round limbed shapeliness and her ready smile succeeded in extricating them from any remaining measure of decent sensibility. Her very presence seemed to enthrall the opposite sex. Her mother was prone to criticize her for what she interpreted as a provocative air. Helen invariably reddened in frustration and embarrassment at the criticism.

She was a natural beauty and could no more control her allure than a wildflower could avoid blossoming in spring. Her mother seemed to harbor resentment, and even jealousy, at the attention given Helen. Helen believed her mother's eagerness to marry her to Shin was intended to remove an irritating impediment to her own search for a mate.

Days after Shin's appearance at the market, Helen heard rumors of his asking around town about her. Before long he appeared on her doorstep.

Mother, of course, observed all the ritualistic measures customarily observed in polite society. She eyed this young caller with motherly suspicion. She even protested at his daring to come "a-calling" unannounced. Her admonitions were never as harsh as Helen would have expected of a truly concerned mother. Mother's rebukes contained enough ire to cause Shin discomfort. He blanched and wavered in his conquest. He weakened in the face of Mother's half-hearted rebukes. Helen viewed his weakness of resolve as a character flaw unbecoming a man of the west.

Mother detected Shin's flagging courage. Worried he would falter, she softened her barrage with poorly disguised reluctance. Her mother shushed Helen's protests at her weakened resolve, instructing her that Shin was to be forgiven. His heart seemed true. Mother assured Helen his awkward manner was likely due to a lack of skill in social discourse than the result of a faulty make-up. She mused aloud that it was likely his devout Mormon upbringing was surely the source of his clumsy manner. She divined that he was true, evident by his youthful courtesy and honest discomfiture at offending the home at such an early stage of their courtship.

When she managed to receive him alone, Mother secretly encouraged young Shin with confidential reports containing exaggerated accounts of Helen's reaction to him. She assured the smitten Shin that Helen seemed more absent-minded and listless since his arrival. She vouchsafed her belief that Helen seemed quite taken with the stalwart young man. Mother's fabricated encouragement emboldened him, and he redoubled his efforts, pursuing her openly and with great relish.

Between his attempts at courtship, Helen complained to Mother that she was not interested in receiving Shin romantically. Her mother quelled her complaints summarily. She reminded her of her limited viable prospects and her diminishing opportunities to leave that dirty town. She attempted to persuade her daughter with an assumed air of concern for her happiness and future well-being. As always, Helen was certain her mother's erstwhile concern was more for her own ends than Helen's.

Helen's resistance weakened about the time the Mormons announced their plans to depart. They announced their intent to make for Hurrah City within a fortnight where they would provision and depart for the territories west.

By this time Helen was properly introduced and it was agreed that she and Shin would be married in time for the journey.

Shin seemed unfazed by Helen's distant manner. With the succor of Father St. Peter's advice, Shin believed she was shy but would warm to him in time. They finally wed two days prior to their departure.

Helen awoke from her reverie with a frown on her lovely face. Her nervous state was a direct reaction to Shin's insistent begging to have relations with her. She had done her wifely duty after the wedding, but she was decidedly not attracted to him in that way. She disliked his ungainly manner during the act, and he bore little stamina. What repelled her most was his demeanor - even his very smell. She had been near other men, and their musk had not repelled her as her husband's did. No matter how frequently he bathed, the odor was unmistakable and unpleasant. When he objected to her unyielding defenses at his advances, his manner of speaking became whiney and complaining. Even among the men, his habit of winding into caustic tirade caused those worthies to cast baleful glances towards him.

His attempts to convince her to rut were equally objectionable and annoying. They had not lain together since starting the journey more than three weeks hence. He was becoming more and more resistant to her deflections and weak excuses. Often, he lingered uncomfortably when they embraced. She feared that each time he did so was the day he would succumb to his animal side and force her to take him inside her.

She struggled with her reaction to him. She was, after all, his wife in the eyes of God. She endeavored to find something within her which would sustain her for a lifetime with this man. She found nothing which could ease her discomfort at his touch.

It was after dusk when the Mormons finally massed the wagons and made camp for the night. Helen had been ready to stop for hours. Their guide, Crease, typically stopped no later than afternoon's end. The late halt necessitated that much of the camp's preparation would be done in the dark.

She climbed from the wagon and began drawing the night's provisions from the rear. Shin would arrive soon, and he would be hungry. She was bent over the cooking fire when a buxom, matronly woman approached from around her wagon.

Myrtle St. Peter, Father's wife, was a stern taskmistress, but she seemed fond of Helen. Among the men she was fearless and, at times, garrulous and of ready humor. With the younger members, she was to be respected and obeyed.

"Helen," she said without preamble, "Shin will be delayed. Could you help me prepare the meal for those not in the work party?"

"Certainly, Mother, has something happened?"

Mrs. St. Peter smoothed her dress as she surveyed Helen's camp handiwork.

"Mr. Cole has taken us to the edge of what he calls 'Tontantin Mesa' and the men are rigging the wagons for a marathon trek through the region."

Helen straightened and considered Mrs. St. Peter for a moment.

"Is that why we travelled so late today?"

"Come dear," she said as she walked away.

Helen lifted the rough iron pot with a tattered rag and followed dutifully.

"According to Mr. Cole," Mrs. St. Peter said without turning. "We had to travel as far today as possible, or we would be 'caught on the Mesa' after dark."

"That sounds a little mysterious, Mother."

"Dramatic to say the least: but we are to travel as Mr. Cole sees fit."

Helen bit her lip. She felt it wise to keep her thoughts to herself. She kept her eyes on Mrs. St. Peter's broad shoulders as she followed. Her instincts troubled her.

As they approached another fire, women bustled about, and children played just inside the fire light's circle. Mrs. St. Peter moved to the fire and stirred the simmering pots.

"Marjorie," Mrs. St. Peter said to one of the Mormon women, "Gather the children. We need to get them fed and to bed at an early hour. We start out before first light."

Marjorie, a thin, dark-haired woman, nodded and went off to wrangle the noisy youngsters.

"Helen, place your pot here."

The camp was quiet, and the fire had burned down by the time the men returned from their labor. Crease led the way in silence.

Shin was close at his heels.

"I don't like it Cole," Shin complained. "If there is something you're not telling us you need to say it."

Shin tried to make eye contact with Crease.

"I am the guide on this trail, and I don't need to break down my every decision for your approval," Crease said without looking at Shin.

Crease accepted a plate of food from Helen with a grunt. He nodded his dismissal to Shin and repaired to a wooden crate where he sat heavily. He shoveled stew into his mouth and chewed, obviously tired.

Travis St. Peter accepted a plate from Helen with a smile and nod. He moved towards Crease. He lifted a steaming spoonful of the stew to his lips and consumed it as he looked down at Crease with a thoughtful gaze. He chewed thoughtfully then swallowed.

"I recognize there is little love lost between you and Shin, but I share his concern. It is curious to me that we would take pains to travel so far tomorrow to cross a region you have assured us is safe. I don't question your authority in this matter, Mr. Cole, but the well-being of my flock is my responsibility."

"Well, as they say, Mr. St. Peter, curiosity killed the cat," Crease took another bite and looked emphatically at Travis. "We will be in the open, in Indian country, is all."

Travis looked over his plate, considering Crease a moment more, not satisfied.

"Again, I ask you..."

Crease interrupted him. His lip curled as he spoke.

"Mr. St. Peter, this here journey ain't a prayer meeting. No matter who you woulda picked to guide you through rough country, dangers are gonna be there. If you and your people didn't expect some hazard on a trip like this, then you are all fools in a fool's fantasy."

St. Peter's brow furrowed at this straight talk from his guide. After a moment more, he turned on his heel and moved towards the fire and his awaiting wife. He was obviously dissatisfied with the conversation.

Percy, Marjorie's husband, took a seat next to his wife and watched silently. Percy was a smallish man with the demeanor of a teacher and the appearance of a rather large mouse. He wore spectacles and was in the habit of looking over the top of the rims when speaking.

Marjorie grasped his hand and said, "Should I be worried?"

Percy looked over the rims of his spectacles into his wife's eyes. He seemed to find his answer in his observation of her lean features.

"Mr. Cole says no. My instincts say yes."

The morning shared the darkness of night when Helen woke to the sound of Mrs. St. Peter banging on an iron wheel ring. The chill air kept her beneath the covers. She cautiously felt for Shin in the dark. The bedding was warm, but he was gone. She relaxed slightly. Fatigue had been her ally the previous night. After making a feeble attempt for her, he gave up and fell into an exhausted sleep.

She rose, fully dressed, thankful for the time saved. She invested the few extra moments gained in an effort to tidy up in case Mother inspected her wagon. She quickly climbed out from under the wagon cover and began stowing those few things remaining unloaded from the night before.

Breakfast was served at Marjorie's camp as supper had the previous evening. Food service was well underway when Helen arrived to help.

Breakfast was a casual affair of bacon, potatoes and biscuits. Drowsy and hungry, families drifted to the serving board before moving away quietly to eat. The hour was early even for these hardy settlers.

The wagon train was under way well before a dim gray line brightened the eastern sky. Shin sat beside Helen on the wagon seat rather than in the saddle of his horse as was his custom. As the dawn colored red and gold, the increased light allowed her to see the tension in his face. He didn't look at her as he concentrated on the task at hand.

"Are things that serious?" she asked.

"What do you mean," he replied a little too casually.

"You aren't riding today?"

"Long day. We need to make good time."

She gave her attention to the horizon as she pondered his unspoken meaning.

The morning grew bright and warm. The wagons moved with a slow steadiness which belied the tension of all within. By degrees, Helen noticed a change in the terrain. Where once they travelled amongst gently rolling hills and feathered greenery, they now entered a region flat as a table with yellow grasses and spare twisted trees. The chief difference to Helen was the lack of birdsong. During her time on the trail, she made it a point to listen to the sound of birds as they gamboled about in their singular duties. She made a game of locating each singer and remembering its merry tune. Since the train had topped the ascent to the mesa, she had heard not a single bird. The absence contributed ominously to her sense of foreboding.

At the front of the caravan she spied a rider making his way back, speaking to the drivers of each wagon in turn.

Shin sat straighter in the seat. Scorn rusted his words.

"What does he want?"

The rider was Crease Cole. He finally reached their wagon and doffed his hat to Helen.

"Push your team, Bruce. We need to pick up the pace."

"These are Oxen, Cole. We ain't got horses in the traces."

Shin gave emphasis to his words with a baleful look at Crease then gave his attention to the Oxen.

Crease looked at Helen. He let his gaze linger upon her for a moment longer than she thought appropriate. Finally, he again touched his hat and moved past them to the following wagons.

"I don't like that fella'," said Shin with a jerk of his head.

"I think he knows it as well as the rest of us, Shin."

"Don't sass me, Helen. I don't reckon this here is going to end well."

Helen peered at him, trying to understand his meaning.

"Tell me what's on your mind."

His jaw worked as he resisted the urge to say more.

"I'm hungry. You got any jerked meat about?"

Helen watched him for a moment. She was decidedly not satisfied with his mute resistance to her concerns. With a shake of her head, she climbed over the seat into the wagon to satisfy his request.

Father St. Peter hunched in the seat of the big wagon. The day was growing hot and he had used considerable energy pushing the oxen. The stubborn animals were not accustomed to the brisk pace and it took great effort and a sustained application of strength to keep the stubborn beasts at that speed. If his thoughts wandered or if he lost concentration on the task, the beasts immediately lapsed into a more comfortable gait.

Not long after midday Father wiped the sweat from his face with a dirty shirt sleeve. His attention focused upon what appeared to be a trellis works in the distance. It was ahead and right of their current heading and was too far for him to make out details. Myrtle noticed his attention to the thing in the distance and shaded her eyes to make out what he was seeing.

"What is that, Father?"

"I cannot say, Mother."

Travis looked ahead. Driving the lead wagon, he could see their mounted guide some hundred yards ahead of the column. Although his face was not visible, the cant of his head indicated Crease was also paying attention to the distant object.

The Sun climbed higher as they came nearer the structure. Heat mounted in shimmering waves, marking this afternoon as the hottest thus far. The early heat was accompanied by the tortured sounds of Cicadas, buzzing in a rise and fall of crisp protest. The train pulled abreast of the structure, but still at a considerable distance. The structures were now recognizable as roughhewn platforms. The platforms were festooned with a variety of hanging objects, feathers, and other distinctively Indian relics.

His face lengthened in horror as Father realized the fixtures of an Indian burial ground. He glanced at Myrtle. He started as she was staring at him full faced.

"Shush, Mother," he cautioned in a whisper.

The distress was clear in her face, but she obeyed.

Helen and Shin stared at the burial stands in stricken horror. Crease had guided them through Indian sacred ground. Helen turned her head slowly from the sacred burial pyres to gauge her husband's reaction to the sacrilege. For once he was silent although his working jaw ground teeth at a furious pace. This uncharacteristic reaction instead of his typical whining diatribe caused her real terror. She sized her husband as a willful critic with little consideration for consequences. This strange self-discipline of restraint shook her to her core.

Riding in the lead, Crease felt his followers' eyes burning into his back. He tried to disguise his frequent looks askance at the burial pyres, but his grim fascination guided his will. He knew he would hear about it when they stopped late into the night.

Throughout his years in this country, he had heard many stories of those who had crossed the Tontantin but had never been here himself. He knew to stay to the southern region of the mesa. Forbidding terrain and his unfamiliarity with the region, however, had resulted in his deviation from established routes.

He felt fear rising in him. He was alone in this endeavor. The Mormon's followed him reluctantly but desperately. Their reluctance was a common companion he kept at bay with sarcasm and a brittle veneer of disdain for the soft settlers. He inhaled and exhaled deeply, trying to salvage his confidence with the logic that it was unlikely they were the first to make this blunder. Additionally, he thought with manufactured relief, it was likely they would remain unseen if they continued to move at this pace.

Crease's mind wandered back to Jake, the old man who shared duties with him in a lonely line shack years ago. Crease shook his head to clear the regret for his actions so long ago that sullied his name. He fled the circle C, taking the old man's hurried advice that he run for it.

Jake was an old man, and he seemed to have always been old – a fixture rather than a persona. Most of the hands regarded him as a drifter, but one wielding the wisdom of a sage. His stories were told with appropriate detail but with the speed of the experienced yarn spinner. His look prompted introspection for signs of weakened resolve or phantoms of shrinking courage.

Crease instinctively doubted the wisdom of anyone who, at his age, was still working line on a cattle ranch. Ironically, what Crease knew of the trek across the mesa was founded at the comfortable edge of a late-night fire, across from the old saddle tramp. Despite his doubts, he felt an undeniable fondness for the old man, and a great confidence in his council. From the first, he counted himself fortunate to have been partnered with so adroit a storyteller. Time moved slowly on the line. A well-spun yarn was priceless in filling the time void with memorable pleasure.

Jake often told stories of his crossing the mesa. One tale haunted Crease now: a tale which accounted the events when Jake had crossed Tontantin Mesa years before it was common for settlers' trains to cross the frontier.

This region belonged to the Lipan tribe. The tribe was fiercely protective and dealt severe punishment to trespassers when discovered.

The accepted route in those early days was known as the Southwest Trail, a much longer but a much safer and easier route. It issued from St Louis and crossed the entirety of Arkansas over to the Red River valley. It finally quartered far south towards the Texas coastal town of Port Arthur where it led west towards the unsettled territories.

A secondary route was created in an effort to shorten the passage. It was a significantly shorter journey than the Southwest Trail, but it crossed formidable terrain below the southern rim of Tontantin Mesa. The primitive lower trail staggered through ravines and blind canyons. Complicated by the treacherous crossing of the seasonal cataract of the Tontantin River, the journey could take as much as three-fold the time it took to cross the same distance over the mesa. The lower trail was the last attempt by whites to make good time west while avoiding the dread Indian raids likely to accompany a Mesa crossing. Although devoid of Indian danger, the lower route guaranteed loss of property and, sometimes, life from the formidable terrain and flooding.

The gamble of danger from possible Indian attack over the Mesa figured increasingly more reasonable when compared to the guaranteed losses from travelling the lower trail

More and more settlers took to the Mesa only to fall victim to vicious Indian war parties. Finally, travelers resorted to hiring armed escorts to see them through the region. The measure was rewarded with a gradual reduction in Indian attacks as braves met their ends to the hardened defenses of the armed escorts.

The result was not solely the product of armed defenses. The Lipan grew more concerned with protecting the living among them from Comanche raids to the north. The insults paid their dead by whites in the south lost much of their interest as they committed forces to defending against the raids. Although the frequency of Indian attacks upon settlers' trains diminished, the travelers cautiously gave the burial grounds a proper berth. The perceived respect for the sacred grounds was enough to reduce the settlers' trespass to a lower priority in defense resources for the tribe.

Jake, however, had crossed the Mesa before the Lipan were so tolerant of the passing of the whites through their protected land. He shivered as he told Crease how, like many who followed over the years, he joined a settlers' train at Hurrah City. The train was led by the Greer brothers. Caleb and Reginald Greer were veterans of the Indian wars and had participated in the Missouri Indian raids. Their history was bloody and chock full of adventure.

They were commissioned to service by a group of prospectors headed for the California Gold fields. The passage was ill-timed in that the start was late summer. The weather favored those who left in spring. Moreover, the late start exposed the traveling party to a greater likelihood of hostile contact from Lipan hunting parties gathering game for their winter stores.

The Greer brothers took the job only after the prospectors offered them twice the normal rate. Jake answered the Greers' call for additional guns. The train was no more than a mile onto the mesa when the first attackers struck. The Greer security detail lost two men though they successfully fought off the raid.

Caleb Greer picked up the pace of march, taxing the pulling beasts cruelly. By the end of the Greer trek, two wagons, eight oxen and twelve fighting men had been left behind.

Crease recalled Jake's story with alarm. Despite the Lipan's reduced interest in passing settlers, and the fact that their seasonal timing was good, they had blundered far north of acceptable routes. Most concerning to Crease was that they were woefully short of fighting men if the Indians were to attack.

The Lipan had not engaged a wagon train for many months. The general rumor was that the Comanche had stepped up their attacks upon the Lipan as with most of the smaller tribes in the region. This was scant relief for him. With no real armed defense, Crease was gambling with the lives of his party, risking that the blind eye turned by the Lipan would continue. His feelings of doubt were all but overwhelming. He was certain he would feel no relief of the strain upon him until he led the settlers' train down the gentle western descent from the Mesa.

Helen watched the horizon with keen eyes, made sharper by a deep-seated dread. Shin sat his seat rigidly. Her attempts at conversation had been rebuffed with monosyllabic replies. She had long since stopped trying to read his expressions. His face was a stoic mask. She knew not whether his manner was induced by fear or something akin to the dread which consumed her energy and shook her self-possession. Anxiety was driving her to seek action – any action. At one point, she considered dismounting the wagon and running alongside to exhaust her surplus of nervous energy. Shin would have deemed this ridiculous. She knew not why, but she didn't want to show her weakness to him.

Although their progress appeared slow, the oxen were flagging as the miles dragged away behind them. She noticed that Shin slowed the animals' pace from time to time, but the respite was scarcely enough to succor the poor beasts. Moisture fell from the animals' broad haunches. Their open mouths dripped like leaky buckets. Helen prayed for the poor animals. She felt some guilt at the selfish nature of her prayers.

The relentless mid-afternoon sun punished the trespassers. Shin pulled up on the reins as the wagon ahead slowed, then stopped. Helen leaned out to identify the cause for their halt. A rider approached from the front of the train. She recognized the rider as Travis St. Peter. He pulled up beside the wagon with grim countenance.

"Shin, saddle your horse and meet us at the front."

Helen shifted in the seat.

Travis looked at her as he spoke to Shin.

"The women need to stay with the wagons."

Travis moved past them to the following wagons.

Shin handed Helen the reins and silently dropped to the ground. He moved to the rear of the wagon where his saddle horse was tethered.

Travis St. Peter collected the big farmer, Kyle Spears from his wagon. The two made their way to the front of the train. Father kept his steed at a gentle lope. He was more at ease behind the pulpit than behind a saddle horn. The journey, however, had given him opportunity to achieve a small amount of skill in the saddle. He learned early that a lope or gentle canter was his preferred mounted gait.

He summoned only the family leaders for Crease's meeting. He was not sure of the topic, but he was certain his foreboding was not ill founded. As he and Spears approached the small group, he could hear the others already in heated conversation.

"Maybe you should take the lead then, Bruce," Crease said, looking askance at the approaching riders.

Shin leaned forward in his saddle, his jaw advancing him in defiance.

"That's your answer?" Shin failed to control his temper as he continued, "I didn't come by that money easy, Cole."

Percy Price, a typically mild mannered, soft-spoken man, allowed some pause before he contributed his response to Crease's statement.

"I ain't seen no Injuns since we left out."

Crease chuckled without mirth.

"You don't regular see 'em. An Injun is somethin' you feel – mostly around the hairline.

"This confab is a waste of daylight and my patience. I called this meeting and I aim to do the thinking and the talking."

Shin laughed harshly and shifted back in his saddle.

"Ain't much wasted far as your thinkin' is concerned. You been saying the same damn thing for the last nine days."

Shin looked towards St. Peter, guilty at his rough language. Travis didn't seem to notice the slight, so Shin continued.

"I reckon you're plumb out of new ideas Cole."

Crease fixed Shin with a hateful look. His next words were deliberate and seemed to come from a measure of consideration for his foe.

"You dumbass hayseed. Your bitchin' and moanin' wears thin. You could ruin a good drunk and a free whore. I reckon you fill them britches with shit every day 'cause you can't figure out whether to drop 'em or not."

Shin shaded red from his forehead into his collar. He made a mighty effort to control his anger but to no avail. He began to climb out of the saddle.

"That's all for you Cole. I'm gonna settle your hash once and for all, you..."

Father sidled his horse up to the left side of Shin's horse to block his dismount. Cole watched the action with a grim smile playing about his hard-lipped mouth. No shade of mirth was reflected in his steely gaze.

Father grunted as his horse bumped Shin's.

"That'll do, Shin."

Father St. Peter leveled a look at Crease Cole, obviously weary of the man's eagerness to deflect any question or doubt of his prowess with threat and ridicule. He took a breath and let it out slowly, holding a hand up to Kyle who was about to voice a slowly formed thought. He took a moment, confident in his control of his men, then again looked at Cole.

"We have been two days with neither water nor forage. We hired you as guide because Bodine was shot, and you were the only man who seemed to know this country and was willing to take the job. Are we on the right path or are we not?"

Father's words were slow and measured. Cole took a like pause, his silent jab at the older man, then spoke with inappropriate disrespect to him.

"Mr. St. Peter, I can't be no more clear with you. I called this meeting because I saw a dust bloom on the hills to our north. We need to drop south or..."

Cole stopped mid-sentence, his mouth agape, his gaze focused at a distance beyond their small group.

Shin was taking this opportunity to add a thought to the conversation, "I'm about sick of your theatrics..."

Shin stopped as Father laid a quavering hand on his knee, suppressing his words. Father turned his head to see what had attracted the guide's attention. His expression hardened and his face paled. To all, he was visibly shaken as he hushed Shin.

Shin moved to turn his head when a hissed warning came from Cole.

"Goddam it! Keep your goddam heads forward!"

If the warning had not been enough, the taking of their God's name in vain drew all heads forward immediately. Father had looked long enough to have seen what troubled Cole. Atop a butte, at scarcely a mile, silhouetted against blue sky, were two Indians on horseback. Their open interest in the settler's train was unmistakable, even at that distance. They seemed completely unafraid of detection.

Cole spoke to the group in a hushed yet urgent manner.

"There are two Injuns on top of that butte at about half a mile."

He touched the side of his head with an index finger.

"Where there's two, there's more. We are gonna, real easy like, get them wagons moving."

Cole surveyed the terrain in the remaining directions unoccupied by the Indian threat. He thought for a moment, his listeners waited breathlessly for his next words. Their worst fears were being realized and they were helpless in their horror.

"We'll be too exposed if we stay the course we're on."

He said this more to himself than as information for the gathered men. He nodded towards the South, away from the Indian threat. He straightened in his saddle with confidence in his decision.

"There," He said, turning back to them. "We'll split that gap to the South and find cover."

Father could see clearly the lay of the land to the South but could discern no gap or even a break in the low, ragged escarpment which created the southern barrier for the Mesa.

"That looks pretty rough country to me, Crease," Father said. "We have wagons to consider."

Cole was already turning his horse towards the South. Over his shoulder he said, "This ain't no time to argue. Get 'em moving."

Helen watched as Shin returned, trying to discern his mental state. He approached, head down, jaw still working, as had become his habit. Finally, when he was close, she saw his eyes were wide and his complexion ashy.

"Shin..." she began.

"Not now," he said as he tied off his horse to the wagon. He climbed up onto the seat beside her and waited silently for the wagons ahead to move.

Helen felt fear rise within her throat. She shaded her eyes and looked around to determine what was amiss.

Shin grabbed her arm and jerked it down. She cried out softly and looked at him in alarm.

Shin returned her gaze from under the brim of his hat. His eyes were ablaze, and she thought she saw a hint of moisture in them. His voice was tight in his anxious state.

"Keep your eyes straight ahead and act natural."

"Is it Indians?" she asked.

"It is Indians," he replied bitterly.

"Oh my God! What will we do?"

"We are getting the hell off of this mesa," he said with a quavering voice.

Helen looked up to see the leading wagons turning south.

"I don't see a way through," she said weakly.

"Me neither."

She was unaccustomed to this type of candor from him. He presented no condescending retort nor deprecating observation — just honesty. She strongly suspected this was the honesty of weak and hopeless desperation.

She felt the blood drain from her ears and a mortal terror gripped her heart like a ghostly fist. Was this her last day? Although unseen, she was certain she felt the weight of impending danger.

The leading wagons adjusted course slightly east as they came nearer the escarpment. Apparently, Crease had found a passable route through the seemingly solid wall, and the leaders were altering their direction slightly to access it.

Helen wanted to look behind her wagon to gauge the pursuit of these unseen foes. With monumental effort she resisted the urge. Her mind, however, created pictures of blood-thirsty savages overtaking the trailing wagons and massacring the helpless occupants. Their wagon was a scant 3 wagons from the end. Again, she fought the desire to look back. She held to the belief that following Shin's order to keep looking ahead would be the key to their survival though there was no logic to it.

Soon their wagon tipped sharply into a steep decline as they began their descent from the flat of the mesa into a rough and unforgiving region of knobby hills and large boulders. As they rounded a sharp bend where the ground sloped alarmingly from left to right, they came upon a wagon tipped onto its side. It appeared to Helen that the driver had guided the wagon too far to the right of the treacherous path cho sen by the leaders. The wagon's contents were spilled through rips in the canvas where the weight of the cargo had rent the fabric. There were no passengers nor were there oxen in the traces. Helen surmised that the occupants had boarded another wagon and the oxen were in tow ahead somewhere.

At a distance, the southern border of the mesa had appeared to be a continuous cliff face. At closer range, the escarpment was a knobby region of sharp hillocks and rough rock formations. The wagon train was forced to zigzag following the most passable routes. Many of those passes between the hillocks were merely narrow cuts at the base of two hills. Frequently, the wagon drivers were tasked with keeping the wagons leveled by balancing wheels on opposite hill sides at roughly the same height. This maneuver put tremendous strain on the axle bearings and the moving parts, causing the taxed wagons to creak and crack, groaning their protest from the inward pressure of the opposing grades.

Their treacherous trek continued for many hours. Towards late afternoon the wagon just ahead of theirs came to a complete stop. Helen saw the driver jump off the tall seat and make his way forward.

Shin seemed undecided for a moment then he handed the reins to Helen.

"Wait here. I'll see what's what."

Shin worked his way forward, stumbling over some rocks and loose debris cluttering his path. Helen watched as he disappeared around the front of the wagon ahead. She stood and looked behind her, surrendering her superstitious belief in the folly of Shin's guidance. The wagon behind them was just coming to a halt but she could not see the rearmost wagon. It was not visible due to the twisting path concealing it behind a hillock. At least, she hoped that was why she could not see it.

As she looked forward again, she was surprised to see Shin returning. He climbed aboard as she moved over to make room for him.

"Percy's wagon broke an axle. We're leaving it behind."

"But Percy's wagon has all the plow shares and implements," she said in disbelief. "How will we plant or harvest?"

Shin shrugged and kicked the dust off his boots. Helen could tell Shin was holding back much frustration at this new development. Not long after, they passed the overturned wagon. It had been tipped onto its side to make room for the remaining train. Shiny farm implements and sharp tools lay on the ground where they had fallen from their places in the wagon.

After a time, they descended onto a comparably smoother region. The hillocks grew farther apart, and tufts of spare gray grasses began to appear more frequently here and there. The next bend brought them to a long narrow valley which fed into a greener region below. The sun was falling low toward the western hills. This was the season where daylight lasted longer, but Helen was fearful they would have to travel after dark.

Helen saw Cole at a distance making his way east towards a flat-topped hill jutting from the edge of the valley wall. She presumed he was attempting to gain higher ground to assess their continued route.

Cole's pride still smarted after the loss of their second wagon. He was aware that their trail difficulties were not over, He needed to gain his bearings and come up with a viable route. He broke from the train after motioning to the lead wagon to continue on its present course. He made for a flat-topped outcropping in order to get a better look at what lay before them.

He climbed the hill and dismounted, bending and straightening his stiff legs. The shallow valley stretched out before him, narrowing as it reached the bottoms towards the river basin. Long shadows crawled eastward to darken the valley floor. He reached into his saddlebags and withdrew a telescopic glass. He opened the device and searched north, scanning behind the train for pursuit. He brought the glass around slowly along the farther valley wall until he was again looking south. As he moved the glass further down the valley, something caught his eye. He slowly moved the glass back until he could make out a slight discoloration on the darkening valley floor. He trained the glass on the curious discoloration, straining to identify the object. With a gasp he dropped the glass from his eye. He couldn't be certain, but he thought the discoloration on the ground was the color of clothing. He thought he made out the indistinct shape of a body within them. Why would a dead man be laying out there? This was no travelled route. The ground bore no marks indicating travel by wagon or horse – at least none he could discern at this distance.

Cole mounted and returned to his place before the wagon column. He would soon know the answer to the mystery of a man lying dead in the middle of an untraveled wilderness. Their route would take them directly past the corpse. He felt his old companion, bitter dread, taking its place within him. They did not need more Indian trouble right now.

CHAPTER THREE

The Bank

He had lain in the tall grass for a long time. He had passed the point where pain was specific enough to identify each of his many injuries. He now dwelled in a region of overall discomfort. He was attended by dark specters of impending death.

Time betrayed him. Where once it was a path, giving cadence to an ever-changing life, it was now a drain: spilling without purpose just as the life which now leaked from him. He had mastered stillness during his time on the ground and he remained stock still even when he imagined sounds of approaching rescuers. He no longer trusted his senses. He had imagined the sounds of footfalls before. The dull ghosts of rattling horse tack had haunted him on several occasions. He had since learned to ignore these phantoms of his retreating sensibilities. His lot was cast. He resigned himself to the hands of those who continually stalked him. With his arms and legs staked to the hard ground, he could do no more than wait for death.

He battled himself for control over his final thoughts. He occupied himself by pushing his regrets and ill deeds from him. He would have an eternity with those. He, instead, searched his mind for the will to pass from this life as a man, not a whimpering cur. As always, his mind was a mighty foe and he again revisited that which ended with him tied down to the ground by leather and wood. He no longer knew how long he had lain here. He had been here in his own waste and filth till he no longer cared. He drew a labored breath while his memories gathered about him. As had been his torment many times before, he felt himself drawn again to the events which ended here. He refused to recognize a vengeful fate as being a part of his condition. His eyes clenched in his effort to stem the memory's return. He groaned as his thoughts moved against his will.

Agua Caliente was founded upon the site of an acrid watering hole, serving only the most desperate of nomadic visitors. The small town had been no more than a way station for cattle trains headed to Kansas via the Chisholm and the Shawnee trails. The land around the foul water tank was purchased by Chance Joiner: a wealthy shipping magnate from Galveston. When his fortunes became troubled due to increased competition and French privateering, he emptied his safe and fled to the comparative anonymity of the Texas frontier.

He founded Joinerville on the site of the useless watering hole. The water tank was known as Agua Caliente because just below its murky bottom lay a petroleum deposit, which continually seeped into the pond's water. On occasion, drunken passersby tossed matches into the water, igniting it dramatically. The skim atop the tank burned for hours until the fuel was exhausted.

To Joiner's chagrin, the name took root. At first it was a jest referring to the volatile nature of the tainted water. Later, those familiar with the place refused to give credence to the fool who built there. Joinerville was too permanent a name for an enterprise popular opinion condemned to failure. How could one take the place seriously, after all?

Joiner didn't see promise in the watering hole itself. However, he did have a stubborn vision. Cattle wouldn't drink the water, but the grass of the valley was plentiful, and the town was an ideal place to provision for the long cattle drives ahead. Doggedly, Joiner opened a general store, a saloon, and a brothel. His vision proved resistant to public sentiment, and it wasn't long before Agua Caliente was an established launch point for the Mexican and Southern Texas Cattle outfits. The General Store was well stocked and suffered no competition for 200 miles in any direction.

Seemingly overnight, the town grew to a respectable size. Newcomers were attracted by the prospect of commerce and growth. Cattlemen favored the spot as a shelter from cattle stealing savages.

Joiner built the bank as a matter of necessity. With great industry comes the need to secure the profits of same. Joiner was no fool. He was aware of the possibility that outlaws would likely view a remote bank as a prime target for ill-gotten gain. To discourage this, he constructed the bank of the sturdy limestone, plentiful in the area. He installed no windows and built only one door into the new bank. He commissioned the safe's manufacture to Boston Safe Company at great trouble and expense. He then employed a retired Texas Ranger to guard the bank night and day. He had a small house built on the grounds, insuring the Ranger's comfort and near proximity to his duties.

In time, the bank became a landmark and a source of pride in that it had never been successfully robbed. Many attempts were made in the early years. Most ended in death from a hail of bullets brought down upon the robbers by the "Ready Men" of the town. Those who survived the Ready Men were hung from an exposed roughhewn beam projecting from the peak of the stone roof of the bank. The bank earned a reputation for being "unrobbable," It was the only bank in Texas to have a standing army at its defense. The Ready Men were so named because the citizens in the surrounding homes kept a rifle at hand night and day to defend the great bank. Chance Joiner tendered a standing offer of $50.00 for any man who would bear arms in defense of his bank. He made good on the promise with every robbery attempt. In a time of rampant bank robberies, an "unrobbable" bank drew depositors from afar. The bank was rumored to house the riches of pharaohs.

Texas is known for its formidably hot summers. It was early, but the Sun was already scorching the dirt path to the narrow boardwalk when the old ranger keyed the tumblers of the lock which secured the stout front door of the bank.

As he did every day, the wraithlike bank clerk passed him without a greeting and took his place behind the secure bars guarding the long front desk inside the bank.

The Ranger locked the door behind the clerk and turned on his heel. He rattled the keys as he walked back towards his little house. His shambling gait stirred hot eddies of dust behind him. He sensed eyes upon him, and he looked up to see a rider seated on a rangy dun. The man watched him openly as he made his way to the back of the bank. The Ranger didn't recognize the stranger but something about him set off his internal alarms. His instincts had many times been the sole reason for his surviving during his storied and lengthy career. This rider demonstrated an open interest in the old ranger and his morning duties. The ranger maintained his casual demeanor as he made his slow way to his little cottage in the rear of the bank. He endeavored to assuage any suspicions of the watching rider. His rifle was at the ready just inside his front door and the pull rope for the alarm bell was within easy reach if this rider turned out to be an advanced scout for a robbery attempt. The ranger felt no sense of worry or panic. The townsmen were as responsive as any army garrison. Their tradition as "Ready Men" was a source of pride, spoken of often at social settings and over family meals.

The ranger turned the corner at the rear of the stone bank. He stopped abruptly as his way was blocked by two armed men blocking the dirt path.

"Howdy, lawman," said the smaller and bearded of the two.

"Howdy yourself," said the ranger. "This ain't a good idea."

"Thanks for the advice old timer."

This came from the taller of the two men. The ranger looked closely at the taller man. There was something about him which carried an innate authority. He seemed at ease and decidedly bore no threatening guise. His blue eyes, however, belied the casual smile on his lips. He appeared to be a man of early to mid-forties. He was powerfully built. His manner was pleasant, but one had only to look for another instant to perceive an intent which wasted no extra effort than that required to feign a courtesy intended only to disarm.

"Turn around," said the tall man.

"I can't do that Mister," said the ranger. He fought a rising fear: a fear he had not experienced since youth. He knew if he turned his back, he would not see the inevitable shot which would take his life this day.

"Suit yourself," said the man of the blue eyes. He pulled back the hammer and shot the ranger dead center.

Hearing the shot, the rider of the dun rode up to the front of the bank. He dismounted and tried to force open the front door. He put a shoulder to it. He bounced back without effect to the thick door. Other riders approached and dismounted.

A bull of a man in shirt sleeves led the group.

"Locked?" was his simple question.

The first man did not reply but glanced at him before giving his attention back to the heavily planked door.

"Step aside," the large man said, moving him irresistibly to the side with a giant hand. He tested the door's strength by pressing the rough wood with his huge padded finger tips. Without preamble, he stepped back, then rammed the door with his better than three-hundred pounds. The door shuddered under the blow. With a cracking complaint, it fell open. Sharp splinters exploded from the thick door's edges. The door sagged heavily upon the lowest hinge which clung with the desperation of a soldier overcome and outgunned.

Men entered the bank in an expanding mass. A quick search found no sign of the bank clerk. The robbers passed behind the teller cage in their search for the clerk and the ultimate prize: the bank safe. In a side anteroom they found the smooth steel door of the stolid safe. One of the robbers moved forward carrying a leather satchel. He dropped to a knee and withdrew the contents of the bag, placing them carefully onto the clean planks of the wooden floorboards. He withdrew and staged an array of surgical looking steel tools, a can of clay putty, detonating caps and fuse cord. Finally, he slowly lifted two glass containers of a clear liquid. He placed them among the other items with great care and apprehension. Meanwhile, the others continued their hunt for the clerk.

Moments later, their leader of the blue eyes and his bearded companion passed through the wreck of the doorway at the front of the bank. He looked at the ruined door, rattling the ranger's keys in his left hand.

Shaking his head, he moved to the back of the bank where his safe cracker was preparing the safe to be blown.

"Where is he?"

The safe cracker kept his eyes and sweat beaded face cautiously on his work as he replied.

"They haven't found him yet."

The leader moved beyond the safe room. He soon joined other robbers, congregated around a locked steel door.

The behemoth, who had earlier broken through the front door, pulled on the steel handle with all his might to no avail. The first man who had tweaked the ranger's instincts turned to the leader.

"The rat's inside. He locked himself in. "

The leader kept his blue eyes on the door as he spoke thoughtfully.

"I'd rather use the combination than blow that safe."

He stroked his chin as he considered his next move. Finally, he turned away. He spoke as he withdrew from the room.

"Beau, stay with this door and kill that clerk if he comes out. Boris, come with me."

Boris pulled the handle one last time before he turned to follow. He cast one last look at the steel door then plodded out of the room. The remaining outlaw pulled his pistol and leaned against the wall.

Franklin Meriwether Tate was an accountant by trade. His home in Boston was modest but arranged and managed according to a very specific credo of careful organization and balance. When he made his tiny bed, special attention was given that the colored squares of the clean but threadbare quilt, crafted by his dear mother, were evenly distributed from the left to the right sides of the bed. If his suit trousers became more faded than his coat, he ensured his coat was repeatedly washed until the shades were identical. The contents of his saltshaker never dropped below the level of his pepper shaker. He even varied his route of travel through his home so as not to wear the floorboards unevenly. To Franklin Meriwether Tate, the key to success and contentment was balance.

His sense of contentment ended four years prior on a breezy afternoon in May. He was called into the office of the principle partner of his employing accounting firm. He entered the dark heavy doors and stood before the expansive desk front of Cornelius Dane Dale, of *Dale, Pernice and Foster, Accountants*. During that short meeting Tate was given his marching orders carefully disguised as a request.

He learned that his services were required at a new bank in which the firm was financially and personally vested. Although he was not offered an increase in salary, he was assured the move would be of a semi-permanent nature and would open a rare door to a junior partnership in the firm – provided he achieved similar results to those he had achieved with their Boston firm.

By week's end he sat a hard bench awaiting a west-bound train at Boston's central rail station. He stayed back as the screeching locomotive passed into the station belching smoke, steam and dust. He watched the arriving passengers disembark before he rose. He was not one to waste time or energy with premature preparation, even in the process of boarding a train. He enlisted the services of a rail porter. His bags were loaded, and he was seated comfortably in first class. From his window seat he held a commanding view of the rail station platform. He busied himself perusing a ledger sheet's figures as he awaited the train's departure. His attention to the figures on the sheet was troubled by the peripheral assault of a glimmer from polished steel passing under his window. This was his first glimpse of the Boston safe with which he would acquaint himself intimately over the next four years.

He and the ponderous safe arrived at a desolate rail station in east Texas where both were loaded onto a freight wagon. He assured the driver there had been a mistake. He protested at the prospect of travelling several hundred miles aboard an open wagon. The driver assured him in return there had been no mistake made. The three-week journey to Agua Caliente would be made by the gleaming safe and slight accountant on that heavily-springed wagon, drawn by eight powerful draught horses.

So it was, four years later, Franklin Meriwether Tate entered the bank and paused as the bent ranger locked the ponderous bank door behind him. He stepped to the desk behind the teller's cage and began organizing his ledgers for the day's work. The paperwork took little time after which he made his way back to the "Storage Room" as it was known to the bank personnel.

The room was a steel lined and heavily doored pantry where priceless heirlooms, permanent bank records or items in transit, requiring temporary storage, were secured. A dowry of negotiable securities and precious gems had been entrusted to the safety of the Storage Room overnight before the security detail moved on through town to their ultimate destination: a society wedding between an eastern debutante and the son of a western cattle baron. The contents of the dowry chest more than tripled the greatest depositors' sum ever housed at the bank.

The hidden storage room was considered more secure than even the bank, more due to the closet's secret existence than its being more unassailable than the famous safe from Boston.

He released the double locks and opened the rough door. On the center shelf was the breadbox sized dowry strong box containing the wealth of kings. Franklin was in the midst of making a note when he heard the gunshot from behind the bank, just outside of where he now stood.

He pushed the heavy door closed and was in the act of inserting the large key into the first lock when he heard the front door of the bank give way. His first responsibility was to the valuable contents within the bank. He immediately decided upon his course of action. He held the only keys to the wealth of the bank. He alone could defend the bank's holdings. Acting quickly, he opened the door and stepped inside the room. He rattled the large key into the interior cradle for the door's lock. He felt and heard the dull metallic catch as the lock engaged.

Within minutes he heard men outside the strong door working to open it. He couldn't make out the words, but their tone was not friendly. Inside the vault was dark as any cave and the air seemed uncomfortably close. He was wedged tightly between the steel door and storage shelves so as he could hardly breathe. He certainly had no room to move. It seemed longer, but it only must have been a few minutes, when the efforts to open the door ceased and all became quiet. The close darkness and confined quarters occupied his mind uncomfortably. He had never before been confined as he was. His imagination could not be diverted from its dominating comparison of his predicament to that of being trapped in a coffin. His typically absent imagination now moved forward and began a disconcerting back and forth with his reason and logic. As a seeping pitch in a dark fissure, his panic grew.

Logic: This was a room to which he had the only key. It was not a coffin, and it was above ground.

The mischievous creative mind attacked him with the hypothetical.

Imagination: This may not be a coffin, but it was dark, confining: and wasn't his breathing becoming more labored? Were his labored breaths becoming less satisfying as if his precious breathable air was turning stale?

Again, the defensive parry of his logical mind: darkness and a confined area could account for all of these.

Imagination: but wasn't it likely where light cannot penetrate, air might also not enter?

In an instant, fully formed panic joined him within his prison, taking up more space than comfortable.

He became aware of the weight of the keys he held. He dared not put them down on a shelf. He might not be able to find them again in the dark. If he accidentally dropped them, he would not be able to bend to retrieve them from the floor. His hand seemed to grow fatigued from the weight. He scarcely believed his dilemma. The smallest of blunders, a slight mistake of happenstance could prove fatal.

In a wave, he was overwhelmed with the irresistible urge to leave this place. Precious light and freedom were only inches from him. The bad men, sure to be waiting, were of smaller consequence compared to the sure death he now faced. The slightest bit of carelessness here would end him. Couldn't he trust his fate to the mercy of men? He represented no threat to anyone. Ultimately, he could use his knowledge of the contents of the strong box to bargain for his life. He was an accountant, not a sentry. He had done his job admirably for years. He could not be blamed for being unwilling to assume this new and dangerous mantle. This situation was beyond his control.

His heart lightened as he realized that whatever he gave up for his life would be recovered by the irresistible force of the Ready Men. Perhaps the bell had already tolled, and the townsmen were now repelling the robbers. Might he be unable to hear the bell from within the muted walls of the vault?

After one last deciding labored breath, he rattled the key into the lock. He fumbled frantically with the mechanism before he twisted the key. The heavy door swung open and he savored sweet fresh air. He did not immediately see anyone in the room. Relief succored his flagging spirits. A rough looking man with a gun stepped before the door and he saw the flash of the pistol. A searing pain penetrated his chest. He felt himself crumble to the floor. To his surprise, he was not afraid. Conversely, he felt a certain relief and final elation. He would not die in a dark steel box. His eyes dulled as life left them. The gunman moved the accountant's body aside with a foot as he began his search of the vault's contents.

Boyd Hutton led these outlaws. He heard the shot from the back room with no change of expression to alter his grim face. He watched his safe man, Henry, work the "soup" into the crack between the safe and door. The gap was sealed with a clay putty. Once sealed, the nitro was carefully poured in. Henry inserted a blasting cap into the top pour space and the fuse was lit. Boyd Hutton and his men moved quickly to the back room where the bank teller lay dead, and the "closet" door was open revealing empty shelves.

A dull thump shook the bank walls. Fingers rubbed sore ears as the outlaws returned to the vault room. The safe front was blackened but had not opened. Boyd Hutton looked mildly upon the safe. His calm demeanor changed to anger as he heard the alarm bell sounding from outside the bank. The gun shot or nitro blast must have caught someone's attention. He turned to Beau.

"What did you get from the back vault?"

Beau grinned and produced a bread box size tin container from his filled gunny sack.

"Must be a fortune in here," Beau said with a stained toothy grin.

"Tie that bag. We're leaving,"

Beau dropped the box back inside the bag and knotted the top. Boyd pulled his pistol, and his men did likewise.

"Time to feed the beast," Boyd muttered grimly and headed for the door.

The five men shoved through the door where their four mounted lookouts had returned. Horses stamped tight circles as the riders searched roof tops and doorways with trained weapons.

"They're organizing, Chief," said the rider of the Dun horse. "They are already blocking both ends of the street."

Hutton stepped onto his horse without a word. His men silently mounted then followed their leader who had urged his mount down the street. The group moved as one at a brisk canter, ready for the onslaught to come.

A shotgun barrel snaked cautiously around the corner of a building. Hutton moved his horse at an angle towards the moving gun barrel. He leaned forward around the corner well forward on his horse. He shot the gun man holding the shotgun through the top of his hat. A second man backed away from the shot leader — brains and gore speckled his face. Hutton shot him dead center. The man fell in a puff of dust with a muted cry.

Hutton turned his mount back into the group. His men were accustomed to this succinct dealing of death by their leader, but they still exchanged uneasy looks among one another. Law was scarce here but it came to quick judgment and even quicker execution. Hutton had just put a death sentence upon all of them. The killing of the bank teller seemed of no consequence compared to the wholesale killing of members of the Ready Men. The outlaws' fate was sealed in either case. It was a certainty that Hutton would tolerate none of his men shirking their duties to commit whatever killings necessary to escape the Ready Men this day.

Mounted Ready Men could be heard approaching from behind. Hutton increased the pace. The trailing posse knew their direction of escape and would seal any retreat. Hutton turned to his men.

"Beau, stay among us. Don't lose that sack."

Beau nodded, his pale face shone with sweat in the morning coolness. The outlaws rounded a left turn at the end of the main street to the onslaught of a volley of rifle shots. Hutton's horse was struck. The sound was like a club to bone. The animal staggered, stumbled and fell. He leaped clear of the dying animal, hitting the ground at full speed. His fellow riders threw themselves from their saddles and fanned out to either side of the street seeking escape or cover. Boyd took aim and shot a head rising for a shot behind the street barricades. Another man leaped away from the falling man and Boyd clipped him in the back with a snap shot.

By this time, bullets hissed around them from all directions. Lead splintered wooden siding and kicked dust eddies from the roadway all around them. Amazingly, none of the bandits were hit. It was apparent they were surrounded. The outlaws looked to their leader. Their instincts led them to cower and await some respite or perhaps a yet unrevealed opportunity.

Hutton spared no look for his men. He set his jaw and pushed himself forward with hands and legs. He made for the barricades which shielded the firing gunmen. Without hesitation, the outlaws moved to follow their leader on this seemingly vain attack upon a well bunkered enemy. As one, the outlaws rushed the barricades, raining lead onto the hiding men. Although well-armed and in possession of the tactical advantage of superior cover, these were still only town folk who had little fighting experience and whose only motivation was a $50.00 reward: a scant trade for a life. The outlaws knew they would either live or die within the next few seconds. That chance for life drove their efforts and, with little resistance other than wild desperate shooting from the townsmen, they crashed the barricade, placing counting shots into the defenders.

Suddenly two of Hutton's men went down. The shots came from behind them, away from the barricades. A cavalcade of mounted ready men burst around the corner from which the outlaws had arrived. The roar of pounding hooves reached full volume as the rear-guard riders turned onto the adjoining street where the battle was in full force. Hutton saw this and turned his fire upon the charging riders. His mouth tightened into a grim line of desperation. His eyes blazed with the fury of the lost. He picked up a carbine lying next to a dying man and fired rapidly, levering rounds smoothly between shots. The mounted men split and sought cover as lead hornets zipped past their faces. A bullet clipped Boyd's hat. The shot came from above him. He dodged left and looked up for the shooter. He spotted a youth perched on a roof top, edging down for a clearer shot at him. Boyd brought the rifle to ready and moved along the eave's edge until the youth leaned out, sighting over the rifle barrel. Boyd fired. The boy's hand lost two fingers and he fell, dropping the weapon. He landed in a puff of dust. Boyd pulled his pistol and shot him in the face.

The outlaws had shot down many at this point and the only danger now lay with the remains of the mounted pursuit busily finding cover. Boyd reloaded his pistol, walking towards the scattering riders. The man of the Dun horse called out to Hutton.

"Chief, they're on their heels. Let's get out of here."

Hutton closed the thumb breach on his pistol and continued on his way.

Beau, holding the sack of loot in a bloodied hand, rode up to the Dun rider.

"Stub, what is he doing?" he asked grimly.

Stub reloaded as he replied with a voice tinged with frustrated rage.

"I reckon he's gonna kill everyone."

Beau seemed more horrified by Stub's statement than the actions of their boss. His mouth hung agape as he stared at the other in disbelief.

"This is suicide," he protested.

Stub spoke to the remaining outlaws over his shoulder.

"Spread out. Pick off the stragglers."

The others paused before following this last order. To a man, they yearned to capture any of the many loose horses about them and speed away towards the safety of open country. Sanctuary beckoned within scant yards of where they stood. Doubt kept them in the fray. No one knew for certain whether the man beside him would or would not shoot him in the back if he tried to escape alone. The hesitation ended and the group reloaded their weapons and fanned out. They moved deliberately with a grim sense of purpose. Hutton's pistol could already be heard amongst scattered return fire from the targeted ready men.

Beau shook his head. Why could so many flee from one man? He drew his pistol and followed Stub into an adjoining alley.

"With pistol at ready, he asked, "What are we doing, Stub?"

Stub turned in the saddle. His face was contorted in frustrated anger.

"When the chief gets his blood up, he tends to take it out on someone. Them 'Ready Men' are the someone today. You'd best shut your mouth and open your eyes and shoot anything that moves."

The outlaws searched the streets and alleys. At intervals shots announced the end of a Ready Man. Three of the outlaws riding together came upon their Chief shooting a man lying on his back with outstretched arms as if to ward off the inevitable bullet. After the shot, he turned to his men.

"Burn it all,"

The three fanned out. They bunched dry straw and pieces of broken plank next to the buildings. They lit the tinder and watched briefly to ensure the task had been done.

Hutton holstered his pistol and moved towards the growing fires.

"We gotta slope."

Hutton mounted a nearby horse and wheeled it around towards an alley leading to the main thoroughfare. Smoke billowed upward into a clear blue sky behind the four riders as they entered the street. The remainder of the outlaws sat their horses watching their leader and company approach.

Stub said to Hutton, "No one else outside, Chief."

"Likely nothing but women and old folk cowering inside of doors," said the big man, Boris.

Hutton nudged his mount towards the broken barricades beyond which open country beckoned. As the group threaded their way through the blockade debris and scrap materials, a volley of rifle shots exploded from within a building to their left. Three outlaws, including Beau, went down under the fusillade. Hutton pulled his pistol but had to lean low and spur his mount forward as a second volley erupted. More of his men fell. A bullet dug a furrow across his shoulders, and he spurred the horse cruelly. The lunge of the startled horse saved his life as a bullet sang over his head nearly parting his hair. He sent a wild shot into the building, but it spatted harmlessly into the wood of a window frame.

Apparently, the Ready Men had planned a more elaborate defense strategy than was at first apparent. This last squad of ambushing gunmen had kept their hiding place even as their fellow townsmen were being slaughtered. They had waited until the outlaws were forced to slow their escape to weave through the debris in the roadway. They knew that then would be their greatest chance to wipe out the gang in ambush. Planners knew the outlaws would breach the inner defenses, or at least suspected it was a possibility. The mounted pursuit was meant to push the outlaws towards the ambush point. They counted upon panic to aid the gunmen waiting there. Most likely the townsmen expected that many of the outlaws would perish at the hands of the first pursuit. This second skirmish line, as it were, was there to clean up any surviving bandits.

All of this flashed through Hutton's mind, though in not so detailed a way. He looked over his shoulder but none of his cohorts followed him. Through smoke and dust, he could make out riderless horses moving pell mell to escape the gunfire and smoke. The outlaw spurred his mount and the horse leaped ahead to a full gallop.

Hutton knew he was wounded but he wasn't sure how serious it was. He had been shot before and his experience told him it was most likely a flesh wound. He hadn't felt the bullet strike a solid blow. Rather, it had felt more like a tearing pain.

Behind him he heard shouting as a posse formed. He took a moment to assess his mount. The horse had a generous space between longish ears. Its gallop was strong but not fluid as he would have liked. At best, this horse was a decent trail pony, but he was certain it wouldn't last long at a forced pace over rough country. His only chance was to make for Indian Territory. The Indians had been restless of late and the townsmen would know that. It wouldn't take them off his trail, but it might serve to slow them for caution's sake. The saddle scabbard under his left leg held a rifle. If the pursuit crowded him too much, they would lose some of their number.

He turned the pony into a dry wash and made his way south towards the Tontantin. Time was not in his favor. The hour was early, and he would have to ride smartly for hours until night fall aided him. He doubted the horse would last that long. He didn't know the region well enough to have knowledge of nearby ranches or settlers, so a fresh remount was unlikely. He held down the horse's pace as he followed the sharp turns of the stony wash bottom.

Wayne Smith sipped hot black coffee. His wife brought him a plate with two fried eggs, thick bacon and cornbread. He sliced away the whites of the eggs with the side of his fork. His toothless grin welcomed the yolks as he lifted each carefully and placed it in his mouth where he broke the sweet yellow with a satisfied tight-lipped grin. He prided himself in never leaving a drop of yolk on his plate. His wife watched the ritual with a tolerant impatience. He looked up at her with pride and his eye lids fluttered several times. He beamed upon her as he swallowed the egg yolks. Smith was also known as Blink. He had drawn the nickname from an unconscious habit of blinking continually. His manner was sometimes compared to that of a startled bird.

His smile froze at the sound of a nearby gun shot. It was rather early for the discharge of a pistol by a drunken or mischievous cowboy.

"The Bank," he said breathlessly.

He rose and went to the rack where he grabbed his rifle. He checked the breach then ran out the front door of his little home which was only a short distance behind the Ranger's house.

He ran as quickly as aged, bowed legs could manage. He took the front steps in one bound and followed the short dirt trail to the street gate, careful to avoid stepping on his wife's flower gardens lining the borders of the narrow path. He wheezed and was short of breath when he arrived in sight of the bank building. He looked down the lane beside the bank and saw several hitched horses prancing restlessly at the front of the bank. At a distance, armed men appeared to be on the lookout. Blink leaped into the brush line beside the road and made his way stealthily towards the back of the Ranger's house. He looked to his rifle then peeked around the back corner of the little stone house. He saw the Ranger face down on the gravel path. A dark stain spread from beneath him. Blink moved towards the ranger hastily, but with caution. He crouched and place a quavering hand on the ranger. The man was dead. Blink was certain a robbery was under way. He fell to the ground fearfully as a muffled explosion buffeted the air. He looked up and around him cautiously. It occurred to him that the sound was not a firearm, but instead, the concussion of a large detonation, say of a bomb or nitro. They were trying to open the famous Boston safe.

He crossed the short distance to the bell tower at the rear of the bank and yanked on the rough rope. The bell peeled sharply in the morning air. He rang the bell only as long as he dared, fearing the lookouts would approach to silence the alarm and silence him as well. He released the rope and ran into the brush to his right, dropping low into the dense leaves.

Smith squatted in the high grass and small trees, mustering his courage. He blinked rapidly as he scanned the area around him. Finally, he heard voices at the front of the bank. He crept along the side of the bank, following the path the Ranger had walked at the end. He peered around the corner in time to see the gang ride away en masse towards the upper end of town. He made his way to the front door of the bank. The door hung at a crazy angle from only the bottom hinge. The interior was awash in floating swirls of smoke from the explosion. Blink saw no one behind the counter. He moved down the hallway and found the bank clerk face down in a pool of blood before the open doorway of a steel vault. Blink had not been aware of the vault until now.

He turned on his heel and ran back to the front door. A small contingent of mounted men arrived at the bank entrance. Blink shaded his eyes allowing them to adjust to the brightness outside the bank.

A lean man with full handlebar moustaches nodded towards the bank interior.

"What's the story, Blink?"

"Ain't pretty, Shell. Clerk is dead but the Boston Safe is still locked. There is a vault in the back room, and it is open and empty. The robbers just headed up town at a clip."

"How many?"

"Not sure, maybe a dozen or so."

"Get your horse and catch up with us," Shell said and wheeled his mount. His three companions followed him towards town.

Blink shambled down the hard-packed dirt street towards his little house. His wife was waiting at the gate. She wiped her hands on her apron with a look of frightened worry around her eyes. She looked him up and down as he approached.

"You ain't shot, Wayne," she informed him. "Who is?"

Blink moved past her towards the stable path beside the house.

Over his shoulder he said, "Ranger and the Bank Clerk are gone. Getting my horse."

She watched him go with a frown.

Blink walked through the broad doorway to his small stables. He lifted a saddle off the rail and threw it atop the stall fence beside which his sorrel mare munched slowly. Her gentle eyes watched him curiously. He brought the bit to her muzzle. She raised her head to avoid the device. He pushed the bit between her teeth. She fought vainly before Blink was able to wrestle the bit into her teeth. Nonplussed at being overmatched, the mare resumed her casual interest in the remainder of the saddling process. He buckled the bridle and tossed the blanket over her hunched back. The saddle was next, then he led her to the outside. He slid his old .30 .40 carbine into the saddle scabbard and mounted as his wife approached.

"Fifty dollars ain't worth a life – yours or another's."

"It ain't just the money, Mother. That ranger was a good man and I liked him."

She considered him with a long level look.

"Go on then," she said.

As if he had been awaiting her blessing, he squeezed his heels into the mare, and she struck a canter onto the dirt road. He passed the bank front. A crowd was formed, busily shaking their heads and talking worriedly amongst themselves. They paused their discussion to watch him as he rode past.

A tight exchange of gun shots sounded well down the road from him. He recognized that the outlaws had reached the barricade. Smith lifted his pace to the tattoo of increased gunfire. He was nearly at the ambush turn when he saw a dismounted man shoot point blank into a man who hurriedly reloaded a rifle. Blink recognized the man reloading the rifle as one of Shell's companions from earlier. The killer saw Smith and drew bead on him in preparation to fire. It was a lengthy try but Blink had the impression this man could make that shot. He yanked the Sorrel's head around towards a side alley as the bullet splintered a post just behind him. Another report from the same pistol sounded and Blink heard a stifled cry from an unseen victim. Blink dismounted and drew his side arm. He wasn't good with a rifle at close quarters and his desire for the bounty had diminished with the big outlaw's uncanny display of marksmanship.

Blink peered around the corner. He saw a group of outlaws shoot into two Ready Men in hiding. Over a roof across the lane he saw gray smoke ballooning from the rear of the buildings facing the street. It was not long before he saw flames licking the inside of two buildings. One was Greer Mercantile and the other was the county land office. He crept around the corner and moved cautiously along the boardwalk. It frightened him not knowing where the shooter had made off to. It appeared to him that the Ready Men had taken a horrible defeat at the hands of these cruelly driven robbers. He knew coming upon the outlaw gang suddenly would be his end.

He turned the corner and saw the first volley of Joiner's ambush guards as they fired upon the milling outlaws. It seemed that every bullet found its mark. Many of the robbers fell from their saddles. Blink spotted the gunman who had taken a shot at him. The big man ducked low and spurred his horse. The horse jumped. The mount and rider disappeared into a dense cloud of drifting smoke from the fires.

Two more mounted but wounded riders were shot by a tight volley from Joiner's men. They fell heavily. One dropped a tied gunny sack as he died.

Blink hurried up the street where Joiner's men were emerging from their ambush point, stepping over the broken window's frame, rifles at the ready.

"I ain't never seen nothing like this bunch," Smith gasped. He was out of breath and blinking like a windmill's shadow at noon. "I think they killed all the rear guard and burned the buildings. They must have been soldiers from the war or some such."

Joiner, a tall lean man with a lantern jaw and jutting brow grabbed him by the nape of the neck.

"Did you go to the bank?"

Blink looked up at him confused.

"I reckon you could say that. I sounded the alarm. That Ranger and the clerk was murdered in cold blood. They tried to blast the safe, but she held. They did get into a vault in the back room and that one was empty."

Joiner realized he was gripping the smaller man with unnecessary force and released him.

"Sorry, Blink."

He turned to his men.

"Mount up, men. We're gonna catch their leader. Blink, you're coming with us."

There was a general rush for horses. Town's people slowly emerged from their hiding to witness the aftermath of the battle.

"Mr. Joiner," Blink stammered, "I ain't ready to ride a long pursuit just yet. The wife..."

Joiner turned a black look upon the man.

"Get on your horse, Blink. You have collected on the bounty on several occasions. You have to earn it this time."

Blink groaned then went back towards where he had left the sorrel mare.

Hutton had been riding for hours. The late afternoon heat and the strain of a forced flight were killing his mount. He had sized up the gelding accurately. The little horse was lacking as a hearty and reliable mount. At first the pursuit had been no more than a distant cloud of tawny dust on the horizon. In time the cloud had grown a dark line beneath made of straining horses and riders. He could tell the posse were pushing their mounts hard. They probably knew of the horse he rode and its inherent weakness. If Hutton was correct in his assessment of this horse, the posse would not have to burn up their mounts to overtake him before he gained the advantage of nightfall.

He nursed the horse's strength: running on foot beside the beast up and down grades. While mounted, he rode as lightly as possible in the saddle, a skill gained from countless hours on horseback. He had been lucky to find a small rivulet upon the ascent onto the Tontantin mesa. The waters of the Tontantin River were still miles to the south. The horse would not have made it this far without his shepherding the animal's strength or the drink from the small stream. The water stop had reduced his lead over the pursuit to less than a mile. His confidence strengthened with his belief the pursuit would have no choice but to stop to water their horses as he had.

The weakening horse unsteadily wound through a region of mound-like hillocks and large boulders. The rough terrain provided no hope of evasion or even a likely hiding spot. Hutton felt slight relief at the cover it provided after his long trek over open country. Soon he descended a gentle slope which broadened into a narrow grassy valley. A scant mile before him he could see the dense tree line which shaded the river's banks. A shudder shook the horse and it staggered. The outlaw knew the horse was taking its last steps. He spurred and whipped the horse with the thick reins. If he could get a little more out of the horse before it died, he might make it to the river on foot and somehow escape with the current. The gelding staggered forward on nerve energy alone. The animal's raspy breathing came with a deep labored sound of suffering. Crimson sprayed onto his muzzle and speckled the grass below. Finally, the horse fell, and Hutton was thrown forward rolling down the hill a short way. The horse tried to rise but failed. Hutton rose from where he had been thrown. He returned to the dying horse. He watched as the horse's efforts to rise slowed then ceased before moving to the saddle. He drew the saddle carbine and turned from the horse.

He couldn't risk a shot to end the animal's suffering. He knew the posse was near, but he didn't want to help them pinpoint his location. He moved towards the river, lifting his pace to an easy run. The downhill made the effort less taxing, but he still had quite a distance to cross if he were to achieve the hopeful safety of the tree line.

The sound of thundering hooves broke over the hill behind him. He turned to see the posse riding down upon him. He heard distant but clear yells of triumph. The posse pressed their mounts to a heightened pace, now certain of their quarry.

They opened fire but the bullets flew wide. The distance was still great and shooting from horseback was difficult in any case.

Soon, Hutton judged that the riders were in range of his weapon. He levered a cartridge into the rifle breach and brought the gun to his shoulder. He fired and one of the horses fell, throwing the rider heavily. The return gun fire increased as they tried to press him to take cover. Bullets spatted harmlessly around him in little spouts of dust. He levered in a shell and shot again. Another horse fell. The rider leaped off but hit a rock and fell heel over head and lay still in the tall grass.

The outlaw heard the leader's voice though he couldn't discern the words. The posse split, flanking him left and right. He was caught in the middle of this valley with no cover nearer than several hundred yards in either direction.

Hutton realized with a grim certainty that he would die today. His jaw tightened resolutely. He would give the beast enough fodder to take some of the attention from him. He levered another cartridge and shot into the left flanking group. One of the rider's grabbed his leg and pulled up his mount. A fresh volley of rifle shots came toward him. This time, however, the marksmen were close enough that slugs whined close to him, cutting the air near his face. He levered the rifle again. He felt no resistance of a round pressed into the chamber. The gun was empty. He tossed the rifle aside and pulled his colt.

Before he could take aim, they were upon him, guns trained on him from all directions. Joiner dismounted.

"Drop the shooter, Mister."

Hutton did as he was told.

Joiner looked up at the first man he saw.

"Blink, get his guns."

Blink dismounted and approached the outlaw carefully. He collected the pistol then backed away cautiously until he reached the rifle lying a short distance away.

Hutton looked around him. Twelve men looked upon him with set jaws and gimlet eyes. Several dismounted and stood just behind their leader.

Joiner said, "Do you know who I am?"

Hutton watched him but made no reply.

"My name is Joiner. You robbed my bank. You killed my clerk and my guard. You burned my town and killed many of my friends."

Joiner stepped closer.

"We might as well learn your name, outlaw. We don't need it to erect a headstone, cuz we ain't gonna. We're gonna erase any trace of you. I'd just like to know a name to curse whenever I see your face in my mind's eye."

The outlaw made no reply. He seemed distracted, as if he were thinking of something else other than his dire predicament. Joiner saw that no answer would come from this aloof scoundrel.

"Can you divine what we are fixing to do to you?"

Hutton focused his gaze on Joiner for a long moment before he looked around.

"Them trees seem a little short to hang me from, so I guess you'll take me back to face trial or a lynch mob."

Joiner's eyes blazed with hate.

"You get no trial outlaw. Ain't no lynchin' gonna save you from the gallows either."

Joiner's men looked at him in confusion.

"We're gonna pep you up a bit then we're gonna give you all the time you need to reflect on your ill deeds."

Hutton looked only at Joiner as the mutterings of the posse grew. In a wink, his fist shot out and caught Joiner full in the face. He then threw himself into the group of men, striking with fist and boot. He surprised the group, but they quickly overpowered him and tied his arms behind his back.

The Sun was near setting before they were through with him. Blink could watch no more of the grisly spectacle. The outlaw must have had at least a half dozen broken ribs. His face was an unrecognizable bloody and bruised mass.

Joiner wiped sweat from his brow with a soiled white kerchief. He pocketed the cloth then pulled his pistol. He checked the cylinder then trained it on Hutton's head as he cocked the hammer back.

Blink took a step forward. "You ain't just gonna murder him are you Mr. Joiner?"

"That's exactly what I am gonna do," Joiner said without looking away from the outlaw.

"You don't want his blood on your hands, Boss."

"He ain't leavin' this valley alive, Blink. Now step aside."

Blink stepped closer to Joiner.

"I saw just what you saw, and I saw more. If ever a man deserved hanging, it is this here fella. We had our way with him. Now let's take him in for his due justice."

Joiner turned slowly and faced Blink. He was unaccustomed to a challenge to his authority. He was intolerant of weakness or reluctance in carrying out his orders.

"Step aside," he growled through clenched teeth, "or I'll give you a taste of what he has coming."

Blink hesitated but stood his ground. Joiner lifted the pistol above his head. Blink shrunk a bit from the impending blow but didn't retreat. A voice stopped Joiner before he delivered the blow.

"*Con permiso, Patron.*"

Joiner looked around him, gun clenched above his head.

A lean mustached Mexican named Fuentes stepped forward from the group. He stepped between Joiner and Blink and looked down at the outlaw as if the raised gun was not of concern.

Joiner was almost breathless with rage. His words were low and menacing.

"What is it, Fuentes?"

Fuentes squatted down to get a better look at Hutton.

He said to the prostrate man, "Good, *Whetto*, you are still awake."

From his position close to Hutton, he spoke to Joiner: "*Senor*, I lived among the Indians for a while. The *Lipranos* are good at only one thing. Two really, but only one of them is good for this man."

Fuentes pulled a long knife from his boot.

"I need wood and leather thongs, Patron."

Joiner hesitated. He was unsure of the Mexican's intent and was wary of rebellion from another quarter.

Fuentes looked up at him.

"Patron, this man does not deserve to die quickly. He must consider his fate as he moves in fate's direction."

Fuentes was known for his odd Indian rituals and prairie wisdom.

By degrees, Joiner relaxed his posture. The Mexican was suggesting a method to what Joiner had said to the outlaw earlier. He felt no challenge, but rather a solidarity with his wishes. After a moment, he holstered his pistol and turned to his men.

"Do it. I have an oilskin in my saddle bags. You two go cut a couple of strong branches off one of them scrub cedars."

Soon, the outlaw was staked and tied to the ground stripped from the waist up. His skin displayed numerous scars from past battles mixed with recent bruises and lacerations from this latest encounter.

Joiner approached Fuentes who stood over the outlaw, his arms akimbo.

"He's tied down, Fuentes. It's your show. Do we leave him or is there more to this?"

"It takes a long time to die out here from thirst, starvation or the weather. He might work himself loose."

"Them stakes are drove deep," said the sweating Blink.

"I have no doubt of that," Fuentes nodded, "There is a way to hurry death, but not so much that this dog doesn't have time to savor it before it closes his eyes."

Fuentes wiped his knife on his boot, then grabbed a pinch of the outlaw's skin over his stomach. He made a small cut. The incision began to bleed. He reached into the wound and pulled a small bit of the outlaw's guts through the cut. Hutton clenched his teeth and a groan escaped him. He struggled with his bonds, writhing in pain. The entrails clogged the hole and slowed the bleeding.

Fuentes wiped his hand on Hutton's nearby shirt. He stood and looked down at the outlaw.

"The animals will soon smell blood. Even the smallest will nibble at his *Tripas*. The larger predators will soon come and make the hole bigger to get at the meal within. You will live through the meal, my friend."

Fuentes laughed with real mirth.

"You made a good choice of this place in which to die. There is no one that will come this way. The trails are miles north and south of here. You will be alone with your friends until they finish you."

Fuentes' smile disappeared. He pursed his lips then spat in the outlaw's face. He turned on his heel and went back to his horse. The remaining posse members looked on for a moment more. One by one, they moved to their horses. Blink and Joiner stood together, looking down at the man.

Joiner kept his eyes on the outlaw as he said, "Well Blink, now you've earned that bounty."

Joiner moved away to collect his horse. Blink watched him then looked back at Hutton.

"Sorry pardner. You came a-robbin' in the wrong town, I guess."

Blink looked at the man a moment more. Hutton lay still, eyes closed to his pain. He gave no attention to Blink. Blink turned and hurried to catch up with the posse.

CHAPTER FOUR

Boyd Hutton

Hutton heard the approaching wagons without any belief they were real. He had learned that delirium made his wild perceptions indiscernible from reality. Even when gentle hands cut his bonds and lifted him from the ground, he suspected he was near enough death that all his senses were in on the deception.

He was laid in the back of a wagon. He could tell that much through the swollen slits which provided him limited sight. The wagon began moving as someone ministered to his numerous injuries. He heard a woman's voice then he heard nothing more.

It was late when he again emerged from the darkness. He felt pain where his injuries had been treated and bound. He tried to sit up. A white-hot spear of hot pain struck him down and he again passed into a region of dark oblivion. When next he awoke, his first images were of the heavy seams of a wagon cover. He moved his gaze painfully until he beheld a brilliant cloudless sky. He resisted the urge to sit upright and instead rolled gingerly onto his side. With effort, he was able to peer out the back of the wagon over the end gate. Behind the wagon in which he rode was a train of nearly a dozen wagons moving slowly. The train followed a trail that curved, allowing him to see the entire caravan following lazily behind.

He fell back heavily onto the blankets with a groan. He glanced to his left, inside the wagon. Beside his bed sat a matronly woman with gray hair. She dozed, her breaths coming in audible sips. She seemed to sense his gaze with a small catch of her breath. She opened her eyes.

"You lay flat 'fore you pierce a gut with them busted ribs."

She was casual in her statement, but her sharp eyes betrayed her concern. To Hutton, she seemed guarded. He made no reply but, instead, closed his swollen eyelids and lay quietly in agony until sleep again took him.

Helen leaned against a barrel just outside the fire's glow. She fought the warm seduction of sleep. They had travelled for a week with scant breaks. Shin had droned on with his continual diatribe espousing the inadequacies of Crease Cole. The men believed, based upon the conversations she had been able to overhear, that the Indian threat was still a concern. They had yet to find a suitable fjord and had been unable to cross the Tontantin River. They had followed the river's winding path farther south than Crease had promised.

Shin confided in her that he was convinced that the guide was unfamiliar with the region and was stalling in the hope he might get a lucky break by which to save face. If her husband was correct in his suspicions, Crease might feel that a lengthy forced march could keep the settlers busy and fatigued, thus keeping many objections at bay. When questioned, Crease replied only that they couldn't risk stopping until they had the river between them and the Indian mesa. He had assured them that the fjord was close. He did indicate that the river seemed to be higher than usual, likely from flooding upstream, and the crossing points were fewer than usual.

From her dark seat she could hear Crease and Father talking about the wounded man. He was mending at a remarkable rate, according to Mrs. St. Peter. The injured man was laid out on the ground near the

St. Peter wagon on a pallet of rough blankets. He appeared to be sleeping comfortably. She had heard him cry out and even lift a hand to ward off some danger his mind had concocted in its delirium. The guide and St. Peter's conversation drew her attention away from the newcomer.

"I ain't never seen him before," Crease said, indicating the wounded man's general direction with a nod.

Travis looked mildly at their guest.

"I daresay," he mused, "he didn't tie himself down to die."

Crease shook his head, took off his hat, and ran a hand through his blonde hair.

"I'd agree with you. He was put there with the intent that he wouldn't be found none too soon."

Crease put his hat back on. He looked directly at the injured man before he spoke.

"Hungry animals or thirst would have done for him if we hadn't happened along: and that was shore lucky for him. His guts hangin' out appears to be the work of Injuns."

The older man nodded his agreement.

"He is healing remarkably, considering the gravity of his wounds," Travis said.

Crease laughed without mirth.

"I should smile."

Travis leveled a searching look at the guide.

"What do you mean?"

Crease picked up a stick and traced a private image in the dirt.

"We may live to regret him mending. Somebody sure as hell thought he oughta pass out of this life in a slow and painful way."

Travis inhaled deeply. He seemed to imagine the suffering which would have accompanied the newcomer's fate had they not rescued him.

Both men reflected silently upon their respective thoughts for a long moment.

Finally, Travis said quietly, "Of that I am certain."

Travis tamped fresh tobacco into his cob pipe then pulled a short stick from the fire. He had placed the stick there with the intent to use it to fire his smoke. He touched the ember to the tobacco and puffed deeply until the flame took. He puffed with active pulls from pursed lips. Satisfied the embers had lit the tobacco, he drew deeply then released the smoke, squinting his eyes at the pleasure of the tobacco. He returned his gaze to Cole.

"Do you think those savages are still out there?"

Crease watched the pipe glow as the old man drew on it once more.

He looked away as he said, "I ain't seen sign of them for two days. If the stranger was victim to angry redskins, we may have more ahead of us. If those who were behind us are still there, I reckon they won't try to brace us during the night. They got superstitions about fightin' in the dark."

Helen had seen Shin walk up unnoticed by the two. He surprised them when he spoke.

"Bodine said that was a yarn. He said redskins don't own time pieces. They stay in a lather twenty-four hours a day and fight at the same pace."

Crease frowned at the ground. He hated the smaller man. He was as unpleasant as a constantly yelping little mongrel dog.

"I reckon you ought to consider that Bodine is filling a hole right now. He ain't one to heed when it comes to advice."

Shin sneered at him.

To Travis he said, "I got a bad feeling about us not seeing them savages on our back trail for the last couple days."

Crease looked up at Shin. He shook his head in disgust. A grim smile curved his lips.

"You better keep your hat on, so they don't take your hair tonight."

His faint smile grew to a genuine grin at this sally. He watched Shin for a moment to ascertain the depth of the verbal barb before he turned his attention to the older man to receive the predictable silent disapproval.

Instead, St. Peter appeared pale and drawn in the fire light. His gaze was fixed on a point just past the fire's glow behind Cole and Shin. The old man muttered something unintelligible as he struggled to focus on what it was that had his attention. Crease and Shin searched his face in confusion.

Travis' eyes widened in recognition.

"We're lost," he gasped.

Shin was in the act of turning to look behind him when an arrow pierced his neck with a grinding sound. He grasped at the arrowhead protruding from his throat and gurgled a bloody bubble.

The Indians sprinted silently towards the group of men. Helen cried out at the violent injury to her husband. Panic ripped at her, but she was frozen in place with fear. The savages were painted from face to waist and they carried bows and rifles. Their hair was odd to her in that the left side was cut short above the ear and the right hung low over their shoulders. The silence of their attack was as terrifying as their very appearance. Her gaze returned to Shin. He still clutched the arrow protruding from his throat. She watched him collapse slowly as if he were under water. His Desperate eyes looked at her, but she saw no recognition before life left them.

Crease leapt to the right and drew his pistol. He brought it to bear but an Indian hit him full on as the muzzle belched flame. The Indian was smaller, but his muscled torso seemed carved from wood. He rolled past Crease, pulling him over with one hand. He drew his knife from a beaded sheath with the other. The Indian came to his feet to give force to the knife blow. Crease, with surprising agility, brought a fist up under the Indian's lean jaw. The redskin fell back. Crease thumbed back the hammer of his colt and shot his foe in the chest. The Indian's body curled and twisting like a snake with its head chopped off. Crease finished him with another shot.

Helen caught movement to her right. Marjorie was half out of her wagon, climbing down desperately. She fell to the ground. She struggled to regain her feet. Finally, she stood up and lunged around the corner of the heavy wagon. An Indian came around from the opposite direction. She ran headlong into the savage. The Indian reacted instinctively, plunging his knife into Marjorie's body to the hilt. Marjorie froze, held upright by the strength of the Indian, impaled on his knife. She put her arms out and held the Indian's shoulders, almost tenderly, as she died. He dropped Marjorie's limp body, slowly withdrawing his knife.

Helen began to weep. She felt herself falling into a black abyss. Her ears buzzed and she felt hot prickles under her skin. Through clouding vision, she saw Marjorie's killer approach Crease from the rear. Crease shot an Indian across the fire. The stalking Indian grabbed Crease's blonde hair and was in the act of bringing the gory blade up for a killing blow. A loud explosion bowed his back and a narrow red stream of blood oozed from a small hole just below his right shoulder blade. Crease whirled around and knocked the wounded Indian to the ground with a sidelong blow. Helen looked to her left.

The injured stranger stood unsteadily and levered another shell into the rifle he held. Crease frowned silently but nodded in gratitude to the injured man then turned to seek out any additional concealed foes.

Another Indian screamed a loud war cry and ran upon the wounded stranger from behind. The bandaged man sidestepped the rush and brought the rifle butt down across the Indians shoulders. The Indian staggered but stayed on his feet. The tall stranger stepped in and brought the rifle butt down. This time the sickening sound of crushing bone and of rent flesh could be heard as the blow landed on top of the Indian's head. The Indian fell on his face. The wounded stranger brought the rifle butt down again and again.

Frightened settlers gathered slowly. Their faces registered fear at the attack, but also reflected horror at such brute rage. The group watched in silence as the blows continued to fall. Finally, exhausted, the stranger stood unsteadily from his assault. Blood flecked his face and mottled his bandages. His breathing came in wet rattles. He stood still, wincing in pain, then he fell unconscious atop the dead Indian.

Helen didn't think she would ever cry again. The brown churn of the river moved briskly, high in its banks. The air was unseasonably cool and bright droplets decorated the long grasses. Water-logged tree limbs sagged tiredly. Not far from where she sat, an old elm tree stood sentry over three fresh grave mounds overlooking the river. Shin, Marjorie and Kyle's eldest son, Caleb lay in their final resting place.

After the attack, the settlers had packed and fled, taking the bodies with them. The men agreed that another attack was possible, and they felt it wise to escape under cover of night. The long trek took them into dusk of the next day when it began to rain heavily. The storm raged as brittle sparks of lightning and the distant roar of thunder pressed them to find high ground and secure their belongings from the strengthening winds.

Crease, still unsettled from his brush with death, shared his relief that the storm would erase all sign of their passing. Rain, heavy winds, and lightning kept them awake most of that night.

The storm broke with the dawn, and the caravan pushed on. They followed the bends of the river south for many miles until it quartered westward. They did not locate a safe place to cross the river until later that evening. That was two days ago. After burying their dead, the men spent most of the remaining time rigging the wagons for crossing – whenever that might be. Crease had since cursed in frustration repeatedly, noting that the rains had raised the river even higher. The swift cataract was impossible to cross, even for a man on horseback. They would have to wait out the swell.

Crease, Kyle, and Percy had departed that day around mid-morning on a hunting trip. Helen suspected they were less set on securing game than they were intent upon giving their minds something else to think about. The deadly attack weighed heavily. Any distraction was welcome. She had never known Crease to seek out the company of any of the other men. She suspected that even he was shaken somewhere below the casual manner he chose to exhibit.

In Helen's opinion, the three were the most unlikely companions for a hunting trip. Kyle was strong but lacked the stealth of a hunter. Percy was less comfortable than she as an outdoorsman. Crease was not given to casual friendships, and he seemed awkward in his attempts to extend friendly courtesy to the other two as they prepared to leave.

Her gaze again drifted to the graves. She regretted the way she had rejected Shin's advances. She tried to relegate her guilt to those things natural for a recent widow. She hadn't loved him as a husband, but she owned an inherent responsibility which demanded devotion and obedience. Her guilt stemmed more from a shameful relief that he would not demand her flesh any longer, than from a sense of regret at not honoring her spousal commitment.

Marjorie had been such a gentle soul. She was quiet and seemed comfortable only when Percy was nearby. Helen, on occasion, had secretly watched the quiet couple. She noticed how a smile would play about Marjorie's lips when the two sat closely together, talking in low intimate tones, and holding hands.

After she died, Percy had held her in his lap the entire night in the wagon in which she and the other two had been left for the hasty flight after the attack. It had been a struggle to take her from him to lay her to rest. His defiance to hold her in the face of the settlers' entreaties was the last passionate effort he had made. He was now an empty vessel: listless and lost. Doubtless, the other two forced him to join them on their hunting expedition. Perhaps they felt his discomfort on the hunting trail would provide distraction for his broken heart.

Helen's attention was drawn by a rattling of someone rifling through the contents of the wagon next to which she sat. She leaned forward and craned her neck to see who was inside. She saw a boot settle carefully onto the ground, then another. The rummager moved towards her side of the wagon with a stilted stride.

The wounded stranger appeared around the corner of the wagon and limped towards the fire. He sat gingerly across from where Helen sat. He lifted a flask to his lips and took a long drink. He closed his eyes, relishing the warmth of the spirits. Helen recognized the flask as that belonging to Crease. He rarely brought it out due to the rancor it wrought among the Mormons.

This had been the first time Helen was able to see the newcomer fully since they had liberated him from his bondage weeks before. During his treatment and recovery, she had brought compresses, poultices or medicines as requested by Mrs. St. Peter. With the swelling of his features and only brief glimpses, she had never truly seen him. The night of the attack, she had been overcome by terror and her memory of him was more of a faceless beast than the distinct visage of a man.

The swelling had reduced, leaving only red traces and a healing cut on his jaw line. As he limped to his seat, she was surprised that he was taller than she expected. She estimated him an inch over six feet. He was broad shouldered with a thickness about him one might mistake for casual weight. Her impression leaned towards his bulk containing hidden strength. She had trouble discerning his age. His blue eyes were dark and clear. His face carried wrinkles but was not deeply lined. His lean jaw line and high cheekbones gave nothing away. She was certain he was late in his thirties, but he could have easily been mid-forties.

She left her thoughts to again focus on him. She realized his eyes were upon her and she started. He was looking directly at her. His gaze was the most penetrating she had ever borne. He seemed to be reading her thoughts. She blushed and gave her attention abruptly to a bit of smoldering wood.

No, she decided, this stranger was older than he looked. His manner was one acquired over years of sizing up others. She felt a strange instinct urging her to be cautious around him. Helen looked down the line of wagons. The settlers were staying within their family groups. Few were out in the open. She was outside her wagon to keep her mind occupied. She feared she would not be able to stand the workings of her troubled memories otherwise.

As she looked on, Myrtle St. Peter peaked around the end of her wagon and frowned at the stranger. She approached, brushing imaginary dust from her hands. One of the other wives, Rebecca - Helen had to concentrate to remember her name - followed contritely.

Myrtle stopped across the fire from the stranger, beside where Helen sat. He considered her silently then took another drink.

"It's good to see you're able to get about," Myrtle said with her hands upon her broad hips.

The stranger made no response but looked down.

"We are awaiting the flood waters to recede enough so as to cross. Myrtle looked the man up and down, critically.

"Don't think you can loaf — injured or not. We all pull our weight."

The stranger looked up at her. His mouth pursed and he worked his jaw. He licked his lips, shook his head, and took another drink.

Myrtle breathed deeply then leveled her most authoritarian mien at him.

"You are blessed by the lord you didn't die. Your violence towards that savage almost ended your life. We are obliged to you, Mr...."

She paused for him to fill in.

He regarded her mildly.

"Do you have a name?"

"Boyd" was his nearly inaudible reply.

"Boyd..." she repeated.

He looked up at her sharply. She realized she had pressed this quiet stranger as far as she dared. There was something about him which moved her to caution.

Boyd looked at Helen.

His voice was level and matter of fact.

"What's your name," he asked Helen, looking into her eyes. His tone was not reflective of friendly curiosity. His query seemed to be intended for fact finding rather than for making acquaintance.

Myrtle answered for Helen. Her preemptive reply was meant to convey its own meaning.

"This is Shin's wife: Helen."

Helen wasn't sure why she said it, but she added, "Shin lies yonder."

She pointed to the three graves.

Boyd looked at the graves then to Myrtle.

"You got any food?"

Myrtle made no reply, but merely looked at the stranger. She was not pleased with the stranger's direct manner. However, she was not sure enough of her footing to take the stranger to task. Her instincts warned caution.

Clearing her throat, Rebecca moved, unbidden, to the nearby cooking fire and ladled stew into a tin plate. She returned and offered the tin and a spoon to Boyd. He stood with a slight groan and accepted the plate. He turned away, seeming to shut out the others around him as though he had closed a door. Without a word, he moved back to the wagon he had occupied since healing well enough to be moved from the St. Peter wagon.

Myrtle watched him go, then looked down at Helen. She didn't know why, but Helen felt her face grow hot as she flushed under the older woman's scrutiny. Myrtle exhaled deeply then turned on her heel and returned to her wagon.

Helen spent much of that afternoon near the river. She sat atop a grassy knoll, watching the churning muddy water chew at the embankment. Branches and small tree limbs bobbed and twisted in the swirling, muddy flume like a boiling pot of vegetables in a beef broth.

She smiled involuntarily at the comparison. She sat far enough from the graves that the trees perched upon the riverbank shielded them from her view. Even shielded from her view, she still found herself casting a dreadful look in that direction now and again. She was surprisingly comfortable in her perch. She was able to lean back against the steep knoll where she sat in a slight depression on a narrow shelf. Long fragrant grasses cushioned her. A more comfortable seat would tax even the most skillful furniture craftsman.

The steady sound of rushing water was a pleasing aural backdrop to the merry songs of golden flumed wrens and mischievous larks flitting about in the low hanging branches of the riverside trees. She roused herself guiltily as she felt her body relax. Her resistance faded as her surroundings lulled her into a pleasant slumber.

A few moments later she awoke, senses strung tightly. What had roused her? She looked behind her and felt a shiver. She warmed through the shiver as the safety of her hiding place reassured her. She lay back and listened, ears straining to detect that which had wakened her so suddenly. Slowly pushing the flowing water's churn and gurgle from her ears, she heard the faint report of hoof beats. Soon she could make out men talking in low voices. She felt fear begin to grow. She shook her head to push the fear from her. She couldn't imagine Indians casually talking with their quarry so near.

The three men must be returning from the hunt, she told herself. Still she could not muster the courage to confirm her reasonable deduction.

The voices and horse sounds passed behind her. The hillock muted the sounds for a time, soon they were again audible as they passed to the opposite side. She moved slowly, keeping to the high grass, looking in the direction toward which the receding riders were headed. She peeked above the grass and saw the three hunters' backs as they slowly walked their horses towards camp.

Helen rose and brushed leaves and twigs off her dress. She made her way back towards camp.

Crease dismounted and tied his horse to the tongue of the nearest wagon. Kyle and Percy did likewise. Crease surveyed the camp. Dinner fires were lit, and the women were preparing food.

Travis St. Peter smoked his pipe as he listened to the talk of two men of his flock. He pulled the pipe from his mouth and nodded to Crease, still listening to the others. Crease nodded back, scooped a cup of water from the drinking bucket. He drank deeply then replaced the cup. He went back to his horse. He mounted then gathered the reins. Kyle and Percy looked at him curiously. Crease surveyed the two for a moment.

"I'm gonna scout the riverbank for our final crossing point before it gets dark. The river is receding quicker than I thought. We might get across some time tomorrow at this rate."

He mounted and rode off downstream.

Kyle unsaddled his horse. Percy watched the big man absently. Kyle looked left and saw Helen approaching from the direction they had just arrived.

"Hello, mischief," he greeted her with a broad smile. He reached into a bucket and withdrew a heavy comb.

Helen curtsied playfully and approached the big man.

"Was down to the river," she said by way of explanation.

"Careless never did anyone good, Mrs. Bruce."

He began combing out the horse's mane.

Helen looked into Kyle's big gentle eyes. He met her gaze for only a moment before he grinned his admission that he was teasing her.

"The stranger came out this morning," she told him. "He didn't say much, but he did tell us his name: Boyd."

Kyle paused. He replaced the curry comb and brought out a heavy brush. He smoothed fur and muscle, starting from the animal's withers, working back. The horse moved involuntarily with the strength of each arching stroke.

"Boyd what?" he asked.

"He didn't say."

Kyle grunted his interest. He looked at Percy, who stood as he had the entire time.

"What do you make of that Percy?"

Surprisingly, the mousy man answered.

"He killed that murdering savage. I couldn't care less if he was Satan himself."

Percy looked down sorrowfully. Finally, he shambled off to his wagon.

To Helen, he looked small and alone.

Kyle shook his head. The horse struggled to stay in place under the heavy buffing of the big man's brush strokes. He kept his attention upon his work on the horse's haunches as he spoke.

"For one, I hope he ain't Satan," His voice was low and labored with his efforts upon the horse's hide.

Helen grinned. Her humor faded when she saw the giant's face held no pleasure.

"I'd better check in with Mother."

He looked at her soberly then nodded as she walked away.

Percy returned with a halter. He put the halter over his horse's head and began unbuckling the bridle. He looked up as Boyd stepped stiffly from his wagon. Percy cleared his throat in warning. Kyle looked at him. Percy nodded in the stranger's direction. Kyle looked where indicated and watched as the man walked slowly towards them.

When Boyd drew close enough, Kyle nodded to him.

"Helen said you woke while we were hunting," His voice swelled with a welcome tone, he hardly felt. "Glad you're on the mend. Crease, our guide, is scouting for a crossing down river. Are you well enough to travel?"

Boyd made no reply. The graves seemed to garner his attention.

Kyle looked at him patiently. He extended a hand to the stranger.

"I'm Kyle Spears."

Boyd looked at him but didn't take his hand. The larger man frowned and lowered the hand. Kyle, however, wasn't one to be discouraged.

"This is Percy Karnack," Kyle nodded his big head at the smaller man. "What's your name, mister?"

Boyd looked at him mildly. After a moment he spoke.

"What are you doing here?"

Kyle didn't like the man's dismissive manner. He spoke to Kyle as if this were his land and the Mormon's were trespassers. Kyle replied, his voice measured and low with restraint.

"We bought rights in the western territory: St. Peter expedition."

Boyd considered the larger man for a moment.

"Expedition," he said thoughtfully. "You missionaries or some such?"

Percy cleared his throat as he stepped forward. He had the air of a man trying to get a better look at a faraway shore through a swirling fog.

"Mormons," he said finally.

Boyd looked away from the men. He seemed to be surveying the camp.

"You ask a lot of questions, but don't give many answers, stranger," Kyle said to the man's back.

The stranger's aloof ways galled him.

Boyd turned and faced Kyle squarely. Kyle didn't see malice in the move, but his short hairs fairly jumped in reaction to an unseen threat. Boyd considered the larger man in a matter-of-fact way. Kyle felt as if an undertaker were sizing him for a coffin. With only a small change in expression, the man turned and stalked away. He grabbed a chunk of bread from a nearby table and climbed back into his wagon.

Kyle turned to Percy, who seemed a shade pale.

The mousy man shrugged as he said, "I guess we'll have to tolerate his bad manners until we are out of Indian country."

Kyle nodded.

"I reckon."

The following morning, the entire camp packed busily for the crossing. After returning from his reconnoiters the night previous, Crease had given his preparatory instructions in a meeting of the Mormon men. He had found the river several feet down from its crest and his opinion was that the current would be sufficiently weakened for a crossing by early afternoon.

Helen stowed the last of her tarps with the help of one of the Mormon men. She wiped sweat from her brow and smoothed her dress, breathing deeply from the exertion.

The stranger, Boyd, leaned against a wagon watching her with a faint smile. She looked back at him in disbelief. How could a man watch a woman labor, and never lift a finger to help? Helen saw Crease approaching the reticent stranger. She made herself busy with her remaining tasks while clandestinely watching the two men.

Boyd took a drink from a flask as Crease approached. Crease started almost imperceptibly as he recognized the flask as belonging to him. Boyd turned to him and gave him a small salute with the flask then took another draw from it.

Crease eyed the flask with annoyance, but he seemed unable to get his head around how he should respond to this flagrant affront. He looked at the man, masking his frustration.

"You're on your feet," he said trying to hide his displeasure. "Good. We can use another man to help us get across the river."

Boyd again lifted the flask and took a drink. He nodded to Crease as he swallowed, then he turned away from the guide. He walked with a casual stride and was soon out of camp, headed towards the river.

Kyle came up from behind and joined Crease, who was watching the man go.

"How far to the crossing?" Kyle asked much of his attention given to the stranger's departure.

"We can fjord the river a mile or so downstream," Crease said, his gaze focused angrily on the stranger. He continued without turning from his study. "Looks like it's been crossed there before."

Finally, he turned to Kyle with a shake of his head to clear his thoughts.

"So, what's the story on our Injun killer," he asked.

"He ain't doin' much talkin' of late," Kyle replied with a shrug.

Crease nodded his head.

"Is that right?"

Kyle put his hands on his hips.

"He ain't doin' much of anything, since you're asking."

Crease pulled out the makings and began rolling a cigarette. He licked the paper, closed it and stuck it in his mouth. He pulled a Sulphur match from a round tin and lit it on the side of the wagon. The whole process took just a few seconds. He pulled on the smoke, exhaled, and picked a piece of tobacco out of his mouth with his off fingers, spitting dryly to finish the job.

"I reckon," he said looking at his smoke, "we'll have to tolerate him till we don't need to no more."

"That's the point Percy and I came to also."

Crease turned to look at Boyd, now at the bank of the river looking on. He drew another deep breath of smoke then blew it out slowly. His face was a study in frustrated anger. Without taking his eyes from the stranger, he threw his cigarette to the ground and crushed it under foot. He turned and went back to his preparations.

Kyle stayed a moment more, watching the stranger who seemed oblivious to all but his thoughts and whatever it was that interested him about the river.

Helen tied the thong, securing the stowed canvas, then moved towards the St. Peter wagon. Without Shin, her chores seemed few. She drew comfort from her work, and she found that if she stayed busy, the haunts which filled her mind at rest, receded during her performance of the menial. Of late, she often thought of her mother and the loss of her father. Was she living her mother's pain? Did her mother feel love for her father or was he a familiar comfort? Helen tried to recall those weeks just after the letter had arrived from General Yancey. Her mother had read it, folded the letter back into its envelope and placed it in her roll top desk drawer. Helen had watched her read the letter's contents, but her mother had waited more than a week to relate to her its portent.

Helen arrived at the St. Peter camp in time to help close the tail gate of their heavy wagon. She looked about for any opportunity to assist. Everyone seemed ready for the departure, so she wandered the compound yearning to occupy her time until the call to move was sounded.

Her thoughts went back to her mother. The recent widow had certainly observed a proper mourning period. From the first, though, her mother had seemed lighter: almost elated. Helen had thought her frequent smiles and more frequent kindnesses towards the daughter an attempt to comfort by example. The ruse, as Helen saw it, failed because her mother had always been so critical of even the smallest aspects of her daughter's life. Helen doubted that her mother possessed the selfless concern required to feel the need to set any example. Her manner of authoritarian rule seemed to suffice in most situations.

None of this soothed her guilt in feeling so weakly the loss of Shin's passing. If anything, her own similarity to her mother's casual air towards her father's death made her feel even more wretched and shallow.

The Mormon caravan moved along the riverbank headed south towards the fjord location. Helen sat upon the seat next to Jason, Kyle's surviving son. Although only 17 years old, Jason was working out as a full-grown man. His strength, from his father's blood, coupled with a keen intellect, made him equal to any task he had been given thus far on their long trek. He was still a youth, however, and he could hardly conceal his delight at the opportunity to share the seat with Helen. She suspected he had a young man's designs upon her. She found his embarrassment funny and endearing at the same time. Although his youth caused her some doubt in his abilities to cross the wagon, she was relieved that she was not required to cross the river alone.

Finally, their turn arrived, and the young man slowly eased the heavy wagon into the river. He clucked to the oxen as they reluctantly entered the churning waters. They snorted in fear as they lifted their heads clear of the water, their necks craned as high as the yolks allowed. A crack of the whip above their back was enough to commit them to the flume.

Helen watched as the water piled against the side of the wheels then up to the lower edges of the wagon frame. The current eddied and fled without pattern or order. It was as if the muddy flow was confused at this strange impediment and panicked to escape the constriction of its progress. Was it her imagination, or did she feel the wagon slide downstream a fraction? She glanced over at Jason. He showed no sign of fear or doubt. In fact, he beamed a boyish grin, enjoying his role as protector of the lovely young widow. He snapped the reins at the oxen with an enthusiastic 'Heeyah!'

The wagon gained the opposite side of the river. It creaked as it rose from the water. The heavy wood issued a splintery groan as the beasts strained to pull the vehicle onto the bank. Soon the wagon achieved dry level ground. Water streamed away leaving only the familiar dry crunch of earth and stone under the heavy wheels.

That evening they camped near the river. The Mormons worked into the night drying those belongings discovered by the marauding river's waters. Goods rigged for the river crossing were unlashed and the wagons were again rearranged to a state for dry travel. It was late when Helen collapsed near the warm fire with a hot cup of broth. She sipped the soothing liquid, oblivious of anything else. After a time, she looked about her. Her eyes slowly adjusted to the dancing shadows and gated glimmer of the crackling fire. Directly across from her sat the stranger. He fixed her with an intent gaze. As their eyes locked, she felt a physical jolt. She got the distinct impression of a hungry wolf eyeing a helpless hare. It took a physical effort, but she pulled her eyes from his.

Her fleeing gaze met the eyes of Crease, wrapped in a blanket. His eyes glinted hotly with what she perceived as jealousy. She looked back to her cup, feeling a light-headed tingle of pleasure. She knew instinctively it was not the glowering look from Crease which had set her nerves to tingling.

She sat there for as long as she could bear. She did not look at him, but she was keenly aware of the stranger's unflinching gaze. She counted the seconds she felt would be appropriate, so she didn't appear to be fleeing his presence. She stood and made immediately for her wagon and the privacy and security it afforded.

Her dreams were troubled that night. She could not recall the dreams the following morning, but she knew she did not feel rested as was normal for her. Her eyes burned and itched from sleepless irritation as she helped with the breakfast preparations.

Her mind kept going to the stranger. She had so many questions about him. He was a mystery to be certain, but she felt an attraction she could not dismiss with rational thought. No matter how she occupied her mind or her hands, thoughts of him were there waiting for her consideration. The thought of him was like the reality of him. It went unnoticed until she looked up or directed her thoughts without, and there he was, taking her in.

By the time she had her wagon secured for the days trek, she was feeling more herself, although there was still an underlying fatigue.

Young Jason offered eagerly to again drive her wagon. She refused gently and kindly, explaining that she needed the work to keep her mind off things. He nodded, seeming to understand, although she suspected he had no idea. He shrugged and shuffled off, his shoulders hunched in disappointment.

Helen watched him go, then mounted the wagon seat, taking the reins in hand. As the wagon before her lurched forward, she snapped the reins and called to the oxen. The gray beasts leaned into their yolks and the wagon eased forward smoothly.

CHAPTER FIVE

Helen's Battle

Helen sat by the fire, dancing flames and warmth lulling her into a pleasant reverie. A blanket embraced her against the cool evening breeze. Her morning's fatigue was replaced with a comfortable sleepiness. She looked about her, her eyes alight with rare good humor. About her lips played a small smile. Father and Mother sat together a ways farther from the merry flame. Kyle and Percy sat together speaking quietly as they had often done of late. Crease sat opposite her. He was also wrapped in a course blanket, leaning against a log. He looked at her when he thought she wasn't paying attention. He was growing bolder in his advances. When she did catch his gaze, he no longer dropped his eyes immediately. They reached for her as she knew he yearned to in fact.

All eyes raised as Boyd sauntered into the fire light. He held the flask, now completely surrendered by Crease. Helen's eyes lowered to the gun belt strapped to his lean waist. There was no respect for property in this man. His browsing of the wagons had apparently turned up the weapon. She felt alarm at how comfortable he seemed with the weapon on his person. The Mormon men rarely wore a side arm and when they did, they did so with an awkward unfamiliarity. Handguns were more a novelty than a tool with these religious men. If weapons were necessary, they preferred the stability of a rifle. Boyd wore the gun belt low and tied off at his right thigh. Even Crease, who wore two guns, seemed aware of them on his person at all times. He sometimes walked with his hips slightly forward as if to bring them to prominence. With this stranger, it was difficult to tell where he ended, and the gun rig began.

She had not forgotten his attention the previous night, and she still couldn't deny her attraction for the dangerous stranger.

She looked away from the newcomer and her eyes, by chance, fell upon Crease who was staring at her with a black look on his face. Since Shin's death, he had become more attentive. His conversations with her, although seemingly all settler business, appeared somewhat solicitous. She was, of course, aware of his poorly concealed stares when he thought she was looking elsewhere.

At some level she found comfort in his attention. He was confident, tall and strong. Her fears towards his intent were allayed in the knowledge that his regard for her would easily cause him to take up the mantle of protector and guardian with her slightest acceptance of his advances.

All of that changed in the presence of the stranger. This new man spoke little but seemed to see everything. In his presence she felt his eyes always upon her. Often, when she glanced to check, his gaze was elsewhere. She knew instinctually that he still was very aware of her despite a lack of visual confirmation. He seemed to have an attention to everything without relying wholly upon his sight. He had a perception which was like a field of awareness rather than a unidirectional attention.

Her fascination with him bewildered and frightened her. Crease seemed an arrogant child in comparison. The stranger was the embodiment of what Crease pretended to be. She suspected that Crease knew he would break upon the rocks which was the stranger if tested. She also knew that his arrogance would numb him to that reality.

Crease must have caught her appraisal of Boyd and was not pleased. He held her gaze long enough to convey his displeasure and a silent warning to follow a code of conduct by which he meant her to abide.

Helen felt herself bristle at the temerity of this man. No matter her comfort at his attention, she was not his to reprimand.

Crease looked over at the stranger. Boyd was taking another long pull from the flask. He seemed unsteady on his feet. Helen was certain he must have been drinking alone before joining the group.

He wiped his mouth with the back of his hand then moved towards Helen. He dropped down heavily beside her on the log she occupied and almost toppled over. He caught himself unsteadily and laughed. Helen cleared her throat and looked down.

"Well," he said, "how are you bearing up this evening ma'am?"

"I am well, Mr. Boyd," she replied still looking at the ground.

He looked at her for a moment. As before, she could feel his eyes on her with an almost tactile gaze. She wanted to cross her arms and legs, but she feared she was only imagining the feeling, and she didn't want to give him any ideas. Finally, she couldn't bear it anymore and looked up at him. His eyes met hers, alight with desire, seeing her as woman. His gaze burned her. Finally, he looked away at the group around them.

"It's too quiet tonight," he said to no one in particular. He turned back to her. "Anyone play here?"

She glanced at Kyle, who was watching their conversation with keen interest.

"Kyle plays fiddle and some guitar."

She was not sure why she had said that. Likely the relief of his distracted attention played some role in it. Guilt needled her as she suspected that she somehow endangered Kyle with her words.

Hastily she added, "But he only plays for worship - to serve the lord."

"Well alright then, Big Boy," Boyd said loudly enough to be heard by all, "Unlimber that fiddle and let's see how she cries."

"This is not the time or the place, Helen," Kyle protested in a deep but low voice. His addressing her rather than the stranger was significant.

"I disagree," Boyd said, unmindful of the big farmer's reply. "Sashay on over and get her out. We need to add a little coal to the fire."

Kyle sat unmoving for a long while. Helen was afraid he would upset the drunken stranger. He finally rose and disappeared into the surrounding darkness with heavy strides.

Boyd took another taste of whiskey then looked around at the others with an expectant smile. He seemed a mischievous, but decidedly dangerous, boy.

Helen glanced at Crease from the corner of her eye. He had Boyd fixed with a dangerous glare. His look troubled her.

She tried to gauge the stranger's reaction to Crease's deliberate glare, covering her survey with a carefree air expected of a naive girl at a merry campfire. Boyd didn't seem to notice Crease at all, even though, the affront was occurring directly in front of him. His gaze, as always, was inward. A smile played at the corners of his lips. She couldn't be sure if he was amused at the prospect of Kyle going for his fiddle or Crease's attempt to intimidate him. It might just be the whiskey, she thought. She doubted the last. The stranger didn't seem careless. Whatever his thoughts, however, they were punctuated at intervals by pulls from the bottle he carried.

She saw Boyd lift his head at Kyle's return, carrying his fiddle in a rough grip, uncharacteristic of the gentle giant. The farmer was strong as a beast. She had seen him lift a wagon on his own when it became lodged in a sink hole. He had loaded sacks of meal onto a wagon with a single hand. Despite his mammoth strength, his voice was deep and pleasant. His brown eyes betrayed the gentle soul of a caring father.

He handled his musical instruments with the gentle grace of a career orchestra musician. This rough handling of his fiddle betrayed the depth of his consternation.

Kyle padded back to the fallen tree trunk upon which he had sat before. He watched the stranger expectantly but with obvious discomfort and disapproval. Boyd returned an innocent look, the flask poised just below his lips. Kyle sat again at his place and waited. His manner was unassuming, and he endured Boyd's attention in mild silence, as he was prone to do. Helen was afraid he would balk. She wasn't sure, but she suspected the stranger could be easily agitated in his current state.

Her fears left her when finally, Kyle snuggled the fiddle under his chin and drew the bow over the strings slowly. The instrument's deep rich voice began soft and low then built as the bow made its long way. Kyle played a tune Helen had heard many times. She adored the ballad. The chord progression was sorrowful but hopeful.

All heads around the fire turned towards the player, the music committing its will upon their hearts. Not a word passed until Kyle concluded the song. Helen glanced at Boyd, next to her. His eyes were far away, and he was completely still. In an instant his visage returned to one of mischief.

"That makes me wanna cry, big boy. You know something with a beat?"

Kyle closed his eyes. Helen thought he might protest but instead he merely replied wearily.

"I could play a little *Hunters of Kentucky*."

Boyd looked at Helen a moment. She started visibly at his solicitous look.

Without looking away from her he said, "I don't recollect that one, but we can try it out."

It seemed the entire camp noticed the direction of his gaze and the portent of his words. There was a general shifting of weight and shuffling of feet. Muttering was heard here and there around the fire.

Kyle sat stock still looking at Boyd, not sure what to do. Boyd finally shifted his gaze from Helen to the reticent musician. His eyes locked in on Kyle and his head lowered just a bit, as if in warning. Kyle brought the fiddle back to his neck and set his mouth as he pulled the bow across the strings.

The tone started a bit sharp and thin but soon the melody rang clearly, and the voice of the instrument peeled honestly and without favor for anyone in particular.

Boyd took a moment to gather the feel of the song. His head moved almost imperceptibly to the music. He drew a sip from the flask, shook the container to check the level of whiskey within. He stood facing the fire. Helen felt suddenly chilled. He seemed to gather the fire's heat all to himself. It must be her imagination that the chill increased with his attention to the flames.

Pivoting smartly, he extended a hand in a feigned formal courtesy and said in a voice draped in alcohol.

"Would you favor me with a dance, Miss?"

Helen retreated slightly in her seated position. The move was involuntary but struck those around her that she recoiled from this drunken stranger. All those around the fire sat silently - fearfully.

With an oath, Crease Cole stood out of his blanket. His two-gun rig dominating his intent.

"Lookey here Stranger," he said through grit teeth, "we're in Injun country, as you know. Maybe we oughta keep things calm tonight."

Boyd regarded him with only slightly more gravity than he would have given a child.

"We got too much calm going around already. Why don't you sit on back down in them blankets like you regular do and leave the rest to me."

Crease's shoulders straightened as he screwed up his courage. His fists clinched and unclenched a couple of times before he spoke. Kyle had stopped playing and the stranger seemed to be growing annoyed with the silenced instrument.

"I reckon I ain't asking," Crease muttered.

Helen felt a real fear touch her like a chill wind on bare skin. She knew instinctively that Crease would back his words with violence. She was just as certain that he would not live through the act. She touched Boyd's arm with a flattened palm. Boyd only half turned his head towards her. Crease had his full attention now. Helen forced a smile at Crease. She desperately wanted to allay his fears and save his life.

"I suppose it would be alright, Crease ...Just a dance."

She now gripped Boyd's forearm and tried to pull him towards a wide space between the fire and those nearby. Boyd didn't move nor did he change his gaze. His eyes were hard and deadly. He seemed to have come to a point of settlement upon his next course of action.

Helen looked directly at Boyd. She spoke to the side of his face.

"It's just a dance, Crease," This was said to Boyd although the message was for Crease.

Crease's stature softened by degrees until he slowly lowered himself back to his previous seated position atop his blanket. He was obviously furious. He also was obviously unsure how to proceed.

The stranger turned to Helen and pulled her close to him. Helen felt uncomfortable at his familiarity and his intimate proximity. Boyd looked down at her for a moment. When the music didn't immediately begin, he glanced at Kyle who was staring - aghast. He seemed to awaken from his stupor and slowly began playing. The song again started slowly but soon, in spite of himself, Kyle began to show his adroit skill with the instrument.

Boyd pulled Helen around the fire in tight circles, never taking his eyes from her. After a moment she felt him pull her against his body. She could feel her breasts compress against his strong frame. She tried to lean away from him to no avail. Her eyes moved away from the stranger and met those of Father St. Peter as they whirled by. His face was ashen in the fire glow and his eyes widened with concern.

Embarrassed at the way she was being handled by this drunken stranger, she attempted to push him away at arm's length. This accomplished nothing other than to improve his position to allow him all of her body against him nearly top to bottom. She heard Kyle's playing falter and his style diminished as he saw how she was being treated.

Boyd looked directly at Kyle.

"Keep sawing Big Boy. We are just gettin' going."

Boyd released her with his left arm and raised the flask to his lips as they danced. She could smell the alcohol strongly. Her nose crinkled its rebellion against the bitter odor. He grinned and offered her the flask. She shook her head and averted her face from the offensive vessel. He returned his hand to her hand, the flask held high between them. She could see he was enjoying this immensely. He leaned in close and spoke in her right ear.

"You dance as good as you look," he remarked and drew a great breath through his nose. He took in her fragrance, her very essence, she felt.

Helen shrunk under this new affront.

"I ain't gonna hurt you," he said.

He released her slightly so he could look into her eyes.

"What are you gonna do now that you are alone?"

"I don't see how that is any of your business, Mister," she replied indignantly. "Let's just finish the dance."

"A handsome woman like yourself needs a man to look after her ...keep her out of trouble."

"What makes you think I need a man to keep me any way, trouble or not?"

"I seen you looking at me. Maybe we are closer than you think."

Boyd grinned at her, obviously emboldened by the whiskey. Without warning, he grabbed the back of her head and kissed her hard, crushing her lips in the exchange.

Helen pulled away with force. She managed to break his grasp. As she attempted to flee, he grabbed violently for her. He managed to catch part of her dress. She could hear the sound of rent fabric as her dress separated at the seam.

Suddenly, she was half naked, her bosom in full view. She screamed and ran a few steps until she fell to the ground in her effort to cover herself. Her fall landed her among some drying dishes and utensils left from the evening meal.

The music stopped suddenly. Kyle stood, setting his fiddle down roughly and without regard. He approached the stranger with purpose. Helen saw Crease rise opposite Kyle.

"You damned Blackguard," Kyle growled. "You dare paw a decent woman. I'll kill you."

Without preamble, Boyd's pistol appeared, and he shot Kyle through his heart. The big man faltered a step then continued forward. He took two more steps then went to his knees. His hands gripped his chest and came away crimson. Boyd was already turning towards Crease as the big man fell on his face.

Crease had his hand on his right pistol. He yelled, "I told you Mister. I ain't gonna tolerate your guff no longer,"

Crease jerked his pistol from its holster roughly. He was obviously unpracticed and poorly experienced with a quick draw. Boyd fanned his pistol, and the gun belched flame. Crease took the impact with a small cry. The weight of the slug shoved him back on his heels. His gun fell to his feet. A look of disbelief filled his face until the pain of the slug replaced the shock with a grimace of anguish. With a shallow breath sounding like a groan, Crease fell forward into the dust and lay still.

Boyd looked around him. His eyes were fairly alight with the excitement of the moment. To Helen's view, he seemed to be enjoying himself. A cruel smile twisted his mouth and his gun hand made small circles as if to relieve a nervous tension there.

"There ain't no call for this, Mister."

Percy's diminutive voice sounded behind Boyd. The gunman turned and saw the small man, opposite him at the fire, standing with his hands outstretched before him in supplication. The entreaty did nothing more than annoy the stranger. He trained the pistol at Percy.

"I'll be the judge of that you mouthy shit."

Fire belched from the muzzle and Percy fell headlong into the fire. Myrtle had sat silently thus far, her hands clutched to her ample bosom, not knowing what to do. With a cry, she rose and ran to Percy.

"Let him cook, Ma'am."

Boyd broke the pistol open and began filling the empty chambers, disregarding the spent brass on the ground. His full attention seemed to be upon this task, but it was apparent he was completely cognizant of his surroundings.

Helen looked away from this violent monster. Her eyes fixed upon the smoking body of Percy, and horror gripped her. All of this, she thought, was her fault. Her friends had died coming to her succor. A burning shame welled up behind her eyes and tears began to flow. She was blinded by them. Her remorse washed over her in a numbing wave. The brutality of the past horrible moments began to take on an unreal cast. She felt she was moving within a hellish dream. None of this could really be happening. The wash of her emotions cleared her denial. Three of their number were dead at the hands of this casual demon. Helen was shocked out of her reverie by the uncharacteristic shrillness of Myrtle's voice.

"How can you be such a monster? We took you in, cared for you. We saved your life. You saved our lives just days ago?"

Boyd closed the chamber of the pistol, with a smart snap and looked up at her mildly. He holstered the weapon. The smile was no longer on his face. He now seemed somber and reflective.

"I saved my own. We all needed each other for a time. Now I only need one of you."

Boyd's eyes went to Helen. He took in her bare chest with lustful eyes. In an instant, she knew his plans for her. He would use her up. He would hurt her. He would ultimately discard what was left of her. All the hopes and dreams she ever had would be stripped away as would be any part of her which might have been pure or precious. A new wave of guilt passed over her. She could see her mother looking at her, shaking her head.

She could almost hear her say, "'This is how it was always going to end.'"

She could see the pity in her mother's eyes. A pity not of concern but derived from long awaited vengeance. All this passed through her imagination as she met the stranger's look unflinchingly. Her eyes finally fell in resignation. Before her, splayed on the ground where her fall had scattered them, were three large knives. She felt her throat tighten and a fury well up within her. She grasped the nearest knife and rose deliberately. She again looked at the stranger, uncaring of her nudity. With a grunt, she ran at Boyd, drawing the knife far back for her attack. The stranger took a half step back and a light of amusement glinted in his eyes. Helen moved more quickly than he expected, and his look of amusement was replaced with a wide-eyed look of surprise and concern. She was on him before he could react to ward off the attack.

The knife descended quickly slicing into his clothing. He turned his body left, giving her a slimmer target. Her thrust cut through his shirt and vest but missed his flesh. Her impetus caused her to move past him, desperately trying to change her line of attack to stay close to him. He shoved her roughly with his left hand as he drew his pistol with his right. With a scream, she changed her direction and renewed her assault upon him. Helen heard the report of the gun and felt a tug at her abdomen. She was surprised she felt no pain, just pressure. The slug's blow sobered her rage immediately. She dropped and sat upon her knees, a look of surprise and disbelief on her face. Boyd holstered his pistol.

Still looking at Helen he said, "Now I don't need none of you,"

The remaining Mormons were silent in their grief. The women cried and clutched one another. Travis St. Peter appeared stricken and paralyzed with horror.

Boyd walked away from the group towards the wagons. He climbed into the St. Peter wagon. They heard him rifling through the contents within. After a short moment, he jumped down holding a small strong box and an empty sack. St. Peter recognized the strong box as that containing the treasury of their group. The stranger's search of the Mormon's wagons had been thorough.

Boyd tossed the box on the ground and moved the contents into the chamois sack he had secured from inside the wagon. He stood straight and moved to the line of tethered horses. He quickly saddled the nearest one. All of this took a scant few minutes during which time no one moved or spoke. They merely watched his actions in horrible fascination. He mounted and guided his horse back towards the fire. He looked at Helen, she sat where she had fallen. The pain of her wound was beginning to make itself known. She held herself with both hands low and to the side. Blood soaked her ripped dress.

The mounted man tipped his hat to the group.

"Adieu."

With that, he nudged the horse away, into the darkness, and out of sight.

CHAPTER SIX

Cab Jackson

The village of Boguillas endured the dogged sweltering sun during the day, reluctantly going about its business with little regard for productivity or haste. The complaining drone of cicadas honed a ragged edge to the swelter. The setting of the sun, however, beckoned the drifters, passersby and ne'er-do-wells from their warrens and into either of two drinking establishments. The dim light of night lanterns and the smoky din of a drunken pianist tended to goad the night folk to a furor of drink and garrulousness inconsistent with the dogma of a sleepy border town. The cattle routes between Mexico and Texas drew quite a variety of the transient through this town.

Two drinking dens seemed excessive for a town as small as Boguillas. Remarkable as the redundancy seemed, the two watering holes served very different clientele. The older and smaller of the two, *La Puebla*, squatted at the southern edge of the small village: its adobe walls displayed rain streaked and bullet pocked character. *La Puebla* offered up the ambiance of a cave. Bare candles lighted the cantina in smudged elegance. Three tabletops balanced upon rough crates, teetering upon the packed and swept dirt floor within the bar. A single smoky-glassed lantern hung from the dark beamed ceiling, suspended by a heavy rusty chain over the bar. The bar top itself was referred to as *El Roble* due to its being no more than a tree trunk, roughly flattened on the top facing side. If one were not careful, when resting his stoneware cup - the preferred vessel of the establishment - he risked the cup settling upon a ragged splinter and tipping over. The bar top was discolored with dark blood stains in numerous spots where many had fallen victim to its rough carpentry.

At one time, before Texas was rested from the grasp of Mexico, Boguillas was a regularly travelled cattle route across the river into the rich region which was known as *Coahuila y Tejas*. In those days, *La Puebla* was the center of the village. To be truly accurate, it indeed had been the village. The structure predated its current role as a cantina. It was, as far back as even the oldest could remember, a line shack for one of the expansive Mexico cattle ranches. Due to its proximity to an established river crossing and watering hole, the primitive structure became a regular stop for drovers and *vaqueros* alike. Eventually, the stop was manned full time and stocked with food and strong drink.

Boguillas proper was, depending upon several factors, sometimes closer to the Rio Grande than at other times. Although, the river signified a tenuous international boundary between the two countries, its course could vary by as much as a mile north or south, depending upon a variety of causes. Heavy rains, drought, rock slides, and even the remains of fallen livestock could alter the route of the river's flow. *La Puebla*, however, was far enough from the river's irresolute path to keep the pub above water, yet close enough to the border that many patrons from Mexico frequented it year-round.

As Boguillas aged, its growth spread in a northerly direction. The second drinking establishment in Boguillas had been erected only a couple of years hence. Unlike *La Puebla*, it was constructed with precision and care. It boasted milled lumber coated in a penetrating wash which fairly choked patrons.

The new Saloon was called the Shady Lady. This unusual name came from the founder, Jason Steed, who had read the reference in a book featuring a Paris night club and brothel of the same name.

On this night, the Lady, as it was called, was in full swing. The night was mild enough that a collective of languorous patrons rested out of doors. Their number, in various states of leisure, lined the front walk boards, seated upon wooden chairs. Spilling light and surfeit noise escaped the crowded saloon, encroaching upon the dark comfort in which the loungers huddled. Cigars and cigarettes glowed random patterns like hilltop signal fires.

A young man rested between two gregarious stockmen. Their conversation was open to his participation, but he remained audience rather than participant to it. His garb was not unlike many of the cowboys around him. His hat rested casually on the back of his head. His tawny hair lay well over his eyes and down his neck. His shoulders were broad and thick. A heavy six shooter hung from his waist. He slouched in the hard chair with crossed legs and high heeled riding boots.

His name was Cabbage Jackson and he had been in Boguillas for just a few days. The events of the days prior to his arrival in Boguillas weighed heavily upon him. Any preoccupation which settled his restive mind was a welcome exercise. The quiet conversation and casual mood among the loungers suited him.

Cab arrived in town nearly a week after making his way south as quickly as horseflesh would allow. Cab looked around him. His blue eyes reflected his contentment. The two neighboring cowmen talked to one another, glancing politely in his direction occasionally as a courtesy. Cab acknowledged the latest passive invitation with a nod of thanks. He pressed his memories from him and focused on the conversation under way.

"That old mare was as ornery as my wife," This came from the stoutly built man to Cab's left. He was dressed in a vest coat and knee-high black boots.

The man to Cab's right drew on a ridiculously large stogie and said, "The egg trick would have fixed that cayuse, Wilkins,"

Wilkins grinned and drew on his cigar. The cherry glowed brightly, casting an orange hue upon the man's lined and crinkled face.

"The egg trick?" he scoffed with a smoky exhalation of mirth.

Cab smiled and glanced at Wilkins' companion. He anticipated a clever story from an adroit yarn spinner. The man of the cigar grew bolder in his expanding audience. He stretched for effect, then spoke with the importance of a man who was accustomed to imparting wisdom to those requiring it.

"Shore," he said. "I had this three-year-old filly. She would always shy when I tried to daub a bridle on her. No matter where or when I tried it, she would turn her head."

He took another pull on his cigar and let the smoke escape his mouth in a slow curl. He studied the cigar with a frown as if it were misbehaving. Finally, he continued his tale with the gravity of one pushing on with a task against unfavorable conditions.

"One day I lifted an egg from mother's egg cooler. She didn't pay it no mind account of a wet spring and them layers was as busy squeezin' out eggs as a cat covering shit on a hot tin roof."

The speaker apprised Wilkins with a knowing squint to his eyes.

"That wife of mine would have had a fit if she had caught me playin' coyote to her layin' hens."

He leaned back, enjoying the attention his tale was garnering from a growing number of loungers.

"Yeah," he drawled. "That sorrel filly saw me coming up the way towards the barn. I remember the day plain enough count of the unusual fair weather we was enjoying for so early in the spring.

"Anyhow, that filly knew I was all about her due to my working with her every morning for a fortnight up to then. I'm not about playing up to a hoss when I'm givin' 'em a proper education.

"There are some who try to baby a young hoss. They take the high road, so to speak. I never prescribed to the school of soft touches and warm looks when it comes to a hoss's upbringin',"

He looked around him for any who would disagree with his philosophy. Finding none, he continued his story.

"You won't see me lungin' a hoss or makin' up to 'em in a circle pen with a soft leather strap in my hand. That kinda thing is what a woman does when she makes a foal a pet. This little philly was gonna be a full growed cuttin' hoss, if I had anything to say on the matter."

He looked over at Wilkins.

"You recollect that full Dunn I sold at the Round Mountain auction?"

He grunted his importance at the event. "Now that was a helluva cow pony. Couldn't have been any less than eighteen hands if he was a inch. That gelding would throw a salt cowpoke flat when he cut short a bolting yearlin'.'"

Wilkins chuckled at the memory.

"Yep. I can see him plain shore, Herb."

Herb smiled through another smoke cloud.

Those listening close at hand laughed quietly and shook their head in disbelief. The idea of an experienced hand being thrown by any horse was suspect to these veteran cattlemen. Wisely, they kept their doubts behind their teeth so as not to interrupt the flow from the storyteller. A well spun yarn was worth much to those long riding men.

"I fetched out that same old snaffle bit bridle I been using on her since the start and come up to her with a feed pail full of that sorghum mix all them hosses like. Well, she goes for that sweet feed like a mockingbird on a grub. Once she muzzles up a mouthful, she pulls up and I set the pail down and reach in my pocket for that egg. I daub the bridle strap around her neck and slide that rig up towards her nose. As I expected, she throws her head. Quick as a wink I take that egg and hit her high and between the eyes with it."

Herb laughs and looks around as if all could see the memory as plainly as he. He didn't seem to notice the looks of incredulity and confusion.

"All that mare heard was the crack of that shell on her hard forehead, and the sight of yolk and white dripping down over her eyes. She thought she had been struck hard and was bleedin' out. She stood there splayed legged and pert near petrified that she was terrible hurt. I eased that rig up over her ears and cinched it up."

Herb's smile beamed satisfaction and ease all around him. He straightened in his chair as one imparting knowledge which would benefit all for no profit or gain to himself.

"That," he said significantly, "was the last time I ever had any trouble with the bridle on that young cayuse."

Cab looked down at his boots and covered a wry grin. The others chuckled amongst themselves. Quiet comments of the fantastic tale soon trailed away in favor of individual topics of interest between pairs, or small groups. In the pause Cab's mind returned to the memories of the last few weeks.

When Cab arrived in New York, he was struck with the impression of a bustling city of scant hope but great opportunity. His exploration ended in the company of a band of youths near the daunted five points region. His companions were cut from a cloth not as clean as it was rough sewn.

A group of more like-minded fellows could not have been found. As fate would have it, theirs were not minds set upon philanthropy nor theological pursuit. These young men were skilled professionals of the lowest order. Highway agency, confidence schemes, second story work, and a vocation of general skullduggery were their stock in trade. Cab fell in with them as a matter of necessity. One must eat, after all.

Cab shook his head at the memory of the gang's demise. At any rate, his welcome had expired as had his prospects. Sharp instincts and quick feet saved him from confinement and hard labor at the hands of those officials serving the state's interest. He exhausted all the money he possessed for a train ticket west. Three days aboard and two station changes transported him to the most unlikely destination he could imagine: the bustling town of Agua Caliente.

Upon arriving in the east Texas town, he procured lodging at a lackluster boarding house, using funds purloined from a wallet lifted outside a train stop during his western journey.

The following morning found him refreshed and eager for the prospects of the new day. He washed at the stone basin in his room, donned freshly brushed clothing, and set out for a morning walk. He was intent upon surveying the town and his prospects within. Surprisingly, the town was not active of an early morning. His time in New York City had been filled with the continuous din of human activity. The sounds of struggling humanity were unceasing, even far into the early morning hours. The noise had been a source of energy and excitement. He held firm to the belief that achievement was the source of providence. Activity was the source of achievement.

As he rounded a corner boardwalk, he turned his head towards muffled sounds of distant gunfire. He instinctively walked towards the sounds of violence. In moments the crisp peal of a bell's toll sharpened the clear morning air. By the time the bell had ceased its ringing, he was near enough the bank to see bandits moving within then out until the group, as one, mounted and began flight towards the center of town. They rode tightly bunched, led by a big man who sat his horse lightly despite his size. Cab could hear activity mounting all around him. The town was up at arms. He saw heavily armed men bolting for cover or vantage to gain a shot at the bandits.

Just ahead of Cab and to the right, he saw a bearded man leaning against the lee side of a building. He held a double-barreled shotgun tightly to his chest. His companion fell back slightly, as if to distance himself from the violent act intended by his companion. The leading man took a deep breath and brought the shotgun to his shoulder as he slowly rounded the corner in an effort to gain a shot at the oncoming bandits. The leader of the robbers drew his pistol and shot the gunman as he cleared the building's corner. The bearded man went down and did not move. The ambusher's companion turned to flee but fell to the leader's second bullet.

Cab felt fear as he realized his tenuous position out in the open as he was. He looked about him in alarm. Quickly he leaped into a narrow alleyway between two closely placed buildings. He meant to put as much distance between himself and the impending battle as he could. He doubted the bandits would make for the western edge of town. That route took them through the heart of the town and would be rife with mustering armed men. He made his way towards that end of town. Behind him, muffled by the buildings between him and the moving battle, he heard a growing number of reports sounding from pistol fire here or a long gun there. The booming explosions of the leader's pistol were unmistakable to Cab. It was as if the leader were firing a special weapon with its own individual voice and caliber. The pistol sounded often, and its voice cried death with every round expended.

Cab was at a dead run when he broke from cover onto the main street. He stopped short, nearly losing his feet. To his left was a barricade of wagons, barrels, tubs, chairs and all manner of common items. Behind the quickly fashioned barrier were at least a dozen men, rifles bristling in the direction from where the gun fighting sounds emanated.

Cab instinctively drew his pistol and several of the rifles shifted in his direction. He quickly turned his pistol down the street, following the lead of the townsmen. His apparent alliance seemed to ease their suspicions and the riflemen again gave their full attention to the approaching menace. Even so, he eased back into the alley from which he had issued. He no sooner re-entered the alley than he heard a fresh fusillade of gun fire. Apparently, the bandits had rounded the turn and had entered the street before the barricades. The men behind the cover of the barricade fired with a deafening volley. The outlaws returned fire, striking many of the townsmen behind cover. The remaining townsmen retreated from the deadly hail from the outlaws.

Cab peeked around the corner. The leader was on foot, his horse dying behind him. A bullet caught the leader's hat and the man took quick aim and killed the shooter. Cab was shocked at such marksmanship, particularly under the duress of battle. He saw him pick up a rifle laying nearby, lever in a shell and fire up towards a roof top sniper Cab could not see.

Horses could be heard racing towards the melee. More townsmen, mounted and shooting, entered the killing zone. The leader shot two rounds into the mass of mounted men. They separated and dove for cover. By this time all of the bandits were giving their full attention to the pursuers.

Cab looked again towards the leader. He was a broad shouldered, strongly built man. He must have been taller than six feet and more than two-hundred pounds. What fear his physical prowess didn't elicit, his determined and deadly mien and violent manner commanded. Cab was unable to make out specific facial features, but he could have recognized the man, at distance, from his manner alone.

The bandits spread out, barking instructions amongst themselves. A squat bearded man cried out orders as the leader disappeared around the side of a building. Sporadic gunfire sounded from all quarters. The outlaws, it seemed, were executing townsmen as they came upon them. Cab had never heard of such a thing much less borne witness to an act like this. Minutes later the outlaws again entered the main thoroughfare. All were mounted, even the leader who had formerly been afoot.

As a group, they made for the direction of the barricade, now unmanned. As they cleared the barricade, a new barrage of gunfire, erupted from a building out of Cab's sight. He knew the gunfire came from within the cover of a building because of the muffled quality of the rifle reports. Several of the outlaws perished under this new attack. The survivors opened fire wildly. The leader fired into the newly engaged gunmen as quickly as he could draw hammer and release it. He spurred his horse, driving the animal to a full gallop. The horse's leap to flight was so abrupt that he resembled a cat taking flight, his hindquarters nearly doubling under his body. The rider leaned well forward and lay low along the horse's neck offering a smaller target for the gunmen.

Cab watched as the remaining outlaws fell like target ducks at a midway shooting gallery. The men died quickly. The ghastly sight was beyond imagining. It was as if the departure of their leader had removed some mystic spell of protection. Until his departure, the leader and his men seemed nearly impervious to bullets. As the leader made his flight from harm, his men paid with their lives. With the immediate threat eliminated, the townsmen gathered in a group before the storefront.

Cab heard parts of the leader's talk, mostly directed at a gray-haired, bowlegged man. The talk ended with hats pulled low over angry brows. As one they moved towards horses. They mounted, and with a shout from their leader, they galloped out of town in the direction to which the outlaw had fled.

Cab watched them go. He stood alone at the edge of the carnage. He looked down and noticed he still held his pistol. He holstered the weapon. He looked up sharply at the sound of a voice from across the roadway.

"Hey, Mister. State your business."

Cab saw three men crossing the road in a rapid and businesslike manner. Cab took a step back.

"Stay where you are, stranger," said the center man of the three. "We don't know you and it seems a little suspicious that you happen to be here just as the bank gets robbed,"

Cab decided that, although innocent of any wrong doing in the bank robbery, his crimes back east were of sufficient severity that even a cursory inquiry would expose him and likely bring to light arrest warrants. He turned on his heel and fled down the alley. He turned right as the three men loosed lead after him. Bullets crunched into the building planks behind him. Directly ahead was a lone horse, dragging reins upon the ground as it nosed about for the scant grasses nearby. Cab was fortunate that the horse didn't bolt immediately upon his hasty approach. Cab grabbed the hanging reins, and the horse jerked his head up, reacting to the violent movement, but too late for escape. Cab's grip was firm. The gelding sidled away from Cab, but he still managed to gain the left stirrup.

Yells of alarm rang out as the pursuit rounded the building's corner. By this time, he was in the saddle and spurring the horse to full speed. He made for a corral fence where he put the structure between himself and potential gunfire. He sent his mount into a ravine and followed its path for some distance before reemerging onto the flat. He hoped the maneuver would throw off pursuit or at least confuse them as to his direction of escape.

By late afternoon he gained the summit of a tall, wooded hill. In the waning light he searched his back trail. He detected no pursuing posse. He assumed the main body, and most qualified pursuit, was arrowing after the tall outlaw. The loss of life, and the attention to the injured may have subdued the enthusiastic pursuit of a less likely quarry. Although reasonable, Cab was not so easily set at ease. He turned his mount and headed south at an easy but mile devouring canter.

For several days after, he rested in hiding during daylight hours, continuing his flight in the cover of night. He subsisted on water, which was plentiful due to a recent soaking rain. On one occasion he was able to shoot a rabbit. He was a fair shot, but he attributed the uncanny accuracy of the snap shot to desperation and luck.

When he field dressed the animal, however, he was disgusted to find it ridden with parasites. He accounted the infestation to the hot time of year. He was able to salvage enough meat, however, to ease his hunger.

Two more days passed with no kill nor any food whatsoever. By the second day of his fast, it occurred to him to inspect the contents of the bedroll and saddle bags on the horse. To his delight, the previous owner had packed for the trail. In the bags he found hard tack, a leather sack filled with nuts and dried berries, and an oilskin containing a half dozen hard biscuits. He laughed with grim humor. He might have starved to death with food at hand, had he not checked the saddle's contents. He surmised that the horse had belonged to one of the outlaws, evident by the way it was outfitted for the trail. He felt it unlikely that a townsman would be situated for a long ride

Cab thought, with relief, "at least I ain't a horse thief." No one would claim the horse - at least no one above ground.

Some days later, he found himself on a small hillock looking down upon the lights of Boguillas. He rode into the outskirts of the town and spent the remaining dark hours of early morning in a lean-to stables with a milk cow and a sturdy but aged draft horse. There was fodder for his horse and water in the trough for him. He woke before the light of dawn and rode into town openly. He was not so much emboldened by a lack of pursuit as he was driven to act as naturally as he could so as not to pique anyone's interest unnecessarily. He had some bills and coins from his previous gain, so he entered a small, quiet eatery on the main street of the small town. He sat at a corner table near the kitchen and ordered eggs, steak, biscuits, frijoles and hot coffee.

When a buxom woman brought him his order, he dug in with relish, shoveling great forkfuls into his watering mouth.

He was nearly finished with the meal when two armed men entered the café. They looked directly at him, then approached him with dutiful strides. One of the men, the older of the two, brushed his long mustaches with his left hand and turned the chair opposite him with his right then sat down. His tall, younger companion moved slightly to his right bringing Cab into his view while keeping his companion out of the way if their interview resulted in gun play. Cab noticed this with interest.

"Howdy, stranger," said the seated man. "I'm Jim Murray and this is Cal Stubbs. We're Texas Rangers. What's your name?"

Cab put down his fork and sipped his coffee. He sat down the cup and leaned back.

"I'm not sure why that is any of your concern, Ranger. Is there a law I am breaking having my breakfast here?"

Murray smiled his reaction without mirth or pleasure.

"You would be wise to cut the sass and answer the question."

Cab looked at Stubbs. His hand rested on the butt of his gun. His lips were set in an impatient thin line.

"Rangers," Cab said with an uneasy smile, "I'm not sure what you think I did but I just rode into town after three days on the road from San Antonio."

He watched the rangers with his best innocent look. The rangers had no noticeable reaction to his claim. Cab studied his plate, thinking hard. He looked up as an idea occurred to him. With a deep breath, he shook his head sadly.

"Alright then. I admit it," He said forcefully. "I am guilty."

The rangers leaned forward a little at his admission.

Cab continued, looking down in shame. He fidgeted with the coffee cup for a moment, gathering his thoughts. The rangers became very still. The tension became a palpable thing.

Finally, Cab spoke.

"I didn't love her," he exclaimed abruptly. "Surely you fellas can understand that."

Cab looked at the two desperately, easily acted due to the danger of his current predicament.

"I was sure her father would be mad that I left her at the altar tha-taway, but I didn't think he would put the Texas Rangers on my trail."

The lawmen eased back a bit. The tale was compelling, and this youngster didn't match the description wired from Agua Caliente. Though not totally convinced, they were obviously amused. Murray shook his head in feigned pity.

"Sorry son, we gotta take you back," he said, winking at his partner.

Cab didn't see the wink as his eyes were lowered in feigned misery, but he knew the rangers had bought his story and were ribbing him. He continued, with his lowered eyes hiding his look of triumph at the success of his ruse.

"Can't we act like I was never here, ranger?"

Cab seemed close to desperation. His voice quavered slightly.

"That proud Mexican will hang me shore."

Cab looked up at Murray with a look of fear and desperation.

Murray could keep up the sham no longer. He looked at Stubbs and they both broke into broad grins. Cab seemed confused, then his face transformed as he seemed to realize the game the lawmen were play-ing. He sat back and laughed nervously.

"You mean to say that the old man didn't send you on my trail?"

The rangers laughed. Murray stood and replaced the chair.

"Son," he said, "We got bigger game to chase than some calf-eyed kid running from a jiltin'."

Stubbs snorted his contempt.

"Ain't no Mexican gonna send a Texas Ranger nowhere: particular on some personal mission of revenge. We ain't no man's lap dog."

Murray patted Stubbs' arm. "Let it go Cal."

The rangers turned towards the door. At the door Murray turned back to Cab.

"Keep your head down, son. Them Messcans hold a grudge for a long time."

Cab cleared his throat.

"Just curious," he said seemingly uneasily, "What did you think I did in the first place?"

Murray gave Cab a look for a long moment. Cab feared he had gone too far. Instead, the ranger nodded significantly.

"We're looking for a robber and murderer we figure is headed this way. He goes by the name of Boyd Hutton. He is pretty well known as a bad man. He is easy to spot. He is a goodly sized hombre, dark hair with gray mixed in, blue eyes, and mean as a rabid skunk."

The ranger thought a moment then said, "He robbed the bank at Agua Caliente and got away. The word is that a posse chased him but never caught up with him. If you see or hear anything, you can find us at the end of the southern road in an old 'dobe shack. Keep out of trouble kid,"

With that, they walked out and headed towards town. Cab sat for a moment, forgetting to breathe. It was a strange feeling, attaching a name to the fearless killer capable of such horrible action. He drew a long breath and exhaled in long, audible relief. He looked over and saw the waitress watching him with interest. She had probably over-heard his conversation and had opinions of her own. He dropped enough coins to pay for the meal and quickly departed.

He mounted and rode into town. Boguillas was small but modernly built. Although his years were few, his wisdom had grown in the face of the chances he took and the resulting dangers he faced. As was his custom, he cased the town, paying particular attention to routes of escape. He saw the ranger's shack as described – a squat dingy adobe affair. Cab surmised they had chosen the southern road from town anticipating that their quarry would make a break for Mexico and chose a post which seemed perfect for reacting to an escape of that type.

Cab altered his course, swinging east, staying at the edge of town. He came to a complex of stock pens and cattle chutes. The yards were empty. Cab steered wide to pass the pens. Soon he came to a slight depression that deepened into a draw some yards beyond the cattle pens. The draw took a circuitous route for some distance before it veered back south following the natural rugged contours of the land. Judging by the smell, the draw functioned as a run off for the stock yards. He guessed the draw fed into the nearby Rio Grande.

Cab completed his survey and rode back into town via the eastern road. After securing lodging at an old Mexican hovel, he made his way towards the town center where he came upon the Shady Lady.

Every night since, he had whiled away his time with passersby and lounging saloon patrons. That had been several weeks hence. One night he sat in on a poker game and won big. That windfall allowed him to loiter with few worries. He wasn't sure why he remained in the dusty border town, but he felt he would need to move on soon. His commitment to activity goaded him towards restless impatience.

His reverie was interrupted by his companions shifting their chairs for a more comfortable posture from which to spin their yarns. They had redirected their conversation to hunting dogs.

Herb was saying. "Well that ain't so. Hunting with dogs requires two kinds of dogs. You gotta trail game with Bay Dogs, and you hold the game with Catch Dogs,"

Cab lost Herb's line of conversation as his thoughts again rose to occupy his attention. His vacant gaze rested upon the dim darkness of the dusty street. A weary rider approached. His fagged mount crossed a shaft of light spilling from a window. Something about the rider was familiar.

With a start Cab thought, 'more than familiar.'

A tingle rose up his spine. The rider walked his spent horse to the tie rail and dismounted. He tied off the horse, stretched, and climbed the stairs onto the boardwalk. The horse stood with hanging head. The rider, although road worn, seemed in much better condition than his mount.

Some of the loungers took casual notice of the new arrival. After he entered the saloon, however, their conversations resumed as before.

Cab watched the empty doorway into which the rider had disappeared. Although darkness and the play of lighting and shadow obscured clear view of his face, Cab was certain this was the leader of the outlaws from Agua Caliente – the man called Boyd Hutton. There could be no mistake in the build of the man. His stride, even fatigued, was unmistakable. There was something about him that seemed changed, however. He seemed to have lost something of the imposing air Cab had noted during the robbery escape. Cab couldn't describe it, but the fearsome outlaw seemed diminished somehow.

Cab sat for a moment deep in thought. His mind whirled at his fate. What were the chances of running into this dangerous outlaw twice in so short a time? Surely, an experienced crook would avoid a crowded saloon if he wanted to stay alive. This wanted man walked into the saloon as though he hadn't a care in the world. Cab smiled to himself. He had heard somewhere that the best hiding place is in plain sight. This outlaw seemed to embrace the philosophy with a foolhardy confidence. Cab was as committed to fate's plans for him as the outlaw was confident in his safety in entering a crowded bar so boldly. He decided to make the acquaintance of this brazen outlaw. He stood and, without hesitation, entered through the squeaky front doors.

Inside, Cab surveyed the room. Cigarette smoke clung to the ceiling like some cowering wraith, giving reluctant berth to the maelstrom below. Cab spied the outlaw leaning on the long bar. He watched the bartender approach. Hutton accepted a bottle and glass from the bartender, dropping a coin on the bar. He made his way to an empty table near the rear of the place. Cab's experience in the bar found the table informally reserved as exclusive refuge for the piano player, and sometimes the owners. As such, the table was typically unoccupied. Hutton sat, pouring his glass full from the bottle. He drank it down in one draught then looked about him. Cab feared the outlaw had seen him. He hesitated, his nerve flagging a bit. He steeled himself, set his jaw and committed his actions to fate. He walked towards the outlaw as the other refilled his glass.

Cab stopped directly in front of Hutton. The man didn't acknowledge Cab's presence. He drained the glass and poured another drink. Cab cleared his throat.

"My name is Cabbage Jackson. Call me Cab."

No reply.

"Do you mind if I sit down?"

Hutton sipped from the glass then sat it down on the table. Cab got his first detailed look at the outlaw. His soiled clothing hung loosely from his thick frame. His shoulders were broad and thick. His hands were blunt-fingered and powerful. He was seated slightly open to his right, giving clearance for his gun, if required. The gun was a heavy black colt sheathed in a stoutly buckled, worn black leather holster. The stranger's eyes rose and fixed upon Cab for a moment. They were dark blue and seemed to blaze as if from an internal fire. Finally, the outlaw spoke. His voice was deep and held a portent of deadly finality with each word.

"You got starch in your creases, boy."

Hutton evaluated Cab for a long moment. He lifted his glass and emptied the contents. He again filled the glass. As he did, he spoke without looking at Cab. His voice held a tone which disavowed any responsibility for future actions resulting from Cab's decision to associate with the outlaw.

"Your funeral."

Cab pulled back a chair.

As he sat, he said, "Generally is. But I think we are talking about yours presently."

Hutton looked up sharply. The eyes had gone cold. Cab could feel fear rising in him. He sensed he was seconds from death.

"Not me," he stammered. "I ain't bracin' nobody. I came over because there are Texas Rangers been in town for a couple days asking about a feller that comes awful tight to your look."

Cab became a bit uneasy at the steady gaze with which the gunman fixed him.

Cab felt his voice quaver a fraction as he continued his explanation.

"I know what it means to be mistook for somebody else."

He laughed hollowly.

"You could say I have a sympathetic ear for that sort of thing."

The stranger continued his unblinking scrutiny. Finally, he seemed to come to some conclusion about Cab and the edge in his eyes dulled somewhat. The younger man was not excited to receive result of the verdict.

Cab said conciliatorily, "The Mexico border is close, and they will be watching for a break for it. I happen to know a cow path that runs a draw and comes out at the river. I could show you."

Hutton finally looked away. He rose from his seat.

"Where are these rangers stayin'?" he asked with a calm resolution which told Cab he intended to seek out the lawmen and deal with them.

Cab laughed despite his fear of the outlaw. He covered the outburst with a warning.

"You don't want to think about that pard. They ain't alone. This fella they are asking about is too big a handful for them to nab without overwhelming numbers. You might get two or maybe even three, but a half dozen would be a load even for a feller with sand such as yourself."

Hutton looked vacantly at Cab. Cab got the impression that Hutton had relegated him to a lesser danger for the moment. His thoughts seemed to be bent upon his decision making. Finally, the outlaw sat once more and poured himself another drink.

Cab nodded grimly from his chair opposite the big man. To his dismay, the outlaw seemed to have decided to stay there, abandoning any tactical action at all. Cab cast a look around him as if foes were already closing in upon them.

"Maybe you don't savvy the grave situation you find yourself in," he said urgently in a low voice. "We'd best slope."

Boyd paid him no mind. He sipped his drink mildly letting his gaze scan the patrons in the saloon.

Cab pulled his hat lower over his eyes and sunk a bit in his seat. Finally, resigned to the outlaw's silent defiance, he asked, "You got another glass?"

The big man pushed the bottle towards Cab. Cab looked around him and retrieved an empty glass from a nearby table. It troubled him none that the glass was previously used by another. He poured and downed the fiery liquid. Cab rarely drank and he winced at the strong whiskey's bitter heat.

The alcohol didn't seem to change the silent outlaw at all. His bearing remained one of singular self-possession. He didn't become any more personable nor any more untoward as he drank. His eye never grew glassy, and he didn't seem to lose focus on his surroundings.

The two sat at that back table until late. The saloon crowd had begun to thin when Hutton rose without preamble. He corked the bottle and took it with him. Cab remained for a moment, unsure whether he was to follow or stay behind. His fascination with the outlaw made his mind and he rose and followed him out to the hitching rail.

Hutton's mount was much improved but still could have benefited from a good feeding and some unsaddled rest. Hutton mounted and turned his horse toward the south. Cab found his horse and mounted.

He caught up with the bandit then took the lead. He altered their direction more eastward. Hutton followed without a word.

The darkness hid them until they descended into the draw behind the stock pens. The two rode along the draw for no more than half an hour before it widened and descended to the gravelly bank of the Rio Grande River. Dim moonlight glistened on the swift flow of the river. The two horses splashed into the shallow river towards the freedom of Mexico.

A gunshot sounded somewhere behind them, and a bullet tunneled under water near the horses' feet. Without prompting from the riders, the horses lurched to a flume thrashing, lunging run. The water impeded adequate speed, but the splashing served to cover their retreat in the dim new moon's light. More shots rang out and bullets hummed dangerously close to the riders. Both fugitives drew pistols and returned fire. They could not see the assailants, but they shot in the general direction from which the rifle reports emanated.

They soon gained the opposite shore. Clattering horses' hooves could be heard across the narrow river as the pursuers descended the gravelly bank into the river. Splashes confirmed that the pursuit would respect no international boundaries. Judging by the displaced water and the sound, Cab estimated that at least four riders, and perhaps as many as six, were giving chase

Cab spurred his horse to a gallop, ascending the slope from the river bed. He turned to check Hutton's proximity. To his dismay, he was alone. Rather than following him, the outlaw dismounted and unsheathed a rifle. He quickly levered a round into the chamber, leveled the weapon and took a shot. One of the riders fell into the river with a shout. He fired again and another lurched forward grabbing his shoulder. The remaining riders moved to separate, but the water made the maneuver difficult and slow. Hutton shot again and this time a horse fell, hit hard.

The Rangers seemed to organize instinctively, perhaps due to the desperate situation in which they suddenly found themselves. The remaining three riders fired wildly: attempting to cover their exposed position from this uncanny marksman.

Cab drew his pistol as he turned his mount back towards the river. He opened fire on the flailing lawmen. His rounds stung the air near enough the rangers to affect their aim. As one, the rangers broke off and fled back to the Texas side of the river. Hutton took aim and fired once more. His bullet hit one of the horses in the haunch. The horse faltered but did not fall, it staggered as it climbed the bank.

Hutton mounted and turned his horse away from the river. He passed Cab and the latter turned his horse to follow. They topped the small rise then began a short descent, gaining safety from enemy fire. They settled their horses to a mile devouring canter, comfortable to their trail wise mounts.

Hutton glanced at Cab. By way of explaining his recent bravery, he said, "This nag never would of outrun them rangers on her own. Too fagged out."

Those were the only words passed for the remainder of the night. They rode until the gray of dawn stained the starless sky. Hutton led them into a small group of rocks, lifted from the desert by some subterranean force of nature. Within the rock formation they found a slight depression and the remnants of a previous camp, perhaps left by other fugitives.

Hutton dismounted and loosened the girth of his saddle. He hobbled the horse near some grasses which braved the solitude of the small hollow. Cab followed the leader's example as Hutton made a fire in the waste of the previous fire spot.

Soon they were seated at the fire, each examining his own thoughts. Hutton produced the bottle taken from the saloon. He pulled a long rapacious draw from it. He offered it to Cab who hesitated a moment before accepting. He drank sparingly from the bottle then handed it back to the outlaw. His face crinkled at the strength of the whisky. He was not given to sprits and the recent danger caused him to value clear wits.

Wearily, they watched the morning brighten. Finally, Cab cleared his throat.

"You reckon we're far enough outside the Ranger's jurisdiction?"

Hutton didn't seem to hear him. He drank again from the bottle.

Cab looked at the fire for a moment then said with a brightness he only half-heartedly felt.

"I always wanted to do this. I have a bad streak." He looked at the older man. "At least that's what my momma always said."

Cab looked at Hutton from the corner of his eye, searching for some indication he had been heard. Hutton made no indication he even knew Cab was there.

"You got a bad streak?" he asked In the way of conversation.

Hutton didn't take his eyes from the fire's merry dance. Finally, he growled a response.

"There ain't no streak in me, kid. I will pay for what I do. I wouldn't pay this high a price for no streak."

Hutton looked at Cab and there was no kindness in that gaze.

"I ought to kill you here, but I don't want to fight 'em off."

He considered Cab for a moment more before resuming his study of the fire.

Cab looked at Hutton with alarm. He was bewildered by the outlaw's off-handed threat. The outlaw seemed to view the younger man as an impedance rather than an ally. Cab finally asked one of the many questions filling his confused mind.

"Who?"

Boyd looked at him again. Cab saw a darkness in those eyes which filled him with foreboding. Hutton grabbed a stick and disturbed the coals.

"How did you happen to be in that hotel?" he asked.

Cab welcomed the change in conversation as a convict welcomes a stay of execution.

With relief he explained, "Passing through, just like you, I guess."

Hutton smiled without pleasure.

"Just like me," he repeated with some thought to the words' meaning.

"Things happen for a reason," Cab said in an effort to create a bond between them, alluding to the fact that fate had joined them.

Hutton's eyes held steady on the younger man.

"It's best not to believe that," he said in a lower tone, as if the words themselves held a power he didn't want released.

"You don't?" he asked incredulously.

Hutton's eyes dimmed as he appeared to lose interest. He stood and walked to his bedroll. He bent and arranged it near the fire opposite Cab's position.

Cab desired to stay in the strong, silent outlaw's presence as long as he could. Although he was afraid of the man, he sensed a tremendous value in his knowledge. Prominent in Cab's mind was the desire to tap into the man's strength and courage.

He considered his next words for a moment then committed to it.

"You ever heard of Agua Caliente?"

Hutton paused in his task for a fraction of a second, his back still turned to Cab. The only reason Cab detected the pause was because he felt any word from him now could be his last and he was alert to every move the outlaw made. Cab tried to cover the bold question.

"Now that fella who led that raid had sand."

Cab wasn't convinced that the indirect compliment would work on this indifferent man, but he had to learn how to speak to the outlaw in a manner which was pleasing enough to keep his company. Hutton straightened from his task but remained facing away from Cab.

Cab continued.

"He saunters into town at bank opening in broad daylight: a bank that can't be robbed, or so is its reputation. He robs that bank and lights out with his gang. After a fierce gunfight, he is the only one to walk away from that hornets' nest of armed men without a scratch."

Hutton's voice was difficult to hear from Cab's position behind the outlaw. Hutton's tone, however, was unmistakable in its tone - low and menacing.

"How do you come to know about that?"

Cab swallowed hard. He was on treacherous ground here.

"I was there. I didn't see much, but I heard the gunfire and heard the stories afterwards."

This last was an exaggeration, but Cab suspected it wouldn't be good for his continued survival to let on that he had seen the outlaw plainly. Hutton seemed to value anonymity above all.

Cab stammered a bit as he continued.

"I didn't see his face or the color of his mount on account of getting there late and what not. But I saw enough to know it went bad for anyone who got too close."

Hutton turned. His eyes were narrow and suspicious. He watched Cab steadily. The outlaw seemed unsure what the truth of the narrative might be.

Cab smiled innocently in the face of this scrutiny.

"Oh well," he said. "We ain't never gonna know who done it."

Cab yawned dramatically. He had pressed as much as he dared. The air was thick with deadly possibility.

"I'm tired. Best hit the hay. Good night, Chief."

Cab rose and moved to his own bedroll. He unfurled the blankets a ways from the fire's light. His fatigue overcame his wariness and soon he plunged into a dark and dreamless sleep.

Cab awoke squinting. The Sun was well up and he suddenly felt a keen sense of time passing. He looked about him. The fire was a soot circle. Beyond, Hutton still slept, wrapped in his blankets. His boots stuck out of the bottom.

Cab stood and began rolling his blankets. He rose from the task and stretched his back. He had grown accustomed to the comfort of a padded bed. He was reminded that the ground was hard and tended to suck the heat from a body lying upon it. He ached slightly. He remained still for a moment to allow direct sunlight to warm his chilled core. He craned his neck then moved to his horse. He lashed his bedroll and tightened the girth strap. The mare grunted and laid her ears back in cranky reaction to the affront.

Hutton stirred behind him. Cab looked over his shoulder. The outlaw was sitting up, watching him.

CHAPTER SEVEN

Quinceanera

Juliana admired her father. Since she was old enough to know him as more than a kindly masculine presence, she had never seen him out of place. His was a mechanism of confidence and strongly driven self-possession. He was singularly strong, decisive and formidable.

He had achieved governorship of Coahuila when she was just a girl. He had held the state without challenge her entire life. The position was only a step below the presidency of the country. The post of governor was one bestowed by the leader of the country himself.

Most governors dwelled in a world of doubt and fear. The career path of a Governorship was as fickle as it was elusive. For her father, Don Guillermo Valadez Gonzaba, however, the position was one he retained with adroit precision. Even the death of her mother, five years hence, had kept him from his duties only a single day.

Juliana knew the truth. The death of her mother changed him. She had heard the cries of despair night after night from her father's private quarters. She saw a marked change in his countenance and a vacancy in his eyes. He had mated for life and for a while, she feared, his life would end to keep that commitment. He did not die, however. His shoulders eventually straightened that small fraction they had bent at her loss. He soon regained his full mien. No one seemed to have noticed the faltering of his being besides her.

Another change took place after her mother's passing. Her role in her father's life evolved to one of closer regard and genuine confidence. He had always commented upon her intellect and prescience in sizing up a diplomatic situation or the true intent of a political foe. In time, he had even come to depend upon her council to a small degree.

As she grew to full womanhood, he had acquired the habit of recommending appropriate suitors. At first the recommendations amused her. Lately she found them tiresome. She knew she was considered attractive by many. She had been attended by a number of hopeful suitors. They invariably were attracted to her lovely features and shapely limbs. Ultimately, they were not equal to her intellect and direct manner. Some of her gifts had been naturally bestowed at birth, mother to daughter. Other traits, she had learned from her father or acquired otherwise through experience in business and politics.

Juliana had only one sibling. Her younger sister, Alida, was a stunning beauty. Her dark eyes hinted at a deep emotional well of mystery and promise to any boy who was unfortunate enough to gaze into them. Her high cheekbones and finely structured face caused even the older men to struggle with their long-ago discarded romanticisms.

This evening was one of a marked passing from girl child to womanhood. Alida was being celebrated with her *Quinceanera*. The celebration was one all girls of breeding and influence looked forward to. The event was of great importance and significance. Juliana remembered hers some years earlier. The celebration had been held in the capital city of Saltillo.

Today, the celebration was being celebrated in San Buenaventura. Alida was summering with their uncle Guillermo and she insisted the event be held among her friends here.

The Governor had protested greatly. San Buenaventura was as far south as one could travel from Saltillo without leaving the state. The governor was convinced finally by his daughter's power over him and the beauty of the quaint village, nestled comfortably in the lovely rolling hills at the southernmost tip of the state.

Juliana's *Quinceanera* had been a huge event where Family and friends had gathered for days prior, crowding inns and local family households. Her father's influence affected much of the attendance, even though Juliana was considered the crown jewel of youthful society. Juliana's mother had beamed and frowned in alternating patterns throughout the gala event.

Juliana watched the dancing and merriment of the crowd below her position upon the raised dais, where she sat with her father and several dignitaries. She sat lightly in her chair with the learned smile of one continually in the public eye. She searched only a moment before she spied her sister. Alida smiled as she spoke excitedly with her fawning friends. Two chaperones, dressed in dark heavy clothing, kept stern watch. They warded off the timid with withering looks. The bolder young men suffered sharp words and firm promises of dire consequences.

Alida looked towards the dais where her family sat, searching out her sister. A musical laugh trailed from her lips. She saw her sister and their eyes met. Juliana smiled and raised a glass to her sister with a small dip of her head. Alida beamed. A companion touched her arm and Alida's attention reluctantly moved from her sister's gaze.

Alida adored her elder sister. In her, Alida saw more than she could ever aspire to. Alida was lovely, but Juliana was fascinating in every part of her make-up. Where Alida was the aim of any artist's attempting at creating the perfect beauty on canvas, Juliana was the enlivening soul of that artist's picture. Where Alida was dainty and round limbed, Juliana was built with a supple strength that was inexorably attached to a continually active mind and poetic soul.

The young girl's thoughts were scattered by the attention of her friends, the merry music and the dancing couples, brightly dressed. She moved through the crowd, followed by her friends. The two chaperones glowered their disapproval as they followed the girls. Their searching gazes silently warned away ambitious admirers.

Juliana watched her sister's entourage melt into the crowd. She felt her father's gaze upon her and looked aside and up into his eyes.

Gonzaba beamed upon her a proud smile and his eyes fairly burst with his love and pride of her.

"It seems only a couple of years since we celebrated your *Quineanera, Meja.*"

Juliana smiled at him brightly, enjoying this moment as much as he.

"So beautiful," he said. "Yet so intelligent. A father could not be more proud. Marriage would see you to the next chapter of your life."

"You flatter me, father," she said with feigned disapproval. "You are the reason I remain unmarried. What man can measure up to you? They all falter in comparison."

Gonzaba laughed and shook his head. He looked over to his trusted aide, Eduardo Chapa. Chapa nodded his grey head knowingly. He had watched the two grow together over the years and was accustomed to the way they teased one another.

"Your mother was much as you are when we first married" the governor continued, "I had not achieved public office, but we had our families' land holdings to manage."

Gonzaba patted Juliana's hand and narrowed his eyes.

"She, like you, had a shrewd eye for business and a talent for dealings."

Juliana smiled sadly at the memory and the loss: her humor stalled for the moment. Her eyes again took in her father's face as she pushed the melancholy from her. She saw sadness working upon him as well.

"I miss her too, Father."

Gonzaba gazed upon his daughter. He smiled sadly but confidently.

"In spite of your doubts, you will soon be married, and I will have to rely upon volition and experience without the advantage of your keen sensibilities to guide me."

"Father," she scolded, "there are no wedding plans currently, and you are more than equal to the task of governing Coahuila without your devoted daughter under foot."

Gonzaba considered her with a gleaming eye. He leaned towards her, and his manner became more focused upon the intent of his words.

She knew this way of his. She was accustomed to his mannerisms and traits of persuasion. He rarely spoke to her as earnestly as she anticipated he was about to.

"I have never missed a son since you spoke your first words to me and captured my heart, my daughter."

She inhaled deeply to quell her rising emotion.

"Today," he continued looking deeply into her eyes, "I wish you were the son I never had only because you will marry, and your husband will take you from me – and my name from you."

There was a thoughtful silence between them as both contemplated the weight of his words. His smile broke the spell and he leaned back with a look of mischief dispelling the darkening mood between them.

"Attend your sister now. Leave politics to the politicians."

He stood and smoothed his coat.

"I must rest for a busy day tomorrow."

He leaned and kissed her on the cheek.

She beamed up to him.

"I love you, Father."

Gonzaba smiled and straightened. He turned to Eduardo who was already standing. The remaining diplomats stood in respect.

"Eduardo, it is late,"

Shaking hands as he sidled down the line of diplomats, Gonzaba made his way from the celebration.

Juliana sat for a moment, reluctant to leave the comparative safety of the dais. She wasn't shy by any means, but she did not enjoy the continual entreaties and clever sallies from admiring men. Even though she was not in Saltillo, she still held no hope that her potential mate was in attendance.

With a deep sigh, she rose and descended the steps onto the level and entered among the merry makers. Most made way for her with respect and not a small amount of admiration. Others, she had to avoid as they danced without regard for their surroundings. Soon she arrived at her sister's side. Alida cried out in joy and clutched her sister's hands.

"Sister, you are still here," she said with great appreciation. "There are many who are missing you."

Her last had a mischievous tone which caused Juliana to frown her disapproval. Despite her misgivings, Juliana's eyes swept the crowd, noticing a small group of brightly dressed vaqueros, keenly aware of her.

Alida looked in the direction to which Juliana looked. Juliana noticed Alida's attention to her gaze and dropped her eyes to her feet.

"So, you look as well," she said lightly goading her stoic older sister.

Juliana blushed slightly as she protested, "I have sweet Fermine back in Saltillo. He is all I need."

"Sweet Fermine," Alida mocked her reference to Juliana's most recent suitor, "is not what you need. He is what Father wants."

Juliana began to resent her sister's insight. Her brown study was interrupted when a murmur grew in the crowd around her. The murmur died into an expectant silence. Although the music played on, the crowd's accompanying silence seemed even more in contrast. Juliana could not fathom the cause of the strange behavior of the crowd. All heads seemed to be turned towards the arched entrance to the village courtyard which made up the center of the small town. She couldn't see through or over the crowd, so she moved forward. As she moved towards the point of attention for the group, the talking and business of party going resumed by degrees. With the relaxing of their focus upon the disruption, the crowd gave way somewhat as they returned to their original pursuits.

She was soon able to see two men – Anglos – standing at the refreshment table. One was a fair-haired young man. The other man, taller and older, caught Juliana's attention. She could not help herself. Despite her desire to dismiss the crashers, she could not resist assessing the elder of the two. He was dressed as so many other Americans she had seen before. He wore rough clothing, worn boots, and a low-slung side arm. She felt a fascination for this man. Her reverie rendered her oblivious to the people and events around her.

Although she looked directly at the American, it was a moment before she noticed that he was studying her also. She looked away with an embarrassed start. However, she lifted her eyes once more and they locked with the stranger's. His gaze was hypnotic. His blue eyes blazed with a fire she fancied was a mysterious glow emanating from the internal furnace which powered the man.

Alida came up behind Juliana and touched her arm.

"Americanos," Alida whispered in her ear. "Father will not be pleased."

Despite her discomfort at the gaze of the American, she couldn't help but say, "Father is not here."

Juliana did not see Alida's mischievous look at this dismissal of caution and decorum.

Alida's appearance seemed to catch the attention of the younger American who surveyed her with a greedy eye. Juliana felt the look was insulting to her innocent sister. Alida was not some cantina harlot to be lusted after by a rough foreigner. She was a debutante and daughter of a great man of power and distinction.

Hutton selected a clean stoneware cup from the stack on the white clothed table. He poured an amount of liquor from his ever-present flask, then dippered cool cider from a large bowl into the cup. His eyes scarcely left the lovely woman's face across the way from him. Cab sidled up beside the older man and he felt an electric charge as he saw the beautiful Alida. To him, she was the embodiment of all he saw perfect in a woman. She seemed to embody all he had ever dreamed of in a woman.

"Sure as Hell," Cab muttered, speaking under his breath, "That is an angel here on Earth."

Cab felt his palms tingle from quickened blood flow. His face grew warm as if he were fairly aglow. He detected his companion's eyes upon him. He thought he sensed the older man's amusement at his reaction to the Latin beauty.

Hutton returned the flask to his pocket. He lifted the cup and drank deeply. While he drank, his eyes moved in a sentry scan of the crowd. His gaze soon returned to the lovely woman across the way.

Cab heard his deep voice sound low and strong.

"Keep an eye on them Vaqueros. They are of like mind regarding your 'Angel'."

Cab's gaze left Alida to take in the potential threat. A group of five young Mexican cowboys eyed the Americans with malicious intent. Cab wanted to laugh at how garishly they were dressed. From their greased and flattened hair to the short tightly fitted vests over brightly colored shirts and gay sashes, he thought, 'these fellas were some real dandies.' They wore tight breeches with *conchos* up the sides, tucked into tall shiny boots. Most of these menacing fellows were armed with long pistols in heavy belted holsters.

Both Americans noticed the mute attention they garnered from the crowd. The music seemed somehow out of place considering the dangerous intent of many of the party-goers. By degree, however, the party returned to a shade of its former revelry.

Cab watched a handsome, well-dressed youth approached Alida. Cab saw him bow slightly as he asked her to dance. She nodded regally and allowed him to take her politely into a dancing embrace. They spun out towards the other dancers. He seemed to be a skilled dancer and she followed his deft maneuvers effortlessly. Cab was transfixed as she moved with uncanny grace and agility.

Even this confident dancer suffered the effect of Alida's appeal. His face registered admiration then embarrassment by degrees. His step faltered at one point when she smiled upon him with enjoyment at his dancing skill.

The couple circled the large dancing area and soon approached the refreshment table where Cab stood. Without hesitation, Cab moved to intercept them. The youth frowned slightly as he divined that the American intended to cut in on his dance but did not alter his course. When they had come close enough, Cab grasped the young man's shoulder and stopped their progress. He doffed his hat with the other hand and bowed to Alida.

"*Con permisso,* pard," he said glancing at the youth.

Without pause for reaction from the displaced dancer, he took Alida into his arms and they whirled away leaving the young man red-eared and fuming.

Juliana watched the boorish act from across the way. She maintained her scrutiny of the American as he danced with Alida, alert for any sign of insult given or liberty taken. Her singular attention to her sister's peril failed to alert her to her own. She felt her hand taken into that of another. She looked down at her hand and saw a large thick hand grasping hers. Her eyes rose with incredulous delay. Her mouth fell open in disbelief as she looked into the face of the tall American.

Although surprised at his brazen approach and uninvited touch, she experienced some pleasure at his attention. He was not fettered by fear of her father's disapproval nor was he struck senseless by her beauty. She had underestimated his size from afar. Near at hand, as it were, he was taller. His waist was not as lean as he had seemed. His broad shoulders had the effect of making him appear smaller. His clothing and appearance were rough but possessed a general impression of being looked after. He had a light stubble upon his face. The new beard growth was dark for the most part, but a light dusting of gray mottled the overall.

She drew an involuntary breath as she looked into his eyes. His gaze was a tangible thing. He seemed to exert a probing force, which Juliana felt penetrated her most protected secrets. She feared he would see into her private thoughts. She felt a slight pang. Would she be able to hide the attraction she instinctively felt for this stranger? She repelled his probing attention with a verbal parry.

"It is impolite to attend a party uninvited," she said, making no attempt to withdraw her hand from his.

His eyes seemed to stir as he processed what she said.

"Invite me."

His voice was deep and resonant. He hadn't spoken with force, but she felt his words as well as heard them. With welcome strength she pressed her position.

"Why would I do that?"

Again, his eyes changed. This time the swirling blue alteration in his look held a tinge of foreboding.

"To avoid embarrassment."

A small mischievous smile played at his lips. He was obviously enjoying her discomfiture.

"Yours or mine?" she asked, bristling at his confident manner.

The American smiled openly at her flare of temper. He moved away, pulling her onto the dance floor. She found herself following his lead without resistance. She quelled her irritation at her helplessness in his arms. She told herself she wanted to know more about a man who could commit such effrontery without compunction. Her justification, however, fell weakly upon the base truth of her heart. She wanted to know more about this man who fascinated her and whose very voice enthralled her.

From the time she had grown to the age of courtship, every young man she encountered was a potential threat to her independence and singularity. Her defenses had been equal to the task of repelling their advances. With this stranger, she was off balance. Her innate ability to deflect a suitor, her insulating boredom at the ham-handed advances of fawning men of all ages failed her. For years she had merely to compare any interested male to her father. She set the benchmark for qualification high enough, that the likelihood of a young man meeting the mark was remote at best. She would not allow herself to be pawned off to an older member of a prominent family for power or position. As such, she also would not fall into the arms of some dashing heir or charismatic dare devil. She prided herself in her intellect and quick wit. Most men were easily thwarted by a woman who could emasculate with words.

This mysterious American captured her interest. She could only describe her impression of him as a powerful surf pounding a rocky coast. He held her with a strength of will she sensed as a real thing. His blue eyes reflected a depth she could not plumb...and something else. Was it an aspect of danger? She could not be sure. None the less, the confusing attraction enthralled her senses. As she fell into his embrace, her world fairly spun before her eyes. She began to feel embarrassment at her predicament of heart and mind.

Hutton looked down at her.

"Your sister?"

Juliana glanced in the direction towards which his gaze had come to rest. She saw Alida, spinning in the embrace of the young American. In spite of herself, she smiled a little at her sister's willing participation in the dangerous adventure in which she found herself.

"Yes," Juliana replied simply. "Your brother?"

The big American laughed with genuine mirth. His laugh was deep and satisfying. He drew her closer to him. She could now feel his body against hers. She instinctively stiffened and she tried to lean away from him as they danced. He was powerful. She could feel the padding of muscle over his large frame. His embrace was irresistible and final. She felt growing discomfort at his familiarity in the intimate move.

She again attempted to press him from her with her arms and moved her feet to create distance.

"You must show more respect," she admonished.

Her mouth tightened in disapproval and her eyes hardened slightly as she looked into his dark eyes.

To her displeasure, his arms renewed their purchase. She was reminded of a Python's coils, moving powerfully to more securely constrict its prey. His voice came husky, and she could hear desire darkening his words.

"You are a woman who fills a Man's head and his heart. You got way more than my respect."

Juliana forgot her intimate condition with him for a moment as she felt surprise in his weakness of desire towards her. His look hinted at his mind's workings in respect to her. His weakness returned to her some control of her attraction towards him. She had to admit that she was desperately seeking just such a chink from which she could thwart him and her feelings.

"You are quite certain of yourself," she said.

"Not as much as you might think," he replied with surprising candor.

She found herself defending her initial impression of him.

"If that were true," she assured him, "you would have never taken me to dance."

Her justification of his audacity seemed to encourage him.

"It's only a dance," he said dismissively

"You know little of our culture, I see."

She bestowed a look upon him which conveyed an appropriate measure of condescension. The conversation was doing much to revive her former strength in condemnation of his effrontery.

Although Hutton did not respond to her retort, his attention seemed fully upon her. She found that his attention was never so keenly focused as to leave him open to approach from a blind quarter.

A squat but strongly built Vaquero approached the two. He reached out a hairy hand towards the big American's shoulder. His progress was stopped short by an abrupt backhanded blow. The Mexican staggered back a step. His face bore a look of surprise and disbelief. He had approached the gringo from behind. As if through the power of some mysterious prescience, the American had turned slightly and delivered the blow, his hand moving as a cat's paw would swat a mouse. Meanwhile, his embrace of Juliana had not been disturbed, nor had she suffered any jolt from the action.

With a growl, the vaquero reached for his long pistol. Boyd shifted his left hand from Juliana's hand and around her waist. His right dipped swiftly to his hip. He pulled the black gun and it exploded flame and roared its angry report. The Vaquero went down heavily, his shimmering shirt darkening from blood flowing from his chest.

Juliana pushed away from Hutton. She shoved with all her strength. He hardly noticed her struggling as he scanned the fleeing crowd. A youth nearby drew his pistol and attempted to get a clear shot at Hutton. The American released her waist and grasped her by the back of her slim neck. He pulled her around before him and fired around her. The youth fell on his face with a groan. Juliana's eyes widened in horror. She realized the American was using her as a living shield, placing her between himself and his assailants.

By this time the music had ceased, and the crowd was in a panic to escape proximity of the battle. Juliana felt her neck nearly crushed in the hand of the stranger. He was incredibly strong, and he was supporting her entire weight with one hand. If he had released his hold, she believed she would have fallen to the ground. Through the confusion, her surroundings took on a strange hue. Actions of those around her, as seen through her hazed vision, took on the look of color as well as movement. Through her clouded gaze she spied Cab approaching them through the crowd. He no longer held Alida. His unsheathed pistol seemed a divining rod, guiding him through the blind shrieking mob.

Hutton pulled her towards him and around until she was in front of him again. From her new position, she could see a third Vaquero drawing his pistol. With horror, Juliana feared the young man would shoot her to get to the American. Her fear was staunched quickly as the explosion of his pistol sounded near her head. She placed her hands over her ears, and she shrunk from the near explosion of his gun. As her hands went to her head, she thought she heard a scream. She realized in shock the voice she heard was hers.

The young attacker moved abruptly aside as Hutton shot. Juliana saw an elderly man fall just beyond the empty space vacated by the Vaquero. Another deafening report and a red hole popped between the Vaquero's eyes. Juliana heard herself scream again. She feared she was dying somehow.

With a lurch, the American pulled her again. This time he did not stop but kept her moving. She realized that he was making an escape and he intended to take her with him. She dragged her feet and grasped his hand with both her hands. She tore at his grip, but she may as well have been chopping the trunk of a tree with a feather. He dragged her backwards and she could see the bystanders. Women in turn clutched stressed fists against their breasts or covered their mouths in horror. Men stood at the ready with arms at their sides. Their useless hands gripped the air as they struggled with a reaction to this base violence. She saw Cab break through the crowd, striking a man from behind who impeded his path. The man fell grasping his head.

The big man pulled her beneath the stone arches of the village's center square. He grunted as he lifted Juliana off the ground and sat her upon a dark horse. He jumped upon his horse with a bound. Juliana braced for a violent start of the horses. Strangely, he waited with gun in hand, watching the entrance to the square. A figure emerged from below the stone arch. The American raised his pistol slightly. He recognized the newcomer as his younger companion and lowered the weapon to a non-aggressive posture.

Once Cab emerged, Hutton tightened his hold on Juliana's horse's reins and spurred his mount. The horses came to a canter as the American turned to her. His face showed no malice or fear. Nor did it carry any sign he had just killed three men and escaped a harrowing encounter. In a level tone he spoke to her, just loud enough to be heard over the sound of rushing air and thudding hooves.

"You won't jump off if you know what's good for you."

Her predicament was becoming more dire as the seconds passed. This man was not going to let her go. What were his intentions toward her? The numbness of fear and duress were rapidly fleeing in the face of dawning dread and horrible possibility.

The sound of gun fire grew behind them. The first shots sounded like they came from the same gun – perhaps it was the younger American covering their escape. Soon the lone pistol reports were answered by a growing fusillade of reports from a variety of weapons. In moments she heard the dull thuds of a fast-moving horse coming from behind them. She could not see the rider in the dark, but she was fairly certain it was the second American.

CHAPTER EIGHT

Pursuit

Don Guillermo Valadez Gonzaba felt his age tonight. His position was a post of reconstruction. Coahuila, although half the greatness she was prior to the war, was his love. A more devoted servant to public office could not be found. The occasion of his daughter's *Quinceanera* afforded him the opportunity to renew ties with his supporters to the south of Saltillo. The morning would bring new opportunity to shore up those ties and gain favor over those opponents emerging to vie for his post as Governor.

Gonzaba picked up an envelope trimmed in gold leaf. The face bore his name and title written with a flourish. He opened the envelope and extracted a folded parchment. He began reading a missive conveying gratitude and admiration. He paused his reading and looked down to the bottom of the letter. He saw it was signed by the town's mayor. His eyes returned to the body of the letter with a smile of amusement. The mayor had been one of his opponents when his governorship was proposed. He now basked in the warmth of Gonzaba's favor. The favor had been bestowed as a means of control rather than any warm regard held for a loyal supporter.

Gonzaba lifted a cup containing hot spiced tea, a favorite of his. His eyes remained on the letter. A flurry of shouts and muffled reports of shots fired halted the cup at his lips. His eyes rose as he listened. In alarm, he dropped the letter and sat the cup heavily onto the table, spilling the tea. The door to his room burst open and Chapa gestured to him.

"Governor," he said, nearly out of breath, "your daughter has been taken by two Americanos."

Gonzaba jumped from his chair with surprising agility and pushed his way past Chapa. Chapa watched his master go past him with mild surprise at the older man's speed and vigor. Gonzaba was not known as a man of action or athleticism. He rarely raised his voice and even more rarely showed his emotions in any sort of physical manner. He closed the door to the room and rushed to follow Gonzaba.

When Gonzaba arrived at the enclosed area containing the festivities, former merriment was replaced with a dark pall which weighed over the entire courtyard. Under this weight was the moan of crying women and the angry mutterings of the men. Many of the group were crowded near the arched entrance. Gonzaba made his way in that direction. He shouldered past the gawkers and soon found himself at the vanguard.

Several men stood looking into the darkness, guns drawn, faces strained. Gonzaba heard the thuds of a galloping horse making away into the darkness. Looking around him, he saw Alida clinging closely to one of her chaperones. Her face was drawn and moist from her emotions. He failed to see Juliana in his scan of the group. Chapa emerged from the crowd.

"They took Juliana, *Senor*."

Gonzaba growled his rage. He grabbed a pistol from a nearby Vaquero.

"Cowards," he cried, looking about him at the confused throng. "You get on those horses and get my daughter back or I will rip the skin from your flesh."

His threat was received with shock and silence.

He trained the pistol on the group, particularly at a rough looking man just before him.

"Ride you dogs."

His voice was low but menacing.

As one, the throng jumped into action. Horses were mounted by yelling men with drawn guns.

Juliana was still in a state of shock at the speed at which her situation had gone from playful and challenging banter to grave and life threatening. She held grimly to the saddle horn of the speeding mount. She was not a skilled rider due to her station. Her lack of experience coupled with the danger of riding at this speed at night kept her mind busy. She could hardly make out the features of the man who rode close to her. She nearly fell from the saddle as her abductor veered sharply from their course and into a dark mass, she soon discovered was a copse of dense trees and bushes.

They had hardly stopped when the man leaped from the saddle and pulled a knife from his person. She could not see from where he had conjured the glimmering blade, but she held her breath with dread as he drew close beside her. He grasped the bottom of her dress and cut strips from the garment. He grasped her hands and tied them to the saddle, firmly securing her. He then quickly and deftly tied her feet into the stirrups.

She wanted desperately to resist. Although she was frightened and felt any chance of escape disappearing with each binding he secured, her voice would not obey her desire to cry out. Her courage had completely abandoned her, so she made no attempt to resist the securing of her limbs. Her fascination at her own submission to this kidnapper was forgotten as she heard approaching hoof beats. With a rush of wind, spraying dust, and the clatter of skidding hooves, the younger man brought his mount to a halt within the concealment of the grove.

The newcomer's voice was low but excited.

150 | CRAIG RAINEY

"They will be hot behind us in a shake," he said watching Boyd finish his binding of the captive.

Boyd remounted and tied off Juliana's horse's reins to a brass loop behind his saddle.

"Follow me. I will show you how to shag a posse."

Juliana was amazed at the steady ease with which he spoke. As before, his voice betrayed no fear or worry. They moved out of the grove opposite from where they had entered. He led them to the right, back towards the Puebla from which they had fled.

As they returned towards town, urgent voices calling encouragement to the pursuers and the sound of horses and rattling tack grew in volume and intensity. Juliana rode between the two men, securely bound. She glanced over to the younger man and saw him looking at the leader. Although she could only see him dimly, she thought she detected concern on his face.

They rode to the lee side of a small frame structure. Juliana guessed it to be a livery or a tool house. The three waited silently until the mounting din of pursuit suddenly exploded into clear noises of mounted and armed men. There appeared at least a dozen riders spurring their horses hell-for-leather in the direction towards which the kidnappers had ridden.

The American led them quickly in pursuit of the posse. They achieved a full gallop, gaining rapidly upon the rescuers. The night was dark, and much could be missed riding at that speed. The leaders of the posse slowed to a gallop, taking in any clue which would guide their rescue efforts.

Juliana watched the American pull his pistol and immediately the weapon belched flame. One of the rear riders fell. The pistol fired two more times in quick succession. Two more riders perished. The younger man wasted no time to join his leader, thinning the ranks of the posse. In an instant, the two had reduced the posse to half of their original number.

The riders scattered, shooting wildly behind them into the darkness. She heard several shouts warning the shooters to avoid harming the captive. Two more of the posse fell to pistol fire before the panicked group jumped from their mounts and to cover. From their hiding places, the cowering men heard the three horses pound past them and into the distance.

The American led the way throughout the night. Shortly before the grey of dawn smeared the ink of night he veered from their south-westerly direction and descended sharply into a dry wash.

Dwarf Junipers hedged the natural ramp. At the bottom, the three moved down a bit further until they were shielded within a shallow depression under the draw's bank near a sharp bend. The leader dismounted and led Juliana's horse into a shallow cave. He cut her bonds with the same evil looking knife she had seen earlier. She tried to dismount but could not. She groaned as the big man grasped her powerfully and helped her to the ground. The younger man dismounted and moved to gather tinder for a fire.

"No fire," the leader said.

The younger man said nothing but sat on a bleached log. He looked at the other two expectantly. Juliana rubbed her sore hands and stretched with a groan. The leader loosened the girth of his horse's saddle. He searched through saddle bags and produced a bottle. He opened it and pulled a swig. Juliana waited for him to say something to her. She craved an explanation for why he had taken her and some idea of what his plans for her were. He didn't look at her at all.

In Spanish she said, "My father will bring all of Mexico down on your heads."

The leader still didn't look at her. The wash in which they stood seemed to have taken his attention completely.

"Talk English," he said without turning. "I know you savvy it."

"You are a fool," she said in English, her eyes afire with rage and fear.

Boyd turned his head only. He seemed to size her up.

"What's your name?"

Her blazing eyes met his, but she said nothing. He turned and approached her, corking the bottle.

She stood her ground as he moved towards her. He stopped: his face inches from hers. She grew uncomfortable at his proximity, but she forced herself to stand firmly.

"What is your name?"

His voice was low and menacing.

She saw none of the solicitous humor he had exhibited before. He was stone – impersonal. Juliana felt tears well behind her eyes, but she refused to weaken in the face of this terrifying man.

He grabbed her face in his big hand and pulled her close. She shook her head to free herself. Still holding the bottle, he grabbed her by the back of her neck and pulled her into him. She felt him against her. His touch nearly burned her skin. She cried out and he shook her. This rough treatment succeeded where his words had not. The tears began to flow, and she hated herself for her weakness.

"What is your name," he repeated. His voice was nearly a snarl now.

"Juliana," she managed to say in surrender.

He relaxed his grip at her answer. He almost smiled as he released her. Rather than pull away, as she had expected, he leaned towards her and inhaled, taking in her scent. He lifted a hand and brushed her hair over her shoulder as he looked her over. Satisfied, he turned and walked back to his original position showing her his back.

"What in hell are we gonna do?"

The younger man had stood during this exchange. She saw that he was tall and rangy. His build was typical of a young range rider. The leader glanced once at Juliana but did not answer.

"We got Rangers in a lather for us in Texas, and now the goddam Mexicans will be after us here. They don't cotton to Gringos making off with their women folk."

"Shut up or go your own way,"

The leader turned and his eyes held the younger man with a deadly steadiness.

"I ain't asking you to stay on."

"It ain't like that, Chief. I just aim to be smart is all."

The leader laughed grimly, no humor appearing in his gimlet eyes.

"A little late for that, boy. You give up smarts whey you came over to my table at that hotel."

The morning was brightening, and Juliana could see both men as clearly as she had been able thus far. She watched the younger man. Although he appeared to appreciate the peril in which he found himself, he seemed accustomed to the leader's manner and was unoffended.

"What are we gonna do with her?"

Boyd drew his gun and crossed the distance between them with large strides. Juliana experienced the impression of an eagle diving upon a field mouse. The younger man gave way but was caught in one of the leader's big hands. The larger man leaned in close.

"There ain't no we when it comes to this girl. Don't forget that. She belongs to me."

Cab looked at Juliana with real alarm on his face. Juliana felt her short hairs stand rigid and a chill prickled her skin. She could not resist the surge of fear trying to press her to panic. Boyd thumbed the hammer on his black pistol, pressed into Cab's stomach.

"I don't think you are hearing me," he said almost too softly for Juliana to hear.

Cab visibly shrank and held up his hands in supplication.

"I hear you, Chief. She's yours."

Boyd considered the younger man for an uncomfortably long moment. Juliana was sure he would shoot the younger man. Instead, he released Cab and walked over to Juliana. She eyed his pistol fearfully as he approached.

"Who's gonna be on our back trail? Who do you belong to?"

She hesitated, not sure what response would save her.

"Talk up," he barked.

"I belong to no man..." she began in Spanish.

"English," he spat out as his rage mounted.

"My father is Guillermo Valadez Gonzaba, Governor of Coahuila."

From behind Boyd, Cab kicked the ground.

"Goddam it," he growled.

"Shut up," Boyd commanded. To her he said, "Was he there when I took you?"

"He will be here soon," she warned in a low but strong voice.

Boyd took a deep breath and moved towards her. His posture indicated impatience with her. She was sure she had pushed this man as far as she dared.

"Si...Yes! He was there."

Boyd exhaled slowly, still watching her, a smile began to play at the corner of his mouth.

In a cautious voice, Cab asked, "You want I should check our back trail?"

Boyd pursed his lips as he thought about this.

"Can't risk being seen while you take a look."

Hutton moved to where the cloth strips lay on the ground. He bent and picked them up. He returned to Juliana and grabbed her arm. He led her away from the shallow cave. He turned to Cab.

"Bed down. We'll wait here for nightfall."

He pressed Juliana down next to a broad skeletal trunk of a tree. He tied her hands behind her to a thick bough of the bleached tree. He stood and looked her over once again. Without a word, he turned and went to his horse. She watched him remove the saddle and hobble the horse. He carried the saddle under the bank's outcropping, dropped it in the dust and lay down with his head on the saddle. Within seconds he was asleep.

Cab retrieved a leather bladder from his saddle bags and brought it to Juliana. He opened it and gave her a drink. She swallowed the cool water and looked up at him. She hoped to find some glimmer of compassion or sympathy. Instead, his face showed no emotion of any kind. He didn't seem cruel as a rule. She suspected he took no chances when around the violent leader. Even asleep, he would not risk angering him.

Cab corked the bag and returned to his horse. He unsaddled the mare and joined his boss under the outcropping.

CHAPTER NINE

Rigo

To Don Guillermo Valadez Gonzaba, the city of Saltillo was his kingdom. The remainder of Coahuila was under his caring stewardship, but Saltillo reflected the essence of his reign.

He had been but a boy when Saltillo, the bustling capital of *Coahuila y Tejas*, became his true love. The awe-inspiring Cathedral of Santiago had been his inspiration. A monument to God and the potential of man, it was inspired by the same strength and character of those first Conquistadors. It was only natural that Saltillo would be the epicenter of a growing and robust region. In those days, *Coahuila y Tejas* was a vast province, rich in resources and geographical presence. He dreamed, even in those early days, of one day leading his people as governor and master of a vast empire.

Sadly, his was not the destiny of the lord of all he beheld. American invasion, albeit blessed by Mexico herself, saw end to his dream. Invaders disguised cleverly as friends of his country: men who used the title Impresario, rather than the more accurate mantle of imperialist, settled in his homeland and peopled their settlements with ambitious and greedy Americans. The sacred trust invested in these northern invaders was repaid with blood and betrayal.

One of the first Impresarios, Stephen F. Austin, had occupied a prison cell in Mexico City for a number of years. If only he had been executed, as Gonzaba's father had requested, San Antonio might have fallen more easily, and the war might have gone a different way.

Today, Governor Gonzaba sat in his grand office in the large stone mansion he claimed as governor of Coahuila. He turned a fragrant cigar in his heavily jeweled hand as he let sweet smoke fall in a wave from his mouth. Before him stood two men who, at the moment, were in receipt of his ire. The most striking was commander of the regional garrison, a uniformed general of Mexico's army federal.

Although not directly under his command and control, General Benedicto was compelled to act on the Governor's behest due to his close ties to the president. The General secretly hated the man. His hatred was to a great degree, fired by his fear of the Governor's power and long reach.

The second man was Gonzaba's longtime aide de camp, Eduardo Chapa. Since that day more than a fortnight hence, Chapa had labored tirelessly, pressing desperate efforts to recover Juliana. His efforts had borne no fruit and he now stood prepared to answer for his inadequacies.

"It has been nineteen days, and no one has seen her."

Gonzaba said this through a fog of cigar smoke. His eyes blazed as rage consumed him from within.

The General cleared his throat. This was his way of controlling his temper. His distaste in answering to a local politician nearly consumed him. Gonzaba saw only the discomfort incumbent upon a poor leader's realization of his own ineptitude.

In a level and controlled tone, the General attempted to soothe the Governor's frustration.

"With respect, they cannot elude our troops for long. We will ultimately close the net."

Gonzaba looked at the soldier. He took in the crisp uniform. He allowed his gaze to admire the broad chest, covered in jingling, glittering medals and military awards. His appraisal of the officer withered to one of contempt as he turned to Chapa. Eduardo bowed his gray head and waited for the instructions he knew were coming.

Gonzaba pointed his cigar at his aide.

"Bring me Rigo."

Eduardo nodded and backed away maintaining his bowed posture. He backed towards the large double doors and let himself out silently.

"Sir?" The General was insulted. "A man hunter? This is a mission for officials of the state."

Gonzaba leaned back as he looked at his cigar.

"Time is against us here. My daughter's honor and purity are a matter of timing."

Gonzaba drummed a thick finger on the rich sheen of his desk.

He paused for emphasis.

"*Ultimately* closing the net is not acceptable."

The general stiffened under his sharp creases. He was not one to tolerate ridicule. He swallowed his rage and attempted to speak reasonably.

"Governor, I can call in more men."

"More men will do nothing more than increase numbers. I cannot see a different outcome because we put more men on the trail."

Realizing the inevitable outcome of the dispute, the general shrugged away any responsibility. He shook his head and laughed slightly, but openly.

"Rodrigo Herrera is a bounty hunter, sir. He is not a rescuer."

"He is a bounty hunter who can anticipate as well as track his quarry. A mindless mob, no matter the training and discipline, is not going to find my Juliana. This task will require a keen mind and instincts."

Gonzaba rose and walked around his desk. He stood before the tall general and looked into his eyes.

"Your men have done all an army can do. My Juliana must be found now, not when it is too late."

The general considered the governor for a long moment. He had his doubts about the Governor's actions but not about his commitment to those actions. The general bowed slightly. His duty was no longer in question in this matter.

"My men will continue their search?"

Gonzaba started a bit at this statement posed as a question.

"Of course."

The general shook his head almost imperceptibly. Perhaps the Governor was not as certain as he appeared.

Eduardo's horse was hand-picked for comfort. His long ears hinted at patience and slow thought. His long neck and commensurately long torso guaranteed a comfortable and stable ride, even at a trot. He stood well over 17 hands, and he never lost his coat, even in hot weather. His lump of a head bobbed to the rhythm of his shambling walk. His long ears waved lazily in an ungainly tempo. The old man loved that horse, so he ignored the occasional comments from his young and spirited companion.

The young vaquero eyed the big lazy sorrel with amusement. His powder gray roan stepped smartly and with barely contained nervous energy. It was as if the little horse was a cauldron containing boiling water, fairly bursting as it sought escape from the mounting pressure within.

The young man himself was of the cut typical of those brash young caballeros. He wore tight conched breeches, a brightly buttoned blouse set off by a red bandana knotted tightly around his neck. He had tied around his lean waist a similarly colored sash. His gun belt and broad brimmed hat were darkest black. His highly polished boots boasted large silver roweled spurs.

As before, his narrow face split into a toothy grin of pleasure. It seemed to Chapa that there was no end to the youth's discoveries in respect to his mount. The garrulous fellow had noticed every fault possessed by horse and rider. His verbose torrent of abuse seemed to have no end. Chapa considered the younger man wearily as he heard the audible inhalation which had proven a precursor to critical observation.

"*Senor*," the youth chided him under the false pretense of timidity. "It is not I who would be the one to ask such a question if it were not your reputation at stake here."

He adjusted his seat upon his prancing steed.

"But, are you not in fear that this poor beast, upon which you ride, may throw a shoe or damage a hoof in light of his fierce attack upon this trail?"

Chapa cast upon the youth a withering look. His energetic reply was trapped in his mouth by the sudden exclamation of the youth.

"This must be the home of the great Rodrigo Herrera."

Chapa held the youth in his judicious gaze for a delayed second before moving his attention to the region before him. Through the scant foliage and scrub junipers he saw a tall, lean man in a corral giving his full attention to a gleaming chestnut stallion. A wide cloud of white dust boiled aloft as the two combatants vied for dominance.

The riders continued up the worn path where it widened as they approached a small frame house. Outside the neatly maintained structure, a lovely ribbon of flower garden edged the broad front porch. A variety of smells reached out to the riders. Although he did not turn his attention from the travail under way in the corral, Chapa recognized the sweetness of wildflowers seasoned with the bitter tang of basil and rosemary.

The wonders of the sensory stage were diminished by his companion's unavoidable commentary.

"This is the great Rigo Herrera?"

The boy's voice conveyed dismay and some disappointment.

Chapa looked aside at his tormentor with mild interest.

"This is Rodrigo Herrera: The man who captured Corona Viejo."

The youth laughed low and shook his head.

"He doesn't look like he could catch fire."

Chapa's eyes returned to Rigo. It was true the man hunter was older than he had last seen him. His current effort had left him dusty, much of which was encrusted in his clothing. Chapa, as before, pressed his annoyance below a threshold above which he might be tempted to counter the terse words of the young man or, more satisfying, to silence the youth for good. Whatever it was about Rigo which failed to impress the other was his companion's mistake to make with the famous killer himself.

"You have as little eye for quality as you have a tongue for respect."

The riders passed the front door of the little house. A woman appeared in the entrance. Chapa and the vaquero saw she was a pretty, young woman, slight of build, but seemingly sturdy. Her steady gaze sized them up from under a covering hand.

Chapa looked again towards the famous man hunter. He and the horse were moist with sweat. The horse grunted and Rigo spoke softly and soothingly. The man had attention only for the horse and his task at hand. He didn't seem to notice the riders, although Chapa was certain he had marked their arrival long before they had seen him.

Chapa checked his horse at the corral gate and dismounted. He glanced at the younger man expectantly. The rider hesitated to dismount. It was apparent his self-worth was elevated on horseback. With a sigh of disgust, he finally dismounted and stood leaning against the gate, his back slightly towards the battle within the enclosure. Chapa noticed this affront but made no protest. Some mistakes were not his to correct.

The old man looked again within the corral. The stallion was a magnificent creature. He was heavily muscled, and a sheen of moisture caused his body to gleam. The stallion seemed so singularly magnificent that even the dust refused to settle on his brilliant coat. Rigo held a strong but supple rope in his right hand and spoke to the horse in reassuring tones. The horse trained his delicately formed ears fully upon the man. His nostrils flared and his billowing breaths came in large powerful drafts. Rigo shortened the rope as he approached the stallion, continuing to reassure the spirited animal with his low murmuring. To Chapa, the large horse seemed to be poised upon steel springs and hair trigger levers. He was certain the horse would suddenly explode into a rebellious tantrum in a violent effort to escape his captor.

Still Rigo approached. Rigo raised his gloved left hand and spread his fingers so the horse could see he concealed no secret threat in that hand. As he touched the stallion, the horse seemed to ratchet down from high alert to the attitude of a mischievous child who had intended pretense but no real harm. Rigo patted him on his large jaw then scratched between his eyes. Rigo laughed and lowered the lasso. The stallion arched his neck and made a half leap at the man. He humped his back and pitched two guarded jumps. Rigo did not give ground and the horse shook his luxuriant main and danced away.

Rigo laughed, showing perfect teeth. He tightened the rope into a smaller loop as he turned to his visitors.

"Forgive the delay, Gentlemen. Horses, like women, require a certain amount of attention," Rigo looked fully at the young vaquero. He seemed to be evaluating this worthy, perhaps making a mental note for future reference.

"One does not insult either for fear of a fall from favor."

This last was said directly to the young vaquero. The youth met the look with defiance only for a moment. His eyes quickly fell to his feet and his entire stature seemed to lose air under the attention of the great man.

Chapa cleared his throat.

"Naturally you are correct, *Senor*," he said pleasantly.

Rigo turned his gaze to the older man. He nodded to Chapa, opened the corral, passed through then latched the gate. He looked at the horse, which had not taken his eyes from his master. Rigo chuckled and turned. He started for the house.

Chapa fell in step.

"Forgive the intrusion," Chapa said glancing at the young vaquero.

The vaquero still stood with the horses, uncertain of his next move.

"Your Governor requires your special skills one last time."

Rigo stopped and looked at Chapa.

"One last time you say?"

He smiled as he searched the other's face.

"He has two daughters, I hear."

Chapa chuckled.

"So, you have heard?"

Rigo waved his hand dismissively. He turned and continued towards the house.

"Come inside."

Chapa summoned the vaquero with a wave. The youth approached leading both horses. The youngster halted before Chapa. He looked at him with an expression which conveyed doubt and uncertainty. Chapa read the confusion in the young man's face.

"He is a man of breeding and station."

The young man looked at him blankly.

"He once ruled this region before it was governed officially. He gave up his ascendancy to governorship for his passion."

The vaquero seemed more at sea than before.

Chapa shook his head and spoke as he would to a particularly dull pupil.

"The hunting of men," he concluded. "He looks at it as the sport of kings, as others view hunting fox or boar."

The young man spoke with a low voice and an uncomfortable glance towards the house.

"But he is known for his cruelty to the men he hunts."

Chapa shrugged.

"He is a man who possesses great intensity."

Chapa indicated the hitch post.

"Wait for me here."

The vaquero shrugged and moved towards the rail. Chapa climbed the stairs to the house. The fragrant garden sweetened the air. He entered the house. He removed his hat and stomped dust from his boots. He moved into the cool dark interior of the home.

The little dwelling contained a rare amenity: floorboards. It was unusual to find a frame house in those climes, much less one so well appointed. Although modestly designed and constructed, Rigo's house was sponsored by powerful money and, Chapa guessed, favor from men of importance. Rigo Herrera was rumored to have been the instrument which helped select men ascend to station and power.

He crossed a lovely oriental rug in the entry room. He craned his neck into a nearby doorway where he saw Rigo seated at a clean table covered with a lace cloth. Rigo greeted him with another smile. He gestured to an empty chair. Chapa hung his hat on the corner of the chair then he sat carefully. Rigo rested with his hands together atop the table. His tapered fingers were interlaced and relaxed.

"We have not been introduced properly, *Senor*," he said gently. "I am Rodrigo Constantine Herrera. And you are?"

Chapa nodded his head slightly. He had not been aware of the man's full name until that moment. The name Constantine held many stories from his boyhood. He pushed the reverie from his mind.

"We have met, but it was an official function many years ago."

Rigo furled his brow, calling upon his memory to serve him.

Chapa raised a hand to dismiss any further effort.

"You were quite the center of attention and I am but a small piece in the game."

Chapa ended his modest proclamation with an equally deferential bow of his head.

"I am Eduardo Chapa, Aide to his Governorship."

Rigo's attention was drawn to movement in an adjoining room. The woman from the porch entered carrying a silver tray. An ornate decanter and two crystal glasses sat upon the polished surface of the tray. Chapa moved to rise. Rigo stopped him with a gesture.

"That is not necessary my friend, *Senor* Chapa. This is Rosa. We stand on little ceremony here."

Reluctantly, Chapa settled and smiled a closed lipped apology.

She sat down the tray and placed a glass before each man. She poured from the decanter and returned it to the tray. She straightened and allowed her gaze to fully inspect their guest.

Chapa was uncertain whether he had rated well with her. She gave no indication by expression nor word. Instead, she gathered the tray and left silently. Both men allowed an appropriate interval before continuing.

"So, what does the Governor require of his humble servant, *Senor* Chapa?"

Chapa brought the glass to his lips and tasted the rich wine with obvious pleasure. He returned the glass to the table and leaned toward Rigo slightly.

"He requires your particular talents in regard to tracking men."

His voice was pitched low as if he were now taming a wild stallion of his own.

"He further requests your presence to discuss this task and matters related to this task, in person."

Rigo raised his eyebrows in interest. Chapa leaned back, his message delivered. He now waited for the reply.

Rigo adjusted his position slightly to the side in his chair. He was more fully facing the older man. He lifted his glass and sipped from it. His eyes closed in relish as he allowed the wine to do its work. Finally, he opened his eyes.

"We leave at once for Saltillo then."

The two men sat for a moment in silence. As one, they lifted their drinks in salute to one another. They drank another sip then replaced the glasses on the lace table cloth. Neither man spoke as they considered their own thoughts.

After a moment, Rosa returned with the tray and decanter. She sat down the tray and lifted the decanter.

Rigo lifted a hand.

"That was sufficient," he said gently.

A short while later Chapa sat his horse next to the young vaquero in the lane outside the little house. Rigo emerged with a small oilskin pack in his arms. He now wore a heavy black belt which supported a long pistol holster on his right hip and a longer knife sheath on his left. The knife sheath was angled slightly forward, and the knife handle was reversed for a right-hand pull.

Rigo stepped off the porch and disappeared around the left side of the house. Chapa and the young man enjoyed the entertainment of a mockingbird's scolding from a nearby tree. The audacious lean bird jumped from limb to limb, whistling and rattling his displeasure at the mounted trespassers encroachment upon his domain.

Rigo rounded the corner from which he had disappeared. He was astride a delicately made black mare. Her blazed face and stocking feet danced and flirted as she approached. She was fresh and obviously relished the task ahead.

Both Chapa and even the self-possessed youth sat in awe of the black mare. She was all points and lines. It took no expert in horse flesh to appreciate this rare beauty. Chapa and the Vaquero joined Rigo as he made his way on the lane before the neat little house. Rosa stood on the porch, watching the three ride away. Rigo did not give her or the house a look as they departed. Once they were out of view of the house Rigo took in Chapa's horse with a keen eye. Chapa sat stolidly under the scrutiny. He steeled himself for criticism from a second tormentor on the return journey.

"A sensible mount," Rigo said finally. "He appears good for a long ride in comfort and ease. His legs and haunches indicate stamina. His ears show his wisdom upon a long trail as well as patience and endurance."

Rigo bent his attention upon the vaquero's mount. The youth sat straighter under this inspection. He was confident his mount would draw the admiration and approval of this keen judge of fine steeds. If a mount as spindly and awkward as the old man's could draw such praise, he could only wonder at what his trim and powerful gelding might inspire.

After a moment of scrutiny, Rigo turned his attention to the trail without a word. A brief look of confused agitation appeared upon the youngster's face. He looked down and attempted to cover his anger. Chapa thought he detected a fleeting smile play at the lips of the man hunter.

The vaquero rode in silence for some time. In his tormented state, he was oblivious to the beauty of the surrounding terrain. More Mockingbirds scolded the riders as they passed within their claimed region. A light, but welcome breeze, scattered displaced oak leaves. A dense matting of pine needles softening their path.

Early summer heat warmed their shoulders during those brief moments when they passed from within the shadows of the lush *Pino Acahuito* and the tall Pine trees. Fragrant wild blooms sweetened the air where sparse underbrush edged the dim trail they followed. The older men seemed to be completely immersed in nature's welcome to these travelers. Finally, the youth looked fully at Herrera.

"It is a great honor," he said with only a hint of his true feelings tinting his words, "to accompany one of Mexico's heroes on the first steps of an historic mission. Allow me to add my name to the list."

The vaquero doffed his sombrero and bowed as he was able in the saddle.

"I am Jose Ale Boneo Vesca of *Cuitzeo* in *Michoacan*, at your service."

Chapa gave the youth a sidelong glance. The youth's formal introduction was surprising in consideration of what he had learned of the youngster's manner on the trail.

Rigo considered Vesca seriously for a moment. His observation was one which extended beyond the rider's words and his carefully assembled garb. He seemed to move aside all pretentions and glimpse his intent. At least, that was how it seemed to the youth as he weathered the great man's scrutiny.

"Many years ago," Rigo said in his pleasant manner. "A great man lived upon a towering butte in a Hacienda of stone and 'dobe. The outer walls were built thick and high by a people long dead.

"That bleak region was an outlying frontier in a violent time many years before. The home was built to withstand a sustained attack from rampaging tribes, displeased with the betrayal of a broken treaty between Cortes and King *Tangoxoán.*"

Vesca looked at the great man in surprise. This story took place in his homeland. His shoulders straightened in pride.

Rigo continued. Although his words were for the youth, his attention was given to his surroundings completely.

"The master of the estate was not a descendant of the Spanish who had built the fortress. His father had conquered a small group of Spanish *Encomenderos* and taken the fortress for himself. He was of the original people who had suffered and died in the construction of the building. They were known as the *Tarascans*.

"This was not a complimentary term but one that remains to this day. In time, the Spanish left the region in search of more abundant wealth. The master thrived in the breach. His fortress made him indomitable. He even refused the King's requests to establish a defensive outpost there. The master easily repelled the King's force sent to liberate the fortress.

"It wasn't until the Spanish installed the tyrant Guzman as president that the Tarascan master again experienced hardship. Guzman sent an envoy to the Tarascan demanding release of the fortress. He claimed the Spanish held claim by rights. The master executed the messengers and hung the bodies from one of the walls at the edge of a tall cliff.

"Displeased, Guzman dispatched a large armed contingent. The force lay siege to the mountaintop fortress, blocking all access and exit.

"The master was not troubled. His supply stores were well-stocked in anticipation of attacks from his own tribe. He held no concern for the Spanish. Their desires leaned towards gold only. They were known to be lazy and easily discouraged in the pursuit of all else. He was confident that interest in him would fade soon enough. He did not know Guzman.

"The troops built a permanent encampment at the foot of the fortress. The master became a prisoner in his own house. Over the next few months, the score of family, fighters and servants trapped there ran out of food and water. A few tried to surrender to the soldiers only to be burned at the stake on Guzman's orders. The remainder stayed, in the end resorting to suicide and cannibalism.

"The troops finally breeched the defenses and found the fortress occupied only by skeletal remains and rats. The removal of Guzman and fears of local superstition left the fortress abandoned for many years. The encampment remained and later became a village called Nueva Galicia. That village eventually disappeared although the region retained the name for a time.

"The point of the story is that the master had inherited a name from the people who lived below after his death. They called him

Vesca. You see, *Vesca* is short for *vescatur* – Latin for flesh eater. Cannibalism was common among the native people back then."

The vaquero hauled on the reins of his gelding. The horse reared, almost unseating the youth.

Rigo clucked to his mare. She turned an ear to her master. Rigo produced the oilskin bag.

"*Senor* Chapa. Would you like a strip of meat? I am feeling hungry."

They laughed as they journeyed on.

The three riders dropped into the lower valley which cradled Saltillo. Hollows and draws sheltered the last remaining lazy mists of the dawn. The lifting Sun glinted upon trees and bushes, bejeweled in night's dew. Their horses' hooves tossed moisture before them in sparkling flumes of reflected sunlight. Below them, amidst a blanket of greenery, the small city awakened with the same reluctance as the night's mists loitering in the hollows.

The young vaquero rode soddenly, his head lolling with the weary strides of his mount. Chapa eyed his hometown eagerly. The beauty of the morning was not lost upon his appreciative eye. Rigo sat comfortably in his saddle as only one wise in patience upon the trail would have learned. His dark mare seemed to have grown stronger on the long journey from her comfortable stable. Her strides were active as a cat's in the fresh dew.

They entered the outer reaches of Saltillo. Shop proprietors opened their doors, brooms at hand, driving away the remnant of the night's disarray. Many beheld the travelers with polite interest as they passed. Those townspeople had long witnessed newcomers. Many were mindful of the anonymity most strangers required as a matter of course.

Near the center square Rigo guided his horse south. Chapa pulled up and hailed him in protest.

"Senor Herrera, quarters have been arranged for you this way."

Rigo smiled as one eager for the start of a great adventure.

"There is no better time for invigorating conversation and a breakfast served upon silver, my friend."

Chapa nodded his agreement.

"As you wish."

Chapa turned his horse. His young companion obediently turned his mount to follow.

"Your assistance has been appreciated, Vesca. I will call you if you are required further."

The youngster studied Chapa's face for a moment, seeking some hidden warning or veiled comment as to his performance. Satisfied, he tipped his sombrero and turned his horse away. Chapa caught up to Rigo as he rode towards the Governor's mansion.

The great stone structure was protected by rock columns bearing black iron fencing. They entered the main entrance to the grounds. Two armed sentries nodded to Chapa in recognition. Their scrutiny of Herrera drew a level gaze from the dangerous man. They were unable to hold his look for more than a few seconds before they turned to study the road for others who might pose a threat.

The men dismounted handing their reins to a young boy.

Rigo eyed the youth with care. He leaned lower and pitched his voice conspiratorially.

"Have a care. She bites."

Rigo grinned and cast a warning look at the black mare. Her ears stood attentively, as if in protest to this slight from her master.

The youth was uncertain if he was the focus of a jest or if he were truly endangered by this striking animal. His young face broke into a broad toothy grin. Rigo handed him a silver coin and turned towards the large double doors of the home.

Governor Gonzaba stood at his desk as the broad doors to his office opened. Chapa stepped in then stood to the side as Rigo entered the chamber. Gonzaba moved around his desk towards the famous man hunter. They embraced warmly.

"Your journey was uneventful I pray," Gonzaba said.

"As if I had slept through the night in my own bed, *Senor.*"

Gonzaba smiled. He indicated a chair before his desk. Rigo moved to it and they both sat. Chapa retreated quietly through the doorway and closed the door silently behind him.

A side door opened and an aproned woman in black and white garb approached the two with a tray. She sat the tray upon Gonzaba's desk and poured tea into cups placing them before the men. She produced a plate of pastries, gathered the tray and disappeared as she had come.

"Rigo, my friend," Gonzaba beamed. "It has been a long time. How is your family?"

Rigo sipped the tea and squinted his approval. He swallowed then replaced the cup upon the saucer.

"They are well, Governor. My wife continues to honor me with her presence and my son honors me with his absence."

"He remains abroad?"

"Despite my wishes."

Gonzaba shook his head knowingly.

"Young men possess great spirit, but rarely the wisdom to wield it."

Rigo considered this as he again sipped from his cup.

"You require me for an important task, Governor?"

Gonzaba opened an ornate wooden box atop his desk and withdrew a fragrant cigar. He offered one to Rigo. Rigo raised his hand as he sat back to listen.

Gonzaba clipped the end and lit the cigar, puffing in great pulls until it was fully lit.

He expelled a large fragrant cloud, looking at his guest through the fog. He seemed to be preparing his thoughts before sharing them.

"As always," he said finally, "I would not summon you for less."

Rigo crossed his legs and regarded the Governor expectantly.

"Your daughter has been kidnapped and I am to return her."

The summary from Herrera only drew a wave of Gonzaba's free hand.

"Six years ago," he began, leaning forward with the gravity of his words. "A man sat in that very seat. His father, who owns one of the largest shipping fleets in all of Mexico's ports, had dispatched him to lobby for an East West overland route connecting ports on both coasts. His company was based in Vera Cruz, which is surprising in itself. He preferred Pacific trade routes."

Gonzaba puffed the cigar as he recalled the memory.

"He said it honored his ancestors, although I believe his father and his father before had created such a trade relationship that he was reluctant to expand beyond what his family had created from many years before."

Gonzaba smiled upon Rigo as he marveled at the folly of the short-sighted businessman. Rigo nodded his understanding.

Gonzaba's voice became conciliatory.

"As we discussed the specifics of his proposal, that door opened and my eldest daughter, Juliana, entered."

Gonzaba pointed at the big double doors and shook his head. He seemed to take great sorrow from that moment when his daughter made her fateful entry those many years ago. He started slightly as he emerged from his reverie.

"You don't know her, Rigo."

Rigo adjusted his place in his seat at the familiar address from the great man.

"She is certain what concerns me is also of interest to her."

The Governor sipped his tea and returned the cup to its tray.

He lifted his hand with a flourish as he said, "Naturally this young man was smitten from that moment. So much so he extended his visit here for several weeks under the guise of making more contacts for business purposes. He spent most of his time making more contact with Juliana than business."

Rigo nodded with sage understanding. He had earned the regard of many women through well invested time and deft conversation.

"He and Juliana spent much time getting acquainted," he continued. "Although the man was ruggedly handsome and of breeding, his advances found no purchase in Juliana's heart. Alas, both sought my council on more than one occasion: he, imploring me to act on his behalf and she, questioning why she was to receive this young man for whom she felt nothing more than a casual interest."

Gonzaba paused to allow his difficult position to impress his guest.

"Alas, the day came when this brazen suitor could find no more reason to stay in Saltillo – at least not if he were to retain any appearance of honor or pride: so, he departed. He did not return for more than a year. His letters, however, arrived almost daily. Juliana replied to the first few, making her intentions clear. He was not to be dissuaded however, and his letters continued."

Gonzaba puffed his cigar and shook his head. His eyes seemed fixed upon some distant point behind Rigo. He placed his cigar in an ivory tray and picked up the tea cup and sipped the liquid within. He glanced at the cup and blanched slightly as his tea had grown cold during the telling of his tale. He replaced the cup and picked up his cigar. He puffed again and shrugged his acceptance of the substitute flavor.

"One day," he continued through a cloud of rich smoke. "She was attending a great ball here in town. She was surprised to see him in attendance. He was not, however, the man she remembered. He was pale and his drawn countenance seemed to indicate that he was laboring under a great burden. At length he came to her and entreated her with his desires. He explained that he could not be whole without her. Juliana pitied him but, nonetheless, refused his advance. Three days later, my guards apprehended him inside my home in the act of stealing my Juliana from her bed."

Rigo shook his head and smiled at the impertinence of this love-struck fool.

"Indeed," Rigo chuckled lightly, "And what became of this impetuous adventurer?"

Gonzaba leaned forward and pointed at Rigo, his cigar quivering in his hand.

I would like to tell you that he was flayed alive. But it turns out, his father's influence stayed my hand and he is exiled from Mexico: nothing more."

Gonzaba leaned back and rubbed his free hand against his trousers as if to scratch an itch of desire to grip the kidnapper's throat.

"Juliana," he said with a deep throated snarl, "was furious at the leniency I had shown him. After showing me her disdain for an extended period – oh she is willful, that one - she exacted a promise from me. I promised her I would never again take her safety so casually as to let an assault upon her person or her honor go unpunished."

Rigo sensed the conclusion of this story and an explanation of its importance. He sat forward in his chair, his lean frame erect and ready to move in an instant.

Gonzaba looked fiercely at the man hunter and growled in a low voice, his words coming slowly and deliberately.

"You will find my daughter and exact an appropriate price for the offense committed against my family."

The Governor sat back and exhaled as if he had just completed a most arduous task.

In a milder tone he asked, "I trust you still possess an admirable level of passion for your work?"

Rigo smiled broadly in confirmation. He was pleased to return the meeting to familiar ground.

"Since we are speaking of extracting a price…"

Gonzaba interrupted him in impatient assent.

"I will double your fee, of course. You leave immediately."

"Of course."

Rigo rose and bowed slightly. To Gonzaba, he had the appearance of a hawk, released of his hood, jess and anklets. He watched as Rigo left him alone in the room. His mind was more at ease, but he still felt restive and would likely feel that way until she was returned safely with her honor still intact.

CHAPTER TEN

Bounty Hunter

Tonight, the big American seemed more on edge than usual. He seemed always on the verge of great expression of rage, but tonight was different. Juliana was learning more about him as the days accrued. Where she had thought him emotionless other than an enraged and brooding exterior, she learned that he was more complex. Upon closer scrutiny, his state of mind and spirit were more easily discernible. Much of what gave away his mood and, more dangerously, his fits of rage, were subtle changes in his blue eyes.

His normal state was a continual and deft scrutiny of his surroundings. He was ever vigilant on the trail. He missed nothing around him. He continually studied terrain, weather, and wildlife patterns with a singular suspicious behavior. He grew wary at even the slightest change in the natural buzz and rattle of this wild country. He rarely slept more than a scant few hours. When he did sleep, he did so silently and awoke with no sound or change in breathing pattern.

Many times, she had emerged from a moment of deep thought to see him lying in his blankets, observing her. His look was unabashed and meaningful. She, on those occasions, would look away as if meeting his gaze would give him permission to take more from her than a look. His abrupt and violent outbursts no longer startled her.

His temper was always close to hand and active. She could predict a fit of mood, sometimes hours before he acted upon his rage. Even the set of his shoulders gave her warning of a change in the man.

They travelled primarily by night, stopping before dawn to camp. They were adhering to that policy that night when Boyd halted sharply. His head was turned towards the east. At close range, the soldiers were easy to detect. The rattling of tack and equipment was quiet compared with the soldiers' casual approach to noise discipline in their conversation. Many times, however, the desert sounds covered the rider's noises until they were surprisingly close. Boyd seemed to have an almost supernatural sensory ability in detecting the approach of the hunters.

From the first he had demonstrated his awareness of an adversary many minutes before she could hear any sound whatsoever. On those occasions even Cab questioned the evasive actions of the leader. His query was typically met with a threat or at least a blunt rebuke and dismissal.

They retreated into a rocky ravine. One warning look from the American ensured her silence although she was unsure who would hear her if she did cry out. The silence of the cool desert seemed as it always was to her. Nocturnal insects chirped and prattled. A light breeze bent the leaves of the surrounding plant life. She eventually heard a very small sound, like the advance of a swarm of insects through lush grass.

She scarcely breathed as she strained to discern the source of the foreign noise. The swarm sound grew into the sound of metal clicks and jangles followed by heavy thuds of mounted horse's hooves upon sandy ground. Soon she heard the low voices of the soldiers. As they passed closely above them, she could make out their conversation.

The American held them there for many minutes after the troop sounds had long faded. Without a word, he moved ahead staying to the soft silt of the draw's bed. Her horse padded noiselessly taking her farther away from liberation.

A hot wave of regret consumed her as she rode the tired horse beneath the overhanging banks of the dry draw. What prevented her from crying out to the patrol? Death might be preferable if it included her captor in the number of the dead.

It had been less than an hour, she felt, since the passing of the army patrol when she saw flickering lights of a village from among the tangle of low bushes and hanging willow branches. They emerged from the thicket and the leader pulled up under the moon shadow of a low building which appeared to be a stable or perhaps a feed stores.

They dismounted. Juliana was growing more accustomed to long hours in the saddle, but she still grimaced her discomfort and her legs protested this new labor of self-support. The American led his horse to the side of the building where a rough door opened into the side of the structure. He tested the door with a hand. It resisted so he gathered himself and brought a heavy foot against the door. It splintered and crumbled inward. He led his horse within. The others followed him.

Juliana entered a region of complete darkness. Her eyes adjusted by degrees. Cab took her reins and pushed her onto a mound of feed sacks, stacked against a supporting post. He led her horse to a rough stall and tied him there. Her eyes went to the open doorway, escape seemed more irresistible since their close brush with the soldiers.

Boyd approached her pocketing a chamois sack she had knew was filled with coins.

"Tie her to that post," he said simply. "I'll be back directly."

He looked down at Juliana but spoke to Cab.

"Keep your eyes and your ears open."

Cab approached the leader.

His voice was low but there was no mistaking its urgency.

"I know why we are here and it ain't wise to take chances."

Boyd fixed him with a look which seemed both annoyed and contemplative. Slowly, a smile pulled at the corners of his mouth. With no further explanation he turned towards the moonlit opening and strode away.

Cab held his stance long after Hutton had disappeared from view. He seemed to be troubled. Juliana had no doubt that the memory of the close call with the Mexican troops was prominent in his thoughts. With a sigh, Cab looked around him. He noticed the faint glow of a window to his right. He moved to the window and surveyed the night beyond.

"Cab," she said quietly.

He glanced at her to make sure she hadn't moved. Satisfied, his attention returned to the night beyond the window. He had a limited view of the town, but he did not see the leader.

Juliana again spoke,

"He will get you killed or do it himself. He has the Demon *Sangri* in him."

Cab didn't seem to be listening.

"The devil's host tracks him," she said with meaning. "He fights them every night."

Cab didn't turn but she could tell by the silhouette of his shoulders in the window's glow he was listening.

"You follow a man who cares more for drink than for your life."

She rose and approached a few steps. Cab stiffened but still did not face her.

"My father would let you live if you released me," she pled: then more eagerly, "No! He would reward you."

She moved to him and touched his arm lightly.

"You would be a hero to him."

She turned him towards her.

"And to me."

Cab looked down at her with interest. She searched his eyes in the darkness for any sign of tenderness. She could discern nothing from his look. She moved closer to him knowing her presence was a powerful force upon men.

Cab leaned towards her. He searched her eyes for a moment. His face was very close to hers now. She felt his breath on her cheek as he spoke.

"I would be long dead before I collected any reward or walked in any parade."

Cab grabbed her shoulders and turned her away. He moved her firmly but gently back to her previous position atop the sacks. He withdrew the familiar cloth strips Boyd had cut from her dress that first night and bound her hands to the post. He tested the knots then moved silently back to the window.

Gannon Lisle was a bounty hunter. Several weeks of hard travel had brought him to this little alley in this dusty Mexican village. Army patrols were thick, combing the region for the three fugitives. It was his experience that when Americans are sought by the Mexican army, it was unsafe for any American in the search area. With this in mind, he endeavored to evade the searching forces as if he were the object of their search.

The man he hunted was not difficult to track, if one relied on more than trail sign. Tracking his man using trail sign or footprints was futile. He was clever at hiding his tracks. He used the terrain and created trail problems with change of direction, switchback and following well-travelled roadways. One must know a man to track a man, and Lisle knew his man.

Lisle nearly lost him this night until he was forced from the hard-packed cow path by a small mounted patrol. The searching squad forced him from the trail and into a silty wash. After the soldiers passed, he continued to follow the draw. A scant few rods beyond where he took cover, he detected the deep and unmistakable impressions of three mounted horses. The tracks were fresh and were unmistakably those of his quarry.

Lisle had slowed his pace. It would have been a mistake to come upon the fugitives accidentally. Hutton was not to be underestimated in an unplanned encounter. He felt his anticipation for the kill growing as it always did.

The infamy of Boyd Hutton was not lost upon Lisle, but he had brought many "terrible gunmen" to ground. Most ended up filling a hole under a cross made of green boughs. All of those he captured, ended up hanging from the supple coils of his genuine *Hojojutsu* braided rope. His was a special rope, obtained from a Japanese immigrant escaping a vengeful Shogun in his homeland. Since then, many had seen their last moments in its supple embrace. Hutton would feel the slow constriction and his eyes would bulge before they grew quiet for eternity.

Lisle soon came to where the cow path began to widen into a passable lane. He saw the distant lights of a village ahead. He moved from the path and carefully made his way through the dense underbrush. He intended to skirt this end of the village. He hoped to discover a side route. The going was level but heavily overgrown with greasewood and cactus.

At length he dismounted and led his horse through the bramble. Even on foot with the aid of a rising full moon he had trouble avoiding thorns and cactus spines. At one point a thorny bush caught his horse by surprise and almost found him pushed headlong into a copse of fire bushes.

He was relieved when he finally came upon a small out building, then the rear of a mud walled dwelling. Through the single rear window, he could see a dim lantern atop a crude table. A man sat, head down, his unshaven face slack, his eyes closed, asleep where he sat.

Lisle moved quietly around the shack and onto the main thoroughfare of the village. There were no more than half a dozen structures, making it easy to locate what he wanted. Directly across from his position was a squat 'dobe building where a dimly lit, wide opening beckoned the weary traveler. Lisle knew his man. Here he would lay in wait for his quarry. Although difficult to track, Hutton had a weakness for drink – and particularly – drinking establishments.

Lisle drew his horse down a dark alley, littered with old broken barrels and wooden crates. He tied his mount then moved back towards the roadway. He took cover behind a stack of dusty shipping crates. He subdued a start as he saw Hutton walking wearily along the thoroughfare. Hutton, although seemingly fatigued, gave his surroundings careful attention. Lisle wondered if he suspected someone might be stalking him. Lisle appreciated his wariness, but he knew Hutton's caution would not be enough to save him this night.

Boyd Hutton entered the dank cantina through a rough doorway from which hung a pair of opened heavy doors. Inside, the smoky lanterns cast a dull glow upon a half dozen patrons. They spoke in low tones within their groups.

The stranger's entrance evoked a sudden silence. The patrons watched the newcomer enter and move to the bar. The stranger tossed a coin on the roughhewn plank which served as a bar top. The bartender, a soft man of voluminous facial hair brought a bottle and a cup. He sat both before the gringo and took the coin.

Hutton poured a large drink then downed it with relish. His eyes glistened as he enjoyed the warmth of the whisky's path to his core. He poured another and lifted the glass as he turned to face the patrons, who still watched him.

He leaned his back against the bar, resting his elbows atop it. The drink was conspicuously held in his left hand. The patrons found it significant that his right elbow was hardly bearing weight allowing the right hand to dangle near his holster.

A small man at the table nearest the door donned his sombrero and cleared his throat nervously. He rose and began to make his way to the doorway.

The stranger pulled his gun casually and held it in the would-be escapee's direction. He didn't aim with care, but he had the air of a man who did not require a keen aim to hit his target. The man gestured with the pistol towards the chair. The small man bowed his head and returned to his seat.

The stranger drained the contents of the cup once again, surveying the room over the cup's rim. Each patron felt as though he were being singled out by that gaze. He seemed interested particularly in the only woman in attendance. The patrons settled more deeply into their seats. Their impression of this newcomer was one of foreboding.

The American placed his pistol upon the bar with a careful gesture. He seemed almost reverent in his handling of the weapon. He poured and drained the cup once more. He sat the cup down then moved around the end of the bar and took his place behind the bar. He rested on his elbows a moment then stood and poured again.

His voice sounded low and menacing.

"You married?"

The men looked about them in confusion. The stranger's voice came again.

"*Tiene un esposo?*"

The girl did not answer but only nodded. She was obviously frightened and the dread she felt was shared by all in the room.

"*Quién es él?*"

The frightened girl looked at him in alarm and still did not reply. She could not help glancing in the direction of a young man seated across from her seat at the table.

The American looked at the young man.

"*Comer aquí.*"

Slowly, the youth rose and faced the gunman. He smoothed his shirt, almost formally, then approached the bar. He stopped directly before the gunman opposite him at the bar.

"How long have you been married?"

The youth replied only with a confused look.

"*Cuánto tiempo llevas unida?*"

"*Senor?*"

Hutton lifted the cup to his lips as he considered the youth. He sat the cup back on the bar and quickly picked up the heavy pistol and struck the boy across his brow.

The boy fell heavily to the dirt floor. The American eyed the other patrons as their murmured protests grew. The room again fell silent.

The American straightened and his voice came as a low snarl.

"I am that thing in the night you hide from."

He looked down to the boy, now rising slowly from the floor.

"You answer or I will take your wife with me."

The boy may not have understood the words, but the intent was plain to him. His words came softly but clearly.

"*Recién casado, Senor.*"

Hutton sat the gun back on the bar with the same reverence as before.

"I want her wedding dress. Bring it to me."

The youth's eyes teared up in confusion.

"*Voy a matar a todos! Traje de novia. Savvy?*"

The youth nodded and backed slowly out the door.

The group remained silent. No one moved besides the dangerous American who lifted his glass periodically. Soon the sound of running was heard from outside. The American placed his cup on the bar and picked up the pistol gently. He covered the door entrance casually.

Out of breath, the boy entered holding a white wedding dress draped over his outstretched arms like a lifeless body. He crossed to the bar with careful steps then laid the dress gently upon the bar top.

The stranger gestured to a chair. The boy moved to it. All in the room waited breathlessly for the next outrage.

Hutton drained the last of the whisky from the cup, corked the bottle, then scooped up the dress and holstered his pistol. He lifted the bottle and walked from the room.

Hutton passed from the close atmosphere of the cantina into the freshening night. He walked with a satisfied smile on his face. He lifted the dress and smelled it deeply. He gave a wagon a wide berth as he made his way back to the edge of town from where he had come. The mechanical sound of a cocking pistol stopped him, his shoulders rigid.

"I am the thing in the night you hide from," a low voice said behind him.

Lisle brought the butt of his pistol down hard on Hutton's skull.

The bigger man fell, the dress flowing from his senseless hands onto the street.

Hutton regained consciousness slowly. He was no longer in the fine dust of the street. He lay in a patch of grass. He stretched his neck to one side, then the other. He could see dimly that he was at the base of a tree in a sparse grove. His hands were bound behind him. He tested the firm knots.

Lisle's pistol pressed against his head.

"Are you afraid?" Lisle snarled, his lips close to Hutton's ear,

Hutton made no sound.

"You will see fear before you see death, Boyd Hutton – the massacre-er of Agua Caliente."

Hutton held his breath for a second in apparent surprise but not fear.

Lisle looped a supple thin rope around Hutton's neck as he spoke.

"You murdered three innocent settlers. You tried to kill a pretty little girl. You son of a bitch - you robbed them settlers and left them to die..."

Hutton croaked something low and unintelligible due to the strangling rope.

"What's that, dead man?"

Lisle loosened the noose slightly.

"What's your name?"

"So, you want to get acquainted."

Lisle pulled the noose taut again. The force pulled Hutton's head off the ground roughly.

"I am the man who tracked you where armies couldn't," he continued, throwing the rope over a sturdy branch. "I am the man who caught you where the Mexican government could not. I am the man who is going to deliver you to the devil for your just rewards. I am Gannon Lisle, in the service of Brigham's *Danites*, you piece of shit."

Lisle clutched the hanging end of the storied rope with both hands and raised Hutton with a mighty pull.

"The Mormon's hired me to track and hang you for what you did to them folks out there."

Lisle refreshed his grip and pulled with all his weight.

Hutton rose to a height where his heavy boots barely touched the ground, his face looked not at his tormentor, but into the darkness.

Lisle grunted with his effort to lift the big man. With one last mighty effort, Hutton's feet cleared the ground.

"You're gonna turn black Boyd Hutton: black as your deeds. This ends you."

Lisle renewed his grip and pulled again. Hutton rose slowly. Lisle pulled until he was almost seated when a shot rang out from behind him. He felt as though a white-hot spike was driven through both of his hands. His grip fell from the rope and Hutton dropped to the ground on his feet. A pencil stream of blood flowed from small holes in both of Lisle's hands.

Cab entered the copse of trees, gun trained on Lisle. The man hunter clutched his mangled hands to his chest. Cab moved to him and struck him across the face with his pistol.

"Take that you bushwhacking son of a bitch."

Cab pulled a long knife from his belt and grabbed Lisle by the throat. He drew his arm back in readiness to plunge the blade. A grunt from Hutton stayed his hand. Still in striking position, he turned his head to his boss.

"What?"

Hutton stood as he had, hands bound behind him, trying to loosen the rope around his neck by moving his head in circular movements.

Cab dropped the man and crossed to Hutton. He cut the twine binding Hutton's hands and stepped back, his attention on Lisle. The bounty hunter rose to his knees bent over, groaning, and holding his hands.

Hutton pulled the rope from his neck and dropped it, letting it swing from the tree branch over which it hung. He walked past Cab to Lisle.

He looked towards Cab.

"Obliged."

Cab nodded.

"You were gone too long. I started out after you when I saw this cuss jump you. I lost you for a time in the dark. I followed this dumb son of a bitch's talk here."

Boyd squatted before the man and watched him for a moment.

"Here," Cab offered Hutton the pistol.

Hutton took the gun and put out his other hand, still watching Lisle.

"The pig sticker too."

Cab looked at the knife then handed it over to Hutton.

"Go back to the girl," he said without removing his gaze from Lisle. "I got business with our friend here."

Cab waited a moment as if to protest. He shrugged and retreated into the darkness.

Hutton threw a glance over his shoulder to ensure Cab had left before he spoke to Lisle in a low, conciliatory tone.

"You ain't gonna like what comes next, Gannon Lisle."

Hutton grabbed Lisle by the shoulders of his coat and dragged him to where the noose hung, swinging lightly in the breeze. Lisle struggled weakly. Hutton released him where Lisle slumped to the ground clutching his injured hands to his chest.

Hutton looked into his eyes.

"I know what waits for me. Do you?"

Lisle straightened as much as his pain would allow and he looked at Hutton fiercely.

"Just get it over with. I ain't playin' the coward in this game."

"You can't help but play the game I pick."

Hutton moved suddenly and violently. He grabbed the smaller man by the throat, turning him towards the darkness.

"You see them just like I do."

His voice held a desperation of conviction. Lisle sensed that he was to avow this man's fears. He remembered Hutton's gaze into the distance as he was lifting him with the rope.

"Don't you lie to me," he continued, shaking Lisle roughly. "I give you to them, they take their eyes off me for a time. It's always that way. I see what they keep on us for. It's in the eyes."

Hutton turned Lisle, facing him once again. Lisle tried to resist but the man was much stronger. Hutton brought the knife up then slashed, slicing through Lisle's clothes and cutting his chest beneath.

Lisle screamed, his chest on fire.

"Now they hear you. Do you know why they like us to hang?"

Lisle struggled to free himself. His useless hands caused him horrible pain when as he tried to push away. He felt himself falling into unconsciousness from his agony. Hutton shook him.

"Not yet, Gannon Lisle. Keep your damn eyes open. They don't like to be seen. It riles 'em."

Lisle could see only Hutton's flashing eyes. Like two flames drawing him on.

"Do you know why they like us to hang," he repeated the question. "They like us to hang because we see but we can't talk. They don't heed talk, but they hate it just the same. I know! You tried to give me to them,"

His head shook as his rage searched for outlet.

"I can't let that go. You gotta hang. You gotta see them."

Hutton slapped the noose over his head and pulled it taut. The sliding rope burned Lisle's neck like the coils of some fiery serpent. Hutton gripped the bloody end of the rope. He hauled Lisle off his feet with one long pull. The smaller man made a strangling noise as he went aloft. He reached for the rope with his bloodied hands.

"You'll wear out soon enough, Gannon Lisle. Them busted hands can't hold."

Hutton moved towards the tree trunk and wrapped the rope around the stub of a broken branch and tied it off. He rubbed his hands against his pants then moved to a position in front of the kicking and struggling Lisle. Hutton watched the man, fascinated at his efforts. With a look of fear, Hutton glanced over his shoulder, as if something were creeping up on him. His eyes return to Lisle. The hanging man's efforts were slowing as his strength failed him by degrees. Lisle's eyes fixed on something in the dark. His hands dropped helplessly to his side. Hutton again looked into the darkness then back at his victim as life left his eyes. With one last look into the darkness, he turned and walked away in the direction Cab had gone.

Cab entered the old stables out of breath. He quickly began gathering the few belongings he had removed from their packs. Juliana watched him silently. Cab seemed overwrought and possibly frightened. He untied her and led her and the horses outside. She mounted at a gesture from Cab. In moments, Hutton appeared silently from the darkness. He carried a white garment in one hand and a bottle in the other. He stowed both in his saddle bags and mounted. Cab mounted beside him.

"Who was that fella?" Cab asked.

"Gannon Lisle, bounty hunter."

Hutton touched his horse with his spurs, and they left the town, headed south.

CHAPTER ELEVEN

Cantina

Gonzaba pulled sweet smoke into his mouth. He held it, letting the aromatic fumes do their work. His eyes looked out to the gentle slopes and close-cut vegetation garbing the nearby *Zaplinamc* Mountains. From his upper floor balcony, he could see the town square below the ornate spires of the Cathedral de Santiago.

He loved Saltillo for many reasons, not the least of which was the cool southeasterly breezes which managed to reach this high desert country from the far away Gulf of Mexico. Saltillo basked under the languid warmth of an early Summer Sun. Gonzaba allowed the cigar smoke to escape him with a gentle release of his breath. His heart was heavy, detracting greatly from a moment he allowed himself on occasion.

He turned from the scene and sized up the men who stood silently, awaiting his words. His gaze was automatically drawn to the uniformed General Cortez, standing rigidly in the center of the room, before his large desk. Ever-present dangling medals draped his broad chest. A long sword clung to his waist within a gleaming scabbard and broad belt. His riding breeches were tucked snugly into the tops of his tall shiny boots. The pearl and gold handle of his heavy pistol rested within the polished holster, belted to his right hip - high and forward, as was his ceremony.

His trusted Eduardo Chapa stood before an ornate Devan, given him by an Indian ambassador some years past. His manner was always one of readiness to spring into action. His 60 plus years were reflected only in the grey frosting at his temples and rugged lines set about his mouth and between his eyes.

Finally, Gonzaba spoke.

"He hung him?"

The general blinked, not sure how to proceed. He was unaccustomed to the Governor's uncharacteristic economy of words.

Chapa cleared his throat politely and said, "Another Americano. A bounty hunter."

The Governor's eyes remained upon the General.

"My daughter?"

Chapa approached to a respectful distance.

"She has not been seen. But the American took a wedding dress with him when he left the cantina."

Gonzaba looked incredulously at Chapa. He looked his aide up and down as he attempted to make sense of all he heard. He moved towards his desk where he rested his clenched fists atop it. He engaged the General fully.

"How could this bounty hunter find men your entire elite guard cannot?"

Gonzaba silenced the General before he could assemble a response.

"Is there word from Rigo?"

This he barked to Chapa. He shook his head impatiently.

"Never mind. We will not hear from him: only about him after he kills these criminals."

Gonzaba raised himself from his whitened knuckles. He drew again from his cigar, considering both men through fragrant smoke. He exhaled audibly.

"If Juliana is dishonored, you know what must be done,"

Eduardo adjusted his position to a more personal proximity.

"*Senor*, there is no reason to believe she is harmed. Even so, she is still your daughter."

"If she is damaged, she will only be a reflection of what my daughter was. She must not be defiled. She will be damned. Rigo must succeed."

Chapa dropped his eyes in acceptance. The General looked about him, uncomfortable with the personal nature of the conversation.

Rigo Herrera stood atop a low butte which rose above the prairie floor. The familiar feeling which invariably accompanied the hunt warmed his senses and lightened his heart. He could have engaged the Americans nearly half a dozen times in the past few days. However, he was not given to carelessness in his craft. Less than a week prior, he had halted his horse under the dangling proof of what carelessness can reap. The bounty hunter's body swung heavily on the evening breeze. That was a picture he would use to steel his resolve.

He shook his head slowly then raised a long looking glass to his sharp eyes. At some distance he could see the three riders headed southeast. He did not fear detection as the setting sun would tend to dazzle the eyes of any of the party looking back in his direction. Indeed, without a glass, it would take an unnaturally keen eye to detect him at this distance. He lowered the glass and sipped from his canteen. He savored the cool water as if it were a rare wine. He corked the vessel.

Over the past day's travel, the terrain had relaxed its complexity of rugged draws and squat crags in favor of smooth grassed plains. Although, the softer ground rendered the American's trail problems useless, he was more open to detection. As a result, he allowed the interval between his prey and himself to grow.

He collapsed the glass and turned towards his back trail. Just over the crown of the hill he came upon the keen mare. Her delicate ears were alert as she had detected him long before he could see her. She nickered and tossed her head. He couldn't contain his enjoyment at the regard paid him by so fine a creature. He smiled broadly and rubbed her neck with his soft gloved hand. He stowed the glass and canteen in a saddlebag. He pulled the reins from the branch from which he had secured the horse and mounted with a stride.

The mare danced as if she had just emerged from her stable. There was no sign of the long trail upon her. He reined her towards the narrow shelf by which he had ascended to his observation point. The mare's dainty hooves seemed to have instincts of their own. He trusted her to find her way down to the flat.

Once he reached the flat of the valley floor, he let the mare have her head. She struck a gentle canter which was her habit. Horse and rider eventually passed the region where he had seen the fugitives through his glass.

Nightfall found Rigo resting against a cool 'dobe wall in shadow. The cantina was smoky, loud and smelled of stale beer. Dusky eyed beauties moved from table to table, offering attention to those who could afford to pay for it. Rank men clustered around squat tables or at the bar, their raspy voices joined in a rusty chorus.

Amongst the whirl and churn of the patrons was an island of calm. A void in which nothing moved. At this storm's eye sat Boyd Hutton, whiskey close at hand. Rigo limited his direct survey. This Americano's senses were keen. He had noticed Rigo as he arrived and dismissed him as one of the many only after Rigo had gathered one of the women into his arms and made theatre of great desire and familiar intent.

As the rotating beam of a lighthouse, the American's attention scanned the room. Rigo eventually fell securely into the background of this man's attention. He had never known a man as attuned to his surroundings as this man. The answer to the preeminent question of how he had stayed above ground so long was in part apparent in his uncanny purview. Rigo suspected that the remainder was a run of uncommon luck. It was Rigo's intent to end that streak this night.

The man hunter drew the girl close to him. She smiled at his renewed interest in her. He was handsome and there was some other thing about him that attracted her. She would be happy to lay with him for free just to spend a moment more in his company. He pulled her with him towards the back door, embracing her tightly against his muscular frame. As they left the warmth of the cantina, she pressed closer to him as the night air chilled her. Rigo drew her around in a smooth movement until she faced him. He produced a handful of coins.

"Go home to your mother tonight," he said with a smile. "Do not return this night."

He held the coins above her open palm but did not release them.

"Do you understand me?"

She returned his smile, unwilling to surrender him so easily.

His hand closed over the coins with a clink of metal.

A look of concern crowded her smile. She grasped the closed hand.

"I miss my mother. I will go see her now."

He pressed the coins into her hand and held her chin with his free hand.

"You are mine for the night. Do not be disloyal or greedy. I will know."

She nodded as well as she could in his grip. He released her and she walked away rapidly.

Rigo moved some yards away from the rear of the cantina. He pulled his bone handled pistol and looked to the load and mechanism.

He would make no mistakes with this one. He holstered his pistol and withdrew a long evil looking blade from the scabbard. He checked the edge unnecessarily. The knife was his preferred weapon and it was never without a keen edge. The knife disappeared back into its sheath with a gesture. He produced the makings and rolled himself a cigarette. He lit it with a stroke of a Sulphur match against a post. He drew the smoke in deeply. He exhaled towards the stars then began walking. A soft murmur from his lips became a love song delivered softly in a rich baritone.

Cab Jackson was on edge, as was his habit during his boss's forays into town. The uncustomary comfort of an actual room with a bed did nothing to ease his discomfiture. Juliana was sitting on the edge of the rickety framed bed. She watched him with casual interest. He drew on a cigarette. His eyes were upon her, but she knew he didn't see her. His attention was focused within. He stepped to the open window and exhaled a thick stream of smoke into the night air. The faint sound of horns and a guitar drifted to them from the cantina not far beyond his view from the window. Juliana looked at her feet then returned to Cab's back.

"Why must he come to town to drink?"

To her surprise, Cab replied immediately.

"He ain't come to town to drink."

Juliana's brow furrowed in confusion. She was about to speak when Cab's voice came again, his eyes still on the dark surroundings outside.

"It was something I heard him say to that man hunter."

He turned from the window and looked at her.

"I hid out and watched him hang him

"*Dios mio*. He hung him?"

"He only did what that son of a bitch was gonna do for him."

He drew on the cigarette, the end glowing brightly.

"Anyhow, Boyd talked about being watched by something most can't see. I figure he's gotta stay close to lights and noise, and what not, to shake whatever he thinks they are."

"His name is Boyd?"

Cab laughed lightly. It was strange to him that they had been together this long, and she had just learned the Chief's name.

"Yeah," he chuckled, "Boyd Hutton. That bounty hunter knew his name and told him so."

"And you," she asked with a nod.

"Oh yeah. I knew who he was when I partnered up with him on the border."

Cab looked at her seriously.

"He don't like being known, I don't make nothing of it to his face."

He looked at her with a manner which convinced her that he was serious.

"Take a hint and do the same if you don't want to see his cross side."

Cab considered her a moment more before he crossed back to the window and flicked his cigarette butt into the night. He returned immediately.

"Sorry, I gotta tie you down."

"Why, Cab? Don't leave me here."

Cab pressed her onto her back in the middle of the bed. He pulled leather ties from his pocket. The scraps from her dress had frayed to the point that she could have rent them with a single tug. The leather thongs were rough and sometimes bit into her wrists, particularly when Hutton tied them. He pulled the bandana at her neck over her mouth. She murmured an unintelligible protest then lay back frustrated.

"The Chief has been gone too long. We gotta slope right quick."

He stood and surveyed his handiwork.

"I'll be back in a shake."

Cab moved to her feet and tied her ankles to the bed posts. Satisfied, he turned and left through the door opposite the window.

Rigo crouched below the window, careful not to lean against the wall. The slightest creak could give away his position. He listened to the conversation within the room. He felt interest at the apparent insanity the outlaw leader was exhibiting to the other two. In a flash the gleaming blade was in his hand. He would dispatch the kid first then deal with the leader. He heard the kid drawing towards the window. Rigo stiffened, ready to strike like a snake once the kid got to the window. A red flash arced over his head. He froze for an instant until he recognized the glow as that of a thrown cigarette. Cab's foot falls withdrew back into the room. He could not understand the rest of the conversation, but he heard Cab open then close the door. Rigo listened as the young man's footsteps crunched on the gravel of the path. He waited until he was sure Cab had left. He moved around the building and entered through the door. Inside, a single oil lantern burned dimly next to the bed where the girl was tied.

Rigo glanced at her before he began his survey of the room, taking stock of his surroundings. Juliana struggled against the leather straps. She tried to speak but could not be understood. Finally, Rigo approached and bent over her, surveying her in a way that caused her to redden beneath her dark complexion.

"Silence *Senorita*. I am here to liberate you from the Americans."

She nodded and she felt tears of relief well up hotly behind her eyes. Rigo blew out the lantern then moved closer. With a gesture, he removed her gag.

"Untie me," she said in an urgent whisper. Her voice held both fear and anticipation. Finally, she would be free. She could go back to her home and her father.

"Silence *Senorita*," he repeated, touching her shoulder firmly. "He cannot know I am here."

Juliana's eyes widened in disbelief. What was in his mind? Their path was clear. Escape was paramount. Opportunity was on their side. This bravado, or whatever it was that compelled this careless adventurer, posed an unnecessary risk.

"He is a dangerous man. We must leave. He will kill you. Take me from here before it is too late."

Rigo considered her for a moment, compressing his lips into a thin line. He mastered himself and his growing anger. He replaced her gag then covered her mouth to quell her loud and violent protests. He leaned in, his dark face close to hers.

"You are certain of your man's prowess. You know nothing of my resolve."

Juliana felt hot shame heat her skin. She writhed at the implication that Hutton was "her man," Again, the tears came hot. Large drops ran down her temples and disappeared into her disheveled hair.

Boyd Hutton rose from his chair. He corked the bottle and turned wearily towards the door. No one gave him more than a casual glance as he passed. He wavered slightly from the effects of the whisky. The musicians played with heightened energy, feeding off the roiling crowd.

He moved into the coolness of the night. His gaze swept the darkness for signs of ambush. He moved around the back of a shop: windows dark, closed for the evening. He reached the back and faced the wall. He opened his pants and sighed as water flowed. Soon the flow ended, and he cinched his pants and continued around the back of the buildings towards the empty house where he had left the others.

Soon he reached the doorway of the single room house. His hand went to the handle. He paused and listened intently. He heard no movement nor talking inside. He stood frozen in place, hand poised at the handle for some moments. Without warning, he manipulated the handle and the door opened with a slight creak despite his effort to support the weight of the door. Inside, he could see nothing other than the dimly lit frame of the open window. As he closed the door, he sensed movement. It was a swift silent movement. His reaction was so quick that he seemed to respond to the movement of air displaced by the attacker's body than to the solid form of the attacker's body.

Rigo moved in fast, the knife held forward and low. The knife penetrated the American's clothing but failed to find flesh as Hutton feinted to the side. Rigo's impetus carried him past the man. He felt a heavy blow pound him just behind the ear, causing him to fall heavily against the wall beside the door.

With impossibly fast reflexes, Rigo arced the blade around and up behind him, in an attempt to hook the American as he evaded the attack. The knife sliced the air, narrowly missing Hutton's neck.

The maneuver opened Rigo to another blow from the bigger man, to the side of his head. Like a bear, Hutton was on him. His left hand grasped Rigo's right wrist in a vice-like grip. The right bludgeoned his torso. Rigo returned a blow to Hutton's ribs. He pulled mightily to free the knife to no avail. The large man was remarkably strong, and he didn't appear to be weakening from the strain of Rigo's resistance.

Rigo moved his right foot around Hutton's legs and pushed. The American fell backwards pulling Rigo with him. Somehow Rigo found himself hoisted around Hutton where he struck the floor under the American. The bigger man's weight landed fully on Rigo's chest, knocking the wind out of him. The impact jarred the knife from Rigo's hand, and it clattered just beyond reach. A powerful right struck the side of Rigo's head. The white light from the blow stunned Rigo for an instant. Hutton stretched out his right hand and grabbed the knife. Rigo reached desperately for the right hand which grasped the knife. It was by the slimmest of chances that he intercepted Hutton's upward thrust without being cut. Rigo grunted as he attempted to wrest the knife from the man. Again, he fought using his entire body to move the bigger man from atop him. He felt himself weakening in the grasp of the American. The darkness hindered either man a clear view of his opponent. This battle was one of blind grappling and aimless body blows, while vying for control of the knife.

Hutton's strength coupled with the advantage of being on top began to noticeably weaken the man hunter. By degrees he was able to bring the knife up Rigo's struggling form until it lay across his throat. Exhausted, Rigo ceased struggling and panted from the strain of combat. The American didn't seem at all fatigued and his breaths were inaudible.

Hutton leaned in close to Rigo's face, the knife blade across his throat.

"What is your name?"

Rigo's reply was only to make a violent move to wrench his right arm from the man's grasp. The American's body tensed where he held Rigo down. The knife pressed more firmly to his throat. The victor's voice sounded low and menacing.

"*Como te llamas?*"

Rigo did not reply. The moonlight filtering through the window cast enough of a glow that he could make out much of the man's face. What he was able to see in the man's eyes struck him mute.

Hutton looked around him. He saw Juliana tied to the bed but failed to see Cab. His eyes returned to his victim.

"You croaked the kid?"

Rigo remained silent.

Hutton nodded as he seemed to decide on his next action. He lifted the knife from Rigo's throat. Rigo's ineffectual grip remained on Hutton's wrist though he was unable to restrain Hutton's manipulation of the blade. Hutton turned the knife's position to one suitable for a downward stab rather than a slice. Rigo felt his opponent's weight shift as he adjusted the knife.

In a violent movement, Rigo shifted left and brought his left knee up into the American's torso. The blow dislodged Hutton, allowing him to roll twice. In that instant he was on his feet. He leapt to the window with two large strides. Hutton gained his feet and pursued. Rigo vaulted through the window, striking the ground with a dull thud. He rolled forward and gained his feet. He sprinted around the building. He fled from the American's pursuit, but more so, he wanted to escape the hot shame of defeat crowding his heart and constricting his throat.

Hutton stood at the window, knife in hand. He waited a few seconds after Rigo disappeared into the night before he returned to Juliana. He removed her gag. Her face was soaked in tears. As he removed the bandana, she drew a long breath with a shudder of despair. He gripped her face in his sweaty hand.

"Where is Cab?"

She couldn't compel her voice to respond. Black disappointment throttled her. Hutton shook her violently, causing her to focus on the moment.

"He went looking for you," she sobbed as she spoke. Her voice sounded husky and strained.

Hutton cut the leather straps with Rigo's knife.

"We are leaving."

"We leave without Cab?"

Hutton gathered the few belongings laid about as he replied.

"I reckon. Likely that Mexican killed him and was after me next. Enough talk, let's slope."

Hutton grasped Juliana's arm and pulled her upright, then onto her feet. He moved quickly to the door. Had she not moved her feet she would have fallen. She was sure that if she had, he would have dragged her outside. He lifted her into the saddle.

Cab entered the cantina. His gaze scanned for sight of Hutton. His entrance drew attention from some of the patrons. One of the women moved his way, pleased to greet him. He raised a hand to her and shook it, warding off her advance. She frowned at him. The next moment she spied someone of interest in a different direction. Her smile immediately returned, and she moved away.

Cab made his way through the smoky room, moving towards the back. Perhaps there was a back room or a rear entry. It was not like the chief to spend his dangerous drinking time alone, but he was out of options. He located the back door and walked through it. The rear of the cantina was empty save the clutter of crates, whisky casks and all manner of refuse left to rot or blow away.

His mouth formed a thin hard line. He was beginning to fear that one of the numerous patrols had captured Hutton. He shook his head to clear the possibility. He had heard no shooting and capture of the outlaw would not be quiet nor without loss of life. So, where was he?

Cab walked around the rear of the cantina and made his way back to the little house. Perhaps he had missed him somehow. He searched the alley ways and spaces between buildings. He was not going to take chances. In moments, he found himself back at the doorway of the squat shack. He drew his pistol. The door was open, the interior dark and silent. He looked towards the copse of trees where the horses were tied. He saw no movement. The moon could not illuminate the depths of the grove adequately to ascertain the presence of their mounts. He moved towards the door cautiously, gun at the ready. He knelt beside the door and peeked in. He saw nothing in the dark room. He leaned against the wall and listened. Silence. No creaking floor boards, no breathing, no stirring of any type that he could detect. Finally, he entered. The room was empty. He turned on his heel and moved quickly to the grove. The horses were no longer there. Cab moved through the grove and scanned the dimly lighted region around him. He was alone. He holstered his pistol, removed his hat and scratched his head.

Rigo Herrera sat upon the ground, his back against a tree. Despite the cool night air, his face glistened with sweat. His entire body was soaked. His clothing stuck to him as if he had just emerged from a swim and dressed without drying himself. He shook his head in despair.

"I was defeated by an Americano," he whispered: as if the admission was an admission of guilt. His chin fell upon his breast. "How does this happen?"

He raised his hands, palms up. To his horror, they were trembling. He clenched them into fists and pressed them against the grass below him.

"Coward."

His accusation was barely audible.

With the groan of a tortured soul, he dragged his weary frame upright. He leaned against the tree to gather his strength. With a push, he forced himself to walk. He moved through the dark countryside back towards the distant lights of town.

His mind returned to his preparation. Maybe the woman was right. His primary charge was to liberate Gonzaba's daughter. Doubts crowded his mind as he questioned his judgement. The young American's leaving the shack seemed to be the first blunder. Afterwards, the failures stacked up rapidly. Had he tried to achieve too much?

He entered the edge of town sooner than he had anticipated. His preoccupation with the night's events had busied his faculties, shortening the journey. He gave no serious thought to further danger from the big American. He would have fled shortly after their encounter. Even a man so brazen as to frequent cantinas while on the run, would make a hasty retreat once discovered. The fugitives had no way of knowing whether Rigo was alone or a part of a larger pursuit.

Rigo grunted his surprise when he stopped before the front entrance of the busy cantina where he had first located his quarry. He thought his path aimless, yet his feet brought him here. He surveyed his surroundings suspiciously. His scrutiny found no threat. He shook his head then continued to the entrance. He entered the rough doors, exchanging the cool night for the warm close din of the bar.

Rigo moved through the cantina, paying little attention to the dark figures around him. His mind still hid within a dark fog of shame and confusion. He wandered without purpose, or so it seemed to him. His feet, however, took him towards a manifest destiny of sorts. He stopped abruptly. His vision cleared as a curtain parts. He had stopped before the very table at which Hutton had sat only a scant hour or so before. The table was occupied by two men who abruptly ceased their conversation and looked up at him with bland consideration. A long silent moment passed where their drinks waited mid-gesture, and their faces were frozen in a look which struck Rigo as amusing. His grim countenance changed by degrees and a grin lengthened his lips and lighted his eyes. The two patrons were unsure how to react, so they attempted to return the good nature of Rigo's changing look. Rigo's voice came strong and level and with a good humor lightening his expression.

"Get out," he said, and his smile matured to full grown.

Confusion complicated their attempts to smile and uncertainty kept them in their seats. These were not fighting men, but they had seen enough trouble in this place to recognize it when it stood before them. In an instant they stood, glasses clutched but forgotten. One of the men reached for the half full bottle on the table.

"Leave it," Rigo said with the same good cheer.

The two did as they were commanded and faded from Rigo's notice.

The man hunter sat in one of the warm seats and looked about him. He was unsure for what he looked, but it was his intention to stay there until he found it. His methods of trailing a man had necessarily included understanding the way his targets reacted in many conditions. Often, he fashioned his movements as his quarry would. Much of what had led him to Hutton had been his proclivity towards haunting lonely bars. At first, the practice had seemed a fluke. Rigo's incredulity at a fugitive exposing his whereabouts so flagrantly would not allow him to see a pattern. His confusion at the practice had stayed his hand on previous occasions. He anticipated a trap might have been laid. He also was suspect of so easy an opportunity, particularly one so easily used to his advantage.

The American was adept at creating trail problems. It was only reasonable to presume he would practice the same clever stealth when exposing himself so obviously. This last opportunity had created doubts confirmed by the young American. What he had overheard within the little house from the conversation between the Governor's daughter and the young kidnapper shone light upon the addled thinking of the older outlaw. Perhaps there was something to the young outlaw's contention that his leader was haunted by some specter, whether spiritual or imagined. Rigo shook his head as he often had since his defeat. Perhaps it was his long-practiced instinct to get inside the head of his quarry which caused him to occupy the very seat in which the American had sat.

His forced occupation of the table had not gone unnoticed. The bartender approached the table cautiously. Rigo glanced at him from the cover of his thoughts but did not acknowledge his approach. The bartender placed a glass on the table, extending his arm to its farthest point, as if he might be burned if he came too close. He left the glass and fled back to his safe haven behind the rough bar top. One glance assured him he was not pursued for some unknown affront. He quickly occupied himself with the business of waiting on the raucous patrons.

Rigo poured the glass full. He corked the bottle and sat it down with reverence. This was his sanctuary. The key to the salvation of his spirit lay within these walls. This table was his confessional. Many would have scoffed at the idea, but he was a man of complexity of heart and mind. He always thought himself a favorite of he who controls providence. His plight had always seemed of special interest to God. Proof of that fact was inherent in his safe delivery through countless dangerous dilemma. He suspected this was a table destined to launch life changing events for him. Here, he was sure, he would find answers.

One lesson he had learned early was that control was a myth. Life was a vast ocean. Some days were calm seas and favorable winds. Other days were tossing waves and violent storms. His boat was sailed with respect for those forces. Ultimately, he went where he was bidden. It was his to make the best of the conditions. An agent of change and a harbinger of wisdom would guide him moving forward. His plight was only to be alert for the signs and remain compliant to them.

Rigo sat at the corner table for the remainder of the night. He moved from his spot only to relieve himself. Just before dawn, the bartender begged him to leave so he might close and gain a small rest before opening again.

The following afternoon found Rigo back again. He drank more of the strong whiskey and even took his meals in that spot. When he was not drinking or railing against the memory of his defeat, he was angry with himself for being there at all. Those angry moments were generally endured in silence and expressed with a firm grip upon the table's edges. His fervor faded somewhat only at the point where the smooth, dank planks creaked in his grip.

There was no warmth nor amusement in his tone. Conversely, she felt his words held an unspoken threat, or at least a warning.

"This all seems pointless."

Her voice sounded stricken and a bit desperate. She found it difficult to control her emotions.

"We travel for the sake of travel – nothing more! We can never be together: not in Mexico – not in the north."

She felt a tingle of shame. The words indicated a context of belonging she did not intend.

He considered her keenly and she was sure he had taken from her last statement what she feared he would. He drank deeply once again. His eyes changed slightly. They seemed to hold a light of amusement. Maybe he was more interested beyond what he had demonstrated thus far. Fear rose in her and constricted her throat.

He sat the bottle down and leaned forward.

"We are together now. You belong to me."

His words were not comforting nor were they delivered with warm regard. He had merely made another statement of fact. He could have said similar words in the same way about the horses.

"I am here because you stole me. I don't belong to you. We are together because I remain captive."

He extended one of his large hands towards her.

"I love you, Juliana. That amounts to something in my book."

His words struck her like a physical blow. Her head reeled. She felt a dizziness which caused the dark night to move around her. She shook her head to clear the pall from her buzzing mind.

"Love?" She spat out the word. She was angry now. Her eyes flashed and she stammered slightly as she continued. "What horrible thing about you has the capacity to contain love?"

She lifted her chin in authoritarian judgement of this animal who dared trespass into the ways of man.

"Where in the murder and selfishness in you is there room for regard for anyone other than yourself?"

Hutton considered her for a long silent moment. He seemed to be taking her in by degree. Her words were only a part of what he processed in their communication.

Finally, he said mildly, "Is that how you see me: murder and selfishness? Am I a beast?"

He grabbed the bottle and raised it. He stopped the bottle's advance short of his lips.

"You don't know nothing about me. I had to become a thing to survive."

These last words were dismissive of her opinion. He drank the bottle empty with a single pull.

"There are many who never became this 'thing' and not only survived, they thrive,"

Her derision was obvious. Her filter was gone.

"You are not the romantic figure you flatter yourself to be."

"So now I am romantic."

Juliana started as if under a whiplash.

"Only in your view," she managed to say.

Hutton flung the bottle into the darkness.

His voice was hardly audible, and she sensed he was growing intolerant of her criticism.

"And what am I in your view?"

Juliana stood, letting the blanket fall to the ground. She balled her hands into fists and placed them upon her hips. Hers was not courage, but bitter resignation. This was her moment. She knew she would not live through the night, but she would strike at this demon with the only weapon she had. She was certain hers was an ineffectual attempt, but at least she would be heard.

"You are a hunted beast," she accused him with all her anger and pain. "You are the most destructive man I have ever met. Your nature is such that you no longer have to kill by your own hand. The specter of death embraces you. It is large and infects those around you, so they are destroyed merely by contact with you."

She felt out of breath as she finished.

Hutton sat looking at her blankly.

"Specter of death," he repeated. He seemed to be contemplating her words.

He stood in a motion. She fought to hold her ground. He moved slowly around the fire towards her. He spoke slowly and matter-of-factly as he approached. His head was down, and his jaw jutted menacingly.

"Some have to be swept out of the way. I am on a path. It is clear to me. It ain't no matter if it's clear to you or not. There ain't no end point to life, except the one. We all journey on. Only the fools think they are where they should be."

He was now directly before her, at arm's length. She noticed his manner had changed somewhat during his soliloquy. Did she detect an attempt to convince her? Was he appealing to her reason? This was the most he had said to her, or to anyone else, since she had been in his control.

"Is Cab where he should be?"

He started a bit at this. She pressed her advantage.

"Did he need to be swept away?"

He now appeared to grow upset. His eyes narrowed and his body stiffened.

"You don't need to speak of that boy," he warned through his teeth.

Juliana lifted her chin with the moral authority of a woman in judgement of a man.

"So now you feel remorse?"

"He may not be dead, and if he is, I didn't kill him."

"Didn't you?"

Hutton stood taller as his anger grew.

"You got a mouth on you," he muttered through clenched teeth.

"What do I have to fear? I will end up dead soon enough, just being near you. I no longer fear death."

"There are scarier things than dying. Dead is easy and natural. Nobody ever tried to die. They just did it, or it was done to them."

Juliana leaned towards Hutton a fraction. Hers was the courage of the lost.

"You speak of love and death in the same breath. You don't know the meaning of love."

She shook her head at him with disdain.

"You mourn Cab. Why? You have caused the death of many. Do you mourn them as well?"

She had pushed him too far. He grabbed her by the fabric of her dress with rough hands. He pulled her closer to him.

"You confuse my patience with weakness. There ain't nothing weak about me."

She could smell the whisky, heavy on his breath. There was something else as well. Was it the smell of death? She mustered as much strength as she could.

"Your weakness is your fear," Her voice was failing her, and her words sounded more like a raspy whisper than the firm indictment she had intended. "Your fear moves you to desperate actions. Your actions define what you are – and what you are not."

The last was spoken softly. Her strength had abandoned her. She felt an incapacitating exhaustion. She wanted to collapse upon the ground. He held her up. He looked into her eyes. Violently, he pulled her body against his. She could feel his strength. She felt how powerless she was, and her spirit flagged.

He moved one of his hands to the back of her head. He pulled her face close, and he kissed her hard. His mouth sought her hungrily. She could feel him harden against her stomach. She wrenched her body trying to free herself.

"No! You cannot do this!"

He grabbed her hair and put his mouth to her neck. His mouth was at her ear.

"You belong to me and you're gonna understand that."

He pushed her backwards to the ground, his body still pressed to hers. His mouth sought hers. She turned her head and pushed without result. His mouth was all over her face and neck. His hands moved to her breasts. He squeezed causing her pain. She cried out in alarm. He rose slightly and unbuckled his gun belt. He dropped it beside them. He unbuckled his belt and unfastened his pants. He gripped the bottom of her dress and began pulling it up around her waist.

She sobbed as she exhausted the last of her strength in resisting him. He pushed between her legs then he grasped himself putting himself in position to violate her. In his moment of triumph, he looked her in the eye. He wanted to savor her expression as he entered her.

He gasped and moved backwards, falling to the ground, his pants around his knees. This thing that looked back at him was not the face of Juliana. This face was a mask of decayed flesh. The eyes were two vacant holes in a darkened mask. The rotten teeth were exposed within torn lips. The hair was a matted web of gray. He saw Juliana's face as a death mask. He knew instinctively that he was seeing what he would create once he had sated his appetite with her. He knew this would be all he would leave for her in the end.

He tore at his pants, trying to cover his exposed manhood. He managed to cover himself as he looked for his pistol. He snatched up his gun belt on the second attempt. He pulled the pistol and cocked the hammer in one motion. He was so overwrought by this horror that he had to give the weapon his full attention just to wield it. He brought the gun on line. Over the sights he saw not the face of a rotting corpse, but instead, Juliana's lovely face had returned.

Her expression registered terror, but also confusion. Her horror at the attack on her was left hanging and ragged. She desperately tried to make sense of why he had broken off his assault, and now was about to shoot her.

He held the gun on her, his hand shook as the horrible vision still haunted him. She pulled her dress down, never taking her eyes from the sightless black eye of the pistol bore. Sobs wracked her body, and her eyes were moist from her tears. His pistol dropped slightly as he regained some of his lost comportment. With a start, he suddenly jerked the pistol back in line with Juliana's face. His countenance was a storm of doubt and mistrust of his faculties. He held the pistol in a rigid arm lock. Juliana was certain of her death. His eyes were maniacal. He didn't seem to be breathing. A long moment passed, and he slowly relaxed his posture. Finally, he lowered the pistol then holstered it. He moved away from her and to his bed roll. He fastened his clothing and lay down, his back to Juliana.

Rigo maintained his strange vigil for several days. He had rejected the working women's advances on previous nights, but this night he was attended on either hand by two buxom young beauties. They occupied their time fawning over him and casting frequent glances beyond to warn envious women who were not so well attended. They had learned the identity of the man hunter and his company was a prized position.

The dark beauty to his left drew close to the great man. Her lips were near enough his face he could smell her rose water fragrance and the life within her touching him through her breath.

"Everyone knows the name of Rigo Herrera," she breathed as she stroked his bare arm.

Rigo's gaze was upon nothing in that room. He was looking afar to see more clearly within himself. Alcohol was doing its work upon him.

"I am Rigo Herrera," he confessed. "It is true. The man lives beyond the name."

"You are a great man still, *Senor* Herrera," she assured him with a passion fired by confusion at his words.

She pressed her bosom against him.

"You are powerful and you are dangerous yet," she purred in his ear.

Rigo breathed in her scent once again as his eyes followed her black hair down to her inviting neckline. He looked into her bottomless eyes.

"You are a lovely flower."

He studied her countenance for some time. She arched her neck as she looked up at him, smiling her pleasure at his attention.

"I ask forgiveness for not noticing before," he said with a look of sincerity. "I am in the jaws of a beast and I have been struck blind."

"I am a woman: no more – no less."

Her manner was well learned and found its mark with the man hunter.

With a sudden movement, Rigo brought his big hand behind her and pulled her towards him. His voice came raspy and heavy with desire.

"Oh, you are more," he whispered where only she could hear. "What my eyes do not see, my years complete."

His mouth covered hers and she felt him kiss her more deeply than any man ever had. Her head grew light, and her heart burned hot.

They separated slowly. She searched Rigo's eyes.

The beauty to Rigo's right watched her curiously. Finally, she spoke to break the spell.

"Consuela, you must be careful."

Rigo cast a hawkish look to his right. He seemed annoyed, but when he spoke, his voice was smooth and sure as it had been before the interruption.

222 | CRAIG RAINEY

"Why must she take care in my presence?"

He turned back to Consuela.

"Are my advances unwanted?"

"*Senor* Rigo," she said, never taking her eyes from his. "No man is more desirable than you," She smiled impishly. "Leticia worries that young Christoph may grow jealous."

She looked slowly away towards the bar where a closely huddled group of three young caballeros watched intently. Rigo glanced at them with a casual dismissive look. He seemed reluctant to lend his view to anyone other than Consuela. The three young men were dressed as was normal in that region for the occasion. Their garish outfits were cut tightly at their narrow waists and broad in the shoulder. Broad brimmed sombreros were ornate with colorful bands of silk at the crown. Dangerous looking pistols hung heavily upon their hips. Their eyes blazed with a combination of fury and unrestrained joy at the opportunity to express that fury.

Rigo noticed all these details in his brief look. Consuela felt she couldn't be sure, but had she seen a glint in the great man's eyes as well? Rigo grasped Consuela and tasted her lips fully and deeply once again. The casual manner of his glance had not gone unnoticed by the three. The subsequent kiss was obviously meant to incite the three youngsters. As one, they stood from their leaning poses against the bar. They approached Rigo's table with deliberate slowness. They separated somewhat, fanning around the older man.

Consuela's eyes narrowed in concern. Her enjoyment faded as peril mounted before her. She moved to separate herself from Rigo. She hoped to defuse the situation by showing a lack of commitment to the man hunter. Rigo, however, drew her close once more. He swept a strand of hair from her face with his free hand.

The three men stopped just before the table. They stood well above Rigo. The youngster in the center wore two-gun holsters. His dark hands clenched and unclenched the air very close to the pearl handled pistol grips. Rigo knew this was Christoph the jealous.

"You are new here, *Senor*," the youth said with impressive calm. Rigo still did not look up at him. "Perhaps you are unaware of who I am."

His gaze took in Consuela with disapproval.

"More importantly," he added, indicating the mischievous girl, "who she is."

Consuela's eyes blazed at his tone and his implication of ownership of her.

"Christoph, I do not belong to you."

He looked directly at her with the authority of their history. He was about to retort when Rigo's voice came low and consoling.

"Shhh, little one," Rigo said. "I need no woman, even a lovely flower, to speak on my behalf for such as these."

By now, the room had grown silent. Many there knew who the dark stranger was. All knew who Christoph was. This was a moment with historic significance for them.

Christoph's hands stopped moving. His entire body grew absolutely still. He seemed to consider his course of action.

"Measure your next words, *Senor*," he warned the seated man.

Rigo looked closely at Consuela as he considered the warning. Finally, his voice broke the strained silence, yet he still spoke to the girl.

"It is measure you request. Let me share with you a belief of mine. Up until recently I believed that some things were manifestly earned and permanently kept. Even one as old as I, am is capable of learning new things, it seems. I now know: that which got you here is no longer sufficient to keep you here."

With a small sigh, he released Consuela.

"You are free, my flower."

The girl rose slowly, suspicious of her easy escape. Her companion stood and moved swiftly to Consuela. They embraced and moved fearfully away.

Rigo's voice continued in the same casual manner. He looked up at Christoph.

"When I was a young man, younger than any of you, I had the gift of being the better of any man in combat, no matter his prowess."

He looked at each of the three with a significant pause in his narrative. The two youths to either side of Christoph shifted their feet slightly as their discomfort and perhaps as their fear grew. Rigo brought his thumb and forefinger together with only a fraction of an inch gap between.

"I learned," he continued, "that it took only this much more effort to best any foe."

He dropped his hand upon his lap in a gesture of futility.

"At first the lesson was lost upon me. I thought my successes would ultimately end."

He looked at his assailants as if they were his council, awaiting their judgment of his tale. They, however, offered no opinion. Rather, they seemed confused and unsure of his intention.

Christoph shook his head and began to fill, in the silence, but Rigo continued, curtailing any response.

"That little measure, however, never failed."

Rigo looked at them expectantly. His expression was one of innocent revelation. He appeared to be seeking their understanding of the moral of his story. After a moment, his expression changed. His eyes grew harder. His conciliatory tone was replaced with one more suited to the danger of his situation. He seemed to have emerged from his reverie in time to notice that before him were examples of the foes to whom he had just referenced. They were no longer insiders in his council.

Christoph's voice finally found purchase within his mouth.

"Was this measure made up of talking your foes to death?"

Christoph's companions laughed at this sally. Some of the patrons chuckled in spite of themselves.

Rigo did not laugh. His face had not changed. His eyes darkened as a thought troubled him for a moment. He frowned as the thought displeased him.

"Again," he said in a voice troubled with frustration, "a lesson learned. Thank you for pointing out yet another mistake."

Rigo rubbed the tabletop as he shook his head. He pursed his lips with self-loathing.

"I ask your forgiveness for killing you, but this is a door through which I must pass to regain that which I have so recently lost."

With a grunt, Christoph realized his situation. He reached for his pistol just a blink before his companions. Even that was not nearly as rapid as Rigo's movement. The man hunter was instantly rising and pulling his pistol. His hand was a blur. He fired three times before he stood fully. The flame from the muzzle blast appeared as a single flash. Only Christoph's pistol cleared leather. It did not rise beyond the mouth of his holster before it dropped solidly to the ground. The caballeros fell as one.

Rigo looked about him at the shocked faces of the bar patrons as he replaced the empty shells with fresh cartridges. He holstered his pistol, dropped two coins on the table, and strode from the room.

CHAPTER THIRTEEN

Murder

Cab Jackson had been in the saddle for the better part of two days. Much of his time since he was abandoned had been spent scouting for any sign of Hutton's flight from the small village. Even in the darkness, Hutton's trail had been plain for several miles outside of town. The trail sign, however, completely disappeared over a region of smooth rock. He dismounted and traced a circular path. He soon realized, with certainty, that he would have much difficulty finding any trace of the outlaw's trail in the darkness.

He retreated to a stiff juniper copse and bedded down in a cold camp. He feared a fire might serve as a beacon for any who would follow the same tracks by which he had arrived at this place. Sleep eluded him for some time after he laid his head on his saddle. Why had Hutton left him? His absence had been for only a few moments. Hutton must have found some way of returning to the hide out without Cab's detection. They must have encountered some unseen danger at the casa during his trip to the cantina and back.

His thoughts fled at a snapping twig in the thicket beyond his camp. His stolen mare shifted nervously. He dared not breathe as he listened. Before long, he heard the movement of some small animal searching for forage or insects.

He scolded himself for his nervous state of mind. He was not a stranger to the outdoor life, but he had grown accustomed to company over the many weeks with Hutton and he was maladjusted to life in the wilderness alone. Eventually slumber gently lifted him from his fears and thoughts and into an oblivious comfort.

He awoke from a dreamless sleep. The sun was already above the horizon. He quickly saddled the horse and stowed his gear. He had little in his saddle bags.

His only provisions were those remaining in the small pack he had reclaimed that night from the dark room. Upon Hutton's departure for the irresistible attraction of the cantina, he had collected a few food items from Juliana's pack for the certain vigil they would endure while awaiting Hutton's return. Juliana's lighter weight warranted her animal's carrying the group's provisions. They had enjoyed a light meal before he closed the pack and laid it on the bed table.

He swallowed some hard tack then bit into a half of one of Hutton's biscuits. He shook his head as he chewed. The chief had few redeeming qualities, but his biscuit making was a sure winner on the trail. He carefully wrapped the remaining food in the pack and returned it to the saddle bag.

Cab mounted then returned to the smooth rock shelf where he had lost the trail the previous night. He circled the perimeter, making wide detours for scrub juniper groves and large boulders. After a full circuit of the shelf's perimeter, he found no trail sign. He came upon a game trail some yards away. Perhaps the packed surface had resisted hoof prints. This he would follow in the hope that the chief had selected that route.

He travelled without sign of his companions for two days. He was no tracker, and he finally gave up the search with a grim reluctance. He convinced himself that he had been abandoned on purpose. He could not fathom a reason for the betrayal, but much of what Hutton did was a mystery to him.

He travelled without an aim for several days after abandoning his search. Afternoon was nearing its end when he topped a rise. Below was a small house. He was elated to see a tendril of smoke floating above a rough stone chimney in the still air. A warm meal and company would do much to lift his flagging spirits.

He scanned the sparse clearing upon which the cabin was built. He saw no sign of movement outside nor within. He dismounted and led the horse towards a stand of scrub brush and trees closest to the house, but still outside the clearing.

Uncertain why, other than a more frequently present sense of caution, he felt it wise to secret his horse and approach stealthily on foot. He hid the mare in the dense grove. The thorny walls of the hiding place were impenetrable, but it contained a low clear area in its center, accessible from only one way. The grasses were down smooth and there were rubbings upon the larger tree trunks.

He supposed this was a deer lair, where the shy animals waited out daylight and poor weather. He tied the mare and she began nosing about for tender grass. He moved back towards the edge of the thicket then followed the tree line to a point where it came closest to the front of the house. He looked about him warily before running across the open area.

He approached the dwelling, his hand resting upon his holstered pistol. He stopped before the little house. He listened carefully before mounting the porch step. He thought he heard a dim shuffling sound from within the cabin. He moved to the front door and stepped to the outside of the door's frame. If a shot was fired through the door, he didn't want to stop it. He knocked, careful to stay away from the thin wood of the door.

"*Ola*," he called with genuine warmth. "I am lost and could use something to eat."

He was sure he heard movement within.

"*Por favor*," he said in a low voice.

The door opened slowly. He looked through the dark crack between the door and the frame. He saw a pair of dark eyes looking up at him. He grinned as he recognized the face of a child.

"Well lookie here" he exclaimed, doffing his hat with a grin. "Where's your mam and pap?"

His good humor fled, and his short hairs tingled, and he looked around with alarm. If the child's folks were away, it wouldn't be for long. The kid was too young to fend for herself and she certainly had not started the cook fire whose smoke he had seen earlier. He moved with purpose, touching his lips with his left forefinger.

"Shh," he said with a smile.

He pressed the door open gently. The little dark-haired girl opened her mouth to protest as she stepped away from the moving door.

"It's okay, little one."

He roughed her hair as he stepped in. He closed the door looking about him. The cabin was crude but well kept. He sensed a woman's hand in the arrangement of things. No man would keep fresh cut wildflowers in a delicate vase, out of place next to a rough clay pitcher in the middle of the home-made table. He inhaled the flowers' sweet fragrance and the stronger irresistible aromas of food cooking in a pot over the fire. He moved to the pot and bent low to smell the delicacies within.

He had no sooner taken this pose than the back door opened with a scrape, and a thin-limbed, dark eyed beauty entered with an armload of firewood. Both he and the woman looked at one another for a moment before she dropped the billets with a low moan. Cab held out his hands before him.

"*Con permisso, senorita,*" he said in his poor Spanish. "*Comida por favor.*"

She rattled off something in Spanish he could not decipher. Her fear gradually evolved into anger, her words built her courage, as the wood was meant to build her cooking fire. Her Spanish torrent gained power as her own words served as a bellows for her heightening rage.

Cab tried to interject politely one time then a second. In despair, he drew his pistol and trained it upon her with pursed lips and a grim shake of his head. Her eyes widened in fear and her diatribe ceased, leaving the room in troubled silence.

"That'll be plenty, ma'am," Cab said with a finality which could not be misunderstood. "Go over yonder" he said, gesturing with the pistol and shovel some of them frijoles onto a plate and behave yourself."

She hesitated uncertainly. Whether she understood or not, she had only a very few options from which to choose. She moved towards the fire hopeful that word frijoles meant to him what it meant to her. She spooned steaming beans and carne onto a plate. She lifted a tortilla from the hot stone and handed the plate over to him, fully extending her arm to maintain her distance.

He gestured for her to sit at the table and took a seat opposite her. The little girl tucked in closely under her mother's arm and watched the stranger with wide eyes. He ate greedily, his hunger urgently compelling him. In moments he had emptied the plate. He rubbed the plate clean with the thick tortilla. A pitcher next to the flower vase in the center of the table was nearly full of water. He poured a stone cup full of the fresh cool water and downed it to kill the heat of the spicy beans.

During his feeding, he had lost focus upon his company as his being was concentrated upon alleviating his hunger pangs. The warmth of the meal and the contentment of a full belly settled him. He again took stock of the two before him. Mother and daughter weathered the scrutiny for a long interval before his attention went abroad to the cabin and its contents. He saw a lever action carbine hooked above the front door of the cabin. A sturdy rocking chair sat nearby within comfortable range of the cooking fire. Upon the rockers were scars from the broad rowels of Spanish spurs. Cab smiled at the thought of the cruelty inflicted by the Mexican who wore them. Those spurs had been the spoiling of many a good horse.

'Mexican bravado,' he thought, shaking his head.

He was certain of one thing. There was a man of the house, and he was a danger. The rifle over the door for quick access, spurs worn in the house even in repose, a beautiful woman and small child left un-attended: all these facts indicated a man of action, confident in the safety of his loved ones, guaranteed by his reputation.

His gaze returned to mother and daughter. They awaited his next move, dread plainly apparent, fear in their eyes and in the hunch of their burdened shoulders. He stood, demonstrating a grave manner he did not feel. He was enjoying the theatre of the moment. He had decided to leave, but it was in his nature to have a bit of fun at their expense. He looked at the two with feigned consternation. Although frightened, he was certain the fiery Mexican woman would take any opportunity to arm herself with any weapon or utensil at hand. He considered her for a moment.

"You are one hell of a handsome woman," he admitted aloud.

She glared blankly in return. It seemed English was useless around her.

His mind moved towards his departure. He didn't want the fiery Latina to arm herself and shoot him in the back when he left. If he sent her outside again, he could gain a bit of time to return to his horse and beat a hasty retreat. He would keep the daughter with him inside, then when she left, he would leave silently. This would buy him more time. He pointed towards the back door.

"*Vamonos*," he said.

She looked at the door and hesitated, clutching her daughter to her.

He gestured with the pistol for emphasis.

She rose slowly, searching his eyes for some sign of his intent. He again pointed at the door. She took the child's hand and began to lead her in the indicated direction.

"No," he said. "Only you. She stays."

He gestured with his left hand as he instructed her.

She grasped his meaning immediately. Her voice rose in protest.

Cab's playful intent was reverting to impatience. He experienced an acute feeling of time passing. His instincts told him the longer he delayed, the more he risked a confrontation with the roweled Mexican warrior. His full belly no longer demanded risky behavior from him.

"Alright," he acquiesced to her protests. "Take her too."

He indicated the little girl who looked at him curiously. As he watched the youngster, he saw her eyes change. Her attention was drawn elsewhere. He looked at the mother. She also seemed distracted. He had less than a second to ponder what caused the change in them before he heard a barely discernable, almost musical sound. He thought perhaps the wind had risen and was disturbing some metallic object hanging on the porch. He saw the little girl look cautiously at her mother.

"*El Torito*," she whispered. Her mother's eyes darkened under furrowed brows.

"Shh, *nina*," she breathed. She looked up at Cab in alarm.

"The little bull," he said to no one in particular.

He directed the full focus of his faculties upon the sound. The jingling grew in volume.

"That's the sound of dolled up tack," he said finally.

The two didn't understand his words. The lovely *senorita's* face changed by degrees. She looked at him with what he understood to be a small evil smile. He could tell she anticipated his demise in the growing sound of the approaching rider.

Cab looked about him more by rote than to actually gather information. He already knew there was no place to hide in the simple cabin. He felt a reluctance to engage the approaching foe in battle. He attempted to comfort himself in assigning his reluctance to his current good humor and not fear of the approaching warrior. He was not familiar with the rider nor his prowess in battle, but he felt no desire to take a life unnecessarily if he could avoid it.

The tinkling of metal was soon joined by the distinct thuds of heavy hoof beats. He guessed that the rider was mere rods away. The rider's noises grew more distinct with closer proximity. He could hear the creak of saddle leather. His jaw lowered. The muscles beneath worked as he came to a decision about his next move. He raised the heavy pistol and pointed it at the mother. He indicated the chair from which she had just stood.

"Sit," he commanded in a low but forceful tone.

She obeyed, but he sensed none of her previous fear. She seemed, at some level, to enjoy his predicament.

Outside, he heard the rider halt his mount then a heavy boot hit the ground. Footsteps approached then mounted the rough porch floorboards just outside the door. The floor planks vibrated as the rider stomped dust from his boots on the low porch. Spurs jangled in protest to the rough treatment. Cab heard the horse toss his head with the tinkling of ornate bridle adornment.

The door opened and a broadly built man with thick mustaches entered. He held a heavy rifle in one hand and saddle bags in the other. He smiled as he looked expectantly for the mother and daughter. He halted when they did not rise to meet him with raucous welcome. His visage darkened suddenly at the trouble in her face. He dropped the saddle bags and moved to bring the rifle into a ready position.

"Hey, Mexican."

Cab barked the words as he cocked his pistol, training it steadily at the man's face. The rifle froze on its journey towards the ready. A tense moment passed with Cab tightening his grip upon his pistol. The Mexican's jaw muscles working in fury and frustration. Finally, the little warrior relaxed his arm. The rifle and saddle bags lowered towards his thigh.

"On the floor."

Cab gestured with the pistol barrel.

The man obeyed, placing the weapon and bags carefully as instructed.

The Mexican raised his eyes to meet Cab's. He spoke to him in heavily accented English.

"I would speak to your foolishness in being here, on this day, but I don't talk to the dead."

His voice was low, and his accent cluttered the words.

Cab shrugged.

"You got tolerable bad timing, amigo."

Cab glanced at the two seated at the table.

They watched the two men with stony attention.

Cab gestured to the man to join the mother and daughter. The man shook his head and obeyed, taking the remaining seat.

"This here can end a couple of ways," Cab explained. "The worst for you would be dead."

He moved closer and scooped up the rifle from the floor, never taking his eyes from his man.

"The preferred way is that you stay sitting with your wife and kid and I ease on out the door, no one the wiser."

The man of the mustaches shook his head in what seemed genuine sadness.

"*Senor*, this is not my wife and daughter. I am brother-in-law to the woman and uncle to the child. It is not my leave you require. My brother will be here soon, and he will not allow you either option you present."

His face split into a stained toothy grin under his thick moustache. A deep laugh rumbled within him. To Cab, although the man's laugh was a pleasing baritone, it was an unpleasant affirmation of his predicament. He felt certain this man could handle himself in a rough situation. He recalled the child's words when she heard the man approaching from outside. She had called him *El Torito* – the little bull.

Cab felt a sense of rising dread. One such man, even held captive, was formidable indeed. The potential of one fiercer and more deadly, added to this current foe, was a dragging weight upon his flagging courage. He felt a surge of anxiety growing within him. He needed to beat a hasty retreat before the husband arrived.

The 'little bull' seemed to read his very thoughts.

"You decide to use your head too late."

He canted his head slightly. His eyes focused beyond the walls of the cabin.

"He approaches."

Cab listened intently but could hear nothing more than the hiss of his straining ears. His frustration rose.

"You ain't gonna rattle me, greaser. Option one is gainin' purchase every time you open your mouth."

"You are rattled already," the man said with a fearless grin. He had emphasized the word 'rattled" due to its unfamiliarity.

Cab considered the man's manner more than his words. Did he seem so ineffectual and benign that his captive would fail to register fear of any sort?

A dark rage rose from his shrinking heart. He had never felt shame as he did now. He recognized in this brazen Mexican a superiority to himself. His pride and his spirit railed against the dark shame, but more particularly, the impressive disregard of the little warrior.

Although most who knew him thought him affable and enjoyed his humor, Cab felt that his true strength of will and his abilities as a fighting man were rarely given credence. He allowed those qualities he perceived within himself to remain inside. The 'little bull's' manner brought such doubt of his long-held belief in himself that he feared he had overestimated his worth as a man.

Frustrated anger crowded his chest and caused a low moan to escape him. His courage was indeed on the verge of flight. A new time limit created an urgency within him to act. He knew in his soul this man was as much a danger to him unarmed and seated at the table as he was to him as captor, standing and armed. The realization dawned upon him that if given enough time, he would be overcome by this man.

Cab's eyes focused from his introspection to full attention upon his prisoner. He started at the look that was returned. The man demonstrated amusement at his discomfiture. He seemed to know what Cab was thinking. A suspicion grew that he was being read like a track in muddy ground. Cab felt blood heat his face. His heart restricted with fear and anger consumed him.

'Little Bull's' arm moved on the table as he shifted his weight.

Cab's flinched and his pistol belched flame. The concussion pounded the close atmosphere of the small cabin. A red stain spread across and down the man's chest. He fell heavily with a grunt.

The woman screamed and the child wailed. Mother fell from her chair upon her knees beside the fallen man. She lifted his head and held him as best she could. Her wet swollen eyes glared at Cab. She yelled at him. Her voice trailed off in a wail of despair.

He could not understand her words, but he held no misgivings in their meaning. The pistol sagged in his hand as he watched the life fade from this vibrant and charismatic character. By chance, his eyes met those of the little girl, whose head he had patted in comforting assurance only a few moments past. He felt a shock as he met her gaze.

The child stood stock still, her arms at her side. She looked at him in horror as if he were a wraith or a dark monster. Her expression was unmoving, and her complexion was cast pale. Cab had the impression of the child standing on the rocks of a stormy coast with angry waves and howling winds crashing about her. In his mind's eye she stood alone, oblivious to the melee. She recognized him for what he truly was.

She would never again look into her uncle's face and delight in his mischievous grin and ready wit. She seemed to accept this at once and focused instead upon the destroyer of the greatest love in her young life.

Cab's breath finally came in a rattle of despair. In near panic, he fled from the room before his vision darkened completely. The damning wails of the young woman were nothing more than buzzing in his ringing ears. He craved relief in the cooling breezes of the approaching evening. He slipped upon the porch boards and stumbled past the snorting and prancing black stallion with the silver adorned tack. He felt the breeze, but relief was not upon it.

He ran towards the copse where his horse awaited his return. He heard that sound he knew would precede his death: the low thunder of approaching horses. As he entered the grove, he heard the cabin door slam against the outer wall.

The sound of the woman's scream preceded the heavy report of a rifle shot. She had retrieved the rifle from over the door and was intent upon finding him with a lucky shot. The leaves and twigs in the upper reaches of the thicket snapped as the bullet passed through.

Cab retrieved the reins and clawed his way into the saddle. More bullets probed the branches, this time lower and closer to him. The sound of approaching riders intensified as they freshened their pace in reaction to the gunfire.

He gave the mare his spurs. She jumped away sideways then rushed away from the grove. In two leaps she was fully stretched in flight. The wind snatched at the rider's breath. Her strides lowered her nearer the ground as she reached for more length of pace.

By the time darkness gripped the wilderness though which he rode, Cab had placed several miles between the murder and himself.

CHAPTER FOURTEEN

Dark Stranger

His uniform rasped against his neck. He had been in it since before dawn. It was just past midnight, and he walked a quiet street in Saltillo. His instructions on handling this matter with the governor were clear, but he still resented owing accountability to a state official. His federal credentials and connections were impressive and vast.

He turned into the gate at the perimeter fence of the Governor's residence. The large house was dark and silent. He frowned at the time he anticipated would be wasted on this task. His bed beckoned his tired body and troubled mind. He walked up the stone path then mounted the broad steps to the tall double doors.

He pulled his uniform straight and craned his neck in the stiff salty collar. He straightened his back and rapped mightily upon the door. The door shook under the blow. He focused his attention inward, listening for any movement he may have incited within. He heard nothing for some moments. Then, vaguely, he thought he heard the slight sounds of shuffling footfalls. The door opened only a few inches and he made out a servant who squinted to clear his sleep shrouded eyes.

"*Si, senor?*"

"Wake Don Gonzaba,"

The *mozo* exhaled audibly.

"The Governor is asleep and must not be disturbed."

I will see the Governor at once."

The General's words were uttered in a low but insistent voice.

The *mozo* looked the General up and down then shook his head.'

"It is late, *Senor.*"

The General pressed a hand against the door, opening it so as to reveal the *mozo*.

"This will be as late as you will see in your life if you don't bring the Governor here at once."

The servant held the visitor with doubtful eyes. His fear of the uniformed stranger finally overshadowed his fear of his master's wrath. He beckoned silently and the General entered. The General clasped his hands behind his back and watched the servant mount the long curving staircase until he disappeared through a large ornate doorway.

It seemed a long time before he heard heavy footfalls. These footsteps were too heavy to be those of the servant. Governor Gonzaba rubbed his eyes sleepily as he descended the stairs. His annoyed look dissipated at the serious look on the Generals face.

"Is there news? Is my daughter safe?"

Gonzaba steeled himself for the worst. A visit from the General – this time of night. Nothing good was wrought at this hour.

The General looked at his boots as he collected his words. Finally, he raised his eyes to meet the Governors. For the first time, he saw a father rather than a politician. He could not help but envision his own precious daughter. He could not imagine what the man was experiencing. His voice came strong but with empathetic warmth.

"Rigo Herrera failed to wrest your daughter from her captors."

Gonzaba felt the news as a physical blow. He staggered a fraction. He searched the General's face for any trace of malice. It was he who had advised against Rigo's involvement. There was no trace of pleasure or hint of prepotency in the man. He seemed genuinely troubled to deliver this news. The General continued after a moment.

"He found her and was making his escape when the Americano came upon them. He struggled with the kidnapper but was overcome."

Gonzaba turned as if to escape. He stopped mid-turn then faced the General once again.

"This man is a drunk and base murderer. One such as he could not defeat mighty Rigo Herrera!"

The General looked about him as if searching for words. He cleared his throat. He could not help himself. He said what he believed.

"The mighty Rigo Herrera is growing long in the tooth, Governor."

Gonzaba inhaled sharply as a hot retort rose in his throat. Instead, he sighed and bowed his head. He waved an ineffectual hand, weakly dismissing his angry reaction to the news. He moved slowly to a nearby chair. He sunk onto it as if exhausted.

"Then she is lost."

His voice was barely audible, and it quavered as he voiced his worse fears. He was silent for a long moment.

The General was not certain if their conversation was at an end or not. He remained in his spot: silent, unsure of his next move.

Finally, Gonzaba spoke. His voice regained some of its authority.

"A decree of death is to be placed upon the head of Juliana as well as this marauder."

The General took a step forward. He could not believe he was hearing this proclamation of death on the man's own blood.

Gonzaba snapped his head forward. His transformation was startling. His mouth was twisted in pain. His eyes streamed tears. His brow wrinkled in the anguish of his decision.

The General opened his mouth to protest. Gonzaba sliced at him with a flat palm, as if to cut off any further conversation.

"You will do as I say," he cried loudly. "You will obey my command. Do you understand me?"

The General locked his heels together. All resentment was gone from him. In its place remained only horrified obedience. He nodded soberly.

"Is there anything further, Governor?"

Gonzaba stood slowly. His strength failed him.

"The reward is only for their death. They do not live through the capture."

The General bowed. He turned to leave. Gonzaba crossed to him. The General waited for him. Gonzaba placed a hand on the Generals broad shoulder.

"Make it known that the two are bandits and murderers who travel together as a couple. Say what you must to create the proper fear, so they are not captured alive. If they are questioned the truth would cause trouble."

The General considered Gonzaba for a moment. His mind spun with the possibilities of what he heard. He bowed again then turned and left the mansion.

As the big doors closed, Gonzaba collapsed to his knees. Sobs wracked his entire frame. The hiding servants retreated respectfully to the darkness of the inner parts of the residence.

Juliana sat in her blankets, propped against the rough bark of a large tree. The camp was dimly lighted by the gray of the dawn. Her back ached as the rough bark stamped its impression upon her skin under the torn fabric of her dress. She sat facing where Hutton slept silently under his blankets, his back towards her. She had been in this position since well before pink had added pale color to the eastern horizon. Her mind was a torrent of confused anguish. Her memory of the assault upon her the night before had lost none of its edge in her memory. The terror of the unprecedented attack maintained an icy grip upon her heart. As unexplainable as his breaking off the violence against her, she felt a grinding apprehension as to how he would behave when he awoke.

She seldom had the opportunity to see him in repose. He was always busy. Even when he sat at the fire or at a distance from her, he seemed busy with thoughts or action. His sleep was singular in the nature of his rest. He made no sound, nor did he move. Before the advancing morning light allowed her view of her captor, she was unsure that he still occupied the spot to which she had seen him retire the previous night.

Once she was able to see him dimly, she experienced a combination of relief in that he had not moved and disappointment that he still remained with her. In her mind, if he had moved his sleeping location during the night, he might have done so as part of an intent to visit some other strange punishment upon her. His departure from camp might have been welcome if his startled reaction had culminated as a more permanent response in abandoning her.

Considering what she knew of the aberrations which haunted his mind, she had considered his departure a viable option. Her active musings drew her further as she surmised his unnatural stillness as a possible result of deadly fear taking him in his sleep.

She had sat watching him for some time: long enough, now, that she was beginning to struggle with the impulse to rise and check him for signs of life. A light breeze rustled the leaves in the trees as the rising sun caused a disturbance in the air. The small variance in the atmosphere with the coming dawn disturbed the sleeper. He moved under the blankets. Juliana noticed she had stopped breathing when she realized he was fully awake. Although his back was to her, she felt the familiar sense of his omnipresent awareness as he detected her as well as the natural surroundings. He did not move, other than a light stirring, but she was certain he was aware of all around him.

He sat upright, his blankets falling to his lap. He remained facing away from her. His hair was disheveled, and he ran his fingers through it, more to rub his scalp than to adjust his coif. Suddenly, his hands ceased their movement and dropped to his sides. He stood in a motion, leaving the blankets disregarded in a heap. He approached the horses. She saw him sneak a glance in her direction, quickly averting his eyes after ascertaining her position. His manner was likened to a schoolboy sneaking a glimpse at a pretty classmate.

Juliana felt no coy flattered reaction to the look. He was no schoolboy, and this was not a classroom. He was reacting to whatever demons still possessed his imagination from the night before. Whatever had saved her from his onslaught previously was not expressed in his actions now. She felt real fear of his summary decision once the comforting light of day renewed his resolve.

Boyd stacked tinder upon the dying coals of the starving fire. In a moment flames licked the twigs with a hungry energy. He placed larger sticks upon the flames then placed the rough skillet he kept in her mount's saddle bags upon the blaze.

His gaze didn't again seek her out. Conversely, he seemed to invest much committed labor into avoiding any glimpse of her whatsoever. In the days since Cab's loss, he had assumed the menial camp tasks. She had not been asked to perform any tasks other than those pertaining to her personal needs.

The leader demonstrated an adroit command of the cooking fire. He rolled his sleeves and mixed the white powders in leather pouches with water from his canteen. In moments, he deposited the dough in the skillet. Soon after, the dough rose as golden biscuits. He removed the biscuits then placed strips of hardtack in a small amount of salted lard in the hot pan. The hot lard softened the dried meat and contributed a pleasing flavor. He did not serve her, even prior to the previous night. She rose and filled her tin plate. They ate in silence. He consumed his portion as a wolf gobbles prey. He wiped the plate with a last bit of biscuit then rose and stowed the plate. He swabbed the hot skillet with an oily rag then returned them to their places behind her saddle. He tightened the girth straps on the two horses then moved to his blankets. He rolled them and tied them securely.

She finished her breakfast and quickly gathered her things. He mounted his gelding and moved away. She hesitated in confusion. He typically sat his horse and eyed her in silent impatience until she was mounted and moving. His departing without his typical impatience was new. She was immediately beset by doubt. Should she wait for him to move well away then attempt escape? Was she being released?

Her hopes of salvation ceased as he pulled up at the edge of a line of brush, beyond which he would have lost her to view.

He did not look at her, but sat still, awaiting her approach. He touched his horse with his spurs as she mounted. He disappeared through a gap in the brush. She guided her mount to follow him. She hardly noticed the bramble pulling at her legs as she rode the big gelding through the brush.

Her mind worked with what she knew of the outlaw for an answer to his behavior the previous night, and his subsequent conduct this morning.

She shuddered, shaking her head to clear the memory. She had very nearly been ruined beyond recovery. She was not a virgin since her youth. She and Fermine had explored each other with a clumsy mimicry of youthful innocence. Embraced in the grasses near the bubbling and laughing creek below her house in Saltillo, the act was brief and curiously uncomfortable.

This assault, however, seemed to issue from hatred in the outlaw, not from love and attraction, as with Fermine. The violence, and her helplessness to resist him, was the most horrible aspect of the attack.

She had gone through her life believing she could protect herself in those private moments of dark fantasy of her youth. She had ever imagined how she would respond to a sexual attack.

Hutton's actions that night were nothing like what she had summoned in her horrible imaginings. Unlike her dark fantasy, where she overcame an attacker with a hidden strength of moral superiority, she learned that she was no heroine with an innate inner strength capable of repelling such atrocities. Her physical resistance was less than ineffectual. The big man wasn't slowed by her desperate struggles. He pressed through her defenses with no more than a gesture. His desire — somehow that word placed too much validity to the act — radiated from him. His touch seemed to burn her.

Juliana swallowed a sob. She couldn't allow herself to give the experience more scrutiny. She feared that door would remain ajar if she opened it too wide.

She looked towards him warily. She could easily observe his manner this morning in the security of his limited attention towards her. Although unclear from where her succor had originated, her attacker had been vanquished. Whatever he had seen or felt which stayed him, he suffered a lasting effect which demanded he keep his distance.

His imprisonment of her seemed, at present, more implied than enforced. She was certain he would revert to his normal state of impending violence if she tested her theory and attempted escape. She sensed the pall, from which he seemed to suffer, was kept close at hand more for his curiosity of the unfamiliar, rather than its holding any transformative power over his ferocity.

She lifted her head from her reverie and carefully searched the broad back of her captor. She hated these moments when she assigned understood and accepted values to a man who had countless times exhibited more animal instinct than the sensibilities of a man. Her thoughts were arrested as he turned in the saddle and held her with a curious gaze. Apparently, his mind was also at work in relation to the strange events of the previous night. His eyes held her for some moments before he turned again and gave his attention to the trail.

As they rode, the sun warmed her back as it climbed higher. Juliana had the sense they were ascending into a higher altitude. The incline was slight but unmistakable. Her knowledge of their location was sketchy at best. They had ridden much at night during her captivity, and she had no skill in reading the stars. She was certain they headed east towards a far mountain range. The mountains appeared blue and dim in the distance. She guessed they were the Western Sierra Madres. If so, they had travelled far. Her gaze again focused on the leader's back. Where was he taking her? Did he have a plan, or did they wander aimlessly? This daily progression towards a destination unknown to anyone but Hutton was the effort of many weeks, possibly more than two months to date. She had long since lost any reasonable accounting of the days.

As the Sun reached its Zenith, Hutton called a halt at a narrow stream where amber waters danced over smooth rocks. They dismounted and rested upon lush cool grass. He produced hard tack and an oilskin containing his ever-present biscuits. They ate in silence, drinking from the clear water of the spring

Each time she rose to drink or just to relieve stiffness in her muscles from the ride, his eyes searched her with an open curiosity. She felt some discomfort in that he seemed oblivious to any feeling of comportment. Where most would limit their scrutiny to brief periods with a break for a natural courtesy to the subject, he seemed to have no such modesty. His gaze never wavered, as if he were inspecting an object or pressing his vision to see some far away, almost invisible detail.

As the Sun surrendered its hold and the early evening began its slow diffusion of the day's intolerable heat, Hutton rose and tightened the girths on their horses. He mounted without preamble and waited for her to follow suit. His demeanor was similar to that of the morning, but he didn't seem as wary of the mystery of her. She mounted obediently and he moved away from the stream, her horse followed without her urging. It seemed even the beast had given itself to the inevitable ceaseless toil of the trek.

They rode well past nightfall. She noticed that once darkness settled over the countryside, Hutton veered south of their easterly path. He continued this deviation for some time before he called a halt. It was clear to her that he was making efforts to evade any who might follow them. As always, he was extremely sensitive to danger at close quarters. She surmised that he was making the tactical move to evade any followers outside his purview.

They set up camp in a small stand of trees nestled at the foot of a low rock shelf. He built the fire and she busied herself with personal comforts. Soon they sat, eating roast rabbit killed with a casual snap shot any marksman would have considered remarkable. Hutton merely holstered the pistol as he moved to collect the bounty of the kill, never looking to her to receive an admiring look. He boiled beans seasoned with the scant fat from the hare. She drank hot coffee and he pulled form his little flask at intervals.

Hutton slowly chewed, looking vacantly into the small fire.

Juliana cleared her throat and set her cup beside her.

"Do you plan to let me go?"

Her voice seemed strangely out of place in this wilderness where no words had passed between them the entire day.

Hutton considered her mildly. He bit into the meat and chewed as he formulated an answer, if indeed his intention was to respond. Finally, he swallowed then drank from his flask.

"I want you to stay."

He said it simply and without passion.

Juliana felt the same frustration she always felt at his vague and noncommittal statements.

He looked at her for a moment then leaned in a bit.

"You don't know how I feel about you. It ain't important that you do."

He chuckled. The sound was unfamiliar, and Juliana swallowed a knot of mounting fear building in her throat. She was feeling a foreboding of a recurrence of the previous night's conversation.

He drank deeply from his flask then corked it.

"I never looked at any woman as more than bed lining or a cook."

He leaned forward and spoke in a lower more sincere tone.

"You fascinate me, Juliana. Everything you do is interesting to me."

He had never called her by name before and the sound of it seemed strange. How comfortably he uttered it. She ventured a question from within her doubt.

"You think you love me?"

He leaned back and watched her. She made a point to continue her thought as gently as she could. She feared his reaction to her words.

"Do you make all you love a prisoner?"

Boyd considered her for a moment. He seemed to give the question some weight. Finally, he shook his head and replied in an equally mild tone.

"Let's just say I don't kill 'em. Maybe you can appreciate that proof."

His humor was lost upon Juliana.

"Then why don't you let me go? If you love someone you make them happy. I am not happy."

Her words came with unintended force and hinted at her frustration.

"You don't know me yet. When you do, you may feel different."

His words were dismissive of her passionate retort.

Juliana looked at him in dismay and utter disbelief at his disregard for their reality. His commitment to his fantasy view of their relationship and why they remained together eluded any reason she could fathom.

A bitter laugh escaped her. Even her fear could not stay her incredulity.

"You do live in your own world, Boyd Hutton."

The big man started slightly.

"I didn't know you knew my name. Cab must have..."

His humor dimmed at the thought of their lost comrade. He studied the ground before him as he searched for his words. Suddenly his head came up and she could fairly feel his senses tingle.

"What do you hear?" she whispered.

"Hush," he said holding out a hand in a gesture meant to silence her. "We ain't alone anymore. Stay close and calm."

Suddenly she heard the sharp sound of a bullet entering his flesh followed immediately by the report of a rifle from the dark of the surrounding wilderness. Hutton collapsed with a groan.

She crossed to him and sat beside him, looking in the direction from which the rifle report had issued. The darkness was complete and there was no moon to give any light whatsoever. She looked towards Hutton's pistol belt and rifle atop his saddle at a distance from them.

"Don't make a move towards that pistol belt, *Senorita.*"

The voice was rough and there was a menace in the stern warning. Juliana thought there might have been a tinge of fear in that command. Her thoughts changed direction when a tall man in chaps and a black vest entered the light of the fire, rifle and gimlet eyes firmly fixed upon the big outlaw. Hutton moved to rise but failed to complete the movement.

The dark stranger looked away from his victim and strode towards Juliana. He grabbed her and pulled her roughly to her feet. She wasn't sure how to treat this new menace. Was he another assailant or a rescuer? He pulled her close and surveyed her face.

"Your father is a black hearted fiend, wanting you dead."

Juliana felt the blood drain from her ears and her cheeks grew hot. Her confusion mounted. Her feeling of growing betrayal gradually replaced her swirling thoughts.

The man continued, speaking more about her than to her.

"You are one fine woman. I ain't gonna waste you. The reward is mine but so are you."

He lay his rifle against a nearby stump, her arm grasped firmly in his left hand. He pushed her down to the ground and began ripping at her clothes. She tried to resist but he was as strong as Boyd. She knew he wouldn't stop for some vision or mental aberration as Boyd had. She felt her skin cool where her ripped clothing left her bare.

He leered at her and put his mouth to her neck and shoulders. He loosened his grip on her as he moved one hand to open his trousers. She moved violently to the side, and he lost his hold upon her. She scrambled to all fours and moved legs and arms, desperately trying to make for the darkness. Her assailant grunted his surprise then leaped to catch her. He grasped the end of her tattered dress and the fabric tore leaving him holding only a handful of cloth. The delay, however allowed him to gain his feet and his long arm shot out and he landed a blow to her back. She fell, off balance.

Instantly, he was on her once again. His breathing was fast and ragged with the effort and his desire. She was on her stomach and could not fight him. Her dress ripped again, and she felt his bare skin against her bare back side. He shoved her down and pressed her face into the dirt. His legs pinned her legs under a painful weight. He lowered himself down reaching between her legs.

A sound like a muffled chunk and a clank of metal on bone stopped his actions. She felt him shudder then he fell aside, his breeches around his thighs. She rolled away from him and ran into Hutton almost toppling him. The big man was on his knees. His head sagged to his breast and his eyes seemed unable to focus.

"Keep your goddam dick to yourself."

With that he fell on his back with a groan.

"Boyd," she cried, pressing her hands against the wound. "Oh my God."

The last was a wail.

She set her teeth against the sight as she ripped his shirt using the bullet hole for purchase for the tear. She used the torn shirt as wadding as she applied pressure to the little hole. She was surprised at the lack of blood at the penetration. She guessed the bullet was blocking the flow. She knew enough about wounds that she was sure of two things. The first was that if he were not bleeding outwardly from the gunshot, he was certainly bleeding inside. Internal bleeding was worse than blood flowing out. She didn't know why, but it seemed she had learned this fact somewhere during her life. The second thing was that the bullet had to come out or he risked poisoning from the slug. Again, she did not know how she knew this. Both facts may be moot if the shot had struck his vital organs. She shook Hutton roughly.

"Boyd. You cannot die. I am alone here."

She shook him again desperately.

"Boyd!"

The big man did not move, nor did he seem to be breathing. She pressed her ear to his breast and listened. All she could hear was her own excited breathing. She tried to hold her breath so she could hear. She thought she detected shallow breathing and even the murmur of his heartbeat. She could not hold her breath long in her current state and she inhaled audibly as she allowed herself to breathe again.

With a start, she turned her attention to the dark stranger. He lay on his side, Boyd's large knife buried to the haft in his neck. The haft of the knife was at an angle where the blade had obviously entered the victim's body in a downward direction. The blade had likely severed tissue and possibly the lungs, stopping only where bone prevented the steel further entry. The man was not breathing, and a large wet muddy puddle of blood grew around the body. She doubted this man would rise again from his wound as Hutton had.

CHAPTER FIFTEEN

Alone

There was no storm of unbridled emotion. He felt no need to justify his actions. Regret occupied no place in his heart. Cab wondered at the clarity through which he perceived his current situation. His desperate flight from the cabin seemed a long time ago. The confusion of frenzied emotions had plagued him only briefly. The mare chewed up miles and left his decent sensibilities behind them.

This was not the first time he had shot a man. The posse where they captured Juliana held that distinction. He did not believe he had killed any of the men he might have shot that night. If he had, though, his victims were armed and prepared for the dangers for which they had enlisted. Through the darkness he could not have been sure of his targets. Before the murder of *El Torito*, not knowing was a weak but effective insulation to a killing. Considering his latest deed, he was now certain that he would have known.

This kill registered with him as if a harbinger had engraved the deed upon the granite that resides within him and every man. Some things could not be forgiven nor washed away. Murder, he now knew, was chief among those indelible deeds. Moral code, conscience, religion, and the laws of men stay the hand. How easy it was to cross the line. Cab marveled at how all men teeter so closely to the brink of the abyss. A single gesture had sent him beyond the boundary of moral conduct. In contrast, it was much more difficult to resist the seduction of such power than to surrender to it. He understood true freedom now. He was unfettered by the restraining iron grip morality exerted upon most men.

The morning dawned gray. A light mist dampened his clothing and freshened his skin. There was a thrill of freedom in his soul. He had read once that "Under the loftiest monuments sleeps the dust of murder," Cab shook his head with a grim smile. He appreciated the irony as he recalled his father's relentless efforts to educate him. He never understood that part of Ingersoll's writings until now. Cab was certain that true power was that which yields maximum results with the smallest of efforts. A twitch of his finger had summoned from his man everything he had ever known, loved or achieved.

Fear, however, was very real. His was not the fear of dread or panic. His fear was no more than a survival instinct within him. He seemed to have added an additional sensory ability. His fear was a warning mechanism. The accompanying jolt of nervous energy which served to heighten his senses did not fetter him with paralyzing terror. That jolt compelled him towards desperate acts of which he would have been unlikely to perform, or at best, he would have only flung himself into before. Now he occupied a region as if travail and difficulty were a normal environment. He felt somehow equal to any task.

The pursuit had dogged him throughout the night. These Mexican devils seemed able to see in the darkness as well as he could see in daylight. He lamented his inability to create an adequate trail problem. He was a novice. All he knew of trail deception was gained from observation of Hutton on the trail. Much of what he gleaned was guessed at. The big outlaw was not given to explanations nor instruction.

His round-abouts and switchbacks had realized only short intervals of silence giving a respite to the distant sounds of pursuit which drove him. Those respites lasted no more than an hour or more before the rumble of hooves and the crackling of yielding underbrush again dogged him.

He looked around him. The dingy glow of dawn hardly improved his visibility. He listened for any sound of approaching riders. He was just beyond a rocky expanse which he had crossed with difficulty. His trek over the hard shale had been alarmingly noisy and clumsy. He anticipated the same racket from his pursuers' trek over the same terrain. Surprisingly, he heard no sound whatsoever. Even the wildlife seemed poised, silently awaiting the inevitable conflict between hunters and quarry.

Cab looked ahead towards the pale gray lightening horizon. The terrain lifted gradually to a region of taller grasses and greater numbers of trees and low bushes. He stopped breathing. Did he see movement? His instincts were taut with fear. Had the pursuers circled the hazardous rocks? He snapped from his reverie and jumped from the saddle. He withdrew the rifle from its scabbard and crouched low. He looked about him for cover. He saw no growth nor rocks behind which to hide. To his left he saw a slight defilade.

He grabbed the reins and drew his horse towards the depression. He led the horse quickly into the low area. He was pleased to discover that the area deepened and widened until he and his horse were securely hidden below a protecting embankment. He dropped the reins and continued along his current path.

He wasn't sure of what he had seen. It might have been nothing more than a bird descending from a tree branch. His instincts told him otherwise. He made his way along what turned out to be a seasonal creek bed. Soft silt muffled his footsteps. The sky brightened rapidly as the rising sun displaced the cool darkness with a lovely promise of a bright and pleasant day.

These features were lost to him in his concentrated efforts upon his investigation of the movement. More accurately, the added hazard of improved visibility troubled him. He was outnumbered in unfamiliar territory. If the pursuers knew the region well enough to circle a known hazard, could they not also know his location as a most likely hiding spot?

Cab gripped the rifle firmly. He considered several options. He could return to his horse and attempt to locate a more defendable refuge. He dismissed this option. His previous survey had been thorough. He had seen nothing more secure than the ravine upon which he decided. Although hidden now, it the hunters had indeed lost him, they would certainly deduce that his progress had halted nearby. They would retrace their steps and ultimately search the creek bed. His time was limited. His remaining course was an offensive maneuver. He had no choice but to move ahead and hope his aggressive tactic would be unexpected and perhaps yield some measure of surprise.

He looked about him once more, then continued stealthily along the silty bottoms. He was pleased that the creek bed quartered south towards where he had seen the movement. He was certain at some point that he would have to abandon the comparative safety of the draw for a more vulnerable path over open country. Fortune was with him in that he could maintain a concealed approach for a time.

Noise behind him caused him to leap against the sheer wall beside him. He trained the rifle towards the sound. He listened intently. He heard muffled voices. They had found his horse.

His mind raced. The silt was an ally when it deadened the sounds of his movement. That same ally was now a foe. His tracks were plainly visible. The hunters would easily follow them straight to him. In an instant he decided his next move. He quickly surveyed the embankment. It was too sheer to climb, and the soft sides would crumble if he tried. He again faced his original direction of travel. He sprinted along the wall. The creek bed turned abruptly towards the south. He could now see the draw made a roughly straight course ahead for many yards. The banks grew lower where flood waters were free to flow and did not cut into the earth as they had where the terrain channeled the water away from its natural course.

He climbed the bank where it lowered to a level just above his head. He jumped to his feet and doubled back towards the inevitable pursuit. He hoped the hunters would follow his tracks along the stream bed giving him the advantage of higher ground. He heard muffled reports of approaching horses' hooves. He levered a shell into the rifle breach and moved towards the high embankment. Four riders rounded the bend. He shot the first pursuer mid torso. The rider grunted and bent low over the saddle horn. Cab levered another round and shot another rider who pulled up hard at the shot. The two remaining riders retreated around the bend.

Cab ran forward but stayed back from the bank. He felt sure weapons would be at the ready and trained upon the nearest vantage above. He covered nearly 50 yards before he risked a look into the draw. The two remaining hunters were dismounted, weapons trained precisely as Cab had expected. He killed the nearest man with an easy shot. The other dove from his cover and sent a snap shot in Cab's direction. The bullet narrowly missed him. The gunman was skilled. Cab sent another shot near the gunman's hiding place. He turned and fled towards where he had left his mount.

Although the morning was bright and beautiful, Juliana's thoughts were dark. She had not the will to fight any longer. She had seen so much death.

The last words of the gunman seared her memory. "Your father is a black hearted fiend wanting you dead."

A reward on her head? Dead? She could not bring herself to believe it. She felt her eyes burn. Tears flooded her vision.

"Papa," she wailed.

She clenched her fists and looked around her. Her fate was not in her hands. Her eyes rested on the prostrate figure of her captor. She rose. With a scream she rushed to the unconscious man. She closed his throat in her hands. His shallow breathing stopped within her grip.

Her words hissed through set teeth.

"The death you deserve..."

He did not resist. He was not there. He dwelled somewhere beyond this place. Her aggression was visited upon an inert vessel. She slowly released his throat and stood. Her anger railed at her. It burned within her, seeking escape. There was no satisfaction in her assault upon the man if he did not suffer.

She returned to the campfire. She felt an urge to prepare breakfast. She realized the impulse was an attempt to escape her mental agony through activity. She was not hungry. She sunk down upon the log where she had sat when they were attacked. Her gaze fell upon the dark patches where Boyd and the attacker had bled onto the soft soil. Her attention was naturally drawn to a nearby copse of bushes. The gunman's body lay within the shrubbery where she had dragged him. Several hours had passed in his lurid company before she finally mustered the courage to move him beyond her sight. The effort was as arduous as it was horrifying. When she pulled him far enough away, she ran from the corpse to the preferable company of the senseless Hutton.

Tenuous life clung within him offering her scant comfort in her lone vigil. Even his still presence, so close to death, caused her eventually to drag Hutton a short way from the fire, to the foot of a nearby tree. The idea of him dying at her side during the night was unnerving. Her efforts failed to comfort her. The combination of the dead, the real possibility that she was to be alone in this wilderness, her torturous thoughts, and those unseen dangers dwelling beyond the firelight, kept sleep from her.

The thin pale line of dawn's advent could not have come sooner to suit her. The lightening eastern horizon scattered the devilish imps at play about her tortured imagination.

Presently, in the full light of day, she watched Hutton, waiting for life to finally leave him. She detected slight movement where he drew shallow breaths.

Again, her heart ached at the thought of her father's betrayal. There was no other label for his abandonment. It seemed only recently she had sat beside him amidst the festivities, both voicing their mutual love and admiration. What agency of change had moved him away from her and to the enemy camp? What did he believe of her to give up on her rescue? Again, tears fought her. She despised her weakness. Finally, with a low moan, she surrendered to it.

"What do I do?" she asked of Hutton. "Wait with you until you die? Leave you here and hope a rescue party finds me before Indians or bounty hunters do. Is there no hope I can talk to them, or would they not shoot me on the spot?"

The man who now lay dead just beyond her camp had given her no opportunity for explanation or entreaty. Her reason told her she would not fare any better with any of those seeking treasure for her death.

She shuddered and her tears flowed freely. Sobs wracked her frame. Her despair was overwhelming. She knew not why, but her thoughts went to Cab Jackson. She did not believe him dead. What had become of him? She missed his company. Where was he now? If alive, had he heard of her assignment as fugitive?

Cab mounted his horse and sent the mare up the dim path out of the creek bed. He glanced over his shoulder as he gained level ground. The surviving pursuer did not appear immediately. Cab moved the mare away from the winding draw at a shallow angle, careful not to show his back to eminent danger.

The skilled gunman was likely the older brother of "*El Torito*," Although leaping to cover blindly, he had twisted his body like a panther and brought his pistol to bear on Cab's position with incredible control. It seemed reasonable that a man with his reflexes and ability with a gun would garner the devilish pride and sure confidence of the woman in the cabin.

The sparse tree line grew nearer. Cab touched spur to the mare's flank and, with flattened ears at this treatment, she quickly placed a copse of low trees between them and the unseen pursuer. This hunter was clever and knew the terrain. Cab had not seen nor heard the four men until the horses gave away their position. He was certain danger was near, and it would arrive from an unknown direction. As he turned the mare back in a lateral direction, reverse to their last course, his mind worked.

What would this clever gunman expect him to do? What did he know about Cab that would guide his judgement? Cab's teeth clicked together at the answer. He remembered the fear he felt in the younger brother's presence. He recalled the knowing grin of recognition *El Torito* had leveled upon him – the mocking words.

"You are rattled already,"

With a low growl in his throat, he turned the little horse back towards the ravine where he had last seen the man. He kept the mare at speed as he entered the draw at the exact spot where he had left it. The mare slipped on the silty ravine bottoms. She righted herself and they sped down the stream bed. They drove around a slight bend and the mare ran headlong into the mounted gunman. Both horses and riders fell hard to the ground, rolling and tumbling, tossing sand into the air.

Cab gained his feet, gun in hand. The Mexican lay on the ground. He groaned and brought a hand to his face, trying to clear his head. The horses flailed dangerously as they gained their footing.

Cab kept the man covered as he approached. He limped slightly, injured from the impact of his fall. The gunman watched him approach through squinting eyes. Cab came to within a rod of the man.

"So now you kill me like you killed my brother?"

His voice was surprisingly steady and calm.

Cab looked into the man's eyes with a blank stare. He felt the pistol buck in his hand and the gunman was dead. He turned and mounted the mare as she snorted and danced nervously from her recent fall. He tightened his knees, and she took up her work once again.

Juliana's efforts to keep life within Hutton had become more than a moral duty to her. The effort occupied her. Determination and commitment to her mission was as consuming as it was peculiar. The battle for her sensibilities raged on within her, although the conflict now occupied a region just below her conscious efforts. Juliana made Hutton as comfortable as she could. She marveled at the man's will to live. She had seen few gunshot wounds in her life, but this seemed grievous. The bullet must have barely missed his heart and lungs. His heartbeat was weak but steady, and his breathing came without a catch or the wet rattle of blood.

Juliana stood from her place next to Hutton. Again, the urge to mount one of the horses and flee consumed her. She felt her breathing quicken and her pulse race. Escape had been her ardent desire for days now. Her chance to act immediately seemed a cruel trap. She felt tears again crowd her eyes. She had horses and the opportunity to escape. Her courage failed her once more.

She moved to the waning fire. She gathered her few cooking appliances and organized them atop a rock nearby. She rose and stretched her back. She ached a little from the cold and from the strain of emotional tension. She wiped her eyes. She detected the color of clothing among the taller grasses just beyond her camp. The dead man had begun to reek. The smell of death was a pall upon the camp.

It was clear she would have to defy the horror she felt. Just the act of looking in that direction gave her a strange rushing sharp rush deep within her. She felt its presence in every moment.

It would not do to have a dead man nearby for a number of reasons. The smell had grown intolerable. The last few nights, she had awakened to the sound of animals rustling in the brush near the body. Most compelling was the chilling aspect of the exposed dead embodied in her mind as a specter, haunting the camp.

She went to Hutton's saddle where a shovel was tied for private business. He was insistent on burying waste.

He once told Cab, 'Play the cat and cover your shit. It draws flies and followers.'

She returned to her place before the dishes, shovel hanging from an arm. Dread crept in. She didn't want to go near the dead man. She knew the body would be ghastly. She looked left. The horses stood together, their view taking in both the dead man and her. Even the horses felt fear.

She rubbed the ground with a toe as she screwed up her courage. Finally, she lurched forward. Her momentum brought her quickly upon the body. She winced and her throat tightened. He lay on his back, sightless eyes to the sky. The knife must have become dislodged during her efforts to move the body. The eyes were hard to look at. The pupils seemed glazed over and the face hung slack. One arm lay next to him, the other lay stretched past his head where she had dragged him. The finger of the splayed arm pointed beyond. The finger seemed to indicate where he wanted to be buried to her prickly imagination. Juliana knew this was nonsense, but she felt haunted by the wishes of the dead man. He appeared to have been fed upon perhaps by one of the creatures she had heard rustling during the night.

She moved to a point in the indicated direction and sunk the spade into the ground. She was thankful that the tool went to the hilt easily. She needed to bury him as deeply as she could. The shovel was not a familiar tool to her. Her digging with it had been no more than a couple of dips in the ground then returning the displace earth. The grave would be more difficult.

She labored for some time before she was satisfied at the depth and breadth of the grave. She again stretched her stiff back and shoulders. She risked a look at the body. Little prickles tightened her skin and her short hairs stood. She did not want to touch it. With a sigh, she grit her teeth and moved to the corpse. She grasped the outstretched arm, using the sleeve as an insulator, and pulled. He seemed heavier than he had before. Her fear must have aided her strength previously. She pulled again, grunting as she did. The body moved and the smell increased in intensity. Bile rose within her throat, and she fought for control. She adjusted her stance and pulled mightily again. After several such efforts she managed to deposit him in the hole. He lay face down in the bottom of the grave. She preferred he was face down. The idea of shoveling dirt over those vacant dead eyes rankled her.

She filled in the hole and moved back to camp. She felt great relief in the completion of her task. It occurred to her to mark the grave, but Hutton's words again advised her.

'Play the cat and cover your shit. It draws flies and followers.'

She didn't know what to scratch into a memorium, nor did she want a crude monument to draw attention more than her spare camp might.

She turned and made her way back to camp. She was near camp when she saw movement some one-hundred yards beyond the camp. Her body froze mid-step. She strained to see what had moved. She saw the movement again accompanied by a familiar sound. She recognized the metal and leather's thick jangle of tack. Her head lifted a bit as she saw a dark head and mane shake just behind the shield of a clump of dwarf junipers.

Was this horse the carrier of a new danger? She shook her head, rejecting the notion. The dead man had approached from that direction the night of the attack. The mount must be his, deserted in death. She moved slowly towards the animal. The brush and grass within her reach had been eaten and the horse looked thin and starved. How had she not noticed the animal before?

She was a small dun mare with a dark mane and tail, and chocolate stripe at her back. She was tied off to a sturdy bough by long reins. Her ears shook away a fly and she nickered to Juliana as she approached. Juliana was surprised that a big man would ride a mount of such diminutive size.

Juliana released the reins and stroked the horse's muzzle. She led her back to camp. She tied her to a bush where the grass was long and lush. She filled Hutton's hat with water and offered it to the horse. The Dunn drank greedily, drawing large draughts noisily. Juliana patted the horse then moved back to the fire.

She lifted the diminished contents of the canteen and drew from it. She slaked her thirst, heightened by manual labor. She lowered the canteen with a concerned expression. She must find a source of water. Their two canteens were nearly empty. She had conserved the water within the canteens until providing the horse with water. Their supply of drinking water was dangerously low now. She looked around her.

She was not strong enough to haul Hutton onto a horse and she had no way to drag him. She might be here for a while. She looked to the remaining contents of their food stores. She found hard tack, four potatoes, flour and soda. She was not provisioned for a semi-permanent camp. Their shelter consisted of three tall trees, beneath which Hutton lay, and sparse scrub junipers here and there. She pulled the long canteen strap over her head and across her body.

With a sigh, Juliana moved to Hutton. She kneeled beside him and checked his rough bandages. The wadding consisted mostly of strips ripped from his shirt. Leather strips once used to tie her now bound the wadding. She set her jaw grimly at the irony. In some way the straps still bound her. His bleeding had stopped, and he seemed to rest comfortably although she detected no break in his unconscious state.

She stood, her arms akimbo. She looked about her. Her next task would be to locate a water source if she could. The surrounding terrain was fairly level, covered in sparse yellow grasses with a spare mottling of the dark green of juniper bushes. Her gaze went to the horizon. She peered intently towards all four quarters.

Of the many aspects of her predicament, there was one of which she was certain. Detection was fatal no matter the form it took. Bounty hunters and soldiers were guaranteed death for her. Indians or desperados would be no better. A woman alone in the wilderness was rare fodder indeed. She felt real fear and anger that her worth in this wilderness had diminished to the worth of her body to satisfy the desires of decrepit men of for food for wild beasts.

Assured in her isolation, she turned her gaze to areas closer at hand. The ground descended somewhat towards the west. Perhaps she might locate a pond or a seasonal rivulet. She pulled Hutton's heavy pistol from its holster. She would have preferred the less murderous saddle carbine, but she was no marksman and liked the idea of a shorter weapon for defense. The black pistol had taken many lives and she felt fear that the black of the steel was more than just aged bluing.

She held the weapon loosely in her hanging right hand as she moved towards the horses. She untied the rangy bay gelding she had ridden before and pulled him away from the string. She mounted and clucked the horse to motion towards the lower area west of camp. Water sloshed in the canteen in rhythm to his shambling gate.

She rode several rods before the sounds and feelings of nature drew her attention from her troubling dark thoughts. There in a tree, a bird sang. Elsewhere, the cool morning breeze freshened and hissed joyously through the long grasses. She inhaled sweet scents of wildflowers and sage. In spite of herself, she smiled slightly. The farther she roamed, the more she felt lighter and free. The outlaw indeed exerted a tangible influence upon her when she was near him. Even insensate he bore influence upon her.

The gentle descent became more pronounced, and she leaned back a bit as the gelding picked his way down a loose embankment. The region fed into a low trough some forty yards in diameter. The bottom, however, was cracked and empty. She entered the dry bed carefully. The horse's hooves hardly disturbed the dried bottoms. She detected no subsurface moisture of any kind. Apparently, rain had not accumulated here for some time.

Juliana altered her course towards the southern rim of the dry bed. Tall grass and skeletal brush barred a narrow ravine which issued towards lower ground beyond the dried pond. She pressed the horse to climb the bank. The gelding clambered as he drew up over the edge. She moved along over a region of grass and bushes. She followed the sharply cut draw as it tacked to and fro as the terrain allowed. She was soon below the bottom level of the dry bed of the pond. Her movement was hindered by an increase in small willow trees and thicker underbrush. She believed this a good sign. Would not more foliage indicate a likely water source nearby? The gelding stopped of his own volition, blocked by a screen of willow trees.

Juliana dismounted and tied the gelding to a thin branch. With effort, she pushed through the screen of branches. She saw a bright reflection among thick grass. She moved towards the flashing narrow line cautiously. She finally came to a small cut at the bottom of a narrow grassy gully. Clear water trickled sprightly below the guarding grasses. She dipped a hand into the runlet. The water was cool. The flow moved around her hand with a shallow but strong movement. She felt there must be a spring nearby. She moved the grass aside and dug out the bottom of the tiny stream so she could submerge her canteen. The silty cloud moved away swiftly, and the little pool filled with clear water. She pulled the canteen free and dipped it into the depression.

Once it was full, Juliana stood. She felt elation at the rare find. Water was scarce in this region. A source of clear spring water was a treasure indeed. She drank her fill and refilled the container.

She capped the canteen and moved up stream. A violent movement beyond and to her right startled her. A tawny form leaped into the screening mass of willows. She recognized the fleeting form of a big cat. She pulled the heavy pistol up too late to fire a shot. She heard a crash of brush and a terrified snort from her gelding. The commotion was violent. She heard branches break, the hard impact of hooves on ground. The gelding groaned a deep and frightened horse cry then Juliana heard rapid receding hoof beats.

Juliana stayed where she was for a moment, unsure of where the catamount might be. Finally, she moved quickly towards where she had left the gelding. She pushed through the brush. The tree where she had tied the gelding was mangled and the ground was torn up where the gelding had exerted extreme efforts to free himself. There was no sight of horse or predator. She felt it unlikely the animal would have killed the horse. This time of year, game was plentiful. She must have surprised the cat as it refreshed itself at the stream. The big cat, frightened, escaped by accident towards the horse who fled in fear of his own.

She returned to camp by a more direct route, noting landmarks as she went. She estimated the spring a distance of some quarter of a mile from camp. She marveled that the gelding had not sensed the cat upon their arrival. The breeze must have been wrong. Maybe the gelding would make his way back to camp. She watered the horses with Hutton's hat. She emptied one of the two canteens but lacked the will to return to the spring.

The day wore on slowly, but the gelding did not return. She busied herself with the limited duties required of the camp then rested against one of the large trees near Hutton. At intervals she checked upon the injured man. She wet a strip of cloth and squeezed tiny amounts of water into his mouth. She was careful that she not choke him.

As the air cooled in preparation of the coming evening, she chewed on a piece of the hard tack and drank her fill of water. Birds drifted west towards their columbaries and hutches as the night arrived. She wrapped herself in a blanket, daring not risk a fire. Sleep was a reluctant companion and she lay restlessly for many hours. Night sounds and strange noises disturbed her until exhaustion finally smothered her senses.

She awoke with a start. The sun was high, and nature's sounds were those of mid-morning. She tried in vain to remember the dream from which she had awakened so violently. All she could salvage was a dim feeling of dark despair and pursuit of an unknown evil agent of harm.

She pulled the blanket aside and shook her head. She looked towards Hutton. His pose was slightly different than the night before. He had moved some during the night. She rose and made efforts to assess his condition. A foul odor assailed her nostrils. She grimaced. He had soiled himself in the night. She pulled back his blanket. His rough trousers were dark at the crotch. This was a situation she had not considered. The corporeal act was to be overlooked in her planning.

Juliana moved away from him to her sleeping area. She sat against the tree and considered her remedies. Finally, she exhaled audibly. She stood and approached Hutton. She removed his blanket and laid it aside. She moved to his feet and removed his boots one at a time. She placed them neatly to the side then moved to his belt. She unbuckled the heavy buckle and released the 4 buttons at his crotch. She turned her head in embarrassment. He was there for her to see. The smell was quite strong. He was soiled and foul. She moved to his feet and pulled the legs of his pants. They came down exposing his naked maleness and caked filth below and around him. She turned away from the sight with a shudder. This level of intimacy was far beyond any she had ever experienced. No love helped her. No desire enhanced her view of him in this way. He was more repellant to her exposed than he had ever been dressed to this point.

She steeled herself to the inevitability of her task and turned back to him. She shook out his trousers as best she could. She took a handful of dirt and dusted the wet areas. She rubbed the soiled areas together from outside the garment. She went to where his long knife lay beside the cook fire stones. She grabbed it and moved towards the saddles on the ground. She pulled one of the pale saddle blankets from under a saddle and cut a narrow strip from one edge. She moved back to the fire and wet the blanket fragment with the remaining contents of the second canteen. She returned to Hutton and bathed him with curled lip, trying to avert her eyes as she performed the task.

Finally, he was clean enough in her opinion. She covered him again and moved back to the trousers. She turned them upside down and shook the dirt from them. She moved to a bush and hung them upon it. She returned to the fire dripped what moisture she could and washed her hands. She glanced back at the outlaw. She fully expected his eyes to be open, his lips contorted in a grin. She would not doubt his ability to go to this length to torment her. He was instead as he had been since being shot.

Days passed in this way. She watched him go through distinct and marked changes in that time. One night she had been near sleep when a cry from him caused her to sit bolt upright - trembling. The cloudy night cloaked the moon and she could not see him. She peered through the darkness in his direction but did not approach him.

The following morning found him unconscious and unmoved from the evening prior. After that night's interruption, he had become more restless. He shifted his position more often. His more frequent moans of pain did not bring awareness. She had called to him on each occasion. And on each occasion, he had not responded. His battle for life raged within him and he fought it alone. She could offer him no more succor than physical ministrations.

The morning of the sixth day found her out of food stores. The hard tack and potatoes were gone. The flour was useless to her. She grasped the pistol she kept close to her at night. She would try her hand at hunting game.

Juliana rose and draped a canteen over her shoulders as was her way. She moved towards the little spring. She had heard movement in the brush around the spring on other visits since the flight of the big cat.

Since that day, she made the journey to the spring on foot. She could not risk losing another horse. Her approach was quieter on foot which might aid in her hunt. She hoped to have a chance to shoot a small animal and satisfy the empty gnawing in her stomach. She walked down the hill towards the line of willows. She held the pistol awkwardly ahead of her pointed slightly downward.

A rustling disturbed the underbrush to her right. She brought the pistol to bear in that direction. She saw something small, furry, and fast move beneath the foliage. The pistol exploded and she fell sideways. The report of the pistol startled her. She clambered to her feet and moved towards her target. She searched the brush but found no trace. No blood nor fur stained the grass. Fear grew in her as she searched. Anxiety crept in as a thunderstorm moves in over darkened hills. What if the shot had been heard? She turned her gaze towards the direction of camp. She made her way out of the low area, searching around her. As she gained the upper level, she scanned the horizon for any movement or suspicious shape. She saw nothing out of the ordinary. She crouched in the tall grass and waited. She drank from the canteen and peered anxiously around her. She remained in her hiding spot until the sun was high. Finally, she rose and made her way back to camp.

By the end of the second day after her failed hunting trip, hunger turned to weakness. She knew she had to eat. Neither Hutton nor she would survive without sustenance. Her weakness grew to the level that even the smallest effort taxed her and resulted in dizziness.

The evening was overcast as she stared vacantly at the grey smoky embers of the fire. Her thoughts were no longer focused upon her plight. She seemed to be in a stupor of sorts. Hunger and weakness dimmed her faculties to all but one instinctual focus.

With a start, she realized her vacant gaze rested upon the two horses. They were well fed upon the plentiful grass around camp. She railed against the idea which had matured since hunger began forming her thoughts. The two horses had been her only company for many days. She was given to talking to them when the solitude became too oppressive. The idea of killing one of them caused her genuine heartache.

She averted her eyes. She drank a large pull from the canteen to relieve her hunger pangs. She wrapped herself in her blankets and began her nightly game of tricking herself to sleep.

The morning dawned with her sitting up. She could not find a way to absolve herself of her sin. She would slay one of the horses. She was afraid to use the pistol because of the noise. She couldn't, however, settle on how and where to stab a horse for a quick and sure death. If she wounded the animal, it might flee. The wounded animal might die and feed only hungry beasts. The prospect of plunging a knife into a living creature was abominable. Something as big and powerful as a horse: was she strong enough to perform the feat? The agony in her belly moved her.

She stood, knife hanging in her hand. The horses watched her with mild interest. The little Dun mare nickered at her approach. She looked away. Might the sensitive creatures divine her intent somehow? She felt her body quake. Her teeth began to chatter. Juliana gripped the knife until her knuckles whitened upon the haft. She breathed deeply, trying to calm herself. She felt a panic welling up within her. What was happening to her?

She remembered her father talking with a group of young hunters. They had experienced similar symptoms. What had her father called it? Buck Fever. She turned back to the fire.

Hunger and frustration churned her insides. Her head slumped to her chest. She always imagined herself a strong woman. Growing up in her sheltered surroundings – or so they now appeared - she could scarcely have imagined a scenario where she would not prevail, no matter the circumstances. Yet here she was, starving to death without the will to remedy it.

She dropped the knife into the loose dirt at her feet. She moved rapidly to Boyd's saddle. She withdrew the black colt from its holster hanging on the saddle horn. She pulled the hammer back and turned on her heel. She strode to the dun horse and shot him in the head. The horse dropped as a loose sack of bones and meat.

The stars seemed to cast a steely light upon her. The night was growing chill around her. Juliana placed another billet on the fire below the spit bearing a generous cut of haunch. The meat singed and sputtered hot fat in protest. Juliana sliced off a strip and filled her mouth full. Grease shone upon her lips and cheeks. Below and to the side, on the fire, boiled a pot of water with strips of meat within. She checked the soup's progress at intervals and was pleased to find the broth was darkening by degrees. She reached into a small chamois pouch and pulled a pinch of salt which she tossed into the broth. Hutton's yen for campfire biscuits facilitated her need for seasoning with his stash of salt and flour.

The broth was soon ready. She poured a small measure into one of the two tin bowls kept in their camp pack. She approached Hutton. Since his injury she had learned to give him water even while he was in this state. He seemed never totally lost in unconscious oblivion. He responded to her care of him enough for her to administer liquid to him. She now blew on a spoonful of the rich liquid and brought it to his lips. His eyes remained closed, but he swallowed the broth. After a half dozen spoons of the horse broth, he stopped swallowing the liquid. She wiped his mouth and stood.

As she walked back to the fire she turned suddenly. Had he spoken something to her? She peered at Hutton for a time. He scarcely moved and that was only the rise and fall of his shallow breathing. This was not the first time she thought she had heard the wounded man speak. Each time, no matter how long she waited, he failed to move or indicate any increased awareness of his surroundings.

She shook her head trying to scatter the imaginings of her desperate mind. She feared that the solitude and perhaps her despair were taxing her troubled thoughts. Was she losing her sensibilities in the isolation of this wilderness exile?

Juliana poured the remnants or the bowl's contents back into the cooking pot. She moved to her blankets, near the wounded man. Her loneliness had driven her to sleep closer to Hutton. The solitude was crushing to her. His company grew more necessary the longer she remained there. She excused her weakness with the idea of being nearby in the instance that he required attention while she slept. She would be more likely to awaken if she were nearer at hand.

The morning broke with a gray mantle. Silent lightning had flashed from great distance during the early morning hours. The dull glow had been enough to rouse Juliana from her troubled sleep. She feared wet weather was eminent. She rose and rolled her blankets. She stoked the remaining embers of her fire and went about cleaning and stowing the remains of her late-night feast.

Guiltily, she glanced at the spot where the horse's carcass lay. She looked more directly. Had the remains been disturbed during the night? She grabbed Hutton's pistol and approached the kill site. She identified the clean edged region from which she had harvested her night's meal. Further away she spied ragged places where the horse had been fed upon by an animal. She was both surprised and frightened that she had not been awakened by the feeding of a wild animal so near her camp. She stood in thought. How could she secure the camp against possibly aggressive animals? She heard a voice behind her. She closed her eyes patiently.

"No more talk, Boyd Hutton," she said to herself. "Your voice is in my head again. I will not lose my mind because of you,"

She turned her attention back to her present quandary. She held her breath, her nerves taut as a string. Had she heard a moan?

She turned abruptly and watched Hutton. His head moved, his brow furrowed in pain. She almost collapsed as she moved towards him. She felt her relief come in a hot wave behind her eyes and within her breast. She fell upon her knees beside him.

He moaned and turned his face towards her. He seemed to sense her presence, but he was unable to open his eyes.

She set the pistol down on the ground and put hands on both sides of his head.

"You still live," she cried in a quavering voice. "No man comes back from a wound like yours. *Dios mio*! Who protects you?"

With a soft groan he lifted his big hand. He clutched her blouse feebly. His voice was just audible enough for her to understand his words. His voice held a dry raspy crackle.

"You did Juliana. They are here now."

He drew a great labored breath.

"You held me here when they came for me. Every night...they came."

His hand fell loosely from her blouse, and he slipped back into the black void.

Juliana sat, watching him for a moment. With renewed hope she moved to the fire and placed a pan of water to boil. She had fallen lax in her care for him. She had long since accepted his death as imminent. Guilt at her weakened faith moved her to action. She spent the next few hours cleaning his wound and his person as well as her strength and modesty allowed. She changed the rude bandages and she moved about the camp, making it more orderly and clean.

CHAPTER SIXTEEN

Love

Juliana couldn't explain her happiness. She wanted to examine the oddity of her emotional condition. Instead, she allowed herself to abide in this temporary euphoria. She did, however, experience frequent instances where her contented state waned, and she looked at herself plainly. Was her state of mind a product of contrast? Had she been under such duress that the newly assumed consciousness of her abductor was comparatively pleasant to her? She again pushed this bizarre conundrum from her thoughts. She had been on the edge of despair for some weeks and the descent into a more relaxed state was a relief to be savored.

She sat across the fire from Hutton. He was propped against a tree with his saddle supporting him. They sipped hot broth from the horse meat she had harvested. Weakness was plain on Hutton. Juliana saw him markedly changed. His broad shoulders sagged noticeably, and his big hands trembled with the effort to bring the tin bowl to his pale lips. He sipped the broth noisily then sat the vessel on the ground with an uncertain motion. He looked down at the bowl for a moment before his sunken eyes rose to look at her.

"Juliana, you have to get me to a doctor. I am dying."

Juliana returned his gaze trying to clear the confusion she felt.

"But you are getting better."

He shook his big head. His closed eyes seemed to be the best he could do to disregard her protest.

"I am awake," he said, "but I am dying."

She watched him, searching his face for the truth behind his words. Since her capture, she had regarded him as indomitable by any force or natural element. This self-professed failing struck her as a statement meant more for its subtext meaning rather than a literal admission of weakness.

"How do you know this?'

Boyd leaned back and inhaled as best he could. He grimaced as he took silent stock of his condition.

"I don't feel pain where I should feel it. Everything is too bright. The world is shining bright before it goes out."

He lowered his head and looked at her, his internal examination complete.

"You gotta get me somewhere."

"You can't ride yet," she said.

He looked around him, squinting his eyes. She assumed he was reacting to the "brightness" to which he referred. He spoke again, his gaze on a downed tree a few yards beyond their camp.

"You gotta make a travois."

She felt herself wither inside. The idea of the effort to again step outside of her abilities was daunting.

He seemed to sense her internal strife.

"Juliana, I will let you go if you do this for me."

Fire sparked in her dark eyes. She felt herself become instantly enraged. He was so weak she could crush him with a rock, and he would be unable to stop her.

"You no longer control where I go. I could have left weeks ago."

He winced at the portent of her words. He saw the truth in them. His eyes raised to hers and she saw a change in them. The amusement she had seen in them ion the past when she had shown spirit of will in her rare moments of exhibited rebellion returned now. She saw something else also. She thought she detected genuine warmth. This was a foreign reaction. His eyes again dropped as he braced himself on unsteady arms.

"I reckon there is still a little life left in me."

He pushed himself more upright.

"It would be a damn waste of them days if I croak now after all your fussing over me. You have to use my knife and cut them two saplings for the side rails."

The following morning found Juliana leading their remaining horse from within the shade of the trees under which their camp had been sheltered for so many weeks. The encampment seemed no longer a part of the surrounding wilderness. It had about it a sense of permanence and an identity beyond the nondescript point amongst thousands of others in which they might have camped. Merely the act of occupation for an extended period made it familiar and permanent as any cabin.

After weeks in the place, Juliana felt a sense of loss. This encampment, her home for so long, had been a stern test of her mettle, but she felt a sense of self she had never felt before. The hardships, the horrors and the mental anguish had made her more. This place had been her field of battle. She had succeeded in surviving much she hadn't thought possible of the former Juliana who hailed from a long-lost life in Saltillo.

So, with some melancholy, she gave the little camp, shaded by the tall trees which had become her home, a final long look. The encampment held a well-worn appearance, displaying its long-term occupation. The ground around the dark fire ring was bare of grass. Small items of refuse remained to commemorate the time spent there. She marked the spot in her memory. She knew she would never return, but she promised herself never to forget.

Juliana walked ahead of Hutton's horse, a long leaning travois dragging behind. The way was primarily silty grasslands, but occasionally he groaned as the long travois frame struck a rock or grass covered log.

Well before mid-day she saw he was weakening. The journey was taking its toll on him. She halted and gave him a pull from the canteen. She felt his forehead. His brow was hot, and his eyes rolled as he fought to focus on her. She led the horse and travois into the shade under a tall tree.

She looked around her. Expansive, unbroken country stretched away on all sides. The midday heat was gaining strength and the rise and fall of the searing song of cicadas buzzed in protest. As she scanned the horizon, she saw the faintest tendril of smoke rising before the dray backdrop of a distant cleft between two gentle hills. Perhaps if she travelled carefully, she could reach the source of the smoke by sundown.

The way was easy except for detours necessitated by the fragile construction of the travois and the grunted protests of the injured man.

Travel was not kind to the makeshift travois. Her novice handiwork was put to the test regularly. Several times she called a halt to their progress to adjust a leather thong tie or to replace a broken cross member. These pauses cost much delay. It was well after nightfall when they arrived at a squat adobe cabin. Lights glowed invitingly from small windows.

The door opened and a thin man of gray hair and a full mustache approached. He stopped before Juliana and the travois and looked her over curiously. She felt too tired to deliver more than a weak smile at his scrutiny. He looked beyond her to the travois. He moved to the injured man and inspected his wound. He stood and looked towards the house.

"Yuvia," he called in Spanish. "Come quickly."

Yuvia, a slight but strongly built woman, must have been close to the door, for she appeared immediately and hurried to her husband's side.

Juliana tried to explain what they likely already surmised.

"He has been shot and he believes he is dying, *Senor*."

"Help me bring him inside," he said finally after looking into Hutton's haggard face.

Juliana moved stiffly towards the couple. With effort, the three managed to carry Hutton inside and laid him in a bed in one of the side rooms of the neat little home.

They bathed his seeping wound, bound it with fresh bandages and cleaned him as well as they could through his groans and weak gestures of protest. Finally, they left him to rest, closing the rough plank door.

Yuvia gestured towards the small table near the home cooking fire. Juliana slumped wearily into a chair.

"Gracias," she said with a tired smile.

Yuvia moved to the fire and filled an ornate clay bowl with a fragrant stew from a hanging pot over the waning cook fire. She sat the bowl and a large spoon before the tired girl. Juliana smiled her gratitude and filled the spoon with tender meat chunks, corn and potatoes. She raised the savory load to her eager mouth. She chewed with heart-felt relish and nodded her admiration to the cook.

Her new surroundings faded into the background as she committed herself to this delicious repast. She finally came to the bottom of the clay bowl and looked around her, taking stock of the neatly arranged little house. It was apparent that Yuvia was fastidious in the decorating of her home. Fresh flowers occupied wooden cylinders here and there. Most of the furniture was homemade but on the far wall sat a lovely rack of narrow shelves above a solid base containing several drawers.

Yuvia and the man took seats to each side of Juliana. They looked her over before Yuvia finally spoke.

"This is my husband, Ricardo, and I am Yuvia."

She looked behind Juliana.

"Maria," she called. "Come meet our guest."

A pretty girl of perhaps twelve years approached the table with a shy smile. Juliana turned and watched her approach.

"This is our daughter, Maria."

"I am Juliana," she said simply.

Maria sat at the remaining chair, watching Juliana with delight. She turned to her father.

"Why is an Americano this far into Mexico, Father?"

Ricardo shushed his daughter.

"It is not polite to ask such things, Maria."

It was apparent to Juliana that the girl spoke that which all three thought.

Juliana cleared her throat as she considered how much she should say. She looked up as she decided.

"Thank you for your kindness. I am Juliana and he is Boyd. He was shot defending us from a bandit."

Ricardo's attention focused partially upon the girl's words, but more her face as if to divine her true meaning.

"There seem to be many bandits about these days," he said gently.

Juliana continued, careful to minimize her reaction to his comments.

"We had not heard," she said simply.

"We feared you may be outlaws until we saw your companion was Americano."

Juliana waited, unsure of his meaning. She smiled as she urged him to explain.

"Many bandits travel with women?"

"Only one that we know of."

Yuvia rose and cleared her throat. Her look for Ricardo gave notice that the conversation was ended.

"Juliana, you and Maria can share her bed this evening. Your man cannot be moved for a few days. We will arrange for your comfort in the morning."

Ricardo pursed his lips. Juliana was certain he was dissatisfied with the premature end to their conversation.

Juliana rose.

"Thank you for your kindness."

In the little bed beside Maria, she soon drifted into the most fitful sleep she had experienced in weeks.

The next days passed slowly with little improvement from Hutton. Juliana watched as Yuvia ministered to his wounds. She felt useless in the company of so skilled a nurse. Yuvia went about her medical tasks with confidence and an experienced manner.

"He does not improve," Juliana observed by way of trying to be involved as much as she could.

"Moving him so soon after the shooting was not wise,"

"He insisted. We had no medical supplies."

Yuvia looked Hutton over.

"He has been shot before. He bears many scars."

She compressed her lips as she worked.

"Ricardo bears many scars."

She continued, giving her work full attention.

"He was a soldier for many years. Was your man a soldier?"

Juliana hid her frown at the reference to her relationship with Boyd. She knew she must be cautious.

"He is not...I mean to say..."

She looked away to gather her thoughts.

"Most men have been soldiers at one time or other," she finally replied.

Yuvia looked at Juliana for a moment. She seemed to weigh Juliana's last words. Finally, she stood and left the room without comment.

After some days of doubtful optimism, Hutton did begin to improve. His color warmed from a sickly pallor to a healthier tone. Gradually he slept more comfortably. He had not regained enough strength to engage in conversation for more than a few minutes, but he was more alert.

Ricardo and Yuvia were cautious in their dealings with Juliana. In spite of themselves, they grew to acquire a genuine fondness for this lovely young woman in so odd a situation. They yearned for more information but waited for her to share in her own good time.

Maria immediately attached herself to Juliana. She was of great delight to Juliana. They sat and talked for hours. Maria was imaginative and engaging. Her frank acceptance of the newcomer and her open regard gave Juliana great comfort and pleasure. The little girl, in many ways, reminded her of her sister Alida.

In those moments when she thought of young Alida, her heart ached with yearning for those days which seemed so long ago. Days to which she knew she would never be able to return.

The evening grew cooler than usual when the soldiers arrived. Ricardo sat in his favorite chair, enjoying the cool air, pulling from his pipe. Through the rising smoke he saw a line of nearly a dozen mounted troops topping a hill from the west.

"Soldiers approach," he said loudly enough to be heard inside the home, but not so loudly that the crisp clear air would aid in reaching the small column of mounted troops.

He waited patiently as the cavalry unit approached. His years of service gave him appreciation for the bearing of this unit, so far from garrison. Their uniforms were immaculately kept, buttons and boots gleamed in the waning light of the early evening.

Juliana and Maria moved to witness the soldiers' approach through a crack between the lovely curtains and the window frame of the window in Maria's room. Juliana's heart threatened to beat a hole in her breast as she waited. She felt a surge of panic moving her to a desperate act. Her recent travails had toughened her bearings, allowing her reason to prevail. She had nowhere to run. She was at the mercy of Ricardo and his family.

The soldiers were a mere hundred yards away when Maria looked over to Juliana. She saw the tension upon her face and in her gripped fists.

"What is wrong, *Senora*?"

Maria smiled.

"Do not be alarmed. Soldiers come by often. There is a terrible bandit at large and they patrol for him and his gang."

Juliana turned to the girl.

"A bandit?"

Maria smiled and her face turned serious as she relished the opportunity to occupy Juliana's attention. She spoke with a little girl's grave manner.

"Yes," she breathed dramatically. "A terrible man! A murderer and thief!"

Juliana shushed her.

"Quietly Maria. What else is said about him?"

Lowering her tone to a mere whisper Maria continued, encouraged by Juliana's keen interest.

"Only that he is to be shot on sight. They say he is accompanied by a woman as cruel as he is himself. No one knows her name, but she is called '*La Mujere.*' A strange name. She carries the decree of death on sight as well."

Juliana felt herself grow faint. She mastered her emotions as the realization of her peril pressed upon her. The man who had shot Boyd had said the same of her. Her father or one of his council must have issued the order. 'Why?' she thought again as she had so many times. She focused again on Maria.

"Your father must not tell the soldiers about us."

Maria looked puzzled and Juliana's mind strained to create a story that would cover her.

"My fath..."

She faltered. She paused then continued as an idea formed.

"This cannot be true," she said, picking up where the girl had stopped. "Why would a woman be marked for death?"

"She is said to be an enemy of the state," Maria said with wide eyes.

Maria gasped with sudden realization.

"Do you believe they would kill you thinking you *La Mujere*?"

Juliana looked at Maria, frightened at how quickly she made the connection between her and the outlawed woman. She had to act before she lost her footing.

"Call your father inside quickly."

Maria rose and rushed to the door. She paused uncertainly.

"You are not *La Mujere*?" she asked hesitantly.

"Of course not," Juliana replied in a sharp tone meant to dismiss so ludicrous an idea. "My fiancée and I are from Vera Cruz. He is a trader. We met and fell in love and now we head north to be married. These men would not have regard for such a story with these outlaws nearby."

Maria gasped with fear and ran to the front door.

"Father. We must speak to you. Come quickly."

Ricardo removed his pipe from his mouth and looked down at his daughter. He paused to consider the request. In the back of his mind, he was certain he would learn the truth about his guests - the wayward couple. In his mind, the urgency and the soldiers' approach could not be a coincidence.

With one look at the line of soldiers, only rods from the house, he followed Maria to her room. There, Juliana sat on the bed. Her face was a study in fear. Her eyes contained a storm of concern. Ricardo waited for Juliana to speak. His face held a grim expectancy.

"Maria told me of this bandit couple," Juliana stammered. "They will not believe we are not them."

Ricardo seemed unmoved by neither her words nor her urgency. She continued quickly.

"Boyd is a trader who came on a ship to Vera Cruz. We met and fell in love. We were headed north to be married when we were laid upon by a bandit."

Ricardo's face was impossible to read. Juliana was unsure if he believed her or not. She continued doggedly.

"I know this seems odd. In Vera Cruz, there is the son of a wealthy landowner. He wants me for his own. When I told him, I was in love with Boyd, he said he would see me dead rather than with another, particularly a gringo. We escaped at night on horseback because his men watched the ships at port."

She stood and took Ricardo's hands in hers.

"Even if the soldiers don't kill us on sight," she pleaded. "Word will get to the son that we are here. It may be weeks before we can move my fiancée."

She stopped, out of breath. Ricardo studied her face. She saw no reaction to her story. He looked towards the front door. The sound of approaching horses and the rattling of equipment drew him away. As he moved to the front door his gaze fell upon Yuvia. She stood facing him, arms akimbo. Her expression was significant in its judgement of him. He looked away guiltily and moved out the front door once again.

As he moved to the porch, he surveyed the soldiers fanned around him before the house. A splendidly dressed man touched his plumed hat.

"*Buenos tardes.*"

"*Buenos tardes, Capitan.* You are far from garrison and the hour is late."

The commander eyed Ricardo unimpressed. He continued his statement without varying his authoritative tone.

"We trailed hoof prints headed in this direction from a camp peopled only by a dead man and a dead horse. We have searched the region with no results."

"Poor company. I would leave as well from such poor company. Who made these tracks?"

"The *Bandito* and *La Mujere.*"

Ricardo registered genuine surprise.

"They turn south? They must feel the noose closing about them. Your efforts may yet bear fruit."

"Perhaps."

The captain studied Ricardo for a time. His manner relaxed as he considered Ricardo. He knew the older man was a soldier of merit in his younger days. The commander had heard the stories of his heroism in battle.

"Have you seen any travelers? One appears to be injured for the tracks were those of a horse dragging a travois. We lost the trail, but it seems they would seek medical aid at the first opportunity."

"Your trackers are indeed legendary if they can determine whether riders are man or woman."

The commander narrowed his eyes at this sally. He would not tolerate ridicule, particularly in the presence of his men.

"There were remains at the camp site which led us to believe a woman was there."

"Of course," Ricardo said with an apologetic bow. "I should have guessed. Forgive my humor Capitan. So, the bandit or his woman is wounded. That will create talk. Capitan, I have seen no such travelers."

Juliana held her breath at Ricardo's words. So, he would help her.

The commander shifted uneasily in his saddle.

"Please forgive me, Colonel, but we must check the house."

"Check my home?" Ricardo repeated.

Yuvia appeared behind her husband. Her face was set, and her body was rigid with outrage.

"The fugitives might be hiding without your knowledge," the commander explained, eyeing Yuvia curiously. His words held little strength of conviction, even to him.

"You believe," she said heatedly, "I don't know who is in my house? As you are aware, the Colonel is a battle honored officer. You insult him with these demands."

Ricardo turned to his wife and took her hand in his.

"Yuvia, El Capitan is only following orders. We have nothing to hide."

Ricardo patted his wife's hand. She looked into his eyes. She thought she saw surrender there. He turned once again to the officer.

"Your men seem tired. Step down and rest if you must search my home, Capitan."

The commander hesitated, unsure of the invitation.

"Your men are weary," Ricardo said with a critical gesture towards the troops.

The commander surveyed his troops sharply. His eye searched for any indication of weakness or fatigue. He commanded only the finest soldiers. Weakness was not tolerated. Satisfied, he set his jaw and turned back to the old officer.

"We will not waste a moment from the trail with our quarry so near our grasp. Adios, Colonel."

Ricardo nodded.

"Adios Capitan. We will keep an eye out for strangers."

"Andale," he called out. The group broke open a path for their commander and followed him as he spurred his horse to a gallop through their midst.

Ricardo and Yuvia watched until the troops were well away. They turned to one another and shared a frightened look.

Juliana collapsed onto her little cot next to Maria's bed. She threw her arm over her eyes to hide her emotional display from Maria. She needed some time for herself, to deal with the slowly draining anxiety which had mounted during those last tense moments.

Maria sat on her bed and waited silently. She was too young to understand all she saw, but she knew enough to give Juliana her time. Maria looked up as her mother and father entered the room. Their faces were drawn and solemn.

Ricardo looked at Juliana for only a brief moment. Finally, he withdrew and returned to his seat on the porch. He lit the cold tobacco in his pipe and drew upon the smoke. His face no longer registered pleasure at the cool evening breezes. His was an expression of deep thought about dangerous possibilities.

Maria rose and moved to her mother. Yuvia took her hand and they stood together watching Juliana.

Juliana sat upright. She wiped her eyes and drew a long breath of relief. Her eyes went to mother and daughter. She searched for words. Her mind was exhausted, and nothing came.

"Thank you," was all she could manage.

Yuvia and Maria waited a moment more. Yuvia turned and led her Maria out of the room.

When Juliana entered, Hutton was sitting upright in the little bed in which he had lain for the past few weeks. He looked out the single window in the room. He looked his old self, but his demeanor was changed noticeably. Of late he piqued when the others entered the room. He replied easily to questions about his physical condition. She had heard him once talking with Maria about horses. She was a skilled young rider and she enjoyed his American opinion on horsemanship.

Juliana placed a bowl of broth on the small table beside the bed. The morning was bright, and he seemed to be enjoying the scene through the small window.

"Do you feel well enough to leave the bed?" she asked with little emotion behind the question.

He did not reply immediately. He pulled his gaze from the window and only watched her.

She felt anger well up within her breast. She hated his silences more than anything else he did as a habit. When her eyes met his, however, she saw something different than the normal hooded interest or near blank critical regard he typically paid when he studied her. His eyes were ashine with something else she had not seen before. His searching gaze did not dissect her. Rather, he seemed to seek her out – to gain understanding of her.

Finally, he spoke. His voice was strong enough, but he spoke with an almost timid inflection to his voice.

"Why did you stay?"

Juliana felt tears well up behind her eyes. Now her anger was real. She felt months of resentment move forward. He didn't seem to see her resentment, boiling like a distant thunderhead. He continued speaking in that same low tone.

"Yuvia said soldiers came for me and you got the old man to lie to them. You told me you wanted to get away. I thought you hated me."

Her resentment became fury at his ignorance. He was arrogant enough to believe her in love with him - or whatever other reason he contrived that a woman might cover for a man. She was proud that her voice came so easily – so evenly and measured.

"I do hate you," she purred, "but now you are all I have."

Confusion was plain on his face.

"My father has placed a decree of death upon my head."

She looked out the door, ensuring no one would hear her. Her voice dropped a scant degree but none of the passion left her.

"You have won Boyd Hutton. You have ruined me and damned me. If I had betrayed you, I would have died for it."

Hutton's mouth moved as he searched for words. He appeared genuinely regretful.

Juliana felt her heart sag in her breast. She turned from him and left him to his confused thoughts.

Juliana's passion was horses. Ricardo won her heart when he brought out his prized possession. The stallion was young, but the qualities he would ultimately develop with maturity were already apparent in his striking lines. He was sleekly built but well-muscled. He would not realize his true breadth and girth for a few more years. Ricardo allowed Juliana to work with the young stud, but only under his supervision. His fear was for the girl. The spirited chestnut had tested him with hoof and tooth on numerous occasions.

Juliana seemed unaware of any portent of danger from the magnificent animal. She held no compunction at exposing herself to the stallion in any regard. She turned her back to him. She approached him directly from front or back. To Ricardo's amazement, the horse did not as much as flatten an ear towards her. It is said that animals and children are the best judge of character. He mused that maybe his personal reluctance to trust her was just stubbornness, or perhaps fear. The horse certainly detected no ill traits from Juliana

She attached the long reins to the headstall and set about lunging the young horse. She saw Hutton sitting on the porch, watching her work the animal. Her anger towards him had reached a point of steady heat, without flare up when she was near him. She was able to remain cordial with him, but she could not affect any warm regard, feigned nor real. She feared that the only person who still believed she was betrothed to the outlaw was Ricardo. Yuvia and Maria were decidedly unconvinced. They had each commented on how odd it was that lovers could appear so distant.

She placed her attention fully upon the horse. He did not like the feel of the long reins on his sides.

Juliana was skilled from many years of working with her own stock, and her manipulations of the reins maintained her authority over the stallion without error. Ricardo nodded unconsciously at her technique.

Juliana pursed her lips as she worked the gleaming horse, her attention fully upon him. She missed her 'boys', the twin geldings given her by her father for her birthday. Reluctantly, she admitted that this stallion was a much better specimen.

She worked the young horse for more than an hour. She was soaked from the effort. The horse showed signs of fatigue also in a slight drop of his proud head and a heavier cloud of dust beneath his lagging hooves. She checked the beautiful horse and released him from the head stall. He turned his head and looked full at her. It seemed that even he was dismayed at his lenient treatment of this new handler.

With a shake of his mane, he pranced away from her as if on steel springs. She turned her back deliberately and moved to the tall fence where Ricardo sat, an unconscious smile curved his lips.

She handed him the tack and ducked between the bottom rails. She walked towards the house, deep in happy thoughts of her work. She looked up as she stepped upon the porch. Hutton's gaze was fully and unabashedly upon her.

"You have a way with horses," he said with open admiration.

She was surprised to feel pleasure at his compliment.

"My father keeps only the best in his private stock."

She glanced back at the corral. The stallion was wheeling as he evaded Ricardo's efforts to return him to the stables.

"This stallion is as close to that quality as I have seen outside of Saltillo."

Boyd cleared his throat. He seemed uncomfortable with the conversation.

"I know you miss home," he said unsteadily. "If I could change things between us I would."

He looked at her earnestly.

Can you ever..."

She cut him off sharply.

"Don't! Don't apologize to me. You had no right to do what you did. I cannot forgive you."

She walked through the door leaving him alone.

Days passed and soon Hutton was on his feet. His strength was nearly as it had been. He helped Ricardo with chores around the little ranch. The only sign of his injuries were occasional groans from morning stiffness and slow stretches at the end of a tiring day.

They sat at the table eating dinner after one of those long days. As was their habit, Ricardo and Hutton sat at each end of the table. Yuvia was seated to Ricardo's right and Juliana occupied a chair to his left, closer to him than to Boyd. Maria found a place squeezed next to Juliana. They ate in near silence.

Hutton laid down his fork with a dramatic exhalation of satisfaction.

"You are looking much recovered, *Senor* Boyd," Ricardo observed from his end of the table.

Boyd shook his head in his own amazement at his recovery.

"Still a little stiff but I am gettin' around better now."

He looked directly at Juliana as he organized his next words. He hesitated and looked down. He seemed to gather himself. Finally, he lifted his eyes and faced Ricardo directly. Juliana wondered if he was avoiding her gaze.

"I think it's time I got on my way."

All eyes looked to the outlaw. Juliana found her voice.

"I...uh...is it not too soon?"

Ricardo stepped in at Juliana's obvious surprise at the announcement.

"I'll need a horse. Would you be willing to sell me one, Ricardo?"

"*Senor* Boyd, you are not yet mended. A gunshot wound is nothing to be taken lightly."

Boyd nodded.

"I've been shot before. Much obliged for your hospitality, but I need to get moving before luck runs out and we draw more attention than we have already."

Hutton pushed his chair away from the table.

"I understand," Ricardo agreed. "The roan gelding is hard-mouthed but good on the trail."

Hutton rose. He nodded to Yuvia, avoiding eye contact with Juliana. He turned and walked to the front door.

"Thank you," Hutton said with his eyes on the floor. He strode from the room into the night.

Ricardo seemed at a loss and leaned back helplessly.

Juliana replayed his words in her mind. He had said I then we. She was confused and taken a bit off balance by this sudden announcement.

Juliana looked at the family one by one. Without warning, she stood and followed him out the door. Her stride and her manner indicated to the others her mental state. She moved with a heavy purposeful stride. Her head was up and her jaw forward. Yuvia and Ricardo shared a moment between them, their silence filled with memories they shared from years ago.

Juliana saw Hutton walking towards the corral. His head was down, and his gait was a shambling walk. His slow steps raised a low dust cloud at his feet. She caught up with him as he paused at the corral fence, resting a foot atop the lowest rail.

"I'm not going with you," she said sharply.

"I know," he replied mildly.

"You know? What do you know?"

She was angry and a bit confused.

"I know this has gone on long enough. You are right. I can't keep someone I love hostage."

Boyd rested his arms on the top rail and placed his chin in his hands.

Juliana looked at him as thoughts and feelings whirled within her. She was unable to sort her emotions into a single reaction to this strange situation in which she found herself.

Anger was prominent but not dominant. She also felt a hurt deep in her breast. Was there a sense of impending loss?

"So, I am free to go?" she asked incredulously. Her voice raised with the heat of anger fueling her rage.

"Go where? I cannot go home. I cannot reveal who I am to anyone."

Hutton maintained his gaze towards the dark corral. She thought she saw a barely perceptible droop to his broad shoulders.

"Your plan is to leave me here?"

"I ain't got no plan. I don't know where I go from here. I just know I am done with all of this."

"Done with all of what? Done with me?"

Her head dropped and her hands hung still by her side. She wanted to be angry. She wanted to curse him. Instead, she felt a profound sense of loss. Was she mistaken about her feelings for the outlaw? She looked up to see him facing her. His eyes worked to understand her. She almost laughed aloud. She hardly knew her own mind.

His voice held a warmth she had never heard from him.

"I will never be done with you, Juliana. I won't forget you as long or as short as I live."

He looked down at his feet. With intent, he turned to leave. Juliana grabbed his hand, stopping him short. His body stiffened as if he were prepared to receive a blow.

He turned his head and looked into her eyes. She stood stiffly, looking at him. Her eyes betrayed her desire to remain resolute and distant.

He pulled her close and kissed her deeply. She moved her arms around him and returned the kiss.

CHAPTER SEVENTEEN

Pis Aller

The whole town came out for the wedding of the Americano and the lovely Juliana. Ricardo had arranged for everything. The wedding was simple and intimate. The reception was as grand as any fiesta the town square had ever held. Mariachis strolled through the crowd leaving smiles and frivolity in their wake.

Tables were arranged in rows at one end of the square. Juliana and Boyd sat together, breathless from the ceremony as much as from dancing together.

As the party waned with the evening's breezes, the newlyweds strolled to their new home. Boyd refused to purchase the little house with ill-gotten gains, so he agreed to an installment loan from Ricardo, to be repaid from his earnings working on the ranch.

Boyd threw open the door and doffed his hat to his new wife.

"May I bring you into your new home?"

She curtsied with a bright smile.

He leaned in and lifted her lightly into his arms. He carried her through the doorway into the adjoining room where a bed was freshly made.

He settled her gently upon it and sat beside her. She lifted herself onto an elbow and looked up at him.

Boyd placed a hand behind her head and brought his face closer to hers.

"Do you love me, Juliana?"

She wrapped her arms around his neck and pulled herself up to him. She kissed him deeply and for a long time.

They separated, their lips only inches from one another.

"I do love you Boyd."

He gazed into her eyes for a long moment, then pulled her to him. They lowered themselves onto the bed and he kissed her with the force of all his feelings for her.

The roan gelding grunted under the ministering of Hutton's brush. His strokes were long and firm. He moved to the other side to give attention to the damp hide and tired muscles of his favorite horse. From his vantage, he could see the little house through the open shutters of the stables. The moon shone upon the fresh paint and cheery flowers decorating the side of the cottage. Lantern light from an open window cast a pale hue onto the ground below. He heard Juliana's sweet voice. She sang a song he had not heard before. Her voice pitched high then low but never lost the warmth within. Boyd paused a moment to enjoy the performance. His wife's voice elicited a change in him. His expression softened and his eyes warmed. It seemed not so long before that he had carried Juliana across the threshold into their new home. To his surprise, they had been wed almost a year. He smiled at the thought.

Her lyrics became more distinct as she approached the window. He saw her from the waist up as she passed the window. She was lovely to him beyond any other. He thought he knew her heart and he reveled in the knowledge that hers belonged to him. Scarcely a year later, nothing meant to him what she did.

He again gave his attention to the horse, whose ears canted back towards him as if to question the master's lax technique. In good humor he slapped the horse's neck then drew a long stroke along the horse's withers. His hand stopped mid-task. His back stiffened and his neck grew erect and taut. He was no longer alone in the dark stables. His eyes lost some of their focus as he concentrated upon the darkened stables behind him. Realization recovered his sense of the present.

"I figured it was just a matter of time," Hutton said without turning.

"Isn't it always?"

The deep tones of an accented voice issued from near the door to the stables.

Boyd turned and saw Rigo Herrera silhouetted in the doorway. The bright moonlight cast a backdrop of pasture and starry sky in stark paleness. Hutton set the brush aside and turned fully towards the man hunter.

"I ain't armed."

Boyd spread his arms to their full length as if to demonstrate the truth of his words.

Rigo smiled and shook his head sadly. His teeth shone in the darkness – a trick of the unpredictable moonlight.

"A mistake. You think so little of me you exercise no vigilance?"

Hutton considered the man. The softness brought on by Juliana's song drained from him as silt drains through a funnel. His face set in hard lines. The merry softness in his eyes was replaced with a steely glint. Finally, Hutton shook his head.

"I don't fear you, anyone, or anything that crawls, walks, or slithers anywhere in this world."

Rigo paused as he absorbed the boast.

"You insult me."

Rigo moved from the door jamb and stood on widely set legs, slightly bent as if he were poised to react to a move from his quarry. His right hand dipped to his hip and gripped the rough bone haft of his large belt knife.

His head lowered slightly, and his mouth tightened into a straight firm line below dark eyes.

"That's one hell of a love for yourself you haul around with you."

Hutton's words issued through clenched teeth. His tone was low and menacing.

Rigo was about to speak.

"Enough talk Mexican. Do what you came here for."

Rigo nodded silently. He thumbed the haft strap from the knife and drew it slowly from its sheath. The movement was not so much theater for his prey as it was pleasure in the act of drawing this most treasured weapon. His heart sang in anticipation of his long-awaited moment of triumph. He raised the evil blade to the level of his chest. He glanced at the knife, adjusting his grip upon it in readiness for the work ahead. He handled the blade with the deceptive ease of one skilled in the art of knife fighting. His confidence was bolstered in how easily his training took him over. Prideful arrogance, destructive self-doubt, desperate fear: all receded to a safe place behind the discipline he had acquired through countless hours of practice and numerous battles.

Hutton did not move at all. He stood impassively, arms at his sides where he had lowered them after showing his absence of weapons.

Rigo lowered his body a fraction, his offhand poised behind his attacking front and slightly aside. He moved smoothly towards Hutton. His approach was deceptively quicker than his effort would indicate. He crossed the distance between Hutton and himself at a surprising pace.

Hutton did not adjust his posture from its casual stance. He watched the man hunter with a steady hawkish gaze.

Rigo's approach continued until he was within striking distance of Hutton. Moving his knife hand up and twisting the blade down, edge forward, he feinted left, executing a fake thrust, meant to gauge his victim's reaction and to put him on guard.

His technique was designed to use the man's reaction against him then counter and execute an upward arc under the man's rib cage. Hutton did not move, nor did he turn to front Rigo. He merely stepped to his left then turned again to face the circling assailant.

The horse snorted and leaped away from the skirmish. His eyes shown large whites and his nostrils flared in alarm. Neither man paid the frightened beast attention.

Rigo readjusted his position, bringing the blade higher and horizontal along his forearm. His manner seemed to reflect his uncertainty at the unexpected reaction of the big man. With a sudden and explosive forward movement, Rigo attacked Hutton, keeping his weight over his feet to maintain balance for the maneuver. To his surprise, Hutton leaped forward and left of him, limiting the blade's range of motion and achieving the safer region of Rigo's weak side.

The man hunter flexed lower at his knees and brought his armed front towards the man. The move was late, and Hutton struck him on the side of his neck.

Rigo lost his center of balance for a moment as the blow moved his weight off center. The split second it took him to recover was enough for Hutton to grasp his right wrist and land a blow to his body. Rigo was, as before, shocked at the strength of the man. His wrist was in a vice and his insides ached from the impact of the hard fist. He felt a nagging worry as the grip reminded him of the failure at his last encounter with the outlaw.

Rigo came up hard with a knee meant for the man's groin. Hutton turned his torso, taking the blow with his leg instead. Rigo landed a left to Hutton's jaw. The blow was delivered ineffectually from the shoulder and with insufficient force to affect the bigger man. Hutton held the knife hand in his left and pummeled his attacker with his right. The blows ended abruptly as Hutton grabbed Rigo's throat and stepped behind him, pushing him back.

Rigo fell over the leg and his back struck the ground with a meaty chunk beneath his and Hutton's full weight. The impact jarred the knife loose and it slid through the dust out of reach of the two fighters. Rigo's breath left him at the hard impact. His throat felt crushed where Hutton's hand had caught much of the weight of their fall.

Hutton rose slightly and delivered a strong knee to his assailant's ribs. Rigo had not caught his breath and the knee blow insured he would not for a moment more.

Hutton stood and moved towards the knife. He didn't hurry. He leaned down and grasped the knife, testing the weight. He turned towards Rigo. The man hunter gained his feet and faced Hutton. His breathing was labored from strain and his sweaty face was caked with dirt where it had met the stable floor.

Hutton's breathing came heavier than normal but he did not seem fatigued. He wiped his left hand on his trousers as he watched his man.

"This is the second knife I had to take from you. What's your name?"

The question held no curiosity. His tone seemed that of an accountant asking a number value on a ledger.

Rigo looked at the man with furrowed brow. His incredulity was obvious in his countenance.

"You do not know who the Governor puts on your trail?"

Boyd shook his head. There was no amusement on his face – only disgust.

"Is there no end to you going on about yourself?"

Rigo straightened a bit at this critical query. He felt hot blood rush to his face. He knew in his heart that his last defeat at the hands of this Americano had not been a chance outcome. He felt genuine dread for the first time in his life. He raised his head and swallowed the bitter fear rising in his throat. His answer was louder than intended and held a whine of protest at the belittling context of the man's words.

"My name is Rodrigo Constantine Herrera, you dog!"

Hutton nodded. He seemed to recognize the name.

"Look around you man hunter."

Hutton indicated the stables with the knife.

"This is a pretty poor way for an important man such as yourself to fade out: in a horse stalls I ain't mucked in a week."

Rigo glanced around him, resentful that he had followed the instructions. He jerked his head forward to face Hutton. He felt every move he made was foreign and awkward. This man had a powerful effect upon him.

Boyd nodded his understanding. He rotated the wrist of his knife hand. The blade moved in small circles. Hutton freshened his hold upon the weapon. He observed Rigo for a moment with an arresting look. He seemed to set the image in his mind for future reference. Even in the darkness of the stables, Rigo saw the change in Hutton's eyes as he came to a decision.

Finally, Hutton spoke.

"I will remember you."

With that he moved towards the man hunter, knife at his side. Rigo clenched his teeth and rushed the man. Boyd feinted to his left and brought the blade up under Rigo's defending arms, plunging the knife to the hilt between his ribs.

Rigo stood straight and looked at Hutton in utter horror and disbelief. The realization of his mortality distorted his shocked face. Hutton grasped the man and lowered him gently to the ground.

Rigo's shocked nerves had not yet felt the pain of the wound, only the unnatural weight and discomfort of the long cold object slowly warming amongst his organs.

Rigo closed his eyes against the certainty of his death.

"Not like this. There is no honor in this. It cannot end like this."

Boyd kneeled next to him, leaning in close.

"Just like this, Herrera," he said in a soft voice. "Your exciting life ends here: no band and no parade. No one will ever know what become of you."

Boyd looked around him then back at his victim.

"I'm gonna bury you in this stables, then I am gonna kiss my wife and eat the dinner she is making for me."

Boyd looked into the man's eyes as the light left them. After a moment he stood and moved over to the far wall where a shovel hung from two pegs. He lifted the tool and returned to the dead man. The bone haft protruded from his body unmoved by heartbeat or lungs.

He pressed the shovel blade into the soft ground of the stable floor. He cast the dirt to the side and again pushed the shovel into the ground. He transferred the dirt to an area where he was creating the pile with which he would fill the hole later. He saw movement from the corner of his eye. His gaze went to the open doorway. Another silhouette was there, again leaning against the door jamb, arms crossed.

"You need any help, Chief?"

Cab Jackson pushed his hat back on his head, keeping his right hand near his holstered colt. Hutton straightened and peered at Cab in disbelief.

"Good god," he breathed. "Cab, I thought you were cold in the ground by now."

Cab straightened and walked into the stables. He halted out of shovel range.

"Come close a couple of times, but I'm still foggin' glass far as I can tell."

Hutton looked Cab up and down. His voice held little warmth and much caution as he spoke to his long absent trail partner.

"So it appears. What brings you to this neck of the woods?"

Cab was surprised at the tone of Hutton's voice. Did he detect a hint of apprehension – perhaps fear? He shifted his weight as he answered.

"Two things," he replied, "One of 'em ended up there on the ground."

He indicated the dead man at Hutton's feet.

"I been tracking this man eater since we split up."

Cab removed his hat and tousled his long hair.

"You sent him on quite a bloody tirade. He was easy to follow when he was around polite society, but he don't hardly leave a track in open country."

"And what's the second?" Hutton grasped the shovel handle more firmly. "You reckon to croak me now? It'll have to wait till I dig this hole."

Cab looked at him for a long time. His face registered deep thought as he considered his reply.

Hutton stiffened behind his dispassionate expression. He saw much in Cab with which he was very familiar. He knew that many of his own victims had seen this same air of judgement in their last moments.

With a dismissive chuckle, Cab's demeanor relaxed.

"You could always make me laugh Chief."

Cab sniffed audibly. The smell of cooking was strong on the freshening night air.

"You seem pretty settled down for a bad man."

Hutton looked towards the ground. He turned his back to the younger man and sunk the shovel once again. Cab watched him dig with mild interest.

"Juliana and I got a nice life playin' out,"

Hutton did not look up from his task.

"She deserves at least that."

Cab produced the makings. Hutton glanced at him as he rolled the smoke with his left hand. The shovel again stabbed the earth. Hutton spoke as he dug.

"You been busy pickin' up where we left off. From the rumors, you have become a full-grown man yourself."

Cab shrugged as he lit the cigarette.

"You took the attention off of Juliana and me."

Cab blew smoke at the ceiling.

"You're done with all that, I take it," Cab said through a cloud of smoke.

Hutton stood up and leaned against the shovel as he considered the youth. His face registered genuine respect.

"I gotta hand it to you kid. You're wearing long pants now."

A sarcastic laugh escaped Cab in a single grunt.

"A lot has changed for both of us."

Hutton shook his head. His expression became sober and his look direct.

"I'm done son."

Cab nodded towards the dead man.

"It don't look that way."

"This here is old business needed tending,"

Cab smiled grimly then pulled at his cigarette.

"Is that how you see me: old business?" he asked through exhaled smoke.

Hutton detected a hint of menace in the question. His eyes met Cab's for a moment. He felt his short hairs stand. The older outlaw spoke with an edge to his tone.

"There ain't no need to take this thing further."

He waited a moment for the younger man's reply. When none came, he narrowed his eyes in resolute acceptance.

"She ends how you decide,"

Hutton's voice had lost much of its casual tone. "I reckon you're man enough for the job however you decide to manage it."

Cab considered his words. He watched Hutton, his cigarette unmoving in his mouth.

"Simple as that?" He finally asked around his cigarette.

Hutton felt his next words were important to his future.

"More easy than simple is how it adds up to me."

In an instant the youth's posture relaxed and he rubbed his hands together, drawing on the cigarette, the ash glowing red. Cab was again the youth Hutton had known on the trail.

"I reckon there is nothing to do but slope then. A clean break is best."

Cab looked at Hutton one last time.

Finally, he said, "Adieu Chief."

He turned and strode through the doors. Hutton heard horse's hooves beating the ground as Cab left.

Hutton sighed and went back to his digging.

CHAPTER EIGHTEEN

Gonzaba

Juliana felt as if she had gone full circle in time. The crowd moved around her with a familiar energy. The music rose and fell on the wind. Instead of Alida, the *Quineanera* was for Maria. Otherwise, the similarities were uncanny. Even Boyd was with her as he had been that night so long ago.

Juliana looked across the crowd and met eyes with Maria. The girl smiled and waved. Juliana returned the smile and nodded approvingly.

She broke her gaze from the girl and found those of Boyd Hutton. He was seated beside her, a leg draped over the other in true cowboy style. His hat was doffed back on his head and a smile lit his features.

"Ricardo knows how to throw a party," he said with warmth. "Maria is goin' to be a woman sure."

Juliana frowned playfully at her husband.

"Juliana is not a woman yet. A *Quinceanera* does not transform. It enlightens."

Ricardo rose nearby and raised his glass. The crowd quieted.

"This is a proud day. My only daughter, today, becomes a woman,"

Boyd nudged Juliana gently. Juliana slapped at his hand and shot a sidelong look at him.

Shhh," she said unnecessarily.

"This is your day," he said to his daughter. "Enjoy."

He turned to all quarters of the crowd with raised glass.

"Salute."

Juliana and Boyd raise glasses with the rest and drank to the toast.

Juliana turned once again to Boyd. His expression was sober.

"What is in your mind, *mi esposo*?"

Boyd reached to her and touched her neck. He played with her hair. She had grown used to his new familiar habits.

"Would you honor me with a dance?"

Juliana smiled and nodded her head in agreement.

He stood and drew her to the dance square. He pulled her to him, and she closed her eyes as he whirled her among the other dancers.

Behind closed eyes she felt Boyd stiffen. The band stopped playing abruptly. She opened her eyes. She looked at Hutton. He stared intently behind her and above the level of the square. She released him and turned.

Soldiers lined the upper balconies of the surrounding buildings with weapons trained on the crowd. To her right the crowd murmured in alarm as space was made to allow for an approaching group of uniformed men. In moments, the group broke through the crowd and confronted Hutton and her. At the center, dressed in full military uniform was her father. He pushed through his guards to the front. He stopped abruptly when he saw her. He looked at her for a long moment.

Hutton stepped aside, drawing the guards' weapons away from Juliana. He looked down upon the shorter Gonzaba and crossed his arms.

The governor frowned at this rebellious posture. He felt some disappointment in the lack of fear on display from the long elusive American outlaw. He apprised the big man critically. Gonzaba, as many before him, sensed something of the predator in the man's make up. The dark celebrity of the notorious outlaw caused him a grim fascination. He allowed himself a moment to assess the make-up of the man who could evade an entire country's efforts toward his capture.

He was tall and his build indicated a physical might inherited from birth. His broad hands belied strength but not clumsy power. His eyes put one on alert. Gonzaba felt himself exposed, as if even now he were giving the man fodder towards his own demise. With great effort of will he did not vary his scrutiny of the outlaw. His ears, however sought the comforting sounds of the massed garrison of troops at his back. His fear angered him. He endeavored to conceal his discomposure with aggression and strength of words.

"You have eluded me for too long," he said with the voice of a leader of men. "Finally, we meet. Your time of murder and mayhem is through."

Gonzaba searched the man's face for any sign of fear or remorse. There was nothing other than a mild look of interest in his captor's actions. Gonzaba reddened. He felt a weakening fear that his very thoughts were on display for the American.

His next words were low and filled with pathos long pressed below his consciousness. Months of fear and dread over his daughter's kidnapping had been stored there. Now his pain issued in words heavy with dark emotion.

"You hang tomorrow."

Juliana reached a trembling hand and clutched Hutton's arm. He did not look at her nor did he return the grasp.

Gonzaba looked his daughter up and down. She had aged during her captivity. Her eyes seemed devoid of the merry light which once illuminated her expressions. Even angry, she always possessed a sparkle to her eyes. He felt his heart sag in his breast. He knew innately that Juliana was ruined. She had long ago accepted her fate and she now abided in a region of resigned durance. He drew a long breath to fill the void deep within him.

He snapped his fingers and two guards moved forward. They carried heavy steel shackles. The surrounding soldiers moved to positions where the guards would not obstruct their aim. Gonzaba's preparatory orders had been clear as had the promise of punishment in the event the outlaw escaped.

Juliana flung herself onto Hutton. She locked her arms around his neck and clung to him. Two soldiers moved in, careful to remain out of the line of fire. They ripped her away from Hutton with unceremonious violence. She winced in pain and a wail of defeat filled the air. The soldiers dragged her away, nearly supporting all her weight as she sagged in utter despair.

The crowd of townspeople muttered. They moved with meager uncertainty. Gonzaba watched the shackling proceed until Hutton was chained hand and foot. Finally, the governor turned away from the prisoner and beheld the angry mob.

"You do not believe me," he said in a booming voice. "I am the head of the dragon, bent on making my way of self-interest no matter the means?"

His sarcasm was not lost upon those gathered there.

"This man," he said, extending an open hand towards Hutton, "is, in your opinion, the victim. Again, I ask: how can so many be fooled?"

Gonzaba moved towards Hutton, completely involved in his theatre.

"Before you stands a man responsible for the massacre at Agua Caliente. Many of you have heard of this, yes? Before you stands the murderer of innocent women and children; thief and con man; the kidnapper of my own daughter more than a year ago — she who lived among you."

Anger darkened his gaze.

"Blood is on your hands. You took him in on his word and your hands share that same blood."

Gonzaba's jaw tightened. He turned slowly towards Hutton.

"Tomorrow you die."

He repeated the death sentence with the strength of authority vested in him. His shoulders sagged and he seemed to lose much of his rage as he addressed his guards.

"Take him to the jail and bind him in his cell. All of you guard him tonight."

He levelled each man with a singularly threatening look.

"Any who allow him to escape shall suffer his fate."

The guards closed upon Hutton and strong arms tore at him. They dragged him towards the square entrance. Gonzaba watched as the guards removed the prisoner.

The heavy jail door opened, and Hutton was shoved roughly into the cell. Some half dozen guards threw him to the ground against an iron post in the center of the cell. They chained his hands and feet around the post.

He did not struggle against the rough handling. His submission earned him no lenient treatment. The guards beat him as their desires dictated. They knew of this prisoner and felt sure there would be no punishment or reprimand for their abuse of him.

Juliana struggled to free herself. The action only caused the guards to tighten their grips, causing more pain. Her tears blinded her, and she could not track where they took her. A heavy door opened, and she was pushed roughly into a long room filled with heavy furnishings. A worn desk filled one end of the room. Long wooden seats with ornate cushions lined both walls. She recognized the room as a city government meeting chamber. A low window hung near the large desk. She rushed to the window and grasped the sash. A uniformed man appeared on the other side. His face showed his stern intent to contain her at any cost.

She shrunk from the window and slouched against the desk. After a few moments her attention was drawn to the heavy door which opened with a groaning creak. Her father entered with two guards.

He paused for a moment, considering her. Finally, he indicated silently that the guards should leave. They retreated through the door, pulling it closed behind them.

Gonzaba crossed the room. He moved around Juliana until he was behind the large desk, as if he were back in Saltillo in his office.

Juliana watched him through wet swollen eyes. She stood from her slouch and faced her father.

"Father, you must listen to me. Boyd is..."

"He is dead. No more of this criminal. My concern has to do with you."

She began to speak. He lifted a hand, and she closed her mouth with a click of her teeth and waited.

"Throughout this ordeal you have had every chance to escape, yet you did not. You have had many opportunities to return home, yet you have not. You have had the choice to be my daughter, yet you did not."

"Father," she pleaded, "I cannot explain it. At first, I could think of nothing else but escape. It is complicated."

Her voice trailed away helplessly.

"Complicated? Tell me of this complicated. Convince me that you are other than a base traitor. Make me believe any of my daughter remains within this creature that stands before me."

Juliana looked desperately at Gonzaba. She yearned to see her father, the man who loved her, who looked upon her as his favorite.

"I am still your daughter" she stammered uncertainly, "I am still your daughter, Father!"

Gonzaba shook his head.

"That remains to be seen."

Juliana moved around the desk with a renewed hope. Her voice was pleading but rational.

"I will go with you tonight, Father. We can be what we were. I am still your Juliana."

Her voice quavered as she fought for her place in his heart.

Gonzaba stepped aside and went past her to the window she had recently visited. He stood looking out, his back to her, saying nothing.

Was he considering her offer?

Desperation was finding purchase within her. Primary in her mind was the duress he must have been under to place a death sentence upon her head. She believed if she could only make him see that she was the same girl to which he heaped those beautiful accolades in their last conversation, perhaps he would...she continued:

"Why do you not speak, Father? I need to hear you say you love me still."

Gonzaba did not move from his position.

Juliana's jaw set stubbornly. Her entreaties were not working. Perhaps a more direct approach would pierce his indifference.

"You want the truth?" she asked with the passion of the righteous. "I'll give you the truth. I am in love with Boyd Hutton in spite of his crimes. He saved my life. There is more to him than the crimes by which you know him."

Juliana watched as her father's back stiffened and his head dropped to his chest. She could not see any other reaction to her words.

She moved closer to her father, ill at ease and unsure of her next move. She placed a quavering hand on his shoulder.

"Father look at me. I beg you. I must see your face."

Gonzaba took a long moment before he turned to Juliana. She was taken aback at his appearance. His eyes were red and swollen. His cheeks were wet with tears. His eyes were dark with strained emotion.

She looked into those eyes with a daughter's open trust. She interpreted his display of emotion as those of a man whose walls were crashing down. She felt certain he must see the sense of it all. He had always trusted her advice –her reason. With a renewed sense of purpose, she moved closer still. She looked into his eyes with all the love and tenderness she felt.

"Father...He is my husband."

Gonzaba fell back a pace as if he had received a physical blow. His eyes shone as new tears welled from within him. He reached a hand out and pulled Juliana to his breast. She felt welcome relief and joy. She missed her father. She missed his embrace, his warmth. She held him tightly, tears of joy and relief flowed as the warmth of her love was finally allowed outlet.

Gonzaba reached into his coat pocket and drew forth a thin dagger. He tightened his hold on Juliana with his left arm. His right moved close in and he drove the razor-sharp tip into her chest to the hilt.

As the blade pierced her skin, she tried to recoil from the bright sharp pain exploding in her chest. He held her with irresistible strength. She felt the cold steel go deep into her body. Her heart felt heavy and sodden. She felt a strength deep within her that she had never noticed, but now knew had always been there, begin to fade. Darkness rose up over her eyes like black water.

The governor lowered Juliana to the floor. He sobbed helplessly while she struggled weakly, the precious life leaving her body. He withdrew the blade slowly from her body. The knife fell from his numb hand.

He staggered backwards a step then he collapsed into a nearby chair. He knew he had killed more than his daughter this day. His instincts told him that the rest of his days would be no more than the laborious passage of time, delaying only that which would end his suffering.

Hutton sagged wearily against the iron post. His face was beaten to the point he saw a dusty slant of light from the dawning sun through swollen slits. He looked slowly around him. Guards sat fully awake, watching him intently.

A door slammed closed somewhere in the larger building which housed the jail cell. The guards stood expectantly. A moment later, the door swung open and Gonzaba, dressed in a fresh suit entered the vestibule outside the cell. Two guards flanked him.

Boyd stood with much effort. He slouched due to his many injuries sustained through the night. His voice reflected his pain.

"I would like to see Juliana one last time to say goodbye, and to tell her that I am sorry for what I did to her."

Gonzaba nodded to one of the guards and the door to the cell was opened. Gonzaba stepped within. He moved close to Hutton. He looked him up and down.

"Within the hour you will be hanged by the neck until you are dead. You will die for those you killed at Agua Caliente; for the murder of those Mormon men; for the men and women you left to die. You will die for the bodies you have left in your wake since you kidnapped my daughter. You will die for the pain and humiliation you caused me and my family. *Senor* Hutton, you die, in particular, for the murder of Juliana."

Hutton searched Gonzaba's face through swollen eye lids. He sought to understand his meaning. He felt fear grasp him with an undeniable truth. He stood straighter, his pain numbed by despair.

"Juliana is not dead. You can't blame her for what I did. She has no part in this!"

"The day you took her, you murdered her. The day she found the thing in you that she fell in love with, you murdered her."

Something in the old man's face eliminated all hope and replaced it with the certainty of loss. Juliana was indeed dead.

Grief weakened him as surely as if he had been mortally wounded by blade or bullet. He felt a dread pall numbing his senses. In an instant his vision cleared. The weakness left him, driven from him as he insulated himself from pain with a learned stoicism. Indifference took its place in him once more. He felt loss keenly, but it held no power over his resolve.

Hutton straightened as much as he was able. His voice was calm as it was before he gave up his ways for Juliana.

"You're right, you proud piece of shit."

A guard moved quickly past Gonzaba and struck the prisoner in the face. Hutton nearly lost his balance, but the chains held him upright. He gained his feet again. Gonzaba placed a hand on the guard's shoulder and gestured that he back away.

Gonzaba moved closer to his prisoner. His teeth ground with rage, his voice was a guttural growl.

"These are your final words criminal. You are not worthy of addressing a man of honor and respect, so make them memorable."

Hutton laughed grimly at the governor's remark.

"This is the truth. It's up to you whether it's worth rememberin' or not. You are right. I took her. You're right. I have killed many men — more than you know. I have cut down everything that ever tried to stop me or slow me down, but not her. I couldn't do it. She never played the coward when she told me what she thought of me, but I couldn't bring myself to break her spirit – to break her heart.

"You did that. You left her with nothing else but me. You put a bounty on her. She would have gladly handed you my head herself. You left her with nothing else but me. In the end, it was your hand that kept her captive. It was your hand that murdered her and now you have nothing. We share that, Governor.

"Now get on with this thing and save me living with the grief you'll have by your side from now on."

Gonzaba stood silently. He felt his anger rise. He wanted to take the man's throat in his hands and kill him here and now. However, his duty was clear.

"Take him out."

The crowds were large. The gathering for Maria's *Quinceanera* had brought attendees from afar. As a result, Hutton was led through crowded lanes towards the church, the largest building in town. A timber was attached to the front pillars, a heavy rope tied to the extended end of the attached plank.

He walked in shackles once more between two large, uniformed soldiers. Theirs was the air of sentries guarding the most dangerous of adversaries. Their eyes searched Hutton as though he might conjure a weapon from his clothing as if by magic. The crowd comprised many who were confused yet curious. The horrible always garnered macabre interest.

Among the observers, yet far enough away to escape detection by soldier or prisoner, Cab Jackson sat upon a sorrel horse. From his vantage at the outermost edge of the spectators, he plainly saw the procession making its way towards the makeshift gallows before the big church. The news of Juliana's death had reached even his ears.

Behind Hutton and his guards, Gonzaba led a cadre of armed soldiers – a dozen in all. Cab watched the Governor with a menacing expression. He had liked Juliana. The senseless killing of so beautiful a woman seemed cruel and decidedly wasteful of a treasure such as her. There was a shortage of rare beauties in this wild district. Taking one like Juliana in the name of misguided honor was, to Cab, a crime against nature.

A heightened pitch in the crowd's murmured din roused Cab from his reverie. The condemned prisoner mounted the low porch at the front of the church.

Cab turned the horse and made his way along the outside edge of the spectators, moving towards the church. His jaw muscles flexed like serpents under his skin as his mind wrestled with his conflicting thoughts.

His odds were acceptable. There were fourteen troops, but they were not expecting an attack to free their captive. Surprise was on his side. Their long weapons were shouldered ceremoniously. He doubted rounds were chambered. A sudden fusillade would easily down half before they were able to ready weapons to fire. Cab guessed the resulting melee of panicked spectators would add enough confusion to allow him to pick off at least three or four more soldiers.

His plan contained merit though he felt much of it was dependent upon factors beyond his control. Luck was a fickle mistress, whose favor changes at her whim. He was not convinced that he should gamble with his life on such tenuous odds.

Hutton mounted the steps, his eyes upon the knotted noose above him. Instinctively, his eyes dropped to the crowd around him. He seemed to search among the spectators for some dark specter.

The soldiers grasped his shoulders and positioned him under the noose. They turned him to face the crowd. They removed the shackles from his wrists and bound his hands behind his back. Two men pushed a large square crate before Hutton under the noose. They took a moment to adjust the crate's position, looking to the noose and back to the large crate repeatedly to get the proper placement. Finally, they stood and moved to the side, avoiding eye contact with the prisoner.

A priest appeared from amongst the crowd. He stopped before Hutton, his bony fingers fingered beads and a cross, stopping their activity only long enough to open a bible to a book-marked page. He murmured in Spanish as he read from the book.

Hutton paid no attention to the priest. He was busy looking around him, past the black frocked clergyman. The priest closed the bible with a solemn amen and moved away.

The guards helped Hutton onto the crate. A slightly built man climbed atop the box and slipped the noose over Hutton's head. He tightened the knot around his neck. He was to the side of the condemned man but looked into his face to gauge whether the noose was sufficiently tightened. He seemed satisfied and stepped down from the crate. The heavy hangman's knot lay upon Hutton's shoulder.

Hutton's scanning gaze stopped suddenly. A movement in the crowd just before him caught his attention. He focused on a spot between a couple who held one another as if Hutton were their son.

A dark face appeared between them, peering at Hutton in the space between their craned necks. The face moved slowly behind the two. Hutton's eyes grew wider as the dark face became part of a dark robed body. The vision moved towards him slowly, looking into his eyes with a dark soulless gaze.

Hutton felt the hangman's rope pull taut. He realized he was leaning away from the sight, causing the rope to tighten. The wraith's face was familiar. He felt tears well behind his eyes. He recognized the face of the approaching specter. It was Juliana as he had seen her in the camp that night. A voice in his head told him what he already knew. She had become what he had made her. She would abide in everlasting torment because she had given herself to him. She approached slowly. He had no place from which to escape her.

Cab had moved close enough that he was certain the soldiers and even Gonzaba himself would notice him. His gaze returned to Hutton, atop the rough crate. He appeared to be terrified. His eyes were wide, and he leaned back, tightening the rope around his throat. He looked about to drop backwards from the box and hang himself. His eyes were focused upon a point before and just below his position.

Cab searched for that which captured Hutton's attention. He saw no more than the gathering crowd. Cab's mind went back to the day he overheard Hutton's narrative for the bounty hunter as he hung him. Realization came upon Cab with a wave of relief. The memories of Hutton's unreasonable conduct on the trail; his risky need to visit saloons and cantinas; and the conversation with the bounty hunter, moved him to an immediate decision. His reason led him to a resolve which galvanized him and insulated him from any feeling of guilt.

He straightened in the saddle. His shoulders relaxed as the possibility of dangerous action no longer troubled him.

"You wouldn't do it for me, Chief."

With that, he turned the horse's head and squeezed his heels. Horse and rider moved away from the town gathering at a lope.

He gained the edge of the village. Behind him he heard the scraping of a wooden box pushed along a rough planked floorboard. He thought he heard timber creaking under the weight of a man.

Cab spurred his mount towards a distant hilltop. He desired to leave Mexico.

ABOUT THE AUTHOR

Craig Rainey (1962 -) is an American actor, author, screenwriter and musician. He was born in San Angelo, Texas and now resides in Austin. His Texas roots hail back to the original settlers of Coahuila y Tejas under Stephen F. Austin. He cowboyed professionally in south Texas. His first published novel was Massacre at Agua Caliente. The book is based upon the award-winning screenplay of the same title. The script has won numerous awards at film and screenwriting festivals including: Best Narrative Period Piece, Most Likely to be Produced as a Movie, and was Official Selection for many more. Craig Rainey won Best Break-out Writer for the script.